The Name of the Sword

Book 4 of *The Gods Within*

*Beware the power of the self-forged blade, for even when flawed,
it can undo the mightiest.*

by

J. L. Doty

TELEMACHUS PRESS

This book or eBook is a work of fiction. Names, characters, places and incidents are either the product of the author's imagination or are used fictitiously. Any resemblance to actual persons, living or dead, or to actual events or locales is entirely coincidental.

The Name of the Sword, **Book 4 of** ***The Gods Within***
This book or eBook is licensed for your personal enjoyment only. This book or eBook may not be re-sold or given away to other people. If you're reading this book or eBook and did not purchase it, or it was not purchased for your use only, then you should return it and purchase your own copy. Thank you for respecting the hard work of the author.

The publisher does not have any control over and does not assume any responsibility for author or third-party websites or their content.

Cover designed by Telemachus Press, LLC

Cover art:
Copyright © ThinkstockPhoto/96635409/iStockPhoto
Copyright © ThinkstockPhoto/89908712/iStockPhoto
Copyright © ThinkstockPhoto/77005529/Stockbyte
Copyright © ThinkstockPhoto/100672861/Hemera
Copyright © ThinkstockPhoto/101137932/Hemera

Published by Telemachus Press, LLC
http://www.telemachuspress.com

Visit the author's website:
http://www.jldoty.com

ISBN: 978–1–942899–10–5 (eBook)
ISBN: 978–1–953757–04–3 (paperback)
ISBN: 978–1–953757–12–8 (hardcover)

Version 2023.11.23

KEpuz!po!EFTLUPQ.6CV292J:
Formatted using eTools for Writers 3.8.8, Nov 22 2023, 16:11:07
Copyright © 2013–2016 by J. L. Doty

Printed in the United States of America

10 9 8 7 6 5 4 3 2 1

The Name of the Sword

Book 4 of *The Gods Within*

Prologue:
When the Steel is Blooded

Properly blooded, the steel is free, unbound, and whole. And he who forged such a blade should fear it most.

All realms should fear the naming of the Unnamed King, for only then will he find peace. Only the consecration of their vows will allow the god-queen to assume her power.

1

The Sacrifice

VALSO STOOD AT the window in his workshop looking out at the inner bailey below, waiting for Carsaris to bring news. Behind him the door opened and he heard the wizard's soft footsteps as he entered the room. Without turning, Valso asked, "Any word from Salula?"

"No, Your Majesty. Nothing since he found the woman in Norlakton. I fear some sort of setback."

Valso dismissed the sorcerer's fears with a casual wave of his hand. "At this point we can overcome any impediment."

His eye caught a bit of motion down below and off to one side. His workshop was on the third floor of the castle, with a commanding view of the city beyond, the inner bailey below, and to one side his family's burial plot. There, he saw the familiar figure of his mother, the twoname Merriketh Alaella, on her hands and knees tending the flowers at his brothers' graves.

His thoughts slipped back to that night 24 years ago when his youngest brother lay dying, and his sister Haleen suffered in the throes of a difficult childbirth . . .

••••

As the boy Valso walked down a dark corridor in Castle Decouix, a scream muffled by the thick stone walls of the building broke the silence of the night. His sister Haleen had uttered such cries throughout the day and would probably do so until her child was born. Valso had gone to some trouble to confirm that the child was healthy, and without his interference would come into this world strong and hale. But for his purposes, it was imperative that the birth appear to be a long and arduous affair, and the spells he'd crafted to make it seem so were doing the job nicely. When the child that eventually lay in Haleen's arms proved to be sickly and weak, no one would question its subsequent death.

He did hope that someday he might find an opportunity to kill Tulellcoe for soiling the virtue of a Decouix princess. But this night he must put such thoughts aside; he must concentrate on the child to come, for his master wanted it born whole and healthy.

He stopped outside the door to his youngest brother's bedroom, his final brother, the last impediment to the consolidation of his power. He lifted the latch quietly, opened the door a crack and slipped into the room. Several healers surrounded his brother's bed, all standing helplessly, wringing their hands and looking upon the dying boy. Valso's grief-stricken mother sat in a chair beside the young boy's bed, her head bowed. None of them took note of Valso's presence, so he stepped to one side and put his back to a tapestried wall

Valso's mother didn't cry or whimper, just sat there with her shoulders slumped, one hand tightly gripping the limp hand of Tarran, her youngest son. The boy's pale and ashen face appeared almost spectral, his eyes closed, his breathing shallow, his skin covered by a fine sheen of sickly sweat.

At 12 years of age—only just a man by clan law—Valso hadn't yet fully consolidated his power. Otherwise, he might have been able to allow Tarran an easier death. He'd been cautious when disposing of his other two brothers. Mikal had died in a carefully contrived hunting accident, while GregorDan had fallen from a parapet and broken his neck. Valso had used a considerable amount of cunning and magic to hide his involvement in both incidents, and afterwards he'd cleaned up by killing a couple of his retainers to ensure their silence. But his mother, Merriketh, powerful in her own right, had suspected, and calmly warned him to stay away from Tarran. At the time Valso had been most concerned about his father, but Illalla merely said, "Be more careful next time."

He'd spent months concocting a poison and administering it slowly in tiny amounts to Tarran. Slight of stature to begin with, the boy appeared to weaken gradually, his illness progressing so slowly that no one noticed anything from day-to-day or month-to-month. But as each season passed his frailty grew, as if his own fragile constitution was the culprit. It was truly a masterwork of murder. Yes, it could have gone easier on the boy, quicker, less painful, but Merriketh watched him too closely, so Valso had had to move with extreme caution, which meant the poor boy had to die ever so slowly. His mother had no one to blame but herself for the boy's long, slow, painful demise.

It occurred to Valso that Haleen had been silent for some time. Tarran might linger on for several more days, and his mother would certainly hope that some spell of healing might turn the tide toward recovery. But Valso knew his concoctions well, and not even he could save the boy now. He had more pressing business with Haleen, so he turned to the door, quietly lifted the latch and stepped into the corridor. Once he closed the door behind him, his concern that he might already be too late quickened his steps as he hurried to Haleen's suites.

He could see nothing of his sister as he stepped into her bedchamber, for a wall of handmaidens surrounded her completely, cooing over her and uttering sympathetic little phrases. To one side of the room a midwife—carefully chosen and bribed by Valso—stood over a small bundle working on it carefully. He stopped by the midwife's side and asked her, "How is the child?"

The child before her lay completely still, with none of the squirming or cries of a newborn. She announced loudly, "A boy child, my lord, but sickly, I fear." She'd spoken loud enough for all to hear.

She leaned close to Valso and whispered, "He's good and healthy, my lord, and whole, and I dosed him with the charm you gave me. He'll not be making any noise."

One of the young handmaidens turned toward them and asked, "He's sickly, is he?" She stepped around the midwife and looked down upon the boy. "He's not moving. Is he alive?"

"He's alive," Valso said, and gave her a cold look. "Don't alarm your mistress with wild rumors. And since I doubt you know anything of midwifery, return to her now."

She curtsied, turned and returned to the clutch of girls surrounding Haleen. She'd seen the boy—no matter how fleetingly—and might recognize the differences between him and his substitute. Valso decided he'd have to arrange some sort of accident to take her out of the picture.

While Valso kept an eye on Haleen's handmaidens, the midwife carefully wrapped the new child in a blanket. She had placed a large valise on the table next to the child. She reached into it, pulled out another wrapped bundle, laid it on the table, then quickly stuffed the wrapped newborn into the satchel, closing it carefully. She unwrapped the new bundle to reveal another boy-child.

With the powers his master had granted him, Valso had found it easy to determine the sex of the child in Haleen's womb. Then, with the midwife's aid, they'd found a peasant with another boy-child who would come to term a few months after Haleen. For a nice sum of money the peasants were more than willing to give up the child—no questions asked. Valso had provided the midwife with powerful charms so that when Haleen went into labor she could induce the peasant-child's birth prematurely, and a sickly child was born. It had all been carefully done.

The midwife nodded toward the peasant-child that lay before them and whispered, "I gave the child the potion you provided, my lord. And I cleaned him up good, like you said."

Yes, she'd carefully washed the filth of peasantry from the boy. "Good," Valso said. The potion would ensure that the child lived for no more than a day or two. A bit more loudly, he said, "Why don't you take the child to his mother?"

She bowed her head. "Yes, my lord."

She picked up the child and turned toward Haleen's bed. The handmaidens parted to allow her through.

Haleen lay overcome by the deep sleep of exhaustion; an entire day and half a night of labor had taken its toll. She roused groggily as the midwife laid the child in her arms. She looked at it once, smiled, then drifted off again.

While the girls spoke of the handsome features the child bore, and of how he looked just like his mother, Valso turned, picked up the midwife's valise and left the room. He paused out in the hall, closed his eyes and opened his soul to his master. Their connection remained tenuous, his master a dark presence hovering at the edges of his soul. He could not fully meld with such raw and malevolent power until he had performed the proper rites, so all he could really relate was a sense of satisfaction, of near completion, a mere impression that soon they would be whole.

Gently carrying the valise, he hurried down to the stables where Salula and Illalla awaited him with two saddled horses. They all knew that Valso dare not call down the power of his master anywhere near Haleen; with the child involved, she would sense it and know. And his weakling of a father was not strong enough to participate in this. But Salula—a faithful servant spawned of the same nether reaches as his master— Salula would accompany him gladly.

They rode hard out of the city, with the child clutched in Valso's arms. The ritual must be completed during the night of the child's birth, so they only had until the moment when the first ray of sun broke over the horizon.

In anticipation of this night, Valso had brought laborers into the forest southeast of the city, and there had constructed a small, one-room, stone shrine. After its completion he had returned to it regularly to give obeisance to his lord and master, slowly building the tenuous connection between them. Tonight that would change.

As they approached the shrine the spell Valso had provided to the midwife wore off and the infant began to wail. Such spells were dangerous to a newborn, so Valso had been forced to use only a modicum of the power at his command. But none of that mattered now; he and his master both sensed the nearness of their joining, and vast joy washed through his soul. Though oddly enough, the child's cries made Valso wonder if somehow it sensed its fate.

Salula opened the door of the shrine and held it for Valso, but dare not enter himself. He would wait outside and tend the horses.

Valso had personally created a small altar for the sacrifice. He had carved runnels in the stone to carry the blood to bowls at its base, blood needed for the culmination of the rite. He placed the child on the altar, and using simple spells lit nine candles placed above it, one candle for each of the Nine Hells of the Netherworld. He returned to the open door, where Salula stood on the other side of the threshold holding Valso's saddlebags. The halfman handed them to him, then closed the door.

Valso retrieved two wooden bowls and an iron knife from the saddlebags; simple, cold iron, a necessary ingredient for this ritual. He placed the bowls on the altar next to the child, then carefully probed the skin of the child's smooth head. It wailed while he did so, and again he wondered if it sensed its fate. He found small tufts of fuzz and cut away two locks of hair. With the knife he carefully trimmed the child's finger and toe nails. He divided and placed the tufts of hair and nail trimmings into the two bowls, then cut and put a lock of his own hair in each of the bowls, with trimmings from his own nails. Lastly, he made a small cut in the child's thumb—it cried balefully as he dripped 13 drops of blood into each bowl. He cut his own thumb and did the same. Then he placed the two bowls at the ends of the runnels he'd carved where they could collect the child's lifeblood.

He unclothed the child and laid it naked upon the altar, then clutched the iron knife in both hands and held it tightly to his chest, thinking only of his master.

He began a chant that he'd memorized, a psalm of words in a language so old they meant nothing to him. He wasn't even certain he pronounced them correctly, though he had no choice but to do his best. And as he spoke he felt the power building about him, felt it coalesce within the tight confines of the small shrine. Valso could exercise more power than any other clansman, certainly more than his weak father. But it was nothing compared to the power he would soon command.

He drifted off into a trance, felt disconnected from the child and the shrine, though his lips continued with the long and arduous chant—he had practiced it hundreds of times in preparation for this. Illalla had found the spell in an ancient text, had spent years deciphering it, though neither he nor Valso could be certain they had all the details right. And Valso's connection to his master remained so tenuous he could not overtly confirm any of their suppositions.

He suddenly realized one of the words meant *blood* in that ancient script, and that another meant *child*, and another *sacrifice*. There was no mundane reason why he should know the meaning of such lyrics, no scrolls or translations available to guide him. But one-by-one the ancient words took on meaning, and the buildup of power in the room accelerated frighteningly. It was time for the next phase of the sacrifice.

He carefully cut the child in nine places, one slice in the middle of its forehead, one on each earlobe, one on each shoulder, one on each hip, and one on the back of each knee; small cuts all, just enough for the blood to trickle onto the altar. Still chanting, he watched it flow with agonizing slowness into the runnels, and along them toward the two bowls.

When the first drop hit the contents of the first bowl, it felt as if a massive bell rang within his soul. As each subsequent drop fell into a bowl the bell rang louder, and power flooded through him, power beyond anything he'd ever experienced. It threatened to overwhelm him, to consume him, and for a moment he faltered, almost forgetting the words of the chant. But then his master came to his aid, wrapping him in a cocoon of malevolence. He knew then that with his master's help, he could control this power in all its magnificent glory, though a demanding erection distracted him a bit.

The drops landing in the two bowls suddenly synchronized. He knew their count without question, and the instant the 13th drops landed into the two bowls, his soul felt as if it would burst.

He reached out, touched his index finger to the nine wounds in the child, collecting a bit of blood from each. Then he touched his fingers to his lips and lost his soul to an infinity of power. Unable to think clearly, moving purely by instinct, by practiced memory, by rote, he raised the knife in both hands high above his head. It was time to stab it into the child's chest, but not into its heart. To complete the ritual he must cut the still beating heart from the child, and drink the blood from its veins and arteries.

Noooooooooooo!

It wasn't a voice, or a word, merely a thought like the whisper of a faint breeze, but he knew it to be a command from his master. In the last few moments their connection had grown stronger, and now he stopped, the point of the knife only a finger's breadth above the child's breast.

Noooooooooooo!

And with that second thought he understood. His master didn't want merely the child's life; He wanted the child alive and whole, a slave for His purposes. Giving Him the child healthy and unharmed would be a far greater sacrifice, and his reward would be to rule the entire Mortal Plane beside his master for all eternity.

Valso lowered the knife, bowed his head, and whispered, "As you wish."

For some time he stood there, not really conscious of his mortal being, bathed in the glorious malevolence of his master. There were no windows in the small shrine, nothing that might allow the world of mundane men to intrude upon this most hallowed of rites, but when dawn came he sensed it and opened his eyes. There was no sign of the child, no blood on the altar, no blood in the runnels, nothing in the two bowls, no blood on his fingertips, or on his tongue where he had tasted it. His master had taken the child alive and whole.

Exhausted beyond belief, he opened the door to the shrine and found Salula standing there, waiting like a ghost at the threshold of its haunt. He stumbled and fell into Salula's arms; the halfman lowered him gently to the ground and propped him up with his back against the wall of the shrine.

Salula said, "A bit of food might help you regain your strength."

No questions from Salula, no concerns, no fears. Valso liked that about him, just cold, hard obedience.

Valso chewed on a bit of journeycake and a piece of jerky, and sucked hungrily at the water skin Salula handed him. When he could again stand—though he longed to lay down and sleep for an eternity—Salula helped him into the saddle. He let Salula take the reins of his horse and he slipped in and out of a hazy doze all the way back to Durin. Illalla met them in the stables, and as Valso dismounted, still barely able to stand, his father asked, "Is it done?"

"Aye, father, it's done."

"And properly?"

"Yes, properly."

Illalla assumed he had sacrificed the child, completed the ritual as it had been written down in the ancient manuscript. But the Dark God had wanted something quite different, and Valso had given it to him. He looked upon his father, a powerful sorcerer by any other measure, but weak and insignificant compared to the power Valso now commanded. He no longer needed this man who had given him life, and there and then he decided not to enlighten Illalla concerning the change in the ritual his master had demanded. That would remain a little secret he'd keep to himself.

Now, time to clean up after the night's events. The midwife would have to die, and the peasants, and that one handmaiden.

••••

Yes, Valso thought, standing at the window, watching his mother tend his brothers' graves. It had been a good night's work, all those many years ago.

2

To Find the Blade

AS THE ONLY person present not of Elhiyne lineage, Cort felt badly out of place. With the exception of Marjinell and DaNoel, the entire family had gathered in Olivia's audience chamber. With Olivia seated on a couch, Tulellcoe, Roland, AnnaRail, JohnEngine, Brandon and Jinella—Brandon's pretty, young wife—all standing before the old woman, almost no room remained for anyone else in the small space. Cort had retreated to the back of the room to remain unnoticed, and she saw that NickoLot had done the same.

Such a strange child, Cort thought, looking at NickoLot. In her late teens and well into womanhood, she was still tiny for her age, a stick-thin waif of a girl. Pretty, with dark hair like that of her grandmother, she had matured into quite a beauty regardless of her slight stature. But her eyes seemed haunted, as if she had experienced too many of life's tragedies, and too few of its joys. And she hid her beauty in black, funereal dresses, with high stiff collars, long sleeves, and always a veil that half hid her face from those about her.

"He was alive," Tulellcoe said, his sorrow a visible smear on his aura. "Alive, and we all believed him dead. And then he truly did die."

Morgin's death, only that morning, had thrown the entire family into chaos. Several of them had felt him depart the Mortal Plane, and they were all still reeling from his passing.

Olivia appeared rather bored with the whole subject. "Of course he was alive. You were a fool to think otherwise."

"You knew he was alive?" Tulellcoe demanded, anger coloring his aura more than the sorrow. "And you didn't tell us?"

"You wouldn't have believed me if I had. And in any case it was just a suspicion. I had no proof."

JohnEngine said, "But if you'd told us we might have been able to help him."

Olivia shook her head sadly. "And how would you have helped him, when not one of us had the slightest inkling of his whereabouts?"

JohnEngine opened his mouth to argue, but Olivia cut him off with a slash of her hand, saying to Tulellcoe, "And what makes you think he is now truly dead?"

Tulellcoe's anger visibly turned to cold rage. "I felt his soul depart the Mortal Plane."

AnnaRail, her eyes puffy from crying, said, "As did I."

Olivia's brows furrowed in thought. She ignored AnnaRail and said to Tulellcoe, "Interesting! I understand his mother sensing his demise, even though there was no blood connection between them. The mother-child relationship can bridge that gap. But you, nephew, what connection is there between you and Morgin that you too would sense his passing?"

Cort revised her interpretation of the look on Olivia's face. It was not careful thought, but rather conspiratorial conniving.

Her words did give Tulellcoe pause, and his thoughts seemed to be elsewhere for a moment. Then he said, "He did once confess to me that when he killed the Tulalane in the sanctum, the power in the sanctum came to him readily, came to him in a way that told me he must have some Elhiyne blood in him."

Tulellcoe's words stunned everyone in the room but Olivia. She merely smiled. Tulellcoe had once described that smile to Cort, and she saw it now for the first time, an avaricious grin of greedy delight.

The old woman frowned in thought and said, "That could explain it; you both share Elhiyne blood, even if his was bestowed upon him by some clansman's whoring."

AnnaRail said, "And you believe he is still alive?"

Olivia shook her head. "I did not say that,"

AnnaRail made no effort to hide her anger as she spoke. "Then what did you mean?"

"I mean only that I have not seen his body with my own eyes, and he has such a penchant for returning from death. So I do not know for a certainty that he is dead. Just as I do not know that Rhianne is dead."

NickoLot flinched. It had been only an instantaneous loss of composure, but Cort happened to be looking her way and saw it clearly. And since she and NickoLot were standing behind the rest of them, it was unlikely anyone else had seen it. If there was any question in Cort's mind about what she'd seen, NickoLot confirmed it by quickly glancing about the room like a thief fearing discovery. Cort looked away from NickoLot before the girl glanced her way, and she pondered what she had just seen. That girl knew something the rest of them didn't, something about Rhianne.

"Do you know something about Rhianne?" AnnaRail demanded of Olivia. Cort had heard she was one of the few who would stand up to the old woman.

The avaricious grin returned to Olivia's face. "I do not believe the girl is dead, though I have no proof of that either."

AnnaRail stepped forward and leaned over the old woman. "Then where is she?"

Olivia sighed, making it clear to all of them that this conversation wearied her. "I do not know. But perhaps, with time, we can find her."

The old woman glanced about the room as if gauging the reaction from each of them, but as her eyes swept past NickoLot, Cort thought she saw them harden for just the tiniest instant, a surreptitious look that no one else saw. Cort realized she wasn't the only one who had seen the young girl flinch.

AnnaRail and Olivia argued quite heatedly, though the stubborn old woman refused to budge. As AnnaRail's anger began to border on something more deadly, Roland intervened and broke up the meeting.

Marjinell's absence didn't bother Cort in the least. After the death of her husband and oldest son, she had turned into quite the recluse. But she did wonder about DaNoel's absence.

••••

NickoLot paused at the door to the suite of rooms Morgin had occupied before being driven from the castle. The first time they had thought him dead, AnnaRail had not felt his soul depart the Mortal Plane, so she had locked the suite and refused to allow anyone to change anything, insisting he would return. But this time Nicki and her mother had both felt him pass. She was glad to find the room still locked, a mundane, mechanical contraption she had no difficulty circumventing. She had already searched the small, single room he had slept in before moving to this suite as warmaster, but it had long ago been cleaned and was now occupied by another. Nicki wanted to search these rooms before someone else did, and before the servants stripped and cleaned them in preparation for a new resident.

She started with the outer sitting room first, searching every bit of furniture, every nook and cranny. She didn't know what she was looking for, was doing this purely on instinct, but when she found a small, copper coin beneath the cushions of a chair, she hoped it had been his, and a plan began to form in her thoughts.

She next searched the small study. Morgin had spent very little time there, but when he had been the hero of Csairne Glen and Warmaster of Elhiyne, Olivia had insisted his suite be appropriate to his station. Nicki found nothing more in the study so she moved on to the bedroom.

She checked beneath the cushions of a chair, pulled the sheets and covers off the bed and shook them out. She ran her hands beneath the mattress, and in the process acquired only a nasty splinter in her thumb. Last of all she stood over a small, wooden chest at the base of his bed. If it yielded naught, she'd have nothing to show for her efforts but the splinter and the single coin.

When she opened the lid she realized she'd uncovered a treasure trove. She found a comb with a few missing teeth, but with several hairs still attached to it. It was an old thing, probably one of the few possessions he'd had as a small child living in the young boy's barracks. She also found a cheap knife, the broken shard of a mirror, a small bronze pendant, four shiny stones polished by the weather, two dove feathers, and an old pair of cheap boots much too small to have fit Morgin for several years now. All these items appeared to be little treasures from his past, and that made them especially valuable for her purposes.

She returned to her own single room, laid the items out on a writing table and looked them over carefully. She must eliminate any that weren't truly his, for they would contaminate the spell she intended to craft.

She started with the copper coin, picked it up and held it to her breast. She summoned power, fed some of it into the coin and thought of Morgin, tried to recall every memory she had of him . . . and nothing happened.

She tried to put her disappointment aside as she next picked up the comb and removed one of the hairs. Again, she held the object to her breast, fed it power and thought of a time when Morgin had picked her up as a small child. She had always enjoyed his antics, making faces at her to get a laugh or a shriek. As with all memories from her earliest years it came to her in hazy and indistinct images, and it was difficult to truly recall his face in detail. But the image cleared, and she saw him as if he stood before her this moment, the young face of a boy at about the age of 12. The screwed up grimace and crossed eyes he made for her evoked a laugh even now.

She quickly determined that most of the items she'd taken from the trunk were his, though his connection to some of them was rather weak. Strongest were the four stones and the strands of hair. He had probably acquired the stones only a short time after first coming to Elhiyne. She decided to work with just the hairs and the stones.

She used two strands of hair to bind the stones into a ring, four stones, each with a delicate knot tied about it. She then pulled one of her own hairs and added it to Morgin's to reinforce the knots. She pulled more power, fed it into the charm she had created, then cleared her thoughts. For this spell to work, she must not contaminate the invocation with her own biases.

She sat for what seemed quite a long time, and slowly a sense of purpose emerged from the charm. She had a brief glimpse of Morgin riding in the Munjarro next to a young Benesh'ere warrior, the two of them crossing the sands together. A moment later they were joined by an older Benesh'ere warrior, then after that a young girl, though she seemed every bit as warlike as the men. Together, the four of them headed toward the glistening, glass-like spires of a city in the far distance. She saw Morgin kissing a beautiful girl that looked much like Rhianne, and yet not. She saw him standing between two armies facing one another across a battlefield; one bore the banners of

Elhiyne, and the other that of Penda. She saw him leading strange beasts to war against dogs who stood on their hind legs and walked like men. She saw many images of him, and from them all she sensed *purpose*, not something that belonged in the past, but rather in the future.

Exhausted, she extinguished the spell and lay down to rest.

••••

Spinning . . . spinning . . . spinning

As Rhianne spun, completely helpless under the control of Valso's spell, she had no sense of the sword. Before, even without the enchantment, the blade had stood out like a beacon in a starless night, and Valso's spell had enhanced her awareness of it even further. But now . . . nothing . . . not the faintest glimmer. Slowly she spun down just as a toy top spins down, and finally collapsed in a heap in the mud, exhausted.

She'd watched Salula kill Morgin just moments ago. He was truly dead, and of that, she was now certain. She'd been mistaken about the skree killing him, but this time she'd felt him die, had sensed his soul depart the Mortal Plane. Laying in the mud with the halfman standing over her, she could not hold back the sobs that racked her body.

"Blast you, woman!"

Salula's rough hands gripped the front of her dress and lifted her to her feet, held her there dangling with her toes barely touching the ground. She opened her eyes and looked into his face, looked into the kind and friendly face of the swordsman France, noticed a runnel of blood trickling down his cheek. But she made the mistake of looking into those inhuman eyes; she saw Salula and had to look away. Wearily, she said, "I tell you he's dead. You killed him, and I felt him die."

He tossed her to the ground and she landed painfully on her shoulder. She had already learned that if she tried to just lay there he'd kick her until she stood, so she struggled to her feet, though the weight of the mud caking her simple, homespun dress made it even more difficult to stand.

"Then where was the body?" he demanded. "And where is that damn sword?"

She shook her head wearily, dislodging several clots of mud clumped in her hair. "I don't know. But that cave was heavily enchanted. In any case, I can no longer sense the blade so it too must have left the Mortal Plane, though that blade is not going to simply die."

He reached out and gripped her arm, turned and shoved her toward the horses. She barely managed to keep her feet as she slammed into the side of one of the animals. Salula gripped her by the waist, lifted her as if she weighed nothing and plopped her into the saddle. He tied her hands to the saddle horn as he grumbled, "Then it's back to Durin for us."

He tied the reins of her horse to his own saddle horn, then mounted up and led her away. The trail down the side of Attunhigh was steep and dangerous, so they moved slowly and it took almost an entire day to get back down to the foothills. As night settled upon them he stopped and dismounted. Still sitting in the saddle, Rhianne considered putting her heels to her horse's flanks and trying to run. But Salula must have guessed her thoughts. Holding the reins of her horse he wagged them at her and smiled. "It won't work, girl. Not while I hold these. And that'll only earn you another beating."

They unrolled sleeping blankets. He lit no fire, clearly afraid of the attention it might draw. Dinner consisted of jerky, journeycake and water. Autumn was not far off, and Rhianne spent the night shivering with only a single blanket to warm her.

In the morning they headed north up the east side of the Lake of Sorrows. Clearly, Salula wanted to stay far away from the Benesh'ere camp on the west shore. They also avoided Norlakton to the north, traveling on game trails through the forest until they reached Gilguard's Ford.

Before crossing the ford Salula turned to her and said, "The God's Road will be heavily traveled. But if you think to call out and get help from some traveler, you'll only get them killed, and gain yourself a beating instead of an evening meal."

Rhianne had no doubt the vicious bastard could make good on such a threat.

From there Salula pushed them hard, slowed to walk the horses only when needed, and didn't stop until well after dark. Each morning they returned to the road at sunup. Travelers on the road frequently took note of the filthy woman on horseback, but if they thought to inquire about her condition, the look on Salula's face turned them away quickly.

Rhianne drifted beyond exhaustion into a state of listlessness, and lost count of the days. It was easier to not think of the world about her, to forget her surroundings and drift off into near unconsciousness . . .

She landed on her elbow and the ground slammed into her painfully. She grunted like some farm animal and rolled onto her back, realizing she'd fallen asleep in the saddle and tumbled from her horse. She lay there for a moment, waiting for the pain in her arm to subside. But then Salula's boot slammed into her ribs, reminding her she must stay on her feet.

Holding her injured right arm tucked into her side, she'd only gotten to her knees when Salula lifted her the rest of the way. He slammed her back against her horse and slapped her hard. "You'll not delay me, woman."

He slapped her again . . . then again . . . He stopped only when she opened her eyes and tried to look aware and alert.

"That's better. If you slow me, I'll just tie you across the saddle like a sack of grain. You'll find a day or two like that very uncomfortable."

Rhianne managed to stay in the saddle, and by the time they reached the outer gates of the city she'd lost all sense of her surroundings. Only when she heard an unfamiliar Kull voice did she return to the present. It was late afternoon, and two Kulls stood among the armsmen who normally guarded the main gates of Durin. One of them nodded and said, "Captain, the king knew you were coming and asked us to await you here." The halfman smiled, though on a Kull's face it looked more like a grimace. "And it's good to have you back."

The two Kulls escorted them through the city to Castle Decouix where Valso awaited them in the courtyard, the little winged snake hovering just above him. The serpent darted toward Rhianne. She'd heard stories of its venom, and flinched as it hovered near her face.

"Massster," the snake hissed, hovering so close its forked tongue almost lapped her cheek. "Ssshe smellsss of power."

"Yes," Valso said. "She's a strong one. But leave her alone for now."

The snake zipped through the air, returned to hover over Valso. Rhianne let out a breath she hadn't realized she'd been holding. She couldn't find the strength to dismount so she remained in the saddle as Salula slid off his horse, dropped to one knee and lowered his head in front Valso. "I failed to retrieve the blade, Your Majesty."

"Come now, Captain," Valso said cordially, which surprised Rhianne, for she had expected anger from the Decouix king. "Rise. Rise and face me."

Salula's leathers creaked as he stood.

"Don't berate yourself, Captain," Valso said. "You were dealing with magics far beyond your comprehension. What of the Elhiyne?"

"I did put my dagger in his side," Salula said. "Deeply. I know that of a certainty."

The little snake hissed, "He'sss dead?"

Salula nodded over his shoulder at Rhianne. "She says he's dead, says she felt his soul depart the Mortal Plane."

Valso looked her way and regarded her. He stepped around Salula and approached her. "Ah, the lovely Lady Rhianne. Such a vision of beauty."

He laughed loudly. "But not so beautiful now. Come, my dear."

He turned to Salula. "Get her off that horse."

Salula gripped her by the waist and dragged her out of the saddle, then stood her up in front of Valso. The Decouix king looked her up and down and walked around her, carefully examining her from all sides, the snake hovering just above him. He stopped in front of her and said, "No, not so beautiful now. My dear, you look like a common peasant—no, worse than a common peasant. And you certainly smell like one."

She hated the man, but his words still stung. She wondered if she would ever be beautiful again, though she doubted she could ever be happy again.

As if reading her thoughts, Valso said, "We'll have to correct that, won't we?" He looked at the magical medallion embedded in the center of her forehead. "And we'll definitely have to remove that unsightly thing."

Rhianne struggled to overcome her exhaustion, to remain alert.

Behind Valso, Salula said, "I did not find the Elhiyne's body. She must be lying."

Valso's eyes narrowed as if he could see into her soul. And maybe he could, for he said, "No, I think she is not. In any case, the Elhiyne is of little consequence now."

"But what of the sword, Your Majesty? She can no longer sense it. Of that, I am certain she speaks the truth."

Valso continued to look into Rhianne's eyes as he said, "That sword is no longer on any plane of existence, for if it were I would know it."

"Then where is it, my king?"

Without looking away from Rhianne Valso said, "Dear girl, where do you think one might go to leave behind all the levels and planes of existence?"

With her thoughts muddled by exhaustion, she couldn't play a game of riddles with Valso. She shook her head, and caked with dried clots of mud her hair swung about her as if the ends were weighted by small rocks. "I have no idea, Your Majesty."

Valso looked back to Salula. "There is only one place it can be, Captain. A very special place, but a place for which I *do* have a contingency plan."

"Where is that, Your Majesty?"

Valso turned toward Rhianne and spoke to her as if she had asked the question. "It can only be in . . . the Kingdom of Dreams."

3

Lost in a Dream

MORGIN DIDN'T REMEMBER coming to the forest; didn't recall walking among its trees to get there, and had no memory of entering it from someplace else. He recalled only that one moment he had been dying in Aethon's crypt, then the next he'd been a whisper of thought rippling through the leaves of this forest. Then, without transition, he stood in the shadows cast by the dense canopy overhead. And he knew without doubt that he stood in the Kingdom of Dreams, though this time he sensed an overriding difference from his past dreams. He knew that his life depended on understanding that difference, so he pondered it carefully, and realized that for the first time he was not dreaming in the Kingdom of Dreams, but actually walking within it.

Somehow he had physically manifested in this strange forest, and he wondered now about his memories of the dark cave and the skeleton sitting on a throne surrounded by the trappings of a great king. He wondered if those memories were merely dreams. But one overpowering need drove him: he must find his way back to Rhianne and save her.

The density of the branches and leaves overhead allowed only the faintest light to reach the forest floor, casting it all in deep shadow, which comforted him. Here and there a small gap in the cover allowed a bright shaft of light to pierce the gloom and cast a brilliant spot on the pine needles and leaves that carpeted everything. He could have been content with it all, but the forest about him left him strangely unsettled, as if it were a living entity and him nothing more than a drop of blood flowing through its veins. It was acutely aware of him, as if he was an intruder that must be watched closely, though he sensed no malice in its watchfulness, so perhaps *intruder* was the wrong word.

Wanderer, a whisper of thought said as it brushed across his soul. *Searcher. Traveler. You have traveled far, and now returned.*

He turned around, thinking to find some stranger or spirit standing behind him whispering in his ear, but found no one. He stood alone in the shadows as a light breeze rippled through the higher reaches of the forest, rustling the leaves overhead and filling his ears with a soft hiss. But he caught the hint of another sound hidden within that noise, so faint that he wouldn't have noticed it had he not stopped to listen. He couldn't identify it clearly, shouldn't have been able to hear it at all, for it was far too faint. But the forest wanted him to hear it and so he did, though he knew only that it sounded human, and sad. There was never any question as to its direction, so out of curiosity, he turned and began weaving his way among the trees. Hopefully, he might find someone who could direct him to the Unnamed King so he could learn his true name. Then he'd have to find his way out of this forest and back to Rhianne.

He walked for quite some time, and the going proved easy, almost as if the forest opened trails before him. As he drew nearer to the sound he realized he was hearing the voice of a young woman sobbing quietly, a voice he recognized. Up ahead he caught a glimpse of something colorfully blue, visible only for an instant as a tree branch swayed to one side in the soft breeze, then hidden again as it swayed back. Ever cautious, he kept a large tree between him and the young woman as he approached her, using the forest skills he'd learned in the far distant past as a Benesh'ere. He stopped behind the tree, then leaned slowly to one side and peered around it.

She sat on a fallen tree in the middle of a small clearing, the sun's rays lighting the grass and flowers and leaves in brilliant splashes of color, framing the bright blue of her dress. He was far to one side of her, could only see her in profile, but he immediately recognized this girl. She had bright green eyes, fair skin and auburn hair loosely bound into a wimple, with a rich cascade of tresses hanging down past her shoulders. Sobbing quietly, she dabbed at her eyes with a small handkerchief. As he looked upon her from his shadows, a lock of hair broke loose from the wimple and floated down over one eye. She brushed it aside with an irritated swipe of her hand, much like one might swat at a bothersome fly, and for a heartbeat he thought Rhianne had escaped from Salula. But then he recognized Erithnae, a very young Erithnae, though his heart wanted to call her Rhianne, while something within him told him that was not her name in this time and place. He felt compelled to put another name to her, a mortal name: Rhiannead.

He released his shadows and stepped forth into the clearing, moving slowly and not wanting to startle her. She didn't notice him at first, didn't look his way until he took another step toward her. But then she looked up, and when she glanced at him she started and reacted strongly. She jumped to her feet, gasped, and with a look of absolute terror on her face she backed away from him. But she caught a heel on something, fell back and landed unceremoniously on her rear in a flurry of petticoats, emitting a very unladylike grunt.

He crossed the distance between them to help her, but she raised an arm to shield herself and cringed away from him. "Please!" she said, gulping air fearfully. "Please don't hurt me."

Surprised by her reaction, even a bit hurt, he stepped back, raised his hands and held his palms out. "You need not fear me. I would never harm you, my lady."

She lowered the arm a bit, but still held it before her and peered over it. She looked him up and down warily, and for the first time he looked down at himself. He wore a modest, leather jerkin over a gray blouse, comfortably loose pants tucked into knee-high brown boots; simple clothing of simple quality, though not the clothing he'd been wearing in Aethon's tomb.

Her brow wrinkled, then she frowned and asked, "You're not the ShadowLord?"

Clearly she feared he was the legendary boogieman. He said, "I'm not the Shadow-Lord of legend, though some have called me that. But that was just a pretend persona I assumed to confound an enemy."

Her frown deepened. "Well . . . you're clearly no monster, and . . . I think we've met before, though I can't quite recall it. Have we met before?"

Oh, he thought, *I could tell you such tales.* But he merely said, "Perhaps."

He glanced down at himself then back at her. "As you can see, I am merely a wanderer who's become a bit lost . . . and a bit confused."

Her impatience grew into anger. "And clearly no gentleman if you just stand there over a lady who's fallen and don't help her to her feet."

"I'm sorry, milady," he said, stepping forward and extending his hand. She reached out and put her hand in his, and when they touched a strange sensation washed through him, as if she were not this Rhiannead, but rather his Rhianne. Memories washed through his soul, glimpses of Rhianne and him, together then apart, happy and sad, the memories of a lifetime compressed into an instant. He staggered and forced his thoughts back to the moment, and by the look of awe and wonder on her face, she had clearly experienced those same memories.

He gently pulled her to her feet, meant to just help her stand, but she stumbled into his arms almost as if by intent. Without conscious thought he wrapped his arms around her as if his actions were dictated by another. He felt her relax and lean into him as she put her arms around his neck and pressed her body against his. They fit together as if the gods had intended them to find one another. Her lips parted, and he leaned forward to kiss her, as he had wanted to do for centuries, and she leaned forward to be kissed. It didn't feel as if he were betraying Rhianne with a strange woman, rather as if he were holding her in his arms.

They both paused at the same instant and frowned, not really kissing, their lips brushing together so lightly it felt like the mere touch of a feather. He thought that perhaps they weren't acting under their own volition, that someone or something else dictated their actions. But if that meant he would be forced to kiss her, he would happily comply.

"We can't do this," she whispered, breathing heavily, though she made no attempt to pull out of his arms. "I am betrothed to the Unnamed King." Again, she brushed her lips against his in that feather-light touch.

He said, "But you're so much like someone else I know. It's as if I've known you for centuries."

"And I you," she said. "Why is that?"

She removed her arms from around his neck, pressed her hands against his chest, but didn't push him away. "I think we are enchanted, but we cannot betray the Unnamed King this way."

He had pressed the palms of his hands into the small of her back, felt her spine beneath his fingers, wanted nothing more than to hold her that way through eternity. But he released her slowly, reluctantly, lowering his arms and dropping them to his sides, though she didn't step away from him, remained pressed against him. He looked into her eyes, saw desire that mirrored his own. Then she slowly pushed at his chest, as if she couldn't merely step out of his arms, but had to force herself to do so. And with a whisper of thought brushing through his soul the forest sighed its disappointment.

They each took one step back. "I'm sorry, milady. I don't know what came over me."

She lowered her eyes in embarrassment, could no longer meet his. "Yes," she said, clearly struggling to catch her breath. "Perhaps it's the forest."

"The forest?"

"Yes, this is the Living Forest." She spread her hands and looked about carefully. "It is called that because it is as intelligent as you or me. Can't you sense it?"

That explained the strange awareness he had of the forest. "Yes, I guess I do. But I don't understand. As I said, I'm lost."

She frowned and looked at him, evaluating him. "Maybe you're a dreamer. It is said dreamers frequently get lost in this kingdom."

"No," he said, shaking his head. "For once I'm not dreaming."

Then he realized who he was talking to. "You're betrothed to the Unnamed King. Can you help me find him? I've lost my name and need his counsel to find it."

He recalled the sigil of the Sunset King, scratched by the claw of a demon in black sand scattered on a yellow stone floor. And beneath it the demon had scratched two crossed swords. But that image brought terrible fear to his soul, and his heart began to pound unmercifully. He staggered, reached out and sat down on the fallen tree where moments before she had sat.

She stepped forward and stood over him. "Are you ill? You look so pale."

He dismissed the symbol of his unknown name from his thoughts, and his heart calmed. "No, I'm okay. Just a bad memory."

He looked up into her face. He had loved her once, still loved her, and now this Rhiannead knew him not, though again he saw that yearning in her eyes, in her posture, in every nuance of her movements. He thought if he pushed the matter, she would again fall into his arms, though reluctantly. But that would be terribly unfair to the betrothed of another man, a king, and he could not betray his Rhianne that way.

He glanced around. The two of them were completely alone, and that was not right. "You shouldn't be here in this forest all alone."

"Oh, I'm not alone." She glanced over her shoulder, then back at him. "At least I wasn't. I have an escort, or I had one. They were taking me to the Unnamed King so we could be wed. But I've lost them."

He looked at the forest about them. It wasn't so dense that one could easily misplace an escort. "I don't understand how you could lose your companions that way. Travel through this forest is not that difficult."

She followed his gaze, turned slowly around, and looking at the trees surrounding them she said, "Ah, but it *is* this forest. One moment the trail was simple and easy. The next it was completely blocked. For some reason it doesn't want us to travel further."

She turned full circle and stood facing him again. "We stopped, and I turned my back on them to go sit on this log, and when I turned back the forest had closed in between us. I heard them crying out, trying to find me, but their voices dwindled into the distance, and I was alone and lost."

"Is that why you were crying?"

"Yes, and . . ." She hesitated, clearly had something else to say, but held it back.

He prompted her, "And . . ."

Her eyes glistened with tears again and she turned away from him. "It's nothing. I'm just being foolish."

He stood, and from behind her he wanted to reach out and take her in his arms, but he dare not. She stifled the sound of another sob and turned back to face him. "No one can claim to have ever met or seen the Unnamed King, and I must marry him. And when I do, I have to become a god-queen."

"Yes," he said. "You're Erithnae? Or is it Rhiannead?"

She shook her head angrily. "It is Rhiannead, and I'm just a simple witch. But I must assume the mantle of Erithnae when I am wed to His Majesty, and I don't want to be a god-queen. And how did you know my name?"

He looked in her eyes and recalled that he had met Erithnae before. "I met you in a dream, but you always seemed happy and content. So I don't think you'll be unhappy with him. And I need to find him to find my name. If we can find your escort, perhaps you'll allow me to accompany you."

"Milady," a male voice yelled, hidden by the foliage of the forest.

She turned toward the sound. "That's Captain Rafaellen. I'm sure he'll allow you to join us."

She cried out, "I'm here, Captain. Here."

She and the captain shouted back and forth a few times, there came some thrashing about in the forest undergrowth, then a soldier in officer's livery hacked through the brush with his sword and stepped into the clearing. He was tall, well built, brown hair trimmed at shoulder length, his chin sporting a carefully manicured goatee.

When he saw the two of them he hesitated, sword in hand, and his eyes narrowed. "Why are you crying, milady?"

An older woman entered the clearing behind Rafaellen, stepped around him and rushed to Rhiannead. "My dear. Who is this man? Is he bothering you?"

"Oh no," Rhiannead said. "Not at all. This is . . ." She hesitated and turned toward him. "You have no name. What shall I call you?"

He tried to say, *I am Morgin*, but when he opened his mouth the words would not come. Time and again he'd learned that in the Kingdom of Dreams he could not claim a false name. But maybe he could do it differently, claim it not as a name, but rather as a simple label. "I am called Morgin," he said, and that did work. "I don't think it's properly my name, but it's as good a moniker as any."

She cocked her head and looked at him oddly. "You speak the ancient god-tongue?"

"No, why do you ask?"

"*Morgin*," she said. "In the old tongue *morgin* is the word for *mortal*."

She pondered that for a moment, then said, "That does fit you. Since you're not the demon ShadowLord, you must be a morgin, so I'll simply call you *Lord Mortal*."

Lord Mortal, he thought, recalling how she and the young boy Aethon had always called him that in his dreams.

Indicating the older woman, Rhiannead said, "This is Mistress Kenna."

Obviously Rhiannead's chaperone, the older woman eyed Morgin suspiciously. He understood her distrust, for he and her charge had been alone and unchaperoned.

Rhiannead quickly explained to Rafaellen and Kenna the circumstances of their meeting, finishing with the question, "How did you find us?"

"This blasted forest," Rafaellen said. "Without warning it thinned out and opened up, as if it had been waiting for something."

Rhiannead said, "Perhaps it was waiting for me to meet Lord Mortal here."

"Perhaps," Rafaellen said, eyeing him skeptically. When Rhiannead explained that he would be accompanying them, Rafaellen gave Morgin a suspicious look similar to that Kenna had given him, and Kenna actually sneered.

Rafaellen said, "Well, at least you brought your own mount."

Morgin frowned, confused by the man's comment. Then he heard a horse neigh, and turned around to find a coal-black mare standing a few paces behind him. She had not a mark on her to break up the unrelieved darkness of her coat. She was saddled and ready to ride, with a sheathed sword strapped to her side, a sword he recognized easily.

He said, "I guess I shouldn't be surprised you're here."

Mortiss neighed again, as if to say, *Of course I'm here. I wouldn't miss this for the world.*

4

Bird in a Cage

VALSO'S WORDS INTERRUPTED DaNoel's thoughts. *My Elhiyne friend.*

Not for the first time, DaNoel regretted aligning himself with the Decouix prince, now king. *What do you want?*

Why, we haven't spoken in some time, and I thought to inquire after your health.

DaNoel could not undo the choice he'd made, so now he must make the best of it. *My health! You have no concern for my health.*

But I do. You do not realize how valuable you are to me.

DaNoel suspected the Decouix couldn't speak the truth even if he wanted to. He bitterly recalled the day he had helped Valso escape from Elhiyne, and what a mistake that had been. Yes, Valso had discredited Morgin, had somehow made that sword go berserk at the meeting of the Lesser Clans. But then Valso had shown his true colors by almost exposing DaNoel's complicity. *If that's true, why did you wake that guard and leave me no choice but to murder him?*

I needed to ensure your commitment—your loyalty.

NickoLot almost discovered me. And now she is suspicious. The little brat limits my ability to aid you. That is all you accomplished.

Hmmm! That is a complication. Perhaps you're not as valuable as I thought.

DaNoel's heart raced as he realized his mistake. He needed to prove his value to the Decouix, for Valso had little to lose by discarding him. He resolved to find some piece of information to yield up.

What of your brother? Valso asked. *Have you had any news of him?*

The whoreson is not my brother, and in any case he's finally dead.

And how do you know this?

My mother grieves for him. DaNoel wondered if AnnaRail would grieve for *him* that way.

You've been mistaken about his death before.

DaNoel decided not to anger the Decouix by pointing out that it was Valso who had been wrong before. *There's no mistake this time. She says she felt his soul depart the Mortal Plane. And others felt it too.*

Interesting! I wanted to see if you could confirm that for me. Rhianne says the same, you know.

Rhianne? She's still alive?

Quite. And as beautiful as ever.

Where is she?

She's my guest.

Rhianne! Alive and accessible. Now that things had calmed down, AnnaRail and Olivia were becoming more serious about finding a wife for DaNoel, and he wondered if they might consider Rhianne. She was certainly prettier than some of the other prospects, and with the whoreson dead, now available. Just thinking about her he began to get an erection. *Will you return her to us?*

Interesting that you care! Only a short time ago you hated her as much as you hated your brother.

He was never my brother. In any case, with him dead, she may have some use.

Ah! You covet her for yourself.

No, not at all.

The Decouix ignored his protest. *Perhaps, if you remain valuable to me, I could give her to you as a reward. Do you want her for just one night, or several?*

I think you should return her to Elhiyne.

Now that is the most interesting thing I've heard you say. I'll have to think on that.

••••

NickoLot knocked on the door to her mother's sitting room. She had learned from the other women that AnnaRail had chosen to spend the afternoon alone, and she feared that her mother would again spend the time grieving for Morgin.

AnnaRail didn't answer immediately, probably taking a moment to dry her tears. When she did open the door her red and puffy eyes confirmed NickoLot's suspicions.

"Nicki," AnnaRail said, smiling. "Come in."

They embraced briefly, and NickoLot felt the tension in her mother's back and shoulders. It was bad enough to lose a brother; Nicki couldn't imagine how terrible it must be to lose a son.

AnnaRail sat down on some cushions in a window box. Nicki sat down beside her and said, "I've asked the servants to bring us some lunch."

AnnaRail's eyes focused on the floor in front of her. "I'm not really hungry."

Nicki had promised Roland she'd try to get her mother to eat something. "You must eat, mother. Starving yourself won't bring him back."

"It's hard to find an appetite."

At a soft knock on the door Nicki rose, crossed the room and opened it. A young servant stood in the hallway carrying a large tray of food. Nicki held the door open and said, "Come in, and place it on that table over there." She pointed to a small table to one side of the window box.

The servant walked past her and placed the tray on the table. She pulled aside a large piece of cloth to reveal two bowls of steaming soup, along with slices of apple and wedges of orange. Nicki helped her arrange them on the table. The servant then curtsied and hurried out of the room.

Nicki sat down in a chair at the small table. "Come, mother, please join me."

AnnaRail rose slowly, crossed the room and sat down opposite her. Nicki handed her the bowl of fruit, then started on the soup. AnnaRail selected a slice of apple, and nibbled on it as if it were an enormous piece of fruit that would take her hours to consume.

Nicki said, "I miss him too."

AnnaRail chewed some apple for a moment, her eyes focused in the far distance. "You know, the first time I thought him dead, I hadn't felt his soul depart the Mortal Plane, so I had some hope he was yet alive. It's almost harder to have gone through that first, and then learn that he is truly, unequivocally, gone."

Nicki couldn't contain herself. "I don't think he is."

"Oh, child, why would you say that? He is gone, and you cannot change that with false hope."

NickoLot recalled the images she had seen when she'd created the spell from Morgin's hairs and the polished rocks. "He is gone. Yes. I too felt him die, but I also think he still has a future among us."

AnnaRail considered NickoLot with a probing look not unlike what Olivia might have used. "What have you done? What do you know?"

The spell had been so unclear and confusing that she was reluctant to speak of it. Nevertheless, she carefully described how she'd searched Morgin's rooms, the few possessions of his she had retrieved, and the spell she had concocted. "I think I saw Morgin's future among us, and in it he is alive and well."

The grieving AnnaRail disappeared in an instant, and the strong and powerful—yet caring—mother that Nicki knew so well appeared. "Foretelling the future is a dangerous thing, easy to misinterpret and be misled. Please tell me the details."

Nicki carefully described the images she had seen, tried to provide as much detail as possible. "I saw purpose and intent, as if they were the future."

AnnaRail toyed with the piece of apple in her hand and stared at it for the longest moment. Then her eyes focused on Nicki and she said, "That was powerful magic you concocted. I won't ask you not to do it again, but do be careful, and you would be wise to have me ward you during such spell-casting."

Nicki said, "There's something else I have to tell you." She had dreaded this moment, and knew she should have told AnnaRail about Rhianne long ago.

AnnaRail lifted one eyebrow and waited for NickoLot to speak.

"When Jinella and I went to Norlakton . . . I discovered that the hedge witch we were sent there to examine was actually Rhianne in disguise."

AnnaRail's eyes widened. "You and Jinella knew this and you kept it from me?"

Her mother almost never grew angry, and Nicki had rarely been the target of her ire, but she felt it most keenly now. "Jinella didn't know. She's never met Rhianne, didn't know what to look for and wasn't strong enough to see through her disguise."

AnnaRail made no attempt to hide her disappointment as she said, "Oh Nicki, you should have trusted me with this. Where is Rhianne now?"

"I don't know."

"Norlakton, eh? We should send someone there to find out. Though I think we should not yet tell anyone else about this. Let me think on it."

"I'm sorry, mother."

AnnaRail gave her a forgiving smile. "You sadden me and hearten me with the same words. I suppose I'll focus on being heartened, rather than saddened."

She tossed the last bit of apple into her mouth, chewed it and swallowed. Then she looked down at the bowl of soup; it had long since cooled. "I feel quite hungry," she said, then picked up the bowl and began carefully spooning the cold soup into her mouth.

••••

Rhianne awoke slowly, didn't want to wake from such a dream. She languished in bed, relishing the comfort of clean, linen sheets, warm blankets and a thick feather mattress. It had been such a wonderful dream.

She reached up and traced a finger across her lips with a feather-light touch, the way she and Morgin's lips had brushed together in the dream. The dream had excited her in a very unladylike way, and disappointed her too. If she could dream that dream again, she would not be so prudent. She would fall into his arms and she would tempt him and tease him, which would tempt her and tease her as well. And she would do so until neither of them could control their passion. Morgin was ultimately too gentle a soul to just rip her clothes off, so she might have to help him a little in that.

Morgin! Dead! Tears filled her eyes as she realized they would never be able to truly take such pleasure in one another. But if she couldn't have him in reality, she would at least enjoy him in her dreams. Though she feared that, in the way of dreams, she wouldn't be able to control them that easily. If she could dream of him again, the dream would probably control her and not she it, and she would awake as frustrated and disappointed as now.

Such a strange dream: she Rhiannead—destined to be Erithnae—and he Lord Mortal. Strange that they had such difficulty simply saying his name, but then, it was just a dream.

"Milady? Are you awake?"

The previous day Valso had assigned a suite of rooms to her, then turned her over to a bevy of handmaidens. They'd bathed her, perfumed her, applied her makeup, and curled and set her hair. Then they'd presented her to Valso, though she was thankful the little demon snake had been nowhere to be seen. Valso had examined her much as he might one of his other possessions. As always, that one blasted lock broke loose from the elaborate tangle atop her head and drifted down over one eye, and he seemed to find that attractive. Clearly he considered a beautiful captive more valuable than one caked in mud and filth.

He commented on her bruises and the broken and chipped fingernails; none of the handmaidens were powerful enough to correct those deficiencies. And while she herself could have taken care of such minor inconveniences with her own power, she had no desire to increase her value in his eyes. No, she would fight him, even if she could only do so in small ways.

"Milady, you must awaken."

She suppressed her tears and tried not to think of Morgin. Her concern now—at least in the living world, not in the dream world—was revenge. She would find a way to avenge Morgin's death on Valso and Salula. If she succeeded in killing them in some way, she suspected it would cost poor France his life, but better that than allow such an abomination to live.

"Milady?"

"I'm awake," she said, making no attempt to hide her irritation, which was quite unfair since these girls were all young and quite innocent. "I'm awake."

"His Majesty requires that you attend him, and we've awakened you with time to prepare."

She opened her eyes; they were sticky with dried tears.

"Oh, you've been crying again, milady. You shouldn't cry."

She hoped Valso wasn't aware that these young girls had heavily romanticized her relationship with Morgin: the tragic lovers, him dead and her alive and grieving. Valso could be so cruel, and the poor things didn't know that she and Morgin had never been truly intimate. Rhianne resolved that she would correct that in the next dream, if she ever dreamed that dream again.

The ritual of applying her makeup, perfuming her and coiffing her hair took hours, but that was the way Valso wanted it. They finished by dressing her in an elegant gown of green brocade with a low front that made even her small breasts appear more ample than they really were.

One of the girls said, "His Majesty chose the gown to match your eyes, milady. And they are very beautiful eyes."

Rhianne smiled and asked her, "What's your name?"

The girl blushed and said, "I am called Geanna, milady."

Geanna appeared to have some authority over the rest of the girls. She always seemed to have little extra bits of information at her disposal. Rhianne strongly suspected that she was one of Valso's spies, and she resolved to carefully guard her tongue in Geanna's presence.

Her handmaidens and servants were organized like clockwork, and just as they finished the last of her preparations, there came a knock at the entrance to her suite.

It threw the girls into a frenzy. They rushed about, lined up, stood here, stood there, until they were all positioned in some predefined order, and Rhianne realized that she'd been naive. They were probably all spies for the king.

Valso entered, the little snake curled on his shoulder. He stopped before Rhianne and bowed with a flourish, which sent the serpent flying into the air. Valso was handsome and elegant, and she hated him for that. "My lady," he said.

The snake coiled on his shoulder as he looked her over, his eyes settling on her breasts. It reminded her of the night he'd turned her over to his Kulls in Castle Elhiyne.

"You are a vision of loveliness," he said, reaching out and taking her hand, flashing gleaming, white teeth in a big smile.

She realized then that she was a trophy, a symbol of his victory over Morgin. Yes, she would definitely find some way of avenging Morgin's death.

Valso looked down at her hand and frowned. "We'll have to do something about that," he said, looking at her broken and chipped nails. He would have his trophy perfect in every way, though she resolved to use her own power to undo any damage he had his healers repair.

He released her hand, walked around her carefully, examining her from all sides and commenting, "Yes, quite lovely, isn't she, Bayellgae?"

"Yesss, massster."

"Always the most beautiful girl at the ball."

He stopped in front of her, and again his eyes settled on her breasts. "In fact, you're so lovely, I might have to bed you myself."

She saw in his eyes that he meant it. It was no jest, and with that realization her heart began to pound and nausea washed up her gut and into her throat. She stepped back a pace, gagged and gulped trying to keep her breakfast down.

Valso must have realized she was close to emptying her stomach, for his eyes widened and he stepped back fearfully, as if he didn't want her to soil his boots. She managed to control her heaving stomach, and took some satisfaction in the look on his face.

••••

Lewendis eyed the Elhiyne border patrol in the distance. His gut clenched with anger as he thought of the last time he'd faced one of them. DaNoel had deployed archers, had used them to send Lewendis running fearfully back to his men, a few of whom had smiled in amusement. Even the grizzled old sergeant who'd led these men for years had had trouble hiding a grin. Lewendis had lost the respect of some of his men because of DaNoel, and he would not allow that to happen again.

The old sergeant didn't approve of Lewendis's plans, so he didn't look at the fellow as he said, "Deploy the archers."

••••

"There, my lord," one of the armsmen said, pointing north. "A Penda patrol."

Alcoa, March Lord and sworn to Elhiyne, looked across the creek that marked the border between Elhiyne and Penda. In the distance the Penda patrol reined in their horses and came to a stop. Both patrols rode forward, though the Pendas stopped about two hundred paces from the creek, and their leader issued orders, pointing left and right. His men spread out in a wide, skirmish line, strung their bows and nocked arrows. *Strange!* Alcoa thought. *And provocative!* He decided not to respond in kind.

He'd had reports from Brandon and JohnEngine of tension on the border with Penda. His own lands, bordered on the south by Aud, on the west by the sea, on the east by Elhiyne and on the north by Penda, were usually rather quiet. The worst he'd had to contend with for quite some years now were the occasional bandit or highwayman, and this new stress with Penda worried him greatly. He was too old for war, was looking forward to a doddering old age.

Following the old formulas, he and the Penda leader nudged their horses forward into a walk. At a hundred paces Alcoa did not recognize the Penda, had not met the man before, though from the description provided by JohnEngine and Brandon he thought the fellow might be the hothead Lewendis, and wondered why the idiot felt compelled to deploy his men in such an aggressive way. They each stopped their horses about ten paces from the creek, and for some reason the Penda appeared openly hostile, as if the two had some personal grievance between them.

"Elhiyne," the fellow said, his voice devoid of any decorum. "What do you want?"

Alcoa refused to be baited. "I am March Lord Alcoa, and you are?"

The fellow lifted his chin proudly. "I am Lord Lewendis." He'd placed great emphasis on the word *Lord.*

Alcoa said. "Greetings, Lord Lewendis. I hope all is well."

Alcoa's politeness clearly took the fellow by surprise. His eyes narrowed as if reevaluating the situation. "I am well."

"And your family?"

"Them too. Is there a point to this?"

The fellow's rudeness seemed more than just a symptom of his prickly nature. Alcoa said, "I am only following the formulas that our clans have followed for centuries."

"Of course," Lewendis said, as if he didn't believe a single word from Alcoa's mouth.

Alcoa continued. "And I have a problem with a pig thief. Well . . . now you have the problem. He crossed into Penda lands about three leagues east of here. He's a heavyset fellow of average height, with dark hair and a jagged scar on his left cheek. If you catch him, I'd prefer that you return him to me alive. We'll hang him ourselves."

"And why should I do your work for you?"

Alcoa couldn't believe his ears. "Why, because we have cooperated in these matters for centuries. And because if you don't, he'll just start stealing your pigs."

Lewendis frowned and appeared disappointed at the obvious logic of Alcoa's words. "Very well, we'll find your pig thief for you, though I can't promise we won't hang him ourselves. Is there anything else?"

At this point they should be trading information about the state of their mutual border, and Lewendis's attitude truly baffled Alcoa. "No," he said. "Nothing."

Lewendis looked him over as if trying to decide whether to have his archers murder him. "Then you'd best hurry back to your men, before my archers grow impatient, and we have an accident."

For some reason Lewendis wanted to provoke Alcoa. "I'll ride back, but slowly and without hurry. And if one of your archers grows impatient and puts an arrow in my back, you'll have to answer to the Lady Olivia as well as your own lord."

Alcoa reined his horse around, doing so with deliberate casualness. Then he nudged the animal into a slow walk, though throughout the ride back to his men, the skin between his shoulder blades itched unmercifully.

5

The Steel in a Bargain

WITH THE WINGED demon snake coiled on his shoulder, Valso held out his arm. "Come, Lady Rhianne."

Rhianne had not expected Valso to arrive at her suite accompanied by Bayellgae. He sometimes used the snake to execute those who displeased him, did so at odd moments, apparently on no more than a whim. She'd heard that the venom of its bite turned the skin black, a dark stain that spread outward from the wound, an agonizingly slow process that consumed its victim body and soul. The pain was reputed to be so great that death came as a relief. She wondered if there was something she might do to protect herself against that venom.

At her hesitation, Valso smiled. She had no choice, so she took his arm, and with the snake's head weaving from side-to-side only inches from her throat, she accompanied the king like some courtesan down to the Great Hall of Decouix. Just outside the hall they met Carsaris waiting for them, a tall, stick-thin skeleton of a man. Rhianne had heard of Carsaris, had met him briefly when they'd returned Illalla to Durin in chains. He was reputed to be very powerful, and a close confidant of the king, though his large, round eyes seemed to be shadowed by fear and distrust. And his thin nose and sunken cheeks only added to his spectral appearance.

Valso positioned Rhianne at the bottom of the dais upon which sat the great throne of Decouix. He put her on the left side, the off-hand side, then brushed the winged snake off his shoulder. It buzzed across the room and settled on a perch. Valso ascended the dais and sat upon the throne majestically, glanced down her way and she saw only malice in his face.

The Great Hall seemed rather bereft of courtiers. There was Valso on his throne, with Carsaris standing beside him on the dais, Rhianne at the bottom of the dais to his left, and Salula at the bottom to his right. Beyond that there were only Kullish guards lining the walls. The hall was a vast space, and its emptiness did not befit the grand court of the king of the Greater Clans. At the far end of the room the two massive doors that gave formal entry to the place seemed diminished by the unfilled distance that separated her from them.

"Please," Valso announced loudly. "If Her Majesty is ready to address me, I would have her come before me as an equal."

He had said, *Her Majesty*. There were no monarchs in the Lesser Clans, and only Valso in the Greater. That left Aiergain, but everything Rhianne had heard of the Mistress of Aud would not put her here conspiring with the Decouix.

Two Kulls threw open the great doors at the far end of the hall. They slammed against the stone walls with a loud crash that echoed through the vast space, revealing a small group standing just outside the hall. The distance was too great for Rhianne to make out any detail other than that they were dressed in an unusual kaleidoscope of bright colors.

Valso's chamberlain preceded them. He stopped halfway down the length of the hall and loudly announced a string of titles for this queen. Somewhere buried in his words was a name, but Rhianne recognized neither titles nor name.

The queen marched forward slowly in a stately fashion. She was followed by her retinue, who seemed a rather unruly bunch. And there was something quite odd about all of them. They walked with a strange gait, and from a distance the skin of their arms and faces appeared to be light brown, much darker than the norm within the clans. Closer yet and Rhianne saw that their legs were misshapen, or rather their knees seemed to bend the wrong way. And their faces were elongated, ending in a strange sort of muzzle very unusual for any person. They stopped a few paces distant, and still Rhianne didn't understand what stood before her.

Then her perception shifted, and she realized she was looking at dogs standing tall on their hind legs, walking like humans. The queen wore a strange hat with holes from which her long, pointed ears protruded, and a floor length gown that hid her legs. Behind her stood two dogs dressed in military garb, with epaulets and symbols of rank decorating their uniforms. And behind them milled an unruly group of warriors.

"Magwa," Valso said. He stood and descended the steps of the dais. "We are honored that the queen of the jackal court has accepted our invitation."

Jackal, Rhianne realized, *not dog.*

"Valso," Magwa said. Her voice came out in a strange sing-song, half way between the howling of a dog and the voice of a human. "Your messenger said you need my assistance in a matter of some urgency. But first . . ."

The jackal queen's head turned slowly and her gaze settled on Rhianne. The malice she saw in the bitch-queen's eyes made Valso's pale in comparison. Magwa walked casually toward her and stopped only a pace away. She examined Rhianne carefully from head to toes, then said, "This . . . I take it . . . is his bride?"

Rhianne struggled to hide her trembling. Valso approached and stopped beside Magwa, grinning at Rhianne's unease. "Yes," he said. "She's a lovely thing, isn't she?" He spoke to Magwa but his eyes never left Rhianne.

Magwa asked, "And she is—what you humans consider—beautiful?" Like Valso, her eyes remained locked on Rhianne.

"Quite so," Valso said.

"And *he* is dead?"

"We never recovered his body, but it appears that he did die."

"And this matter of some urgency?"

"There is a sword, a very important and unusual blade. It is no longer on any plane of existence, so it can only be in the one place that you are uniquely qualified to invade."

"And that would be?"

Valso finally took his eyes off Rhianne and turned his head to look at Magwa. "The Kingdom of Dreams, my dear."

Magwa continued to stare at Rhianne. "And why should I assist you?"

Valso's words were almost a smug insult. "Because it will make our mutual master happy. And if you do not, he will be sorely displeased."

"But the Living Forest will oppose us."

"Our master will see that the Living Forest does not hinder you."

Magwa nodded slowly, accepting his words with indifference. "Very well, we'll get your blade for you. But I do have a price."

"And that is?"

If a jackal's face could be said to grin, Magwa's did. "I never had the opportunity to exact my revenge upon her husband, not in a properly long and drawn-out fashion. I killed his Benesh'ere alter-ego quite a few centuries ago, but that was too quick and not at all satisfying. So when I bring you this sword, you will give *her* to me." She nodded her head, indicating the jackal warriors standing behind her. "So that I can give her to them."

For the first time Rhianne truly looked at the warriors standing behind Magwa. The eyes of every one of them were locked on her, and in their faces she saw their anger and hatred; she saw her fate.

"They too want revenge," Magwa said. "So her death will be long and slow in the making."

"Done!" Valso said happily.

Rhianne did not faint, but her knees gave out and she could no longer stand. No one bothered to catch her as she fell to the cold, stone floor.

••••

Chrisainne kept Valso's odd little charm in a pouch around her neck. The coin was much too important to just leave lying around, for without it she'd have no way of contacting him, would have to wait for him to contact her. Interestingly, while she was not a weak witch, she couldn't sense even a hint of the magic he'd poured into it, which impressed her even further with his strength and power.

Alone in her room, she sat down in a chair, then kissed the coin and closed her eyes to wait.

After several moments Valso said, *I'm busy, so make it quick.*

Your Majesty, the situation on the border should begin to heat up nicely. Apparently, Lord Da-Noel is as much a hothead as Lewendis.

Good. You're doing well, girl. Keep up the pressure. I'll get back to you later.

Valso withdrew from her thoughts.

An hour later BlakeDown had her pinned against the back wall of the stable when Valso returned to her. *You have done well, girl. My compliments.*

Thank you, Your Majesty. I am pleased that you are pleased.

BlakeDown pounded in and out of her with his usual lack of grace or finesse. She had recently become rather adept at communicating with Valso while in the presence of others. It was especially easy to do so with BlakeDown while lust clouded his mind. "Oh, my lord," she cried out, pretending that his crude and unskilled efforts brought her pleasure.

I take it you and BlakeDown are enjoying yourselves?

No, Your Majesty. I see to it that he enjoys himself, but at lovemaking he is a graceless pig, so I must pretend.

Well then I feel even more indebted to you, girl.

No, Your Majesty. Please don't feel that way. I take great pleasure in serving you, even if I take none from him.

BlakeDown's efforts grew more frantic, he grunted loudly and jerked spasmodically as he spilled his seed inside her. She cried out again, pretending to climax along with him, thinking she'd have to check the charms she had concocted to prevent pregnancy.

When BlakeDown had finished he held her pinned against the wall for some seconds while he caught his breath. Then he withdrew from her, stepped back, reached out and grabbed a fold of her skirts. He wiped his penis on it, and said, "Girl, you are a wonder! How you bring such pleasure I cannot fathom."

She blushed purposefully and said, "And you, my lord, return the pleasure ten-fold."

He pulled up his pants, tied the laces carefully. Then he leaned forward, kissed her on the cheek and clutched one of her breasts, squeezing it like an apprentice cook might knead bread. "I have a meeting with one of my liegemen, so I must leave you." He turned and strode out of the stable.

Such a consummate actress, Valso said.

It is necessary, Your Majesty.

Perhaps, when you return to Durin, I might personally show you real pleasure.

That would only be added reward for me, Your Majesty. But until then, I will continue to lead BlakeDown down the path to war.

Be careful, he said. *Not too soon. I do not want open war until the time is right. For the time being, let's keep it at just a skirmish or two.*

Yes, Your Majesty. I value your guidance in all matters.

As you should. Don't fail me, girl. Keep the blister irritated, but don't pop it. Do this properly for me, and you will be quite happy with your reward.

Thank you, Your Majesty.

Valso withdrew from her mind. She pulled up her smallclothes, retied the laces, arranged her petticoats and her skirt, then laced her blouse.

While BlakeDown had brought her no pleasure, the act of pleasuring him had aroused her greatly, and she needed to sate her own lust. Time to find that stable boy.

••••

Clearly, Captain Rafaellen considered it his duty to keep Morgin and Rhiannead separated, while Kenna hovered over her constantly. Rafaellen had a troop of 12 soldiers, a reasonable escort in friendly territory. He placed Morgin at the rear of the column with a squad of his soldiers while he, Rhiannead and Kenna rode at the head of the group, with scouts ranging ahead. As they rode Morgin tried to draw out the soldiers near him, but they were a tight-lipped bunch, so he quickly gave up and rode in silence.

He longed to be near Rhiannead, was drawn to her by the flood of memories that had come at the touch of their hands. Was she aware of Rhianne, as he and Morddon had been aware of one another? Throughout that day he recalled his memories of haunting the ancient Benesh'ere warrior's soul. In the far-distant past they had fought as one in the Great Clan Wars, fought alongside archangels and griffin lords, and together suffered the Archangel Metadan's betrayal. Was Rhianne hidden there somewhere in Rhiannead's soul, and could he learn from her Rhianne's fate at the hands of Salula? He needed to return to Rhianne, to rescue her from Salula, but how did one get out of the Kingdom of Dreams and return to the Mortal Plane? The Unnamed King would know the answer to that, another reason to find him.

Throughout that day, Rhiannead repeatedly turned about in her saddle and glanced back his way. She must have done so a hundred times, and each time Kenna and Rafaellen took note of it, and each time he saw their distrust of him deepen. And each time he found it harder to believe that she was not Rhianne.

That evening they camped near a small brook. Morgin unsaddled Mortiss, let her drink her fill, fed her from the troop's supply of oats, then tethered her with the rest of the horses. While Rafaellen and a few of his soldiers pitched a tent for Rhiannead and Kenna, Morgin and the rest collected rocks and assembled two fire pits. One of the soldiers pointed Morgin to a seat at the pit farthest from the tent, farthest from Rhiannead. Morgin carefully chose a position from which he could watch her, though it was a torment to do so since it only fueled his desire to speak with her, to learn if she knew of Rhianne. And she, either by chance or design, sat down in a spot where she could watch him.

They prepared a simple meal, a soldier's meal. Morgin chewed on some beans, and a tough biscuit, and some jerky that had been cooked in the beans but still had the consistency of leather, and he watched Rhiannead, though he tried not to be obvious about doing so. He had loved her for centuries, though he didn't understand how he could love anyone for such a length of time since he was mortal, or *morgin* in the old tongue.

Morgin and the soldiers bedded down in the open, and when he finally crawled into his blanket, it had been a long day filled with frustration. Before he closed his eyes he noticed that Rafaellen's soldiers positioned their blankets so they formed a clearly defined defensive wall, surrounding him and separating him from Rhiannead, who had disappeared into the tent with Kenna. Or was she Rhianne?

No, he would not allow himself to be fooled by her looks. But it all seemed so confusing.

••••

Throughout the day Rhiannead tried not to think of Lord Mortal, and yet a part of her cared nothing for the obligations of her birth. She sensed another being within her soul, a manifestation that had come upon her only when their hands had touched, a young woman from Lord Mortal's past. She realized now that the flood of memories had come from that other being, and that she and Lord Mortal had been separated, and longed to find each other again. Without conscious thought she glanced over her shoulder to look at him. And when not doing that, she could think only of that almost-kiss they had shared, and she longed to make it a real kiss—or was it that other presence within her that longed to make it a real kiss? She tried to stay focused on the trail ahead of her, but time and again, without even realizing it, she glanced his way.

"Milady," Kenna said. "You must move with caution here."

"I don't know what you mean."

"Do not allow a handsome stranger to turn your eye away from your duty."

"Trust me, Kenna. I know my duty well."

"You may know your duty, child, but I think you do not know your heart. Be careful, and do not allow yourself to be tempted so."

Rhiannead knew that Kenna was all too right. And yet, that other woman who haunted her soul cared so much for Lord Mortal that she would defy all convention to be with him. Oddly, Rhiannead felt the same, though she knew she must resist any such inclination.

That evening Rafaellen and Kenna hovered over her as she ate dinner, then all but confined her to her tent.

6

Intruders in a Dream

NICKOLOT CLOSED THE door to her room, latched it and turned the key in the lock. Then she placed the charm she had prepared over the latch and activated it with a bit of saliva, an arcane protection far more powerful than any mundane lock and key.

She had eaten a quiet dinner with AnnaRail and Jinella, Brandon's pretty, young wife. Jinella still had no idea that the hedge witch she'd interviewed in the inn in Norlakton had been Rhianne in disguise. And if she learned of it she'd probably blame herself for Rhianne's absence, thinking that if she'd recognized her she could have helped her in some way. Nicki liked Jinella; she was kind and pleasant, with not a hint of arrogance about her, and unlike most clanswomen she didn't question Nicki's strange and rather unflattering choice of attire.

NickoLot sat down at her small writing table. Most strong witches maintained a well-stocked workroom for practicing the arcane arts. AnnaRail had even offered to make something like that available to Nicki, but Nicki had declined. A piece of her wanted to remain a little girl, didn't want to acknowledge that she had grown into a very powerful witch.

She opened a small chest she kept under the table, and from it retrieved the items she had found when searching Morgin's rooms. She laid them out before her: the old comb with a few missing teeth from which she'd extracted several of Morgin's hairs, the cheap knife, the broken shard of a mirror, the small bronze pendant, the four shiny stones polished by the weather, and the two dove feathers. She'd stored his old boots in her own closet since she couldn't think of any real use for them. Clothing rarely had any strong connection to its owner.

The collection frustrated her. There must be some significance to all the items, but only the comb, hairs and stones had any strong ties to Morgin. The cheap knife, the shard of mirror, the pendant and the feathers; what did they mean to Morgin that he valued them so? He *must* have valued them to have kept them all these years. But time and again Nicki had tried to glean their connection to him, and found it tenuous at best. She had resolved to try one last time.

She hoped to use the hair to make a stronger connection to the other items. She pulled one strand of hair from those she'd extracted from the comb, pulled one of her own hairs and carefully wound the two together, then shaped them into a witch's knot. The hairs didn't want to hold to such a complex pattern, so she stuck pins into the wood of the table to maintain the shape. She had chosen the witch's knot because, unlike so many symbols used in the arcane arts, it did not represent the feminine powers, but rather an inversion of those powers, which should help make a stronger connection to Morgin.

She picked up the knife and examined it carefully. The blade was just a bit longer than her middle finger, ending in a needle-sharp point. It had been crudely formed, a straight slash of metal without the lines and shape common to a well-made blade, with an edge that dulled quickly when used. JohnEngine told her the blade was forged of soft iron, and would only hold an edge for a brief time. The handle—*hilt*, JohnEngine had called it—had been poorly repaired at some point. It had probably once been wrapped with leather, but was now padded with nothing better than dirty strips of cloth.

She cleared her mind of all stressful thoughts, recalled with pleasure the funny faces Morgin had made for her when he was a young boy of seven or eight, and she a small child still staggering around on unsteady legs. And with those happy thoughts to calm her, she looked again at the knife so she could recall from memory every facet of its nature. Then she pressed it against her breast with her left hand, and placed the tip of the ring finger of her right hand in the middle of the witch's knot.

She took a deep breath, let it out slowly, closed her eyes and drew power. She fed power into the witch's knot, and into the blade, and opened her mind to whatever thoughts or images might come. She sat that way for an unknown time and nothing happened, so she fed a little more power into the knife and was rewarded with a faint image. She saw a street that could be part of any large city, filled with people and horses and carts. She only caught a momentary glimpse before the image shifted, and now she confronted an angry mob. Then it shifted again to an alley, choked with refuse and debris.

She felt weak and lightheaded, and knew she had fed too much power into the knife. But when she tried to stop, it drew more from her, sucking it out of her soul hungrily. It had a desperate need for raw power, and she didn't think she could control it, feared now that it would drain her completely and leave nothing but a lifeless husk seated at her little writing table.

No, child, we're here to help you.

She had never before heard Olivia speak kindly, and to hear her do so now was the strangest of sensations. She felt Olivia's power as the old woman wrapped a spell about the knife, shielding her from it. And then AnnaRail wrapped her in the warm blanket of her power.

NickoLot opened her eyes. She still held the knife clutched to her breast, with the tip of her finger still centered on the witch's knot. AnnaRail stood on her right, Olivia on her left. It did not surprise her that either of the two could easily thwart the arcane lock she'd placed on her door. She sighed, lifted her finger out of the witch's knot and placed the knife on the workbench.

The cold indifference had returned to Olivia's voice when she said, "And what were you at, child?"

AnnaRail reached out and picked up the knife. "Isn't it obvious?"

Olivia scanned the items on the workbench. "I've never seen these items before. What is their significance?"

NickoLot shrugged. "They were Morgin's. He valued them in some way."

"Ah!" Olivia said. "Summoning the dead, are we?"

Nicki and AnnaRail had agreed that they would tell no one of her prescient view of Morgin walking among them in the future, but Nicki had no easy way of explaining her actions now.

AnnaRail came to her rescue. "No, mother. Morgin played a significant role in events that will shape the future, and we're trying to understand that. Nicki and I have discussed this." AnnaRail's eyes narrowed as she looked at Nicki. "We also agreed that she wouldn't attempt such powerful spell-crafting without my knowledge."

NickoLot looked at Olivia. "I thought you wouldn't approve."

Olivia frowned. "Me? Not approve of powerful spell-crafting? Why, child, I've encouraged you every day of your life to push yourself. You clearly have far more ability than most, and you have the control to exercise it properly. What I disapprove of is your recklessness. I won't stop you from such spell-crafting, nor will I disapprove of it. But you should have your mother, or me, present to ward you."

AnnaRail added, "She is right, daughter. But you're wrong about these items. They didn't all belong to Morgin. Not truly."

Nicki frowned and looked at her mother, trying to understand how she could be so wrong. "Of course they were Morgin's. They were in a chest in his room."

AnnaRail leaned forward and carefully slid the comb, polished stones and hairs to one side. "These were Morgin's. The rest . . ." She waved a hand, indicating the knife, pendant, shard of mirror, and feathers. "Rat was carrying the knife when Roland found him. The rest I retrieved from his lair. So in many ways they did not belong to Morgin. Rat valued them in some way, and they belonged to him."

••••

Chrisainne hated stitchery, found it a boring drudge. But on this quiet afternoon she must sit with Theandrin, BlakeDown's wife, and pretend she found it rewarding. She'd much rather be riding that strong, young stable boy. He'd proven to have quite a bit of stamina, and she took far greater pleasure from him than she did from that pig BlakeDown, or her own husband for that matter.

Theandrin put her stitchery hoop down and sighed. "I tire of this," she said. She had clearly been quite beautiful when younger, was even now, in middle age, a handsome woman with pale-brown hair and attractive blue eyes. Chrisainne had gone to considerable trouble, had employed the best of her magic and powers to ensure that the older woman heard not the slightest hint of her seduction of BlakeDown.

Chrisainne put her hoop down. "Yes. It isn't the most entertaining of pastimes."

Theandrin stood and walked over to the room's single window. Looking at something outside in the castle yard, she said, "I worry about this border situation with Elhiyne. It grows less stable every day, and neither of us can afford war. But each day seems to bring a new escalation of the tension, as if someone actually wants us to war. And my husband refuses to keep me informed of the latest developments. I'm forced to listen to rumors from the servants, and I do not like conjecture."

If only Valso could hear Theandrin's words, he'd be even more pleased with Chrisainne. "Yes, Your Ladyship, it is troubling. But surely no one would want to see war between us, at least no one in the Lesser Clans."

Theandrin turned a bit and looked at Chrisainne. "You're quite right; no one in the Lesser Clans. But the Decouix king would like nothing more than to see us tear each other apart."

Chrisainne's heart beat just a little faster. "Do you believe that Valso is interfering in some way?"

"No. I've carefully checked all our border lieutenants and everyone else involved. And I've put certain safeguards in place. None of them are working for Valso." She extended a hand. "Come, child. Bring an old woman some comfort."

Chrisainne stood and crossed the room, took Theandrin's hand in both of hers. "You're cold," she said. She clutched the older woman's hand close to her breast and rubbed it to warm it. The courtyard below the window bustled with the daily routine of the castle.

"Thank you, child. Thank you. It must bore you to have to keep an old woman company this way."

"Not at all, Your Ladyship."

"Oh come now, child. Certainly you'd rather be in the stable loft under that stable boy, letting him ride you like a brood mare."

Chrisainne froze and her heart went cold. "What do you mean, my lady? I don't understand." She tried to release the older woman's hand, but Theandrin wrapped her fingers about Chrisainne's wrist in a painful grip.

"Don't play games with me, girl. I know everything that goes on beneath my roof."

Chrisainne focused on the courtyard below. She dare not meet the older woman's eyes, and prayed she only knew about the stable boy.

"You bedded the boy, and you bedded his master to keep him quiet. Well . . . I don't think there were any beds involved, were there? Let me see, the stable boy had you on your back in the straw. And his master . . . what did he do, just stand you up against a wall?"

Trembling, but thankful that there'd been no mention of BlakeDown, Chrisainne said, "It was a foolish dalliance. I don't know what came over me."

"Oh, I know what came over you," Theandrin said. "And I want you to do me a favor. The next time you fuck my husband, I want you to learn all his thoughts on the Elhiyne border situation. It's deteriorating rapidly, and I want to know everything. So come to me afterwards and tell me what you've learned."

"I . . ." Chrisainne said as her gut clenched with fear. "I—"

"Don't speak, girl. Just listen."

Chrisainne clamped her mouth shut.

"That's better. Now you have to be careful here, if you want to survive. If my husband hears you've been soiling him by mixing his seed with that of stable hands, he'll have all three of you murdered in rather short order."

Chrisainne continued to stare out the window, though in the corner of her eye she saw enough to know that Theandrin turned her head to look her way. "And be careful not to find yourself with child. You're what . . . the tenth of his playthings to have come along. I don't really know; I long ago lost count. And I'm not counting the whores and barmaids. There was one girl, some years back, quite a pretty thing as I recall. She lasted all of three years, but she grew careless. Or perhaps she thought she might garner favor by bearing him a child. It doesn't matter. Neither my husband nor I will allow such a complication to muddy the waters of the Penda inheritance. The poor girl, and her unborn babe, died of a horrible accident. Such a shame!"

Theandrin slackened her grip and released Chrisainne's wrist. "Let me be clear about this, girl. You will do as I say, or I will tell my husband of your dalliance with the stable hands, and we'll be rid of you in rather short order."

Theandrin turned, though Chrisainne did not turn with her and remained standing at the window looking out at the courtyard. The older woman stepped out of sight, and Chrisainne heard the patter of Theandrin's feet as she crossed the room. But the patter stopped before she opened the door.

"Oh," Theandrin added. "And be sure you fuck my husband again sometime before tomorrow afternoon. I do so want that information . . . and sooner rather than later."

••••

Your Majesty, you must awaken.

Morgin opened his eyes, and in the darkness that enveloped him he considered lighting a candle. He'd get dressed, clean up his room, get a quick bite to eat, then join France for some sword practice in the castle yard.

Your Majesty.

The voice of the shadowwraith brought him back to the moment. France! Poor France, haunted and possessed by Salula. When Morgin did awake from this dream, he had to save France as well as Rhianne. But he couldn't just kill Salula. He'd learned from experience that all he'd accomplished the first time was to slay Salula's host. So simply killing Salula would kill only the swordsman, and not the demon.

There is danger.

Danger? Rhiannead! Rafaellen! Kenna!

He wrapped a shadow about him and sat up slowly. There was no hint of light in the eastern sky, so he guessed sunrise must be some hours away. The shadowwraith Soann'Daeth'Daeye, hovered above him, and oddly enough, he saw it clearly, even in the dark. Shaped much like a man, it had no face to speak of, only the poorly defined shapes of head, shoulders, arms, torso and legs.

Nearby, one of the soldiers snored loudly. Another grunted in his sleep. At the far end of the camp, a lone sentry paced back and forth in front of the tent. But other than that, all remained quiet and still.

Morgin whispered, "What danger?"

An old one, Your Majesty. Come, we'll show you.

Still wrapped in shadow, Morgin pulled on his boots, gripped his sheathed sword and stood carefully. None of the soldiers sleeping nearby sat up to challenge him, and the sentry near the tent continued pacing back and forth. He quickly counted the sleeping forms on the ground, accounting for Rafaellen and all his soldiers, so the captain hadn't posted any perimeter guards. No real need to do so in friendly territory.

He left his blanket behind and stepped carefully between two sleeping forms. He had observed these men through the day. They were experienced soldiers, so even the slightest of sounds might alert them. He used all of his Benesh'ere forest skills to move quietly to the edge of the camp and slip into the forest beyond.

Dozens of shadowwraiths awaited him. He considered getting Mortiss, but he couldn't saddle her and ride out without alerting the entire camp. So he buckled on his sword and followed the shadowwraiths on foot into the forest.

The shadowwraiths flitted through the branches of the trees in a simple, straight, easterly direction, as if they had no substance that could be hindered by mundane materials like wood and earth. The undergrowth of the forest was thin enough that he could have tromped through it, but it was easier to keep to small game trails, which forced him to zigzag back and forth. With his shadow sight he had no trouble following the wraiths in the dark.

They led him to the remnants of a well-organized camp, now abandoned. Situated near a small stream, it had the look and feel of an efficient encampment carefully laid out by a group of disciplined soldiers. He counted six fire pits, long since cold, and by that and other signs he guessed there must have been three twelves of them.

"Who are they?" he asked Soann'Daeth'Daeye.

We know not, my king. We can sense only their spoor, and we fear they are a danger to the Living Forest.

He recalled the way the forest had closed in about Rhiannead and her escort. "A danger? So why does the forest allow them to travel without hindrance?"

There is some enchantment about them, some power that masks their presence from the forest's awareness . . . and from ours. It is an old and deadly power.

Morgin searched further until he found the latrine pit. It had been carefully covered over with dirt, standard procedure for a troop of disciplined soldiers. But that did not mask the odor.

Dogs, one of the wraiths said.

"No," Morgin said, shaking his head. From an ancient memory he knew these foreign soldiers were not mere dogs. "No . . . jackals."

7

The Forest's Desire

THE SUN HAD just begun to lighten the sky as Morgin approached Rafaellen's encampment, but he heard the captain's voice raised in anger long before he got there.

"How did he slip away without you seeing?"

"I don't know, Captain. I'm sorry."

Another voice said, "He left his blanket behind."

Another added, "He left his horse too. So he's probably coming back."

Morgin approached the camp cautiously wrapped in shadow and stopped at the edge of the clearing near the tent. Rafaellen, Kenna and the soldiers stood over his abandoned blanket at the far end of the camp, arguing heatedly. Just a few paces away Rhiannead stood near the tent watching them, her back to Morgin.

Rafaellen's distrust of Morgin spilled out of every word as he berated the sentry. His misgivings might prove to be a serious problem, so Morgin considered slipping back into the deep forest and hiding among its shadows. He could follow them at a distance and retrieve Mortiss when opportunity presented him with a convenient moment. But they needed to be warned about the danger of the jackal warriors.

He checked his shadows carefully, then stepped out of the forest near the tent just behind Rhiannead. The overhanging branches of the trees threw shadows all about the tent, so he stepped partially behind it and dropped his shadows. He whispered, "They're angry with me, eh?"

She started and turned quickly to face him, but the fear on her face disappeared when she recognized him. She stepped quickly toward him, joined him behind the tent, and standing there no more than a pace away, he forgot everything and wanted nothing more than to touch her. Again, he sensed the forest's influence acting upon them both.

"Where did you go?" she asked.

"To do a little scouting. There is an old danger in the forest and Rafaellen must be warned."

"I know," she said. "The jackals. She wanted me to warn you."

She wanted me to warn you. That had been an odd way of putting it. And how had she known of the jackals? "Who is *she?*" he asked, but he made the mistake of looking into her eyes, and then he cared nothing for her answer.

"It's doing it again," she said. "The forest."

She raised a hand toward his face, extended a finger and traced the line of his jaw. And as before, when she touched him, a cascade of shared memories flooded through him. They danced together at a ball where they'd met, and later she hurt him, a wound of the heart, and he had returned the injury in kind. He recalled the kiss in the stables—but then he remembered that it hadn't been Rhiannead he had kissed.

She gasped, lowered her hand and shook herself. Her eyes narrowed and she spoke as if angry with him, spoke in a voice that sounded as if she were Rhianne. "I promised myself I would do this."

She reached out, grabbed him by the shoulders, pulled him toward her and kissed him with passion and heat and desire. He wrapped his arms around her waist as she pressed her body against him. She showed no restraint as their tongues danced together hungrily.

The kiss lasted an eternity, and yet it ended in the blink of an eye. Their lips parted, but she remained in his arms, her lips brushing against his cheek. She whispered, "We shouldn't do this."

He said, "It's the damn forest." He didn't add that he was glad the forest kept throwing her into his arms, though he knew he shouldn't betray Rhianne this way.

She said, "And I don't understand that. It is said the god-queen and the Unnamed King cannot truly come into their power until they are wed. I—"

"Ahhh!"

Kenna's shout startled them both, and they jumped apart like two children caught playing kissing games. Again, the forest sighed its disappointment.

Kenna marched up to them shaking with anger. "What are you doing?"

Rafaellen and his soldiers quickly surrounded them.

"It's the forest," Rhiannead pleaded. "It keeps driving us into each other's arms."

Kenna stepped between Morgin and Rhiannead as if she needed to protect her. "Impossible, you foolish girl. The forest would not press you to betray its master? You were raised from birth for one thing, and one thing only."

"That's not important," Morgin said, turning to Rafaellen. "There is danger in the forest, and we must be ready to defend ourselves."

Kenna swung out and slapped Morgin across the face so hard he staggered back a step. Two soldiers grabbed him and twisted his arms painfully behind his back.

Rafaellen drew his sword and leveled the tip beneath Morgin's chin. "What danger are you talking about?"

"He's lying," Kenna said. "He's making up a story so we won't punish him for touching the betrothed of the Unnamed King."

Rafaellen's eyes narrowed and he considered Morgin carefully. "We'll let the Unnamed King decide his fate."

Kenna hesitated, clearly unhappy at the thought of not killing Morgin right then and there. But then her eyes widened with calculation. "Yes. We'll take him before the Unnamed King for a proper trial, then hang him."

Still holding his sword tip beneath Morgin's chin, Rafaellen demanded, "And what is this danger you speak of?"

Morgin struggled in the grip of the two soldiers. "Jackal warriors," he said.

Rafaellen frowned with skepticism. "Dogs?"

"No," Morgin said. "Jackals, and they are warriors to be feared. They're an abomination that walks on two legs like men, and they carry weapons."

"I tell you he's lying," Kenna said.

Rafaellen looked at Morgin silently for a moment, then spoke to the soldiers holding him, "Bind him, then let's break camp and get out of here."

While three of Rafaellen's soldiers bound Morgin's arms behind his back, another unbuckled his sword and handed it to Rafaellen. The captain looked at it curiously, gripped the sheath in one hand, the hilt in the other, and exposed half its length. Examining it carefully, he said, "Not much of a blade. A poor man's sticker, at best. Not even worth keeping."

He slammed the blade back into the sheath, then tossed the sheathed sword into the undergrowth at the edge of the camp.

Morgin flinched. He hated that blade, but he also feared it being free and not under his control.

Rafaellen turned to two of his men and said, "I don't believe him. He's probably just making it all up, as Mistress Kenna says. But let's not take any chances. While you're scouting, be alert to any danger."

The two men mounted up, spurred their horses into a gallop and disappeared up the trail. Morgin sat on a log with his arms bound behind his back while the rest of them broke camp. When they were ready to go two soldiers boosted Morgin up into Mortiss's saddle while one held her reins.

Rafaellen spurred his horse forward and led the way out of the camp. The soldier holding Mortiss's reins handed them to Rafaellen's sergeant. The man spurred his horse forward and they followed the captain.

••••

After they had gone, and silence settled over the small clearing, something moved in the brush where Rafaellen had tossed the sword. A harsh grunt broke the silence, the kind of sound a wild animal might make. Then the brush parted, and a small, filthy, feral child emerged, wearing dirty rags and dragging the sword behind him.

••••

NickoLot didn't normally enjoy riding, but JohnEngine had picked out a gentle mare for her, and the scenery was wonderful. After two days on horseback they and their escort of two twelves of armsmen were nearing the Lake of Sorrows. And while the day had turned out to be a bit hotter than she preferred, pacing the horses at an easy canter put a comfortable breeze in her face that kept her cool.

She reached into her blouse and patted the hilt of Rat's crude little knife, just to confirm she hadn't lost it. Roland had helped her fashion a sheath for it so she needn't fear cutting herself. She now carried it with her everywhere and didn't let it out of her sight. Her instincts told her it held some importance she couldn't define, and yet the way she feared losing it bordered on the irrational.

She and AnnaRail had tried a number of spells in an attempt to locate Rhianne, but such invocations were notoriously unreliable, especially if someone with any power chose to block them. After repeated failures they concluded that Rhianne still wanted to remain hidden. So they agreed that someone must make the trip to Norlakton to bring her back, or at least learn of her whereabouts. Nicki had been determined from the start that she would go, but the leader of such an expedition would have to be a male member of the family. So they brought JohnEngine in on the secret of Rhianne's clandestine life as a hedge witch. He had been absolutely livid that she'd kept such a secret from him, and to show his anger he placed her in the middle of the column surrounded by armsmen, with him at its head. He refused to even speak with her for the entire trip, always communicating through one of the armsmen. *Tell the Lady NickoLot something or other,* he'd say, with her standing right next to him. *Ask her this, and tell her that.* Well, he'd just have to get over it. She'd had her reasons for keeping such a secret, and upon reexamination, they were still sound.

Up ahead, JohnEngine pulled his horse off the road and disappeared from sight. Moments later Nicki and her armsmen reached that same point and turned onto a cart track, nothing as wide and open as the Gods Road, but still well-traveled and wide enough for them to ride two abreast.

When she and Jinella had made the trip in the spring, they'd ridden in the comfort of a carriage and traveled at a much more leisurely pace, with Brandon leading the expedition on horseback. They'd both been glued to the carriage windows, trying to take in every sight they could. But most were just fleeting glimpses, and when one of them saw something of interest on her side and called out to the other, by the time they switched places it was usually too late. This time, however, riding in the breeches of a young boy, on horseback, in good weather, Nicki found everything of interest, especially the Benesh'ere camp.

JohnEngine chose a path that kept them out of the camp itself, but they passed rather close to it. Nicki saw hundreds of whitefaces walking about in their dune-colored robes, their white-skinned faces framed by coal-black hair. And then they passed the camp and headed for the north end of the lake.

It had only been a few moons since she'd last come to Norlakton, so as expected nothing had really changed. She was looking forward to seeing Rhianne again, and AnnaRail had told her to insist that Rhianne return with them, so she was also looking forward to the ride back. At the edge of town JohnEngine reined his horse to a stop, and as the column bunched up he turned to one of the armsmen riding beside Nicki and said, "Ask the Lady NickoLot, which way to this hut?"

Nicki had had enough. "Stop being such a child. I'm sorry I didn't tell you earlier, but Rhianne swore me to secrecy."

JohnEngine didn't relent. To the armsman he said, "Ask the—"

"Oh shut up," she snapped. "Just follow me."

She dug her heels into her horse's ribs, and taking them by surprise she left them all behind. She rode through the center of the small town and headed straight for the hut at the far end. But as she rode up to it her excitement at the prospect of seeing Rhianne again collapsed into despair. She stopped outside the hut and a moment later JohnEngine caught up with her. "Damn," he said.

The door to the hut stood partially open, attached by only one leather hinge and askew at an off angle. One of the shutters to the hut's single window had long since disappeared, and the other remained ajar, with cobwebs filling the corners of the window.

Nicki dismounted, her heart pounding with fear. As she started toward the door JohnEngine caught her wrist. "Wait."

"No. I have to see."

JohnEngine held her wrist in a vice-like grip and said to the armsmen, "Check it out. Make sure it's safe."

The armsmen swarmed in and around the hut, and a few moments later their sergeant stepped out of it and declared, "No danger, my lord. But something bad happened here a while back."

As Nicki entered the hut, from what she recalled of her previous visit, she saw that most of the hut's possessions had been stripped. One of the few items that remained was the small, wobbly table in the middle of the room. It had a large, dark, brown stain on it, with an even larger stain on the floor beneath it.

"That's old blood, my lord," the sergeant said. "A lot of it. Someone died here. That much blood, probably a slit throat."

It took great effort to hold back her tears as she said, "Let's check with the innkeeper."

They found Fat John standing outside his inn, wiping his hands on a grimy towel. A nobleman riding into town accompanied by a troop of armsmen would have caught everyone's attention.

"The witch," JohnEngine said, hooking a thumb over his shoulder. "The one that lived in the hut. Where is she?"

Fat John's eyes widened at the question. "I don't know, Your Lordship. She disappeared one night, a little less than a moon ago."

Nicki did the math, and turned to JohnEngine. "That would have been shortly before Morgin died."

JohnEngine ignored her and said to the innkeeper, "And the blood?"

"Her servant, Your Lordship. Braunye was her name, murdered the same night Mistress Syllith disappeared."

JohnEngine and Nicki took rooms in the inn, while the armsmen set up camp at the edge of town. That night, as Nicki lay in her blankets trying to find sleep, she found some solace in the fact that it hadn't been Rhianne's blood. She fell asleep clutching Rat's little knife to her breast.

••••

Chrisainne straightened her petticoats as BlakeDown walked away. She regretted ever letting him stand her up against a wall. That seemed to be the only way he wanted to make love now. Well, *make love* was probably not the right phrase for what they did.

It had not been difficult to meet Theandrin's schedule. The man's sexual proclivities made him easy to control. Interestingly enough, it was easier to manipulate him when in the presence of others. She'd wear a gown that exposed her ample cleavage, then flash a little ankle when only he was looking her way, and pass her tongue seductively over her lips. If she did that when they were alone, he'd just bend her over some piece of furniture and take her then and there, in an almost bored and detached way. But a few gambits like that when in the presence of others drove him insane, as if the need to wait fanned the flames of his lust until he almost trembled with the effort to control himself. When she did that, she could count on him to hunt her down as soon as he got away. And in that brief time before she let him have her, he would tell her anything she wanted, or accept almost anything she proposed.

Chrisainne stopped in her room to change into a clean dress, but looking in a mirror she noticed that BlakeDown had smeared her makeup a bit. She washed her face carefully, reapplied her makeup, then put on the dress.

She found Theandrin out in the west garden, discussing their supply of herbs with the chief cook, a buxom, middle-aged woman in a simple peasant dress with her hair tied up in an unglamorous bun. The cook had made it clear she did not like Chrisainne, though Chrisainne was confident the woman had no inkling of her relationship with BlakeDown. Her dislike was probably based on some perceived slight. In any case, a chief cook in any high-ranking household wielded a fair amount of power, so Chrisainne always tried to be on her best behavior around the woman. She stopped five paces from the two women and waited to be acknowledged, her eyes downcast. They took an interminably long time discussing herbs, but eventually Theandrin turned away from the cook and approached Chrisainne.

Chrisainne curtsied and bowed her head. "Your Ladyship."

"Come Chrisainne. Walk with me."

They locked arms and began strolling leisurely through the gardens, though Theandrin steered them carefully away from anyone else present. "So," the older woman said. "What did you learn?"

Chrisainne had to be careful. If she appeared too knowledgeable regarding the deteriorating border situation, Theandrin might realize she had an acute interest in exactly that. The first lady of Penda was not stupid, and such realization could lead to other more damning conclusions. So Chrisainne must appear to be a girl with no interest in such matters, and clearly ignorant of the politics involved. And such a girl would not know which bits of information were the most valuable. Chrisainne said, "Your husband doesn't seem to be concerned about the situation. Is it really that bad?"

"Oh girl, are you really that stupid?"

"But I don't understand these things, my lady."

"Well you'd better learn quickly. Did he say anything about ErrinCastle?"

Theandrin appeared to have accepted her pretense as a stupid, young girl. Now, give her something she already knew. "He did mention something about reviewing assignments for patrol lieutenants."

"Yes, he's been overriding ErrinCastle's choices. Did he say why?"

Time to give her something she might not know. "He said something about wanting more forceful leaders in charge so they wouldn't be pushed around by the Elhiynes."

Theandrin stopped, turned and looked at her. Chrisainne met her eyes with a look of confusion. "Did he now?" Theandrin said.

"Yes, my lady. Is that important?"

"It's his pride and his rivalry with Olivia. If she says black, he says white, and she's no better. The men he's chosen are not forceful; they're just hotheads, and if we're not careful this enmity will lead to open war. That would weaken both of us."

Theandrin turned and began walking again. "But that's not enough. I need more information than that. Keep at my husband, and learn what you can. But I'd also like to know what orders he's given to that hothead Lewendis, so seduce him as well."

That caught Chrisainne so off-guard she squeaked, "My lady!" She forced herself to calm down and said, "Surely you don't mean—"

"Surely I do, child."

"But Lord Lewendis is so . . ."

Theandrin smiled, was clearly enjoying Chrisainne's discomfort. "He really isn't very attractive, is he? Bit of a yokel, eh? But you're not going to seduce him because he's attractive, you're going to seduce him to get information. And this is not a request."

Theandrin smiled, released her arm, turned and left her standing there.

Chrisainne couldn't speak, couldn't believe what she'd just heard. Lewendis! How could she get out of this? She couldn't just pack up and leave. That would displease Valso, and BlakeDown would want an explanation, and Theandrin would give him one. No, she couldn't run away from this. But as she stood there watching the older woman cross the garden to the castle proper, she realized that there was no practical reason to seduce Lewendis. She could learn from BlakeDown what orders he'd given the fellow, and Theandrin certainly knew that. In that moment Chrisainne realized that Theandrin's decision to force her to seduce an unattractive bumpkin was simply an act of petty revenge. And if she didn't do something about it, in short order Theandrin would probably have her on her back beneath half the men in Penda.

Chrisainne's disbelief slowly turned into anger. She would take great pleasure in putting a dagger in the old woman's back; no, in her gut so she could see her killer face-to-face. And with that thought, a possible solution occurred to her. If Theandrin were to have an accident, something tragic and lethal, that would solve all of Chrisainne's problems.

Chrisainne had never killed anyone before and knew she'd have to think carefully on the method and means, so she resolved to do her homework before taking any action. But she would need time, and she couldn't stall Theandrin that long, which meant she couldn't avoid seducing Lewendis, and possibly a few others, if Theandrin pushed it.

Very well, my lady, she thought. *I'll fuck Lewendis, but you're going to pay for that indignity with your life.*

8

Prisoner in a Dream

RHIANNE AWOKE, FRUSTRATED beyond belief. Rafaellen and Kenna and the jackals all seemed to be conspiring to keep her from her dream Morgin. If not for the forest she probably wouldn't even have kissed him. How wonderful it would have been if she and he had been on their own in that clearing, alone in the forest with no enemies or chaperones about. She could have had him all to herself.

She sat up on the couch where she'd been napping. Shortly after lunch she'd dismissed her handmaidens, then sat down, leaned her head back and closed her eyes, hoping to find Morgin in her dreams so she could warn him of the jackals. She wasn't sure she needed to, since he was dead and lived only in her dreams. And in any case, it hadn't been necessary since he'd somehow learned of them on his own. But still, she'd been happy to see him again, to touch him, to hold him.

The jackals! Certainly they were real. Rhianne had seen Magwa and her retinue with her own eyes, had heard her talk in that distorted imitation of a human voice. But were her dreams real? They felt real enough, and yet there was no question in her mind that she'd sensed Morgin die, and he didn't have to be alive to haunt her dreams. And where was this Kingdom of Dreams if not on some level or plane of existence?

When Magwa and Valso struck their bargain to retrieve the sword, the bitch queen had said something about killing Morgin's Benesh'ere alter-ego centuries ago. Had they faced one another as enemies in another life, in some far distant past, or dream? In this dream Morgin sounded as if he knew the jackals well and was not surprised that they walked upright like men.

She thought back and realized that in the last year and a half she and Morgin had been in each other's presence for only two brief moments. The first had been last spring in the Great Hall when they'd brought Illalla back to Durin in chains, and Valso had stolen Olivia's triumph by having his Kulls throw a beaten and bloodied Morgin to the floor in their midst. Rhianne had defied Olivia, had sat down on the floor of the hall and held Morgin's head in her lap. He'd been semi-delirious, kept mumbling something incoherent about a *vast chasm of power*. And since then she'd only seen him that second time, less than a moon ago, high up the side of Attunhigh on a shelf of rock just outside the crypt of some ancient king, just before France—Salula—had killed him. Rhianne thought that Morgin might have some rather fantastic stories to tell.

"No!" she said, standing, shaking with anger and frustration. She would not be drawn once again into some misguided hope that he still lived. When that happened, it hurt so much to remember that he was truly dead. Her dreams were just dreams, that and nothing more, though apparently the place where all dreams began and ended could somehow hide that sword. If Morgin were truly still alive, and somehow hidden in the Kingdom of Dreams with the sword, Valso would have sent Magwa after *him* as well, with orders to capture or kill him. No, Magwa was after just the sword, because Morgin lived only in her dreams.

By the light from the window and the long shadows it cast, she knew she'd slept through a good portion of the afternoon. Shortly she would be called to dinner and she needed to prepare for that. She called in her handmaidens, had them change her gown, pin her hair up in the more formal style necessary for dinner, then freshen her makeup.

At dinner that evening Valso was rather expansive, playing to his audience of sycophants. That suited Rhianne nicely; had he made her the center of attention it would have thwarted her plans. She nodded politely when needed, was careful not to overcompensate by smiling too much, or being too pleasant, all the while her attention focused on the small roll of leavened bread near her plate. She tore it in half, nibbled on it a bit and concealed half of it in her hand as she lowered it to her lap. She'd chosen her gown because it had a small pocket hidden in the folds of her skirt. She slipped the piece of roll into it.

Later that evening, she hid it beneath the clothing in a small chest. She'd need more than just half a roll to survive when she made her escape. She was under no illusion that she'd be able to squirrel away enough to keep well fed, but she'd need something to take the edge off her hunger. She also had her eye on some of the servants' clothing. If she tried to travel in the trappings of a lady of the court, she'd be discovered rather quickly. But she'd noticed where the servants hung their homespun clothing out to dry after a heavy rain. And hopefully she might also come across a coin or two she could steal. A piece here, a piece there, and soon she'd be ready to make her move.

••••

The bindings that held Morgin's arms behind his back were tight enough that his hands quickly grew numb. He considered spurring Mortiss into a run—she'd know what to do, and with the element of surprise she might yank her reins out of the sergeant's hand. But without the use of his hands and arms it would be difficult to remain in the saddle during a mad dash down a small game trail in the dense forest. He'd probably end up with a broken neck, so he abandoned that idea, though he had no other options.

Mortiss spluttered, as if saying, *I'm not the one who got us into this mess.*

He recalled the kiss he'd shared with Rhiannead that morning, and he thought he should feel guilt at betraying Rhianne that way, but it didn't feel like betrayal. No, he'd kissed Rhiannead with a clear conscience, and he felt no remorse now. It occurred to him that kissing Rhiannead had been identical to kissing Rhianne. He thought of one, then the other, and tried to recall the feel of the young woman in his arms both times. They were indistinguishable, this Rhiannead and his Rhianne. His hands had held her slender waist, and he'd been so conscious of her small breasts pressed against his chest—

Mortiss neighed, *Keep your mind on the trail.*

He said to her, "They're identical in every way."

She shook her head, *Of course.*

He'd seen nothing of the shadowwraiths since returning to the camp that morning, but he sensed them now, fluttering just out of sight in the forest on either side of the trail. At least Rafaellen had heeded his warning of the jackal warriors, even if he had his doubts. Should an attack come, he wondered if the wraiths might help him escape his bonds.

By midday, when they stopped for lunch, his arms had grown numb to the shoulders. Two soldiers helped him out of the saddle, and while a third held a sword point beneath his chin, they removed his bonds. They sat him on a rock, his arms useless, floppy appendages, and as circulation returned he closed his eyes and grimaced at the sensation of a thousand needles puncturing his skin.

While they ate a quick lunch of hardtack, jerky and water, Morgin overheard bits and pieces of a short conversation between Rafaellen and his sergeant. Apparently the scouts they'd sent out that morning had not returned.

When they finished the meal the soldiers retied Morgin's arms behind his back. Again, they boosted him into the saddle, but just before they rode on Rafaellen said to his men, "Shields up. Be alert."

Rafaellen and his men each had a small shield strapped to the side of their horses. They unbuckled them now and raised them. The trail was wide enough for them to ride three abreast, so they sandwiched Morgin, Rhiannead and Kenna each between two soldiers. The soldiers on the left carried their shield on their left arm, and those on the right on their right arm, creating a wall of shields to protect them all.

As they rode, Morgin tried to be alert to every sound in the forest not of their making. And frequently he thought he saw some movement behind a tree a short distance off the trail. But nothing happened, and he realized he was jumping at shadows and the play of light in the forest, a foolish thing to do.

Mortiss neighed, *You're frequently a fool, but not in this.*

With dusk approaching Morgin tried be alert to every noise or movement without overreacting, and he heard the sound a heartbeat before he saw its cause: the unmistakable hiss of an arrow in flight. The shaft thudded into one of the soldier's shields. Another arrow slammed into the side of a horse, and another into the back of a soldier.

"Forward," Rafaellen shouted, and spurred his mount into a charge. The sergeant dropped Mortiss's reins and they all followed. Charging down a forest trail under any other circumstances would be sheer idiocy, but they had to get out of range of the archers and Morgin knew Rafaellen had no choice.

With his hands tied behind his back Morgin leaned forward in the saddle, and prayed that he'd not be unhorsed and break his neck. But leaning down like that he saw very little and had to trust Mortiss's instincts. He heard the clash of swords and shields and looked up momentarily, saw that they'd ridden out from beneath the rain of arrows and were engaged with mounted jackals.

The soldier on his right went down, opening up his flank. A mounted jackal warrior charged in and swung his sword in a flat arc. Morgin ducked beneath it and barely missed losing his head.

Mortiss reared and slammed into the jackal's mount, then charged past him and into the denser forest off the trail. Morgin clamped his knees into her sides as she struggled through thick brush, then broke into the clear. He heard the sounds of the battle behind him, looked back and saw that the forest had closed in about him. Apparently the forest would not allow him to return that way, though with his arms tied behind him, he and the forest were in agreement on that.

Rhiannead! "I have to free my arms and get back to protect Rhiannead."

Mortiss ignored him. As she trotted away from the battle and the forest closed in behind them, the sounds of the fight diminished until he heard nothing but the wind rustling through the leaves of the forest canopy.

••••

Rhianne's dream had turned into a nightmare. Several of Rafaellen's soldiers were wounded or killed in the first moments of the battle, and in the chaos that ensued two jackal warriors separated her from the column. One reached out and tore the reins from her hands. The other leaned toward her, wrapped an arm about her waist and pulled her from her mount. "You're coming with us," he said in the distorted, yowling sing-song of a jackal speaking as no animal was meant to.

She cried out as he lifted her and laid her across the neck of his mount like a sack of grain, then spurred his horse away from the melee.

This Rhiannead, this girl whose soul she rode in a dream, frustrated Rhianne to no end. She acted like a weak-willed child, and Rhianne would not allow that.

The jackal brought his mount to a halt and shoved her off his horse. She hit the ground off balance and fell unceremoniously to her knees, surrounded by mounted jackals.

"Did you find the blade?" their leader demanded.

"No," one of them said. "Certainly, no one fought with it. And after we scattered them we searched their pack horses—nothing."

The jackal captain cocked his head and asked, "Did any of you notice the one that was bound?"

"Bound?" one of his dogs asked.

"Yes, one of their own, riding among them with his arms bound behind his back."

"Yah," another said. "I saw him. Didn't pay him no heed cause he was no threat. What about him?"

The jackal captain cocked his head the other way as if considering that question carefully. "There was something familiar about him, an old memory that wants to surface, but I can't place it. And that horse of his, that mare; she had a nether scent about her, something old and familiar."

"What are you saying?"

Their leader shook his head. "I don't know. But I don't like this."

Rhianne sat there shocked beyond belief, while Rhiannead cried tears of frustration, her thoughts a maelstrom of questions. How could the jackal captain have recognized Morgin? This was just a dream; that wasn't supposed to happen.

"Well then," the jackal leader said, looking down at her. "At least we have her, and she'll make a good bargaining chip."

••••

Nicki recoiled from the disgusting little creature that stood in front of her. Dressed in filthy rags, it smelled worse than any sewer in Anistigh, and she feared that even being near it might infect her with some miasma. But when she saw that it dragged a sword behind it, her curiosity flared.

The little creature stopped in front of her, held out its hand and hissed in a cracking, guttural voice, "My knife. Give me my knife."

At first Nicki didn't understand what it meant, but then she realized her hand still clutched Rat's knife to her breast. By that she understood that she still lay asleep in the inn in Norlakton, and she and this creature inhabited a dream.

She'd been too young when Morgin had first come to Elhiyne to understand any of the stories and descriptions of Rat, and by the time she'd been cognizant enough to do so, some years had passed and the subject just didn't come up. She had never realized how truly degrading his existence had been, had even romanticized it a bit, made up an image of him in her mind's eye: a clean and healthy urchin of the streets, with just a smudge of dirt here and there.

"Rat," she said, "is that you?"

"My knife." He shook the outstretched hand to reiterate his demand.

She hesitated, didn't want to give up the blade. But it had originally belonged to him, and perhaps, in his hand, it would serve some purpose she couldn't fathom. She reversed the knife, held it by its blade and extended the crude hilt toward him. He wrapped his fingers about it, then took it gently from her hand, as if concerned that he might cut her or harm her if he snatched it away quickly. She'd sharpened it carefully, and knew that it could cause a nasty cut before the cheap metal dulled.

Suddenly she and Rat stood in the midst of the Benesh'ere camp with whitefaces everywhere.

"They knew him," Rat croaked.

Nicki slammed awake and gasped. She sat up, looked at the hand still clutched to her breast and saw that it held no knife. She threw on a robe, marched down the hall and pounded on the door to JohnEngine's room until he answered, bleary-eyed and confused.

"Wah . . . wah . . . what's going on? What's wrong?"

"We're going to see the Benesh'ere."

••••

JohnEngine stubbornly refused to take Nicki to the Benesh'ere camp. But then she told him about the dream, about Rat, and about how she'd gone to sleep clutching his knife to her breast—and awakened without it. JohnEngine insisted on searching her room, and after finding no knife he demanded, "Are you sure you brought it?"

"Of course, I'm sure," she said. "I'm not delusional."

He gave her a look that said he wasn't so sure about that, but he relented.

While JohnEngine returned to his room to dress she threw on the riding clothes she'd worn the day before. She retrieved a few charms she had prepared in advance, most importantly the truth charm. It wouldn't work well on a clansman with any reasonable skill at the arcane arts, but the Benesh'ere had no such defenses. She met John in the hall and they headed for the stables.

He and Nicki and their escort of armsmen rode out to the Benesh'ere encampment. The whitefaces were all about, in the town, between the town and their camp, in the forests around Norlakton. And they had posted no sentries, at least none that were apparent to her. But there came a moment when they crossed some invisible line, and they both felt a level of tension in the air that had not been there an instant before.

A tall whiteface carrying an unstrung bow stepped in front of their horses and said, "Good day, plainfaces. What brings you to our camp?"

Nicki thought she recognized the man, as if they'd met before. But that couldn't be, for this was the first Benesh'ere she'd ever faced. She reached into a pocket and triggered the truth charm.

JohnEngine said, "I am JohnEngine et Elhiyne, son of Roland and AnnaRail, grandson of Olivia, and this is my sister NickoLot. We are seeking news of our dead brother, who was named AethonLaw et Elhiyne. But you might have known him as Morgin."

"Dead, huh?" the fellow asked.

Nicki said, "Yes. I felt him die, but he wasn't among us when it happened so we don't know what befell him."

The Benesh'ere shook his head. "Never heard of him."

The truth charm tingled in the recesses of Nicki's soul. She leaned toward JohnEngine, leaned close enough to almost touch her lips to his ear, and whispered, "He's lying."

JohnEngine asked, "And may I have your name?"

The man smiled in a rather friendly way. "I'm Jack the Only."

"Well, Jack the Only," JohnEngine said. "Why do you lie to us?"

The man looked back and forth between John and Nicki. "Why do you assume I'm lying?"

"I don't assume. I know, because my sister here is a powerful witch, and she knows when a man lies."

The whiteface's eyes narrowed as he looked at NickoLot. "Are you practicing magic?"

Her patience had evaporated. "Of course I'm practicing magic. I practice magic as naturally as you breathe."

"I've met a lot of men that stopped breathing, even helped a few get there."

"And I've helped a few get there with my magic."

The whiteface threw back his head and roared with laughter.

Nicki added, "We're here because we loved our brother and we want to know what happened to him. Please help us."

The whiteface's laughter died. "And you have a temper just like your brother. Come, follow me." He nodded toward their escort. "But leave them behind."

The tall whiteface spun on his heel and marched toward the center of the camp. JohnEngine hurriedly ordered their escort to dismount and remain at the edge of the camp, then he and Nicki spurred their horses into a walk and followed.

Jack the Only led them to a large pavilion, stopped outside it and called, "Harriok. Branaugh. It's Jack. I have two plainface guests. May I enter?"

They waited in silence for several heartbeats, then the tent flap was thrown aside and a young woman stepped out. She wore an ankle length, hooded robe, not the sand colored breeches and knee-high boots most common among the whitefaces. She was pretty in a plain and simple way, but she carried herself with an air of rank and authority that would have stood out even on the plainest of women.

"Who are they?" she asked.

Jack glanced over his shoulder at them as he said, "They claim to be the brother and sister of some plainface named Morgin. They say their names are JohnEngine and NickoLot. They *say* all that, but who knows."

The woman nodded and looked at them as if trying to determine the truth of their claim. "Do they now?"

"And they say he's dead."

She paused for a moment, still staring at them, then said. "Get the others."

Jack turned and walked away.

The woman said, "I am Branaugh. Please join me in my home."

She called a young girl named Yim to see to their horses, and they entered the dark interior of the tent. She had them sit on cushions and served them tea, and NickoLot was about to broach the subject of Morgin and Rhianne when the tent flap was again thrown aside. A young man stepped in and introduced himself as Harriok. Like Jack, there was something strangely familiar about him.

Before Harriok could sit down a crippled old man with snow-white hair entered the tent. He supported himself on one side with a crutch, and on the other by leaning on a middle-aged woman. Olivia had described Angerah to her many times, so NickoLot didn't need to be told that the leader of the Black Tribe had joined them.

Angerah sat down on a cushion and said, "How do we know you are truly who you claim? Tell us of this supposed brother of yours."

JohnEngine gave a physical description of Morgin while a steady stream of whitefaces entered the tent, each interrupting him briefly while introductions were made.

Their warmaster Jerst said, "Yes, yes, yes. Anyone can tell us what he looked like. Prove to us you were his kin."

Nicki said, "He killed a lot of men and Kulls in the last few years, but he didn't like killing, hated it, in fact." She told them of the battle in the sanctum when the two of them had fought the Tulalane, and Morgin had killed the twoname. While she spoke more whitefaces arrived and it grew rather crowded.

Jack said, "I believe them."

Jerst's daughter Blesset said, "I don't. Anyone smart and clever could have learned these things about him."

Nicki hadn't paid much attention to the girl when she'd arrived, just one among many in the shadowy interior of the tent. But as the whitefaces argued about whether they could believe the claims of the two plainfaces, she looked at the girl more closely. Like Jack and Harriok she felt she should recognize the young woman. And then it hit her like a clap of thunder: Blesset was the whiteface girl who had accompanied Morgin out on the sands in Nicki's prescient vision. And with that, she realized Jack and Harriok were the other two.

In the midst of the heated argument, JohnEngine and NickoLot were, for all intents and purposes, ignored by their hosts. As Nicki tried desperately to understand her vision, someone from outside threw the tent flap aside, though when no one entered and it settled back into place, she assumed it had been just a gust of wind. But JohnEngine looked up and frowned, though there was nothing there to look at, or to cause one to frown. Then he stood, and still looking at nothing he said, "Old sir, please take my seat."

A strange disembodied voice cackled and laughed. "Why thank you, young man."

The room went completely silent. Someone said, "Toke, is that you?"

"Aye," the disembodied voice said. "And this young fellow is kind enough to offer his seat to an old man."

NickoLot watched JohnEngine's cushion compress as something she could not see sat down where only the moment before he had been seated. Then the strange disembodied voice said, "Well, I guess we have our answer. It appears he can see as well as his brother. And like his brother, he sees all, and yet sees nothing."

9

Unwelcome Visitor

"STOP, DAMMIT," MORGIN shouted at Mortiss.

This time she complied. She simply came to a stop in the middle of the forest and stood there without moving, almost throwing him from the saddle. She didn't even snort some nasty remark.

With his hands tied behind his back it was awkward getting out of the saddle. He had to throw his right leg over the saddle horn, pull his left foot out of the stirrup and slide off. He landed off balance, and fell to his face in the dirt and leaves of the forest floor. He lay there for a moment panting.

Dusk was quickly turning into night, and Morgin wanted to have his hands free by nightfall. But how?

He rolled onto his side, got one knee beneath him, and grunting and swearing he made it to his knees. More grunting and swearing got him to his feet.

He had a knife stowed in one of Mortiss's saddlebags. Using his teeth, he managed to untie the laces on the saddlebag, but couldn't get to the knife. He tried everything, even tried using his teeth to pull the saddlebags off Mortiss's back, but they were too tightly secured.

He gave up on that and stepped back from the horse. An idea occurred to him. "Do you think you could chew through the ropes with your teeth?"

She neighed, *Don't be ridiculous.*

With darkness fully upon him he curled up on the ground and closed his eyes. Sleep eluded him for a time, but then exhaustion pushed him over the edge and he slid into a restless slumber.

••••

Morgin dreamt of Rat. Somehow the filthy child had found his sheathed sword and dragged it behind him on a barren plane of emptiness and misery. Morgin ran after him trying to catch up, but running was awkward with his hands bound behind him.

He stopped and shouted, "Rat, wait."

The creature stopped, turned about and looked Morgin over carefully from a safe distance.

"It's me," Morgin said, and he tried to say his name but he couldn't speak it.

Rat circled him like an animal trying to determine if it faced a large predator. Then he slowly approached Morgin, stopped two paces away, and reached into the filthy rags he wore. When his hand emerged it held a wicked little knife, and Morgin stepped back a pace.

Rat stepped forward, and Morgin hesitated. He recognized that knife, remembered trying to cut a purse with it so long ago.

"Turn around," Rat said in a barely understandable grunt.

Morgin didn't want to turn his back on this thing from his past, not while it held such a weapon. But then he realized he really had no choice in the matter, so he turned about and waited for whatever would happen.

••••

JohnEngine cringed as every whiteface in the tent shouted at once. For some reason the old man's cryptic statement about *seeing all and yet seeing nothing* drew a strong reaction from everyone. Even NickoLot appeared stunned, gaping at him with her eyes wide and mouth open.

Standing in the midst of a lot of shouting Benesh'ere, JohnEngine felt rather exposed. He didn't understand why they had turned so angry, knew that if their anger drove them to violence, he and Nicki stood no chance. He looked again at the old man seated on the cushion he'd occupied only a moment before.

Like most Benesh'ere men and women, this fellow they called Toke wore loose-fitting, sand-colored breeches made of a coarse cloth and tucked into knee-high boots. He also wore a knee-length robe made of the same material, gathered at the waist with a belt of intricately woven cord and strips of leather. His hair had long since turned a white to match that of his skin, and while the top of his head was bald and shiny, a thick mane of it still grew out of the sides and back of his skull to cascade down over his shoulders. He looked up at JohnEngine and smiled, though like one of Olivia's fearsome grins it didn't bring him any comfort.

Angerah bellowed, "Will everyone please shut up?" The many arguments in the tent died slowly, and when silence ensued Angerah asked, "You see Toke?"

JohnEngine looked down at the old man and asked, "I assume your name is Toke?"

"Aye," the old man said.

"What am I missing here?" he asked the fellow.

"John," NickoLot said. "I see no one sitting before you, merely an empty space where you were sitting, though I do see a depression in the cushion as if someone is sitting there."

Toke said, "Your brother told us we could trust you two, and a few others. But we had to be certain you were who you claimed to be. Wouldn't want to give some Decouix agent any real information."

JohnEngine didn't try to hide his confusion. These whitefaces were a crazy lot. "My brother was here?"

Harriok spoke up. "Yes. I saved his life and he saved mine in return."

Jack added, "And he killed a lot of Kulls."

"Aye," Jerst said. "He was good at that. He came among us, taught us a bit about steel, then left. Shame he had to die."

The Benesh'ere turned out to be a terse lot, not very good storytellers. They told him and Nicki seemingly unrelated bits and pieces, and JohnEngine reconstructed the tale of Morgin's time among them from that. But clearly he didn't understand the half of it. The whitefaces didn't know how Morgin had died. He'd left them and not returned. And they knew nothing of Rhianne.

He and Nicki shared a meal with their hosts, then Branaugh sent Yim to retrieve their horses.

JohnEngine climbed into the saddle, but while he waited for Nicki to mount, the strangest thing happened. Harriok approached him and said, "When next you see your brother, tell him we're still waiting for him to right the seventh wrong."

"Wait," JohnEngine said. "You mean he's alive."

"No," Harriok said, giving JohnEngine an odd look. "Of course not."

"Then how am I going to see him again?"

Harriok didn't answer, just shook his head, turned and walked away.

Crazy Whitefaces! JohnEngine thought.

When next you see your brother . . . That statement haunted him.

••••

Chrisainne lay in bed and breathed a sigh of relief as Valso withdrew from her mind. The first time he'd penetrated her thoughts that way she hadn't known the limits of his reach. Could he actually read her mind? Could he rummage through all her memories, know her most private thoughts and desires? Since that first time she'd carefully experimented, allowed specific pieces of important information to surface in her thoughts, bits that would certainly elicit a reaction from him. Then she had held back mentioning them for a brief time, and he had not reacted. Later, when she did tell him, she got the expected response. She had concluded that for him to receive anything, she had to think words as if speaking them.

Still, it never hurt to be cautious, so when in contact with him she was careful to be certain she never allowed dangerous or incriminating thoughts to cross her mind. He was not aware of the stable boy and stable master, nor that Theandrin had somehow learned of her affair with BlakeDown, or that Theandrin was blackmailing her.

She pulled the covers up tightly around her neck and closed her eyes, confident she could control the situation.

••••

Something pulled Theandrin out of a restful sleep. Her bladder wasn't demanding that she make a trip to the privy, and no dream or nightmare had disturbed her enough to wake her, so what had done so? The fact that she asked that question meant she hadn't just awakened of her own accord. Something must have triggered one of her perimeter wards.

She threw back the covers, stood and pulled on a pair of slippers, then walked to the window. She unlatched and pulled back the shutters, and by the position of the moon she guessed it to be late evening, well before midnight. The night was warm and dry and quiet, and the castle about her silent. She neither saw nor heard any evidence of a disturbance that might have awakened her, and that aroused her curiosity even more.

She turned away from the window, lit a candle near her bed and pulled on a robe, then opened the door to her rooms and stepped out into the hall. Walking down the steps to the ground floor she found nothing out of the ordinary. She took a small lantern from the kitchen and used the candle to light it, then walked out into the castle yard.

A guard on the parapets saw her and called out, "Your Ladyship, is there something you need?"

"Not at the moment," she said. "But if I do, I'll let you know."

She crossed the yard to the wall that surrounded the inner bailey. She'd made these rounds hundreds of times in the 30 years she'd lived in Penda, and almost didn't need the light of the lantern to guide her, though without it she might stumble over something unseen in the dark.

She stopped at the first monitoring ward, meant to trigger and alert her should anything attempt to breach the castle walls. It had no physical manifestation in this world, and she'd designed it to be invisible to any eye but her own. Perhaps someone who rivaled her in power might detect it, but she'd been reinforcing this ward and others like it for decades, so they'd have to surpass her by a considerable amount to thwart it.

And even then, she'd probably have some sense that it had been altered, no matter how slight. But to tamper with it, one would have to do so from within the castle walls, for any attempt to do so from without would trigger it immediately.

After careful examination she determined that no one had *tampered* with the ward; of that she was certain. And yet, something about it was off, like the sound of a bell with a small crack in it. She reinforced it, reset it, then moved on to the next. Through the years she had placed a total of 13 such wards so that, when triggered, she'd also know the location of the breach, and she found every one of them slightly off in that same way.

They hadn't been triggered, and yet they would respond that way only to some penetration of the castle. But any physical breach would have triggered only those wards nearby. What would disrupt all 13 of them? And not trigger them fully?

After repairing the last of the 13, she stood staring at it and pondering that question. She concluded that the breach must not have been physical. No thief or invading army had climbed the walls to plunder her home. So what non-physical entity had done so?

She returned to her bed and lay awake into the wee hours of the morning considering that. If she modified the wards so they triggered on just *any* non-physical intrusion, they'd alert her every time someone cast a simple spell. She'd definitely modify them, but she had to be specific, and to do that she'd have to experiment; perhaps have them trigger on a non-physical intrusion by anyone not of Penda Clan. Catching this thief would take some time.

••••

Rhianne stood at the window in her parlor and pondered again the events in her dreams, which had grown less dreamlike each time she returned there, and now had the look and feel of their own separate reality. She could picture Rafaellen and Kenna easily, and even recall distinguishing features among the jackal warriors. And Morgin had felt disturbingly real in her arms.

To return to the Kingdom of Dreams as frequently as possible she now took several brief naps throughout the day, along with the longer sleep at night. At first she had simply wanted to escape her own reality, to return to her dreams where she might find herself in Morgin's arms. What difference did it make? Morgin was dead, and being Valso's prisoner didn't bode well for her own longevity. So what did it matter if she enjoyed a few moments of pleasure before Valso took her life as well. But somewhere, in the middle of one of those dreams, it had all become too real. She couldn't recall the specific moment, but at some point she had come to believe in her heart that Morgin lived, that he had somehow departed the Mortal Plane without dying, and made his way to the Kingdom of Dreams. Funny, how her heart had come to realize the truth while her mind still consciously denied it. And now that she knew for a certainty that Morgin lived, she had to think of some way to help him. She had a unique ability to slip back and forth between this world and that of the Kingdom of Dreams, and she must now think of some way to use that to his advantage.

She recalled that moment when she'd first seen him on that shelf of rock in the side of Attunhigh, shortly before Salula killed him. He'd been struggling to lift a heavy stone, with his sword leaning against a boulder far to one side. She'd been following the nether scent of that cursed blade and its power, and that sense pointed not at the steel sword lying to one side, but at the man grunting with effort to lift the stone. The blade had been benign, lifeless, powerless, while the malevolent power she sensed had drawn her to the man. Had she been following the man and not the blade?

It struck her what a danger she posed for Morgin. Only she knew he still lived; even Valso believed him dead. So she must guard her tongue in the most diligent fashion, for if she slipped up, and gave Valso even a hint that Morgin had survived Salula's attack, it would be as if her own hand wielded the knife that struck him down.

"Milady?"

Rhianne turned to find Geanna standing just within the threshold of the room. "Yes?"

"There is a young woman who wishes to speak with you, a Vodah girl named Xenya. Shall I show her in?"

The nobility of the Greater Clans had been conspicuously absent during her captivity in Durin. She had spied them occasionally from a distance, but they had avoided her so far. She couldn't blame them; she had no illusions as to what her ultimate fate would be in Valso's hands. And if *she* had been a noblewoman from any of the Greater Clans, she too would fear the dangers of associating with one of Valso's enemies. So Rhianne thought it odd that one now wished to see her. "Yes, let's find out what she wants."

Geanna's eyes narrowed with disapproval. For some reason she thought Rhianne should refuse to see the young woman, but a mere handmaiden dare not argue the point.

When Xenya et Vodah entered the room she stopped a few paces short of Rhianne, curtsied deeply and bowed her head. "Your Ladyship," she said. "Thank you for seeing me."

Rhianne guessed Xenya to be about 16 years old, a pretty girl with blond hair and hazel eyes. She wore her hair loose, cascading over her shoulders in long ringlets and curls. She'd chosen a gown with a high, tight collar and billowing sleeves, heavily embroidered in rich, Vodah blue.

Rhianne said, "Please, stand. I am no queen before whom you must debase yourself."

Xenya stood and smiled, though the smile did not extend to her eyes. They appeared strained, and Rhianne thought she saw fear in them. Or perhaps Xenya was merely uneasy in her presence.

Geanna hovered behind her, so Rhianne said, "Thank you, Geanna. Would you be so kind as to bring us some tea?"

"Yes, milady," Geanna said, then turned and left, though she obviously did so with some reluctance, clearly wanted to listen in on the conversation.

Rhianne asked Xenya, "What can I do for you?"

The girl dropped the smile. "I met your husband when he was a . . . guest . . . of His Majesty. I met him several times, though I didn't get to know him at all well. I'm sorry he died."

It was the first mention she'd heard of Morgin since returning to Durin, as if all of Valso's courtiers wanted to pretend he'd never existed. "What did you think of him?" Rhianne asked.

"He was handsome, and nice, but not comfortable with his nobility."

A insightful comment from such a young girl. *Young girl!* Rhianne thought. *I'm barely half-a-dozen years older than her.*

"No," Rhianne said. "He was never comfortable with titles and such."

Xenya looked at Rhianne uncertainly and said, "But he was quite powerful, my lady, and a skilled and ruthless fighter."

That was a curious thing to say. "Why do you say that? I can't imagine where you would have ever seen him fight."

Xenya turned her head slightly and her eyes flicked to one side, a momentary glance that appeared to be an involuntary reaction, as if looking to see if there might be someone present to overhear her. She considered Rhianne for a moment, then said, "Valso forced him to fight a Kull almost daily, to the death. They were brutal contests, with no rules, and he forced many of us to watch."

"But how could Valso *force* him to fight? Morgin would have simply refused."

"He tried to, but each day Valso selected a Kull and gave the halfman permission to kill your husband if he didn't fight back. I'm afraid I was . . . unkind to your husband. I couldn't see beyond the brutality. But near the end I saw how much he hated the killing, and realized he was merely trying to survive."

Morgin had always disliked brutality, and to force him to be brutal himself—Valso had figured out the one way he could hurt Morgin the most. But Rhianne wondered why this girl had come to her. "Why are you telling me this?"

"Because, my lady, now *you* are a . . . guest . . . of His Majesty. I've seen the way he looks at you. When Valso admires a beautiful thing, he quickly becomes obsessed with possessing it. He'll want you to come to his bed. And if you're not inclined to do so willingly—well, he is enormously powerful. No matter how much he may disgust you, he'll cast a spell upon you that will make you long to please him. You'll go to him happily. You'll willingly commit any act he desires, no matter how disgusting or degrading you might find it. When you're with him, pleasing him will be your only desire. And afterward, after you leave his presence, you'll return to your normal state of mind. And recalling what you've done, you'll come to hate yourself."

There could be no doubt that Xenya spoke from first-hand experience. Rhianne tried to think of something to say to console the girl, but nothing came to mind beyond trite reassurances.

Xenya continued. "It would almost be easier if he allowed the obsession spell to possess you afterward, when not in his presence, permitting you to live in mindless oblivion. But he takes his pleasure only in the torment of your abhorrence. And at that, he is a true master.

"I just wanted to warn you, my lady. And now, if you'll excuse me, I should go."

Xenya didn't wait for a reply. She curtsied, turned and quietly walked out of the room.

Rhianne hadn't paid much attention to that voracious look in Valso's eyes when Salula first dragged her back to Durin. Valso was not a sexual creature, and she couldn't imagine him desiring a woman that way. Even when he'd commented, *I might have to bed you myself,* while the thought had revolted her to the point of nausea, in retrospect, she'd concluded he'd merely been taunting her, in that way he had of making everyone about him fearful and uneasy. Then this conversation with Xenya; the young girl probably didn't realize how insightful her comments had been. Valso cared nothing for sex; to him that was merely a means of possessing a woman, making of her a piece of property that he owned, an object he could keep or discard on a whim.

Rhianne had thought Valso could no longer surprise her, but the fear and self-loathing she'd seen in Xenya's eyes had sent a chill through her heart. That Valso would do that to one so young was beyond forgiveness. At her age she should be indulging in fantasies of dashing young men vying for her hand.

Rhianne might have been overcome with pity for the poor girl, but now that she had become Valso's next target it was imperative she keep her sympathies in check and focus on some sort of defense of her own. She was more powerful than most witches. And yet she had glimpsed hints of Valso's power, and knew that when she tried to resist him he would easily overcome any defense she might devise. But if she couldn't protect herself by directly opposing him, perhaps she could do so indirectly. Could she prepare some hidden defense, something he wouldn't anticipate, something that would drive him from her without overt resistance? She'd have to think on that carefully, plan ahead and prepare just the right defense.

She caught a glimpse of her image in a mirror. The gown her handmaidens had picked out for her pushed her small breasts upward, emphasizing her desirability. It had been trimmed in elegant brocade with splashes of Elhiyne red, and it highlighted her trim waist and shapely curves nicely. While her servants were dressing her that morning she hadn't given it a second thought, for it was all very appropriate for a pretty, young clanswoman. To find a handsome, well-to-do husband, young girls were encouraged to display their finer attributes. And only as they approached the age at which those qualities dimmed did they start wearing high collars and showing less skin. But there was no one in this castle whom she wanted to impress with her desirability. Time to make some changes in her wardrobe.

When Geanna showed up with the tea, Rhianne had her summon the rest of her handmaidens, and she made them bring out her entire wardrobe and parade the dresses before her. She'd had no say in the selection, and since none of the gowns and dresses were inappropriate, she hadn't thought to speak out one way or the other. She had dresses of different colors, some more formal and some less, some for evening wear, some for the afternoons, dresses for a stroll in the gardens, even a few riding dresses. But they all had that one thing in common: they showed more of her than she preferred.

She asked one of her handmaidens, "Does the palace have a seamstress on hand, or must I summon one from the city."

The girl said, "We have three seamstresses in the palace, Your Ladyship."

"Well how soon may I see one?"

"We should be able to have one here right away. His Majesty has ordered that you shall want for nothing."

The speed with which the seamstress arrived surprised Rhianne. The woman brought samples of cloth, saying, "I already have your measurements, Your Ladyship. So all you need do is select fabrics and styles and tell me what you want."

Rhianne ordered a few dresses with high collars and long sleeves. The seamstress smiled, nodded and agreed with everything she chose, though she did look at her askance once or twice.

Geanna pleaded, "Are you sure, milady. These dresses you've chosen are not terribly flattering."

Rhianne insisted, and the seamstress left with orders to have the dresses ready as soon as possible.

10

Shadows Revealed

MORTISS WOKE MORGIN with a loud snort. Dawn had come and his arms were still numb to the shoulders. But when he rolled over they flopped loosely free, with cleanly sliced remnants of rope still clinging to them. Rat! He looked down to where he'd lain through the night. Rat had left his sheathed sword lying beside him.

He sat down on a small boulder, and grimaced with pain as the feeling in his hands and arms slowly returned. Once the pain receded he stood, flexed his fingers and stretched his arms, thinking he needed to hurry back and make sure Rhiannead had not been harmed. When he could fully use his arms again, he took up his sword, looked up toward the sky and said, "Thank you, Rat."

He had no trouble finding his way back to the site of the ambush; the forest probably wanted him to find it. He found a couple of dead horses, two dead jackal warriors, and the contents of their pack horses strewn haphazardly about. He recalled that the jackals didn't bury their dead, just stripped them and left them for the crows. He found no dead humans, though certainly he'd seen at least three go down. And when he looked more closely he saw that someone had carefully sorted through their supplies. Some of Rafaellen's soldiers must have survived, retrieved their dead and scrounged food and other essentials from their provisions.

He took Mortiss off the trail and paralleled it on foot. Within a hundred paces he spotted four cairns of rock, obviously the graves of members of their party. He dearly hoped Rhiannead did not lay in one.

Another two hundred paces and he smelled a fire and heard voices in the distance. "Wait here," he said to Mortiss, wrapped a shadow about him and advanced carefully, again using all of his Benesh'ere forest skills.

Rafaellen sat on an old stump near a meager fire, Kenna bent over him applying stitches to a nasty gash in his forehead. "Blast!" he swore. "That hurts."

Morgin counted eight of his soldiers still alive, four with obvious injuries, and four apparently unhurt, all seated around the fire. They hadn't pitched a tent, and of Rhiannead he saw no sign.

When Kenna finished doctoring Rafaellen, the captain stood and pointed to the four uninjured soldiers. "You four and me, we're going after those dogs to rescue the princess."

To the four injured soldiers he said, "And you're taking Mistress Kenna back to the Unnamed King. Tell him what happened here and ask him to send help."

Kenna opened her mouth to protest and he silenced her with a look. He turned to one of his uninjured soldiers and said, "You're our best tracker. Can you find their trail?"

The fellow grimaced, "I'm not really a tracker."

Morgin dropped his shadows, stepped out onto the game trail and said, "I can track them."

Kenna jumped and shrieked, while Rafaellen turned and several of his men jumped to their feet. A few of them drew swords, but Rafaellen snarled, "Put those blades away. He didn't cause this."

He asked Morgin, "Can you really track them?"

Morgin nodded. "I've done so before, a long time ago."

Rafaellen nodded. "Good enough. We'll settle our differences after we've rescued the princess."

••••

NickoLot and JohnEngine spent one more day in Norlakton. They questioned Fat John and anyone who'd had any dealings with Mistress Syllith. JohnEngine took a few armsmen and rode out to the miner's camp to question them, but at the end of the day they had nothing. One night Rhianne's servant had been brutally murdered, and Rhianne had disappeared, and no one had seen or heard of her since.

Throughout the two-day ride back to Elhiyne, NickoLot considered all that they had learned from the Benesh'ere, which was little indeed. JohnEngine had been surprised to finally understand that the old fellow he saw was actually invisible to the rest of them. But the story of Morgin's time among the whitefaces was a confusing mash of bits and pieces. Then there was her vision; how did Harriok, Jack and Blesset fit into Morgin's future? And there was that cryptic statement Harriok had made to JohnEngine as they were leaving, *When next you see your brother . . .*

JohnEngine had told her about it, and she'd asked him, "So they think he's alive?"

"No," JohnEngine said. "I asked him outright, and he said, 'No,' then looked at me like I was crazy for asking. Those whitefaces are all just plain bloody crazy."

It fitted the prescient images of Morgin she'd obtained during her spell-casting. But she'd promised AnnaRail she wouldn't tell anyone of that little experiment, so she said nothing to JohnEngine.

After they rode through the gates of Elhiyne, JohnEngine dismissed the armsmen, and he and Nicki immediately sought out AnnaRail. Unfortunately, they found her in her chambers with Olivia and Jinella, the three of them seated and discussing the coming harvest. They'd have to wait to get AnnaRail alone.

She stood and welcomed each of them with a hug. "Welcome back," she said. "How did the trip go?"

Nicki kept her mouth shut and let JohnEngine speak. "It went . . . as expected," he said.

Olivia rolled her eyes. "Oh come now, young man. Don't be evasive in my presence. I know why you took the trip to Norlakton. So speak up. Did you find Rhianne?"

JohnEngine shook his head. "No. But we went to the Benesh'ere camp and learned a bit about Morgin."

Olivia leaned forward almost threateningly. "Why did you go to the Benesh'ere camp?"

JohnEngine nodded toward NickoLot. "Nicki had a little visitation from Rat, and he told her to go there."

NickoLot found herself the center of attention, and wished that JohnEngine had kept that bit of information to himself. She told them of the dream she'd had.

AnnaRail asked, "And he wanted his knife back, that crude little thing he had when Roland found him in Anistigh?"

"Yes."

"Why?"

"I don't know. I had it in my hand there in the dream, and I assumed he recognized it, considered it his property and wanted it back."

JohnEngine told them of what they'd learned from the Benesh'ere about Morgin, which, in the telling, sounded even more disjointed and cryptic than it had in the whiteface tent.

Jinella asked, "Why were you looking for Rhianne in Norlakton?"

Nicki had no choice but to tell her the truth. "The hedge witch in Norlakton was actually Rhianne in disguise."

Jinella's eyes widened and she said, "Oh dear. She fooled me rather nicely."

"Yes," Olivia said. "She's proven to be quite powerful, perhaps one of the most powerful in the clans, so don't blame yourself for that."

AnnaRail asked, "But what did you learn in Norlakton?"

JohnEngine described the small hut and the blood they found there. "Apparently, her servant was murdered quite brutally. They found her still seated at the table, but there was no sign that Rhianne had been harmed, so she was probably abducted by whoever murdered the girl. And that was shortly before Morgin died. We questioned everyone we could, and no one has seen or heard of her since. She just vanished. Would any of us know if she's dead?"

Nicki said, "She's not dead."

At such an adamant statement, both AnnaRail and Olivia looked at her pointedly.

JohnEngine asked, "How do you know that?"

"I just do. At least I think I do."

"You *think*," JohnEngine said. "How can we be certain?"

Olivia's eyes narrowed and she leaned forward looking only at NickoLot. "Child, you're thinking of a prescience spell, aren't you?"

Nicki lowered her eyes, feeling like a little girl caught sneaking a sweet from the kitchen.

"Good," Olivia said. "That's an excellent idea. I applaud your initiative."

Surprised, Nicki looked at her grandmother. "But I have nothing of Rhianne's to use as a focus."

AnnaRail and Olivia exchanged amused glances. "Oh dear girl," Olivia said. "Your mother and I have bits and pieces of every one of you."

Olivia shooed JohnEngine and Jinella out of the room, then turned to AnnaRail. "It'll be best if she does this where she practices most of her spell-casting, so take her to her own room. I'll meet you there with something of Rhianne's to help her focus."

On the way to her room, AnnaRail said, "I do hope you were going to ask our help in this."

Nicki answered truthfully. "I was going to ask you, but maybe not grandmother."

As Nicki sat down at the small writing table in her room, Olivia joined them. On the table the old woman placed a wrinkled piece of linen with a dark, brown stain on it. Olivia said, "I collected a little blood when she cut herself once."

She and AnnaRail discussed the spell, decided Nicki should rub some of her own blood into the stain. Nicki pricked her finger with the tip of a sharp knife, and dripped seven, dark red drops onto the linen. She heard Olivia summoning wards as she rubbed it in carefully with a finger.

"Think of the near future," AnnaRail said. "Think of Rhianne, and think of the two of you together."

Nicki closed her eyes, fed power into the old and new blood on the piece of linen, and with her mother standing next to her, feeding her strength, she immediately felt herself slipping into a trance.

She saw a sad Rhianne from the past, then an old Rhianne, wrinkled and gray, but happy. She saw Rhianne standing in a magnificent court, in a great hall, and on the throne above her sat a king in Decouix white. But this king wore the head of a goat with blood-red eyes, and from him radiated malevolence and hate.

The goat king turned his head and looked at Nicki. It said, "This is not your future, child."

Terror flooded into her and she screamed.

"It's all right," AnnaRail said.

Nicki opened her eyes, found that she had fallen out of her seat and lay on the floor, her head cradled in AnnaRail's lap, Olivia standing over them. Her pounding heart slowly calmed, and she got control of her breathing.

AnnaRail stroked her brow softly and asked, "What did you see?"

Nicki described the throne room and the monster. AnnaRail helped her stand, then sit down again at her small table. The two older women quizzed her for some time, were most interested in the fact that the monster king wore Decouix white. At some point they appeared to come to a mutual decision. They looked at each other carefully and nodded their agreement at some unspoken conclusion.

"What?" Nicki asked.

AnnaRail said, "She's in Durin, probably Valso's captive." She looked at Olivia and asked, "Tulellcoe?"

The old woman nodded. At the look on Nicki's face, AnnaRail said, "We'll tell Tulellcoe what we've learned here and ask him to go to Durin and investigate."

Olivia said, "Once we tell him Rhianne is Valso's captive in Durin, I think we'd have trouble stopping him."

••••

One of Rafaellen's wounded soldiers could neither walk nor ride, so they set about building a litter for him. Morgin said, "While you're at that, I'm going back to the site of the ambush."

Rafaellen made no attempt to hide his distrust and assigned one of his men to accompany Morgin. With the fellow following him closely, Morgin headed back down the trail, walking slowly and examining every broken branch and displaced leaf for any sign of the jackal warriors. When they reached the site of the ambush he circled it carefully and found the position on the trail where Mortiss had carried him away from the battle, with two mounted jackals chasing him. He continued circling the periphery of the carnage, looking for any sign of the jackal troop's withdrawal. The guard that Rafaellen had sent to keep an eye on him turned out to be a nuisance, looking over his shoulder and questioning everything he did.

Morgin found several places where two or three horses had broken away from the trail. But on closer examination he determined that each was the result of an individual combat that had become separated from the melee. He found a spot on the south side of the trail where the brush and undergrowth had been trampled by the hooves of many horses. He followed that spoor for about 50 paces to a spot where a wide swath of undergrowth had been trampled; he'd found the place where the jackal troop had regrouped after the battle. With more than 30 riders, he had no difficulty picking up their trail, which headed southwest.

Morgin's guard said, "I need to piss. Stay within sight."

He walked about 20 paces away, a distance that would give him plenty of warning if Morgin tried to attack him. He turned his back and began unlacing his breeches.

Keeping an eye on the man, Morgin whispered, "Soann'Daeth'Daeye, are you here?"

The shadowwraith coalesced in front of him and dropped to one knee. *I am, my king. What do you desire?*

"Can you tell me where these jackals are?"

No, sire. We are of the forest, and like it are blind to their presence.

Apparently the wraiths could sense the spoor of the jackals, but not the warriors themselves.

"Can you sense the princess?"

No, my king.

Whatever magic the jackals were using had masked the princess as well. Morgin would have to track them without the aid of the forest or the wraiths.

He and his guard returned to the trail and found Rafaellen and the three remaining soldiers waiting for them. "Come," he said to the captain. "I've found their trail. You can ride with me, but have your men hold back about a hundred paces. I don't want to stumble into any surprises."

He considered telling them of his shadow magic, but recalling Rhiannead's fearful reaction when she thought she faced the ShadowLord, he rejected that thought as soon as it occurred to him. The last thing he needed was superstitious soldiers constantly fearful of him when they needed to focus their fear on the jackals.

Tracking the jackal troop proved to be easy. They made no attempt to conceal their tracks, and with more than 30 riders they left a very visible trail. As Morgin followed them he grew increasingly uneasy about that. By midmorning he suspected they wanted him to track them, so he pulled up and turned to Rafaellen. "I don't like this."

"Why?" Rafaellen asked.

"It's too easy. They want us to find them. They're after something, and it's probably not the princess if they're willing to let us catch them."

"You think maybe another ambush?"

"Possibly."

Looking at the trail the jackals had left, Morgin revised his opinion of the situation. He needed to move with more caution, needed to go forward protected by shadow, but he didn't want Rafaellen to see his abilities in that regard. "Go back and ride with your men. I can move more silently without you."

Rafaellen shook his head. "No. I'm staying close to you."

Morgin turned to face the captain. "You're going to have to trust me."

"I do trust you, but not that much."

They locked eyes for a long moment, and Morgin realized he had no choice. He wrapped himself in shadow and Rafaellen gasped. Then drawing his sword as he danced among the shadows, he stepped out of one immediately behind the captain and pressed the tip of his sword between the man's shoulder blades. Rafaellen froze.

Morgin said, "If I wanted to betray you, or murder you, do you really think you could stop me?"

Morgin lowered his blade, stepped back a pace and said, "Turn and face me."

Rafaellen turned around slowly, and the fear on his face surprised Morgin. The man's voice trembled a bit as he said, "ShadowLord."

Morgin shrugged. "I suppose so. But if I am, forget all the legends you've heard. I have no intention of harming you or your men, or the princess. So do as I say."

He pulled another shadow, knowing that in the soft light beneath the forest canopy he would seem to disappear. Rafaellen gasped again, and Morgin stepped from shadow to shadow until he stood about ten paces farther down the trail. "Do as I say, Captain, or you'll hinder me, and that will endanger the princess's life."

Rafaellen returned to his men and it appeared that now the captain would obey Morgin's orders. Morgin climbed into Mortiss's saddle and pulled a shadow about them both. He nudged her forward, moving more cautiously now that his suspicions had been aroused.

11

The Track of the Jackal

SEDUCING LEWENDIS PROVED to be rather easy. He was a bit of a yokel, and had never really had a lover as beautiful—and as talented beneath the sheets—as Chrisainne. And to her surprise, he turned out to be a gentle and caring lover. He was not the most handsome of men, but he took great care to be certain she enjoyed herself, and she did. Between him and the stable boy she almost had enough lovemaking in her day to keep her satisfied. If only she didn't have to fuck that pig BlakeDown.

She felt the touch of Valso's mind close at hand, so she quickly put such thoughts away.

The weather here in Durin is atrocious, Valso said. *It's been raining all day.*

It's rather pleasant here, Your Majesty, she said. *Though it saddens me that you must suffer such dreariness. But I do have some good news to report, and that might brighten your day.*

And what is that?

I have seduced one of ErrinCastle's lieutenants, one of the hotheads his father forced upon him. She had thought long and hard about this, and decided that she could use Lewendis to her own advantage with Valso. *His name is Lewendis, and he can be quite volatile. But he's also easy to manipulate.*

Chrisainne heard the skepticism in Valso's tone. *But it sounds as if he's nothing more than a low-level lieutenant. So how is this good news?*

Through him I have more direct control of the border situation. I can directly influence his thinking, keep him from starting a war too early, but when you decide the time is right, I'll have him start it at your pleasure. How much of a war would you like him to start? An all-out bloodbath, or just a skirmish?

Oh Chrisainne! I like you. I like you very much.

And with that, Valso withdrew from her mind.

Yes, Lewendis: a pleasant surprise wrapped in a crude country package. And while she took enjoyment from that surprise only because Theandrin had forced her to seduce him, Chrisainne wouldn't let that stop her from killing the woman.

A rather surprising thought occurred to her: why stop with Theandrin? Theandrin first, then wait a year or so, and ErrinCastle could follow her, some sort of accident. At that point, with no other offspring, BlakeDown would be desperate to sire a new heir. And he'd have Chrisainne close at hand, a beautiful, young noblewoman in the prime of her fertility. She'd have to do something about her own husband. It might look suspicious if he died, and then shortly afterward she married BlakeDown. Better to kill him off sometime between Theandrin and ErrinCastle. If she did this right, she could be the mistress of Penda and mother to its heir. She'd have to put up with BlakeDown and his piggish rutting—or perhaps not. Once she bore a son to inherit the leadership of Penda, and maybe a spare, she'd have no further need of BlakeDown. And with him out of the picture, there'd be no one to stop her from taking all the pleasure she desired from whomever she chose, for she would be the Lady of Penda, with no lord to gainsay her.

Yes, she just needed to set her sights higher, and be willing to take whatever steps were necessary.

••••

"Pheasant tonight," Theandrin said, standing in the kitchen, reviewing the meal plan with the cook. "Boar tomorrow evening, and how about—"

Something triggered her special ward, sending a jolt through her soul. She staggered, reached out and gripped the back of a chair.

The cook frowned and took her arm. "What's wrong, milady? Are you ill?"

"No, I'm okay."

"Here," the cook said, pulling out a chair. "Sit down. I'll get you some water."

"No," Theandrin said. She had to move quickly. She turned and marched out of the kitchen, saying, "We'll finish this later."

She'd created a new ward, designed to trigger on a non-physical intrusion, and she had to get to it before the effect dissipated. She strode through the castle proper, servants scurrying out of her way. She marched up to the second floor and into her bedroom.

She retrieved a small chest from beneath her bed, placed it on the bed and opened it, its only contents a small, silver pendent containing a lock of her hair and 13 drops of her blood. She lifted it out of the chest, pressed it tightly against her breast and closed her eyes.

She felt nothing for several heartbeats, but as she concentrated and focused her magic, a faint and indistinct impression washed through her. She saw a white light far in the distance. It slowly approached and grew in intensity until it shone with such brilliance it flooded the landscape of her thoughts, almost swamping any other feature. But not quite, for beneath it she saw two shadows, one green, one blue, both nothing more than a blotch of color beneath the overpowering white radiance. The vision slowly faded, until nothing remained to be seen but the back of her own eyelids. She opened her eyes to consider what she'd just seen.

There was no mistaking the white of Decouix, and that made sense. If she must guess who might place a spy in the Penda Court, the two prime candidates were Olivia and Valso. But she'd seen no Elhiyne red, just the white of Decouix, the green of Penda, and the blue of Vodah. The white and green she understood, a Penda traitor reporting to the Decouix, but how did Vodah fit into this?

Valso probably had a few of his Vodah lackeys sneaking about. They'd keep a low profile, probably pretend to be Penda, or any of the other Lesser Clans. She'd have to check nearby inns, put together a list of possibilities. It would be someone who had been inside the castle walls at the moment the ward had been triggered.

If she couldn't track this intruder down by simply looking for Vodahs lurking about, she'd have to strengthen her special ward. But then the intruder might detect it when he triggered it. Maybe she could add something to it to give her a sense of direction, or location.

What would she do with the culprit when she found him? She'd have to think on that.

••••

Morgin rode at a slow pace with his attention sharply focused on the track left by the jackal troop, Rafaellen and his men following at about a hundred paces. The forest thinned out and the jackals no longer needed to ride in a single column. That worried him, for if a small group split off from the main troop, he could easily miss the signs of them doing so. He had slowed to a walk when he heard a noise to one side of the track.

He and Mortiss froze, and the only sounds to break the silence were the soft rustle of the forest leaves, a little noise from Rafaellen and his men, and the faint sing-song sound of a jackal's voice lowered to a whisper.

Turning only his head, and doing so slowly, Morgin looked in the direction of the jackal's voice. He saw nothing for several heartbeats, then caught a glimpse of motion behind a large clump of brush to one side of his track. An ambush, and he and Mortiss had walked right into it. If not for his shadows he'd likely be a dead man now.

The play of light beneath the dense forest canopy was ideal for shadowmagic. So he released Mortiss's reins and draped them across her neck. Conscious that even the creak of his saddle leather could give him away, he gripped the saddle horn, and moving slowly he swung his right leg over Mortiss's rump. He cautiously lowered his right foot to the ground, then lifted his left foot out of the stirrup and lowered it, careful not to snap any twigs or make even the slightest sound. He leaned toward Mortiss's ear and whispered, "You take the jackals we spotted. I'm going to check the other side for a second bunch. And start the killing just as they spring the trap."

Crouching low, and reinforcing his and Mortiss's shadows, he edged toward the side of the track opposite the jackals he'd spotted. He hadn't detected any jackals on that side, but they were smart enough to set up an ambush with a proper crossfire, and there were several clumps of brush that could easily hide a second group of jackal warriors.

Rafaellen and his men were quickly approaching so he didn't have much time. He drew his sword slowly, glanced back once and saw that Mortiss had left the track, though whether she chose to obey his orders was always a question that would only be answered when the time came.

Walking in a crouch about 20 paces outside the track, he paralleled it, danced from shadow-to-shadow and checked anything that might hide a jackal. He found one standing behind the trunk of a tree, two more a few paces away behind a large bush, all holding strung bows and nocked arrows, their attention locked on Morgin's companions as they approached. He couldn't be certain he'd found them all, and he had no more time to search further. So he stepped into a shadow behind the two and waited. Using surprise he'd try to kill them quickly, then go after the one behind the tree.

The jackals were smart enough to not wait until Rafaellen and his men had crossed directly between them; too much chance that a stray arrow might miss its target and continue on to strike friend rather than foe. No, they'd surprise their enemy just before they reached that point. But since Morgin's targets were spread out, he couldn't wait for that.

He guessed the jackals would strike when Rafaellen was about ten paces out, so he moved when they were at 20. He held his sword in a two-handed grip, stepped forward and swung it down at an angle at the jackal on his left. It bit deeply into the warrior's neck where it met his shoulder. At the same instant Mortiss cried out a scream from netherhell, and the deep brush on the other side of the track erupted in a maelstrom of barking jackals and enraged horse.

Morgin's sword stuck in the jackal's spine and he lost a precious moment tearing it free. He swung it around at the second jackal, conscious that the third remained unchallenged at his back. His sword crunched into the side of the second jackal's head as he saw the flash of an arrow streaking toward his allies.

He spun away from the two jackals he'd killed just as the third stepped out from behind his tree and swung a sword in a flat arc. Morgin ducked beneath it, stepped into a shadow, danced among the shadows while the jackal slashed his blade about blindly. Morgin stepped out of a shadow behind the dog, lunged forward and buried his blade in the jackal's back.

The jackal grunted and stumbled forward, sliding off Morgin's sword. It turned about and faced Morgin, stood there swaying from side-to-side, its tongue hanging limply out the side of its muzzle. Then the light of life left its eyes and it slumped to the ground.

No more jackals came at Morgin, and the other side of the track was silent so he concluded Mortiss had done her job. But a few hundred paces distant a jackal howled out a cry that must have carried for leagues. One of them had gotten away to warn the others.

Morgin bent down and wiped his sword on the jackal warrior's tunic, then walked out into the track. Rafaellen and three of his men were standing over the body of one of their companions, the shaft of an arrow protruding from his chest.

Mortiss walked up to them still wrapped in shadow, and only then did Morgin realize he hadn't extinguished his shadowmagic; he quickly did so. One of the soldiers looked at Mortiss, then at Morgin. He stepped back and said, "Devil horse . . . devil horseman." He finished by making a sign with his fingers, a useless symbol that peasants believed would protect them from evil.

••••

JohnEngine reined in his horse and looked carefully at the Penda border patrol. They were a good five hundred paces out, but even at that distance he saw that they had doubled their numbers—not a good sign. That could force him and Brandon to double theirs. They needed parity on the border, a careful balance that discouraged ill-thought action.

The Pendas rode forward and halted about two hundred paces from the border, a winding creek that sliced through the flat fields of the western Elhiyne lands. It was no coincidence that two hundred paces was just within bow shot of the border. The Penda lieutenant deployed his men in a skirmish line, with archers on the flanks, and only then did he ride forward.

JohnEngine had no choice but to respond in kind. He arrayed his men carefully at a like distance from the border, though they were outnumbered two to one. And when he rode forward to meet the Penda lieutenant his horse sensed his unease, and danced a bit from side-to-side with skittishness.

When JohnEngine recognized Perrinsall, the tension in his shoulders eased a bit. The Penda lieutenant was a reasonable man, not a hot-head like Lewendis. With about 20 paces separating them, Perrinsall nodded politely and said, "Greetings, Lord JohnEngine."

JohnEngine heard strain in his voice that had not been there the last time they'd met. "Lord Perrinsall. I hope all is well."

Perrinsall shrugged, obviously uncomfortable with the situation. "Tell Alcoa we caught his pig thief and stretched his neck beneath a tree."

JohnEngine said, "We'd have preferred to stretch his neck under an Elhiyne tree."

"I know," Perrinsall said. "But he tried to steal some Penda pigs, so BlakeDown ordered his execution then and there."

Clearly, Perrinsall had chosen to give JohnEngine a carefully edited version of the incident. "Well, as long as someone hung the bastard."

"Trust me, he'll not be stealing any more pigs."

JohnEngine knew he must ask the next question carefully. "May I ask why you've doubled the men in your patrol?"

Perrinsall grimaced. "Orders from Lord BlakeDown."

A terse, simple answer, without elaboration. Perrinsall likely had no further details upon which to elaborate. "Well I thank you for hanging the thief. Good day, Lord Perrinsall."

"Good day, Lord JohnEngine."

As JohnEngine rode back to his men he considered the situation carefully. It would not do to have such a discrepancy between the size of the Penda patrols and the Elhiyne. That alone might encourage a hot-head like Lewendis to act rashly, and start a war that none of them wanted. As a matter of caution he and Brandon would have to double the size of their own patrols.

••••

Rhianne's suite consisted of five rooms on the second floor of Castle Decouix. She had a sitting room in which to entertain guests, a bedroom and a bathing chamber, with a smaller, second bedroom in which two of her handmaidens slept. That allowed them to be close at hand should she need anything, even in the middle of night. It also allowed them to watch her closely, day and night. The sitting room opened into an outer foyer meant to provide privacy to the rest of the rooms. Any potential guest who knocked on the outer door would be greeted by one of her handmaidens, who would then find Rhianne and privately tell her who had come to visit, and Rhianne could then choose to see or not see the person. At least, that was how it was supposed to work.

A set of doors in the sitting room opened onto an outer balcony that overlooked the castle yard. It was high enough to see beyond the castle walls, and the castle had been built on a hill in the center of the city. So during rare moments when not forced to endure Valso's company, if the weather was good Rhianne enjoyed standing there, watching the inhabitants of Durin going about their daily business. The distance was far too great for her to make out fine details, but the sun warmed her nicely, and she could fantasize about being free to go about her own errands and chores, wending her way through the crowded streets below.

Down below a bit of movement caught her attention, a noblewoman wearing a hooded cloak walking at an unhurried pace across the inner bailey. She reached the far side and walked up the steps to an entrance in one of the towers. She paused there, turned about, and though her features were hidden by the shadows beneath her hood, she seemed to be looking Rhianne's way. Then she reached up and casually pulled the hood back. Rhianne recognized Valso's sister, Haleen, the Mad Whore as Valso had dubbed her. She looked at Rhianne for a moment, then turned and stepped through the entrance into the tower.

A strange woman, touched by madness, Rhianne put her out of her mind. But on this day she could not put Xenya et Vodah out of her thoughts.

Her new dresses had not arrived. The seamstress made one excuse after another for a series of delays, but Rhianne soon realized the woman was operating under orders from the palace, and would delay the dresses indefinitely. Valso wanted his lovely prisoner looking her best.

Rhianne had a growing sense of her own power, and like most strong witches she could perceive, to a limited extent, the level of power in others. But one had to be careful about taking that at face value, for many of the strongest developed the ability to mask their power and appear weaker if they chose. Living among her enemies, she had decided to be prudent, and now allowed others to see only a hint of her true capabilities; she assumed that most of those about her did the same. However, even with that uncertainty she was fairly confident she could draw more power than anyone else in Durin, except for Valso, and maybe Carsaris.

Like everyone else, Valso masked his capabilities, but in tiny moments of distraction—as when he looked at her breasts hungrily—Rhianne had glimpsed a level of ability in him far beyond anything humanly possible.

Strong compulsion spells twisted the heart as well as the mind until the victim could no longer distinguish between her own thoughts and desires, and those manufactured for her. They frequently left the unwitting permanently warped beyond healing, and, as with Xenya, haunted by memories of acts willingly performed. It was not uncommon for the target of such a spell to find release only in suicide.

For that reason resistance to compulsion spells was included in the basic defenses taught to young wizards and witches. After Xenya's visit Rhianne had concocted a charm that would alert her to any compulsion laid upon her, and another to help her resist it. But would they work against someone as powerful as Valso? Or would she seek his embrace willingly, completely oblivious to her own revulsion of the man?

"It's a lovely day, isn't it?"

At the sound of Valso's voice Rhianne gasped and jumped. She spun about and found him standing on the balcony only a pace behind her. She'd already learned that the protocol of being properly announced by one of her handmaidens didn't apply to His Majesty. But the way he moved so silently through her rooms unnerved her.

"Jumpy, aren't we?" he said.

She thought his eyes flicked momentarily toward her breasts. But then, in her new-found paranoia, she might simply be imagining that. "You startled me," she said.

"I should have been more careful."

She almost said, *Oh no, Your Majesty, think nothing of it.* But she was not in the mood for polite banter. Saying nothing, she stepped around him and walked back into her sitting room. She heard him follow her, suspected that she heard him only because he wanted her to. She crossed the room, hoping to put the entire length of it between them. She stopped near the unlit hearth and turned about, relieved to find that he hadn't dogged her heels all the way across the room.

He stood just within the room, framed by the doorway to the balcony. Oddly enough, it occurred to her that he was quite handsome. He had dark, almost delicate features, with black hair framing a strong face, and a trim, well-shaped figure, with no lack of muscle to fill his tunic. He now sported a carefully trimmed beard, not a big, bushy trail of curly whiskers like Wylow and BlakeDown, but a thin line of black stubble that traced the edge of his chin. Very much in the latest style, it emphasized the strength of his jawline.

He asked, "Are you being treated well?"

"Yes, my lord. I lack for nothing, though there is this seamstress who is rather slow in delivering some dresses I ordered."

"I'll look into that," he said, walking slowly toward her. His stride had a confidence to it that most men lacked, which added to his attractiveness. He did carry himself with the bearing of a king.

He stopped in front of her at less than a pace, an intimately close distance, and for some reason that didn't bother her. His eyes settled on her breasts, and he made no attempt to conceal the hunger in his look. That flattered her a bit.

He turned to one side and held out his arm. "I must go. Why don't you see me out?"

She took his arm and walked beside him, out of the sitting room and through the foyer. Geanna waited for them at the door. The girl opened it and held it for the king.

Valso stopped, turned toward Rhianne, took her hand and lifted it to his lips. When he kissed it she felt a tingle run through her, and wondered what it might be like for him to truly kiss her, not on her hand, but a hot, passionate kiss on her lips . . . and maybe elsewhere.

He released her hand, smiled warmly, then stepped through the door.

The instant the maid closed the door, Rhianne staggered back and bumped into the wall. She couldn't believe what she'd been thinking, and Xenya's words came back to her. *It would almost be easier if he allowed the obsession spell to possess you afterward . . . permitting you to live in mindless oblivion.*

Geanna looked at her, a knowing smile on her face. And Rhianne thought of the way Valso had smiled just before leaving. At the time she'd thought it a warm and friendly smile, but now she realized it had been a cold smirk of satisfaction.

The charms she'd prepared had not helped her in the least; the one had not alerted her to Valso's spell, and the other had not helped her resist it. Stunned, she walked unsteadily back into her sitting room and dropped down onto a couch.

How could she stop him? She had to assume that Geanna had reported Xenya's visit, and Valso could easily guess at the topic of their conversation. So in all probability he'd anticipated what she might do to defend herself, and he'd defeated her charms effortlessly.

She'd have to come up with something more creative, something no one would expect, some surprise that Valso wouldn't anticipate. But what?

12

The Reality of Dream

WHILE THE THREE soldiers buried their dead companion, Morgin told Rafaellen, "We killed six of them and they killed one of us. They can afford the six and we can't afford another. And the damn jackals have some sort of magic that makes them invisible to the forest and the shadowwraiths, so we'll have little warning of another ambush."

"Shadowwraiths?" Rafaellen asked.

"Allies," he said, "though not the most ordinary of friends."

Rafaellen's frown deepened further, and he said, "You mean the shadow beings."

Morgin said, "You're not going to like this, but please don't overreact."

He looked away from the captain and called out, "Soann'Daeth'Daeye, please show yourself."

Hundreds of tiny shadows detached themselves from the canopy of leaves, not one larger than the palm of Morgin's hand. They fluttered through the air of the forest toward him like butterflies, and when they reached him they swirled about him in a giant, cyclonic maelstrom. Around and around they churned, a cloud of shadows that slowly shrank until it converged into a spot just in front of him. Then one-by-one they joined together and coalesced into the familiar form of the shadowwraith.

Rafaellen took a fearful step back, a reaction Morgin had anticipated, and the reason he allowed them to learn of his affinity with shadows in bits and pieces.

Morgin said, "Do not be alarmed, Captain. As I told you, it is an ally."

When the wraith had formed completely, it dropped to one knee in front of Morgin and bowed its shapeless head. A whisper of thought brushed across his mind as it said, *My king.*

Rafaellen put a hand on the hilt of his sword, but didn't draw it. "But what kind of an ally?"

Morgin feared Rafaellen might spook and do something stupid. "I think they're the defenders of this forest. I've run into them time and again . . . in several lives, and they've always aided me when they could."

Rafaellen maintained his distance and circled the wraith. "Okay, so how might they aid us now?"

"Did you hear it speak?"

"I heard nothing."

"It would have been merely a thought that brushed through your mind, not a sound for your ears."

Rafaellen looked at Morgin suspiciously. "Then I guess I did hear something. Did it call you *king*?"

Morgin shrugged. "I am the ShadowLord. I guess that makes me king of shadows."

When Rafaellen's three soldiers saw the wraith they reacted with superstitious distrust, but calmed when Morgin told them, "The wraiths will accompany me, not you. You'll have nothing to do with them directly."

To Rafaellen he said, "You and your men ride about two hundred paces behind me."

Rafaellen grimaced and said, "At that distance we could lose you."

"Don't worry about that. The wraiths will be watching you, and if you stray they'll guide you back on track."

Rafaellen looked at Soann'Daeth'Daeye unhappily. "I don't think we want these things watching us."

"These *things*," Morgin said, "are as much a part of this forest as the trees and undergrowth. Like it or not, they've been watching every move you've made since you entered this kingdom."

Morgin didn't feel like arguing the point, so he turned away from the soldier and climbed into Mortiss's saddle. "I'm protected by my shadows, so I'll ride ahead, and if I discover another ambush, I'll send a wraith back to warn you. Hold back and let me take care of them."

One of the men asked, "You and the devil horse?"

Morgin grinned. "Devil horse and devil horseman." He didn't wait for a reply, just spurred Mortiss on.

••••

As Morgin rode through the forest he kept his attention split between the tracks the jackal troop had left, and the trail ahead, and anything that might hide a jackal warrior on either side. Because of that he rode directly beneath the next ambush without realizing it. He was trying to decipher the tracks on the ground when something above him moved, causing a slight rustle of leaves overhead. Again his shadowmagic had saved him.

He nudged Mortiss forward another 20 paces, amazed at how she could move with such unnatural silence, but then he would never have applied the word *natural* to Mortiss. He dismounted, summoned a shadowwraith and sent it to warn Rafaellen, to tell him to halt and not advance further. Then he backtracked on foot, and stopped beneath the tree where he now suspected a jackal hid. He waited, counting his own heartbeats, and just short of one hundred he heard a jackal overhead whisper, "Any sign of them yet?"

In the next tree over, a jackal answered, "No, nothing yet."

And in the next, "I ain't seen nothing either."

Morgin waited another ten heartbeats, but no more responses came. So there were three of them, up in three trees, probably archers. The jackal captain knew what he was doing. When Rafaellen and his men came into view, from a safe distance these three would shoot one or two arrows each, then retreat. In just a few such ambushes they could whittle Morgin and his companions down to nothing.

Morgin crept back to Mortiss and retrieved his bow, strung it, stuck three arrows in the ground in front of him, then squatted down to wait and watch. One of the jackals moved a bit, another adjusted his position, and the third scratched at something. It didn't take long to identify the location of each of his three opponents.

He stood, pulled an arrow out of the ground, nocked it, raised, pulled, aimed and released. The jackal grunted as the arrow punched into his back. Morgin shot the other two arrows as rapidly as possible, and dropped all three jackals out of their perches. He found one still alive, so he dispatched it with a sword thrust.

By early afternoon he'd uncovered two more ambushes, killing nine more jackals in the process. But mid-afternoon the hoof prints of the jackal troop converged into a single group. He dismounted to examine the tracks more closely, saw that the prints overlapped and seemed pointed in every direction, as if they had milled about for a time discussing something. The prints then led off in a tight column in a different direction. He guessed that scouts foraging ahead had returned to the troop to report something.

Morgin followed the tracks on foot, Mortiss trailing behind him. A few hundred paces further on he heard a horse splutter and neigh up ahead, though it was difficult to tell how far sound traveled in the forest. He turned back to Mortiss and whispered, "Stay here. I'm going ahead."

Morgin reinforced his shadow magic, crouched low and moved forward, stepping carefully from shadow-to-shadow, bush-to-bush and tree-to-tree, using his forest skills to travel silently. The forest lent its shadows well to his kind of stalking, as if he and it were old friends. After a hundred paces he saw bright sunlight glinting off something shiny up ahead. Another 50 paces and he realized he was approaching a large clearing that allowed the sun's rays to penetrate the dense forest canopy.

He heard a horse splutter and stomp its hooves, saw more movement in the clearing. He coursed left and right, making sure he didn't leave a sentry or two at his back. He stopped behind a large boulder about 20 paces from the clearing, peered around it to one side and saw several jackals trying to calm a string of about two dozen horses. Soann'Daeth'Daeye materialized beside him. *We sense nothing, my king.*

That many horses meant the entire jackal troop had probably stopped in the clearing, so Rhiannead must be there too. Morgin whispered, "Go back to Rafaellen, tell him to leave one man behind with the horses, and he and the other two should come forward on foot. And tell them to bring their bows, and move quietly."

When Rafaellen and his men joined Morgin they all moved forward together, and while they proved to be adept at moving quietly through the forest, one of them must have made some sound or been spotted by a sentry. They were still several paces from the edge of the clearing when the jackal captain called out, "You who walks in shadows, I know you're out there. If you want the princess back alive, come forward and show yourself."

Morgin wasn't foolish enough to just stand and expose himself until he knew more about the situation. With hand signals Rafaellen instructed his two men to spread out, then he and Morgin moved forward to the edge of the clearing. It proved to be quite large, creating a wide open space with no shadows at hand.

The jackal captain stood at its center, holding Rhiannead as a shield in front of him, his left paw clutching a clump of dress at the back of her neck, his right holding a knife to her throat. Behind him stood the remaining warriors of his troop holding swords, shields and pikes. He called out again in that yowling, sing-song, dog voice, "Stand forth, I said, or I'll cut her throat now. You have something I want, and I have something you want. So we can strike a bargain and both walk away from this happy."

Far to one side Morgin spotted Mortiss standing perfectly still at the edge of the clearing, a dark, black shadow among those of the forest. He whispered to Rafaellen, "I don't know what I can do, but tell your men to have their bows ready and be prepared to move."

As Rafaellen scrambled away to deliver the message, Morgin drew his sword, stood, and stepped into the clearing, though he didn't advance. About 20 paces separated him from the jackal captain. "What do I have that you want?"

The jackal captain smiled, an oddly familiar sight that Morgin recalled from Morddon's past. "That sword you carry; my queen wants me to bring it back to her. Give it to me and I'll let you and your princess go unharmed."

From that same past Morgin knew better than to trust the jackal. He knew full well that if he gave this dog his sword, it would just butcher him and Rhiannead together. He could make his own shadows and try to reach him, but he had to move from shadow-to-shadow, and with 20 paces to cover, the jackal would slit Rhiannead's throat long before he got there.

No, my king, a thought flittered through his mind. *All shadows are but one. To walk in one is to walk in them all. Make them where you need them and I'll show you the way.*

An enraged nether scream from Mortiss broke the silence of the moment, and she burst into the clearing at full charge, headed straight for the warriors arrayed behind their leader. Startled, the jackal captain looked her way and lowered the knife a hand's breadth from Rhiannead's throat. Without time to consider his actions, Morgin cast a shadow of magic to one side of the jackal captain, then another about himself. So-ann'Daeth'Daeye materialized in the shadow with him, and for a moment he felt as if falling from a great height, then in a heartbeat he stood in the other shadow.

Mortiss hit the troop of jackal warriors just as Morgin stepped out of the shadow beside their captain. The jackal's moment of inattention gave Morgin the only chance they had, though the gap between the knife and Rhiannead's throat left no room for error. Morgin sliced down with his sword and severed the jackal's wrist, removing paw and knife in a single stroke. The jackal howled and stepped back, gripping the stump of its arm with its remaining paw, blood spurting all over Rhiannead.

Morgin grabbed her by an arm and spun her toward the edge of the clearing just as two jackal warriors broke loose from the pandemonium around Mortiss. "Run," he shouted. Then turned to face the jackals.

The jackal captain backed away while his two warriors advanced, both carrying swords. Morgin had no foolish fantasies about his ability to fight two of them at once, but he had to give Rhiannead time to get clear, so he stood his ground as they attacked.

They came at him with a nicely coordinated move: one lunged at him with a direct thrust, while the other swing his sword out in a wide arc. Morgin parried the thrust while trying to side-step the other's swing, knowing he had little hope of success. But an arrow hissed past his ear and thudded into the chest of one just as Mortiss slammed into the other. She rode the jackal down, and as she galloped past him Morgin grabbed her saddle horn, pulled himself clumsily into the saddle, struggled to get hold of her reins and almost ran Rhiannead down at the edge of the clearing before he did so.

He pulled Mortiss about to shield Rhiannead from the jackals while she crossed the last few paces to the clearing's edge. As he and Mortiss stood their ground, Rafaellen's soldiers loosed one arrow after another at the jackals, keeping them occupied. Only when Rhiannead stepped out of the clearing did Morgin spur Mortiss after her.

Just outside the clearing Morgin and Rhiannead met Rafaellen and his two soldiers. Rhiannead had a small trickle of blood at her throat. Alarmed, Rafaellen examined the wound quickly, then declared. "The bastard's knife just nicked her. It's nothing to worry about."

"Then take her," Morgin said. "Get to the horses and run. I'll delay the jackals."

"No," Rhiannead pleaded. "They'll kill you."

Morgin had no time to argue with her, so he simply pulled a shadow about him and Mortiss, then spurred her back into the clearing. He'd done this kind of thing before, in another time, another life.

••••

"You must awaken, Your Ladyship. Dinner will be served shortly and your presence is required."

Rhianne had trouble shifting her thoughts from the chaos of the clearing in her dream, to the quiet of Castle Decouix in the late afternoon. Sitting on the couch where she'd napped, she opened her eyes and lifted her chin. The young girl who'd awakened her started, her eyes widened and she put a hand to her mouth. "Oh dear me," she said.

Rhianne asked, "What's wrong?"

Geanna stepped around the girl and her eyes widened too. "Oh, my lady, you've cut yourself."

Rhianne didn't feel any pain. "I've cut myself? Where?"

Geanna retrieved a small mirror and handed it to Rhianne. Looking at her reflection she saw a slight trickle of blood on her throat where the jackal captain's knife had nicked her. *No,* she thought. *That was just a dream.*

Once her handmaidens determined that it was a small, shallow cut, the excitement ended, though they speculated a bit on how she might have cut herself. She now knew she could no longer deny the reality of her dreams. She shared some sort of existence with Rhiannead, and must accept the fact that Morgin had survived Salula and was now trapped in the Kingdom of Dreams. Could she help him fight off these jackals, help him find his way back to the Mortal Plane? Could she coax Rhiannead to be more forceful? Rhianne reminded herself that the girl in her dreams couldn't be more than 16 years old, and was just as flighty as she had been at that age. But Morgin's life, and hers too, hung in the balance, so perhaps it was time to take the girl in hand, to guide her down the proper path, though she'd probably have to be a bit forceful in that.

She mustn't forget that blade. It had been only a momentary glimpse, there on that shelf of rock in the side of Attunhigh, the blade lifeless, while radiating from Morgin she sensed the power she had always thought came from the blade. Had it always been him? Was the blade nothing more than a piece of lifeless steel? Somehow she had to communicate to Morgin her doubts about its power.

She suffered Valso through dinner, with his boasting and the occasional taunt, but she dare not steal any food. After dinner the evening proved tedious at best, and when she finally retired for the night, she found it impossible to sleep. Somewhere near midnight she lay in bed listening to the soft snoring of the youngest of her handmaidens sleeping in the other room with Geanna. She could have had the girl dismissed for that, but she needed such sounds this night. The girl wasn't terribly loud, but she made enough noise to help mask any sounds Rhianne might make.

She slid back the covers and pulled on a pair of slippers, then retrieved a pretty shawl from a chest at the foot of her bed. It would provide more than one use: she could bundle what few possessions she needed into it, and when it had served its purpose, it was nice enough that she might sell it for a bit of coin. And beneath it she retrieved one of the rolls she'd hidden away. She couldn't confirm it in the dark, but she suspected that by now it had grown a bit of mold. She'd eaten worse.

She'd hidden the next roll high in one of her closets behind some shoes, but it was no longer there; one of the maids must have found it. She'd stolen a few pieces of dried meat from the kitchen by sending a kitchen maid on an errand during the slow time just after lunch, and that too had gone missing. Well, she'd go a bit hungry, but perhaps she could bring a few extra scarves to sell.

She pulled on two sets of small clothes. They were much too fine for her disguise but the parlor maid's skirt she'd stolen would hide them nicely, and she might need them for warmth. But the maid's skirt was no longer behind the chest where she'd hidden it, and the moth-eaten, homespun cloak she'd acquired had also gone missing.

As she sat down on the edge of the bed Geanna emerged from the maid's quarters carrying a small lamp that cast a faint, dim light across the floor. "Does my lady want for something? I see you're partially dressed."

They'd anticipated her, and Valso had probably not needed any magic to do so. While Valso kept Rhianne busy almost every moment of every day, Geanna and the girls had had hours to scour the suite, and had likely discovered everything she'd squirreled away, one piece at a time—well, all but the single roll hidden beneath the shawl.

"No, Geanna. I'm just restless. Go back to bed."

"Yes, milady."

The girl turned, but as she did so the lamp briefly illuminated her face, and Rhianne thought she saw a rather unpleasant smirk there.

As Geanna closed the door to her chamber, Rhianne sat there and nibbled on the roll.

13

The Bite of the Obsidian

MORGIN CHARGED BACK into the clearing on Mortiss. The chaos and pandemonium she'd created earlier had just begun to clear, with the jackals trying to calm their panicked horses. He charged into their midst, and with a giant nether shadow bucking and kicking horse and jackal alike, the horses panicked again. But an arrow nicked Morgin's shoulder, reminding him he could die as easily as any jackal. And outnumbered better than twenty to one, that would be his fate if he didn't move quickly, so he spurred Mortiss out of the clearing. He'd not had time to take an accurate count, but he thought he recalled another four or five jackals down, two Morgin had cut down with his blade, the rest victims of Mortiss's hooves.

"Damn you," the jackal captain shouted. He quickly arrayed six pike-men at the edge of the clearing, facing outward with their pikes set.

The long handle and blade of a pike would be deadly to a charging horse, so Morgin tried to circle around and come at them from a different angle. But they easily followed the progress of a warhorse charging through the forest and repositioned themselves against him. He had no choice but to withdraw, so he decided to wait for them in the forest, where the deep shadows beneath the canopy would be to his advantage.

While the jackals regrouped, he rode Mortiss a few hundred paces along the track Rafaellen had taken. He found a large thicket of brush and trees with deep shadows, entered it, reinforced his own shadows, and waited for the jackals. To follow Rafaellen they'd have to ride right past him.

He heard the jackal captain shouting orders at his dogs, demanding they move faster and get organized. He heard the neigh of skittish horses still not fully calmed after their ordeal with Mortiss. He heard grumbled curses and angry yowls, and one-by-one the jackal warriors led their mounts out of the clearing on foot, then mounted up and regrouped. "Let's ride hard," their captain ordered, and they spurred their horses into a gallop.

Morgin drew his sword and waited in his shadows. The thunder of the jackal horse's hooves grew to roar as they approached him, and they passed within ten paces of his position. As the last jackal rode by, he spurred Mortiss out of the thicket and into their wake. Riding hard, the jackals constantly glanced right and left and forward, clearly expecting Morgin to attempt some sort of ambush and not looking for a large, black shadow to join them from the rear. With several strides separating him from the last jackal in the troop he spurred Mortiss harder, trying to close the distance between them. Little by little the gap narrowed, Mortiss struggling to fill her lungs with air in time with the staccato beat of her hooves. They were almost side-by-side with the last rider before the jackal finally glanced his way, and in the moment it took him to realize he should have been looking back all along, Morgin swung his sword out and chopped into the dog's face. He tumbled off the back of his horse, and with no rider his horse slowed and dropped back.

Morgin took his place and spurred Mortiss harder to catch up with the next jackal. He took that one out in similar fashion, but as his sword bit into the dog's muzzle one of the jackals ahead looked back and howled out a warning. Their captain reined in his horse, bunching them up, and Mortiss slammed into the horse in front of her. The jackal mount went down while Mortiss staggered and sidestepped, Morgin desperately trying to remain in the saddle. A jackal sabre sliced along his left forearm and he cried out at the pain, though a piece of him thanked the gods it had not been his sword arm. Mortiss donkey-kicked a horse behind her, crushing its skull, then broke free from the melee, and with Morgin clutching at the saddle horn she charged ahead of them up the trail.

"After him," the jackal captain shouted.

••••

"We have to help him," Rhiannead pleaded. Rafaellen had her by the wrist, was all but dragging her to the horses. They'd only covered a few paces when the screams of that nether horse erupted from the clearing again, accompanied by howls from the jackals and the sound of swords clashing. "We can't just abandon him."

Rafaellen stopped and rounded on her. "Your presence will only hinder him, and he's buying you time to escape. Don't waste such a precious gift."

Realizing he was right she swallowed her pride and tried to keep up with him as they ran.

A mounted horseman loomed in front of them, and for an instant Rhiannead thought they'd been outflanked by the jackals. But then she recognized the rider as one of Rafaellen's soldiers, a string of horses trailing behind him.

Rafaellen lifted her into a saddle. "We lost one of my men in an ambush, so we have an extra horse for you."

The screams and cries from the clearing went silent, then the jackal captain called out a curse, though the distance muffled his words.

"Stay with me," Rafaellen said, then spurred his horse. Rhiannead dug her heels in and followed him as he led them back along their track at a gallop, the soldiers following behind her. They rode hard for about a thousand paces, then Rafaellen slowed his horse to a canter and the rest of them did likewise.

"We have to pace the horses," he said. "And we'll count on Lord Mortal to slow the jackals."

Behind them they heard a jackal howl, then cries and shouts and the ring of steel blades. Rhiannead saw pain on Rafaellen's face and realized it troubled him to abandon Lord Mortal. He said, "The wraiths will help him." His confidant air of command had disappeared.

"Wraiths?" she asked.

"Yes. Shadow beings of some kind, shaped like men but with no features. He calls them shadowwraiths, says they are the protectors of this forest, and he commands them."

"He commands them?"

"Yes, he is their lord."

Rafaellen opened his mouth as if to say more, but he hesitated for a heartbeat of indecision, saying only, "Keep it at a canter. As long as he harries them they won't catch us."

••••

NickoLot stood by the window in her room looking out at the castle yard below. She watched DaNoel gather with several other young men. They each took up a practice sword, stretched and warmed up for a bit, then three pairs of contestants squared off and began trading blows. DaNoel stood among the other young men watching from the sidelines.

As word had spread through the family that they believed Rhianne was Valso's captive in Durin, there had been quite a range of reactions. Roland had expressed sorrow and sadness, and wondered if they could ransom her. The moment Tulellcoe heard, as expected he immediately began making preparations with Cort to go there, and did not need to be asked. JohnEngine wanted to gather an army and start a war, while Brandon wanted more details—Brandon, always the careful planner. But DaNoel hadn't reacted at all, had just said, "Oh yes," and gone about his daily routine, almost as if he'd already known. All of NickoLot's suspicions had boiled back to the surface, reminding her that she had yet to get to the bottom of his deceits.

Several times now she'd watched DaNoel join the young men for practice. Those watching from the sidelines, and not participating, might slip away for a few moments to do something, but they always returned. However, the contestants exercising their skills were committed, and would fight on until the matches ended. Old Beckett, the weapons master, timed each match with a small hourglass, so she had a good idea how much time she'd have.

DaNoel did not participate in the next round of matches, and Nicki's impatience fueled her nervousness. Not until the third round did DaNoel square off with an opponent. Nicki allowed the contest to proceed for a bit, waited until he was well into it before turning and walking out of her room, trying to keep her pace even and calm.

DaNoel had locked the door to his room with a simple spell. She'd gone through this same exercise two days ago simply for the purpose of carefully analyzing the lock spell. She would have no difficulty merely circumventing it, but when she finished she needed to restore it. He mustn't know someone had searched his room; he'd probably guess who.

She'd prepared a charm in advance, and used it now to open the lock without deactivating it. She stepped into the room and closed the door, then began carefully searching. To her delight she found a horse-hair brush with several strands of hair. She carefully plucked them free and wrapped them in a small silk handkerchief she'd recently had laundered; it wouldn't do to contaminate them. Working with nothing but hair limited the type and strength of the spell she might craft. With nail clippings, saliva, or even bits of dandruff, she could tie it to him much more intimately. But she dare not take the time to thoroughly search his room, and a cursory search of his clothing turned up nothing more that might aid her.

She opened the door a crack, checked to make sure the hall was empty, then stepped out. She closed the door and used the charm to reset DaNoel's lock. Again, she forced herself not to hurry.

Back in her room she closed the door and set her own arcane lock, one much more powerful than DaNoel could summon. She sat down at her writing table, unwrapped the handkerchief and looked at her small bonanza. She counted more than 20 hairs.

After plucking some of her own hair, she braided two of DaNoel's hairs with one of hers. Working slowly, she produced five braids, then applied a bit of saliva to each. While the saliva was still wet she fed power into the braids and chanted, "Let the deceiver be deceived, and the deceived enlightened." Repeating that seven times for each braid, she closed off her power and set the spell.

The next time DaNoel joined the other young men for sword practice, she'd place these charms in and around his room. She wasn't sure what she might accomplish, didn't know what these spells would reveal, but she had to try.

••••

Morgin reined Mortiss off the game trail they'd been following, let her pick her own way a dozen paces through dense brush, then pulled her to a halt and dismounted. He dropped a deep shadow about them both, then sheathed his sword, pulled his belt knife and cut a strip of cloth from the hem of his tunic. Using it as a makeshift bandage, he bound the cut on his forearm.

Twice now he'd waited in ambush for the jackals with his bow strung and a nocked arrow. Each time, as they charged up the trail, he shot one arrow when they came into view, killing a single jackal. But his purpose had not been to kill jackals; he needed to make them wary, and the occasional arrow encouraged them to move slowly, buying Rafaellen time. Now it was time to change tactics, for he'd be a fool to attempt the same type of ambush three times.

The forest gave him an uncanny sense of Rhiannead's location. She and Rafaellen had turned due north, while the jackals had to ride east for some distance to regain the trail before they could do likewise. If he could cut diagonally toward Rhiannead, he could get ahead of the jackals and have enough time to prepare a real ambush.

He turned north, hoping to find a game trail leading that way, and the forest opened up before him. Branches moved aside and underbrush withered as he looked on, leaving a trail that matched his need perfectly. He mounted up and spurred Mortiss forward, and as they travelled up the trail it closed behind him.

The Living Forest! He'd forgotten it had a will of its own.

••••

Morgin pushed Mortiss hard for about two leagues, and the game trail the forest had opened up for him led him unerringly to the trail Rafaellen and Rhiannead followed, the trail up which the jackals would have to come. From the forest he sensed Rhiannead two or three leagues north, but he didn't have a similar sense of the jackals to guide him, didn't know if they'd come charging up the trail in the next instant, or if he could plan his ambush at his leisure. At best he hoped he'd hear their hoof beats a few hundred paces before they arrived.

On impulse he whispered, "Soann'Daeth'Daeye, are you near?"

The wraiths coalesced out of the shadows of the forest, and all knelt on one knee before him, their shapeless heads bowed. Their leader spoke, its words no more than a whisper of thought brushing across Morgin's mind, *We are always near, my king.*

"Send someone north to Captain Rafaellen," he said. "Warn him that I'm only a few leagues behind him, and that I'm going to ambush the jackals."

Yes, Your Majesty.

"And I know you can't sense the intruders, but if I draw my sword, you know I am among them. Shield me if you can."

The shadowwraiths dissipated into the forest.

Morgin retrieved a length of rope from his saddlebags, then chose a spot in the trail where it narrowed a bit. He tied the rope to two tree trunks so it spanned the trail about knee high. The shadows of the forest canopy hid it only a little. An intelligent rider would see it easily, pull up and not blunder into it. But Morgin added his own shadows to the rope, hopefully turning it into a deadly trap. Either they'd see it anyway and pull up, which would give him good targets, or they wouldn't, and he'd have even better targets.

The faint rumble of hoof beats in the distance broke the silence of the forest as he unstrapped his quiver and bow from Mortiss's saddle. He only had six arrows, but that would have to do. He swatted Mortiss on the rump and said, "Hide. And do what you can to help."

As the sound of the hoof beats grew from a faint rumble to an approaching roar, he sprinted up the trail about 30 paces, found a safe spot behind the trunk of a large tree, strung his bow, and waited.

He had an unobstructed view for about a hundred paces down the trail, easily saw the jackals as they came into view, the jackal captain in their lead. But about half way to the rope the jackal raised the bandaged stump of his right arm, and reining in his horse he shouted, "Halt—halt."

The jackal troop bunched up, but they were disciplined soldiers, and to Morgin's disappointment they stopped just short of the rope. Morgin nocked an arrow as the jackal captain nudged his horse forward the few remaining paces to the trap, leaned out of his saddle and looked down at it. He threw his head back and laughed. Moving as slowly and silently as possible, Morgin drew back the bow string.

The jackal captain barked, "It almost worked, man of shadows. But we know to watch for shadows that exist where none should."

Since the rope trap hadn't worked, Morgin might take down one or two jackals at most, but he'd need to escape, and where had Mortiss gone?

At that moment a dark shadow stepped out onto the trail behind the jackals. Mortiss no longer needed to charge into the jackal troop to create chaos, she merely brayed angrily to let their horses know she was there. The jackal mounts realized the demon horse was near and panicked, even though she did nothing but stand calmly in the trail and watch them, stomping her hooves a bit to encourage them. The horses in the rear neighed and whinnied and bucked against those in front of them, forcing the entire troop forward. The captain's mount was the first to hit the rope and trip, bringing the horse down and sending him sprawling. Three more horses followed him.

Morgin heard snapping limbs and braying jackals as he stepped out into the trail, raised his bow and shot an arrow. He loosed all of his arrows in rapid succession, recalled doing the same as Morddon against a bunch of Kulls in a distant past.

One of the jackals carrying a lance spurred his horse into a leap over the rope, dodged around the twisted pile of horses and dogs, lowered the lance and charged up the trail. Morgin tossed his bow aside, drew his sword, and a cloud of shadowwraiths enveloped him completely, obscuring the entire trail, and likely saving his life. He dodged to the side as the jackal rode past, struck out with his sword in a desperate attempt to deflect the lance, landing on his side in the trail.

He scrambled to his feet, but heard another set of hooves charging toward him, turned and found Mortiss bearing down on him. She slowed enough for him to grab her saddle horn as she raced past; he yanked himself into her saddle, but went a bit too far and almost fell off the other side, though he at least managed to keep hold of his sword. A blade hissed past his face as he tried to right himself. He struck out blindly as Mortiss kicked and screamed. She reared high and crushed a jackal's skull with her hooves, charged and slammed into another's horse, knocking animal and rider into the brush. Then she broke free and charged up the trail.

Morgin finally righted himself in Mortiss's saddle. He sensed several steel-tipped arrows arcing his way, and with his steel magic swatted them aside like annoying flies on a hot summer afternoon. He thanked the gods he'd escaped relatively unscathed. He was thanking them wholeheartedly with the wind in his face when the arrow slammed into his back. It felt as if he'd been stabbed with a red-hot poker, and pain washed through him with such intensity he couldn't even cry out. He looked down, saw a hand's breadth of arrow shaft protruding from his chest, its obsidian warhead glistening with his blood. It was off-center to the left, so he hoped it hadn't damaged any vital organs. But it had punched clean through him, through ribs and muscle, a grave wound, perhaps a mortal wound.

He swooned forward in the saddle, barely managed to hold onto consciousness as behind him he heard the jackal captain shout, "Damn you, shadow fighter. Damn you to the ninth hell."

14

Sabian

CHRISAINNE ROLLED OFF Lewendis, her bare breasts heaving as she lay on her back catching her breath. "That was quite . . . enjoyable, darling."

He sat up next to her, leaned over and kissed her cheek, then her neck. After she got rid of Theandrin, ErrinCastle, BlakeDown and her husband, she'd keep Lewendis around. As he kissed her breasts she became aroused again. But she had work to do, so she pushed him away, doing so gently so he'd not feel rejected. "Let me catch my breath, darling."

Leaning over her he said, "When I'm near you I can think of nothing else."

She ran a finger along the line of his jaw. "My husband is far from here—hunting, I think—so we have all night. I just have to return to my own room before the servants awake. We mustn't fuel their gossip."

She slipped out of bed and stood, purposefully didn't cover herself because it kept him in a constant state of distraction. She crossed the room to a small table, poured two goblets of chilled, summer wine. As she returned he couldn't take his eyes off her breasts, and even after she held one of the goblets out to him, it took him a heartbeat to pull his eyes off them and focus on the goblet. He took it from her and gulped at the wine.

She needed to get him talking about the border situation. "Before you . . . distracted me, you were angry at one of the Elhiynes." Always best to play dumb and let him lead her into it.

"Not just one of the Elhiynes," he said. "All of them. They're arrogant, and they look down their noses at me."

Valso wanted her to escalate the situation. She leaned forward, kissed him on the cheek and said, "I haven't met too many Elhiynes, but the few times I have, I've seen that myself. They shouldn't be allowed to get away with it."

She knew he particularly disliked an Elhiyne named DaNoel. She'd never met the fellow, so she lied. "I met Lord DaNoel once, and I found him quite egotistical."

Lewendis's face reddened with anger. He gulped the last of his wine, stood, crossed the room and poured more. He returned to her, saying, "He's an arrogant bastard. When we meet on the border he doesn't even acknowledge my nobility."

Lewendis could barely make claim to nobility; if Valso hadn't enriched her dowry, she'd have had to marry someone like him. She put on a show of anger as she said, "You shouldn't put up with that. The next time he slights you, you should show him that you're a man to be reckoned with, bloody his nose a bit, give him something to think on."

"Yes," he said, almost growling the word like a beast. "Yes, I will."

She reached out and caressed his manhood. "I think I've caught my breath."

He grinned, took her goblet and returned both to the table. Talking about DaNoel had gotten his blood up, and he proved to be quite energetic.

When they finished, Lewendis fell into an exhausted sleep. Chrisainne lay awake beside him, and when certain she could get away with it, she cast a small spell to deepen his sleep. She slipped out of bed, felt her way to her clothing, retrieved Valso's coin from a pocket in her cloak. She kissed it, returned the coin to the cloak, then slipped under the sheets to wait.

Chrisainne, my dear. You've done as I asked?

Yes, Your Majesty. I don't think he'll kill DaNoel, but he'll certainly start something.

Excellent! We'll have—

Chrisainne felt a spell activate, felt Valso's connection to her snap like a twig breaking, and her heart went cold. She took one heartbeat to understand what she could of the spell, sensed only that it tasted of Theandrin.

She climbed out of bed, bundled up her gown, underclothes and slippers, merely threw on the cloak and didn't bother to dress. She opened the door to Lewendis's room just a crack, saw no one out in the hall, stepped out, closed the door behind her and rushed toward her own room. At each intersection she stopped, peered around the corner first, then continued on. Not until she closed the door to her own room, stuffed her clothing underneath her bed, then climbed beneath the sheets, not until then did her heart stop racing.

••••

Theandrin marched down the hallway carrying the new charm she'd made. Her inquiries had yielded no Vodah spies lurking about, at least none who'd been inside the castle walls at the right moment. And yet her wards had been triggered repeatedly. So she'd modified her special ward, increased its sensitivity and added this charm to it, which she hoped would give her some sense of location.

She paused at the intersection of two halls, thought for a moment she saw someone disappear around the far corner to the right, but realized she was jumping at shadows. She closed her eyes, let the charm guide her to the left.

She turned and walked more carefully since she was getting close. Half way down the hall the charm pulled her unerringly to a single door. She stopped outside it, and glanced about to orient herself.

Rooms in this part of the castle were neither spacious nor elaborate. She assigned them to minor clansmen, those of lesser nobility, and she racked her brains to recall to whom she'd assigned this particular room. Could it be Lewendis? She'd have to confirm it with her staff in the morning, but she was almost certain of that.

That certainly added up. If Valso wanted to see war between Penda and Elhiyne, what better way than to have a hot-head spy put in charge of a border patrol. From now on she would keep a close eye on young Lord Lewendis. She really should know a lot more about the man, especially with Chrisainne spreading her legs for the fellow.

It occurred to her she hadn't really gotten that much information from Chrisainne, just bits and pieces, and frequently something she already knew. Time to have a talk with that girl, lite a fire under her. But that would have to wait for morning.

••••

Morgin managed to hold onto his sword and sit up in the saddle long enough to sheath it. He turned slightly so the arrow's obsidian warhead wouldn't stab Mortiss in the neck, then leaned forward and wrapped his arms around her. "Try to catch up with Rafaellen," he said, though saying even that much cost him dearly.

He drifted in and out of consciousness, trusted that he could stay in the saddle, trusted that she would continue up the trail and stay ahead of the jackals. Hopefully, she and he had done enough damage to them that they'd have to lick their wounds a bit before following.

When he slammed into the ground the pain came on so intently he rolled onto his side and vomited. He lay there for several heartbeats, didn't have the strength to sit up.

Mortiss nudged his ear with her muzzle and snorted loudly. *Get up, fool.*

"Yah, I know," he said. "I know." He rolled onto his stomach, rolled onto the arrow shaft protruding from his chest and heard it snap. The pain that came with that sent him back into unconsciousness.

Another loud snort in his ear. *I said get up, fool.*

But he couldn't get up so he ignored her, drifted off to a place with no pain . . .

Mortiss bit his ear.

"Ahhh! Blast you." He struggled to a sitting position. "What did you do that for?"

She neighed angrily.

He struggled to his hands and knees, and stopped there for a moment to think the situation through. As long as he remained on the ground, she wouldn't let him sleep, and he longed for sleep. But she'd let him doze if he managed to get into the saddle.

He got one foot beneath him, then another, but he still had both hands on the ground, didn't feel steady enough to stand up straight, knew if he did so he'd probably just fall down again. Mortiss stood only a step away, so he straightened up and staggered toward her, caught hold of her saddle horn and held on to that to keep upright as waves of pain washed through him. He stood there for a few heartbeats catching his breath. The arrow shaft protruding from his chest was now a splintered stub. He carefully reached around to the shaft in his back, learned that he'd snapped that end off too, probably when he'd first fallen out of the saddle.

As the pain receded he realized that climbing all the way up onto Mortiss's back might be beyond his strength. He leaned his head against her saddle as he felt consciousness slipping away . . .

"Lord Mortal."

"Wah," Morgin said and opened his eyes. Miraculously, he'd remained standing beside Mortiss.

"Lord Mortal."

He turned toward the voice and saw Rafaellen standing beside him. "You're injured."

"Very . . . observant of you! Fell out of . . . the saddle, can't get back up into it."

Rafaellen! Without the princess! "What are you doing here? Where's Rhiannead?"

"We were close enough to the castle that I knew she could get their easily. I sent her on with my two men. I came back for you. I don't leave a man behind."

"The jackals will be along soon."

"I know. Let's get you in the saddle."

Morgin could raise his foot and put it in the stirrup, but he didn't have the strength to climb into the saddle. So Rafaellen got behind him, put a shoulder beneath his butt and hoisted him up like a sack of potatoes.

Rafaellen pushed them hard, or at least as hard as they could go with Morgin slumped in the saddle, Rafaellen riding beside him and trying to keep him from again falling out of it. But each bump in the trail, each turn, each twist, sent a jolt of pain through Morgin's back and chest, which, oddly enough, was of some benefit. The constant pain kept him from slipping away into the blissful mindlessness of unconsciousness, allowing Rafaellen to push them even harder.

"It's still not enough," Rafaellen said, looking back over his shoulder. "They're not far behind us, and they're slowly catching us. It's a three-way race."

"Three-way?" Morgin asked, trying to sit up straighter so Mortiss could ride faster.

Rafaellen reached out and touched Morgin's back, not on the wound but somewhere below it. He held his hand up for Morgin to see; it was drenched in blood. "Yes. Will we make it to Sabian? Or will those dogs catch us before we get there? Or will you bleed to death before that?"

"Pull off the trail," Morgin said. "Let's not make it easy for them."

"The undergrowth here is too dense."

Morgin reined Mortiss to a stop, and Rafaellen pulled up a dozen paces ahead. "What are you doing?"

With the hooves of the jackal's mounts pounding out a thunderous roar not far behind them, Morgin looked up at the canopy of leaves overhead. "Dammit, forest, open another trail for us." Nothing happened, so he added, "Please."

The brush at side of the trail squirmed and moved, some of it shifting to the side, some simply ungrowing, receding into the ground as if it had never been.

"Well I'll be damned," Rafaellen said. He spurred his horse up the new trail.

Morgin looked up at the canopy again and said, "And close it behind us. Please."

Morgin followed Rafaellen, looked back and saw the forest dutifully obeying him. But about a hundred paces on they encountered the shadowwraith Soann'Daeth'Daeye standing in the trail, and they pulled up.

Sabian is sending armsmen to deal with the intruders, mortals who can fight them. It raised an arm, pointing north and said, *This way.*

Morgin turned to Rafaellen. "You said Sabian. It said Sabian. Who is Sabian?"

"The castle of the Unnamed King. It's the seat of his power, and the heart of the Living Forest."

With the jackals off their trail they rode cautiously, side-by-side, so that every time Morgin drifted toward unconsciousness Rafaellen could reach out and give him a gentle shake. At one point they heard the ring of steel in the distance, and shouts and cries of men and jackals and horses, clearly a pitched battle.

"Sounds like help has arrived," Rafaellen said.

Morgin struggled to even say, "Huh?"

"That would be the Unnamed King's armsmen, met up with the jackals, I would guess."

Rafaellen stood up in his stirrups for a moment and scanned the forest. "We're close, very close."

Morgin drifted off again into a sea of pain. But then Rafaellen shook him hard, pointed up the trail and said, "Look. We're there. Sabian!"

Morgin opened his eyes, squinted and concentrated carefully on the forest in front of him. But no matter how hard he tried, he saw no grand castle, no walls, no stone, no mortar. He should be the one hallucinating, not Rafaellen. He was about to give up and turn away when he recognized a vague shape that hinted at the lines of a battlement. But it was no more than the way in which the branches of two trees intertwined. He looked closer, and saw that among the branches there were vines and leaves and flowers woven together so intricately they formed recognizable shapes. And even though the density of their weave was such as to create a solid wall of vegetation, the trees were not choked by the vines, but lived among them healthy and hale.

It dawned upon him that he was looking at a wall, and now that he saw it, he recognized windows and arches, turrets and battlements. But this wall was not made of stone and mortar, it was formed of the inter-grown life of the forest, hundreds of trees tied together by millions of vines and leaves and flowers: a castle both grand and enormous. Morgin could barely whisper as he said, "I see it now."

Rafaellen dismounted, stepped lightly off the trail and stood expectantly before the wall of vegetation, though since there was no gate or door his actions perplexed Morgin. But then the vines and branches squirmed with life again, separating, parting, exposing layer after layer of forest growth. Finally there appeared a small hole in the midst of the activity. It widened and grew and took on shape, and where only moments earlier the wall had been impenetrable, they now stood before an entry capped by a high arch.

Rhianne—or was it Rhiannead—rushed out from the castle followed by retainers and servants. She stopped beside Morgin, looked up at him and said, "You're hurt!"

Morgin looked into her eyes—bright green eyes—and that was his last conscious thought.

••••

Rhianne knew she couldn't support Morgin as he slumped out of the saddle, but she wouldn't allow him to simply tumble to the ground. Still, it surprised her how quickly she crumbled beneath his weight.

"No," she said, unable to pull herself out from beneath him. "I am not Rhianne. I am Rhiannead." But drifting through her mind was the constant thought that, *I am also Rhianne.*

A fat and ponderous man dressed in some sort of official palace livery marched out of the castle. He shouted orders and issued commands, contributing to a general sense of pandemonium. Two servants pulled Lord Mortal off her, and under the watchful eyes of the fat fellow, they placed him on a stretcher. Only then did she see the broken stub of an arrow shaft protruding from his chest.

"Get him into the castle immediately," the man ordered.

Rafaellen helped her to her feet, and they caught up with the servants just as they crossed the threshold into the castle. To Rhiannead's surprise they stopped there, and placed the stretcher on the dirt of the castle yard, then stood there and looked on as if waiting for something.

She turned to Rafaellen. "What are they waiting for? Shouldn't they summon a physician?"

Rafaellen looked ill as he said, "My lady, that wound is mortal. There is nothing a physician can do. He will die."

At Rafaellen's words the fat fellow turned about and gave them both a scornful look. "He will not die within these walls. He cannot die within these walls, for Sabian will not allow it."

Rafaellen demanded, "And you are?"

The fat fellow lifted his many chins and sniffed. "I am Kinardin, Lord Chamberlain of Sabian."

Rhiannead looked down at Lord Mortal, then stepped around Kinardin. She knelt down beside this man she had met in the forest, and her eyes settled on the stub of an arrow shaft protruding from his chest. But as she looked at it the shaft quivered and jerked, and for several heartbeats she feared he struggled in the final throes of death. She reached out to him, but Kinardin leaned down and gripped her wrist.

"No, my lady," he said. "Allow Sabian to do its work."

The stub of arrow shaft now appeared to be completely still, and it took her long moments to realize it moved, but so slowly her eye could not discern any motion. Little by little it withdrew from his chest until it stood up like a small branch that had sprouted from his ribs. Then it withdrew the last, final bit and flopped over on his chest. The servants about her sighed in unison.

Kinardin ordered the servants, "Get him to his suites, bathe him. After this ordeal he'll sleep deeply tonight."

To Rhiannead he said, "And you, young lady. We have a suite of rooms arranged for you."

As the servants lifted Lord Mortal's stretcher Rhiannead straightened. "Will he live?"

Kinardin frowned, didn't bother to answer her, turned and left her standing there.

15

In the Court of the Unnamed King

FROM HER BALCONY Rhianne watched the shadows in the city lengthen as the sun settled toward the horizon. She had napped again that morning, napped to return to the Kingdom of Dreams, only to be awakened by Geanna to dine with the King at lunch. She had tried to nap again that afternoon, but Valso demanded her presence at a reception for some of his nobles. At least the day was nearing its end.

Movement down below in the castle yard caught her attention, and again it was Haleen et Decouix. This time she had not covered her head with a hood, but as before she paused and looked at Rhianne for a moment before continuing on.

Behind her she heard Geanna approaching, so she turned to face the girl.

Geanna curtsied and said, "His Majesty is here to see you."

Valso having himself properly announced; what a surprise! "Then show him in."

Rhianne stepped off the balcony to await Valso in her sitting room, and when he entered, even she had to admit he could be quite handsome. She curtsied, saying, "Your Majesty."

"Rise, Rhianne," he said, casually waving a hand.

She stood. "What may I do for you?"

He wandered over to the hearth in which a small fire burned, for even this time of year the northern climes could hold a chill. He toyed with a vase there, and looking at his back she realized his shoulders were somewhat broad. He was a man of average stature, but he didn't lack for muscle, and he kept himself trim and fit.

He turned around to face her. "I have a question for you?"

She crossed the room and stopped a few paces from him. "And what might that be, Your Majesty?" She saw why her handmaidens spoke of their handsome king with such admiration. But they didn't truly understand him, didn't know enough to despise him as she did.

"Why do you spend so much time in these rooms?" he asked. "You sleep in the morning, then sometimes again in the afternoon. You should get out more. It seems unhealthy."

"I am surprised you are concerned with my welfare."

"But I am." He frowned. "Listen, when this is done, and I rule all the clans, it will be time to put our differences aside. You are a powerful witch, and will be an influential member of whatever clan you end up in. Of course, we'll have to find you another husband—I might even have a certain Vodah in mind—but it will be time for us all to move forward, not look to the past. So yes, I am concerned with your welfare."

That certainly sounded reasonable, though it was all based on the premise that Rhianne was no longer wed, that Morgin had died. She couldn't really blame Valso for his ignorance, though oddly enough she felt a bit disappointed when he'd mentioned some Vodah as a possible husband. It vexed her that he showed no interest himself. She'd certainly take pleasure in turning him down. At least she thought she would, though again it struck her that he was quite handsome, and perhaps she wouldn't take as much pleasure in that as she thought. She wondered what it would be like to kiss him, turned away from him and tried to put that thought out of her mind.

She heard him take a step toward her. "You seem troubled, my dear."

He stood close enough to her that she felt the heat of his body, and she thought again of those strong shoulders and his trim waist. She turned to face him, found that he'd stopped at a distance close enough to be intimate, and to her own surprise that didn't bother her.

She said, "I . . . ah . . ." But looking into his eyes she was at a loss for words, and could think only of his unnatural beauty. And though the distance separating them was little more than a hand's breadth, she stepped forward and stopped just short of pressing her breasts against his chest. She reached up and traced a finger down the line of his jaw, wanted to kiss him with almost desperate desire.

He looked down at her breasts, at the cleavage exposed by her low-cut gown, and she saw the desire in his eyes.

"Yes," she said, but a part of her, buried deep within her soul, screamed, *Nooooo!*

He said, "Turn around, my lovely Rhianne."

She turned about, turned her back to him, and she felt him fumbling at the laces and buttons on her gown.

Nooooo!

His fingers moved deftly, and the top of her gown loosened to the point where she had to hold the front up with her hands.

Nooooo!

She turned back to face him and saw the hunger in his eyes. She wanted him so badly he didn't have to prompt her to lower her hands, and the top of her gown fell just a bit more, now showing an indecent amount of cleavage and all but exposing her breasts completely.

Nooooo!

He reached up, hooked a finger into the top of the gown and lowered it even more. Now, basically naked from the waist up, she wanted him, needed him.

Nooooo!

He smiled, reminding her of a predatory animal at the moment just before it struck down its prey. She knew what he was doing only because he allowed her to; it heightened his pleasure to see his prey stricken with terror, but powerless to do anything about it. He leaned forward, squeezed her left breast with his hand and kissed the nipple of her right breast.

Her gut tightened as nausea flooded through her abdomen, then her dinner boiled up and she vomited on the back of his head. He straightened, screaming, "What! What!"

Another wave of nausea hit her, but this time she spewed bile straight into his face. He staggered backward, stomach fluids and bits and pieces of half-digested food dripping from his face and arms and tunic.

Another spasm hit her and she vomited on the floor, then collapsed there, gagging as wave after wave of nausea hit her. She closed her eyes, gulping and swallowing as her stomach slowly calmed, heard Valso shouting at her handmaidens.

The spell had taken hours of preparation. She couldn't use a charm-based spell, for her spying handmaidens would find it and report it to him, as they had probably done before. So it had to be wholly concocted of her power. It had to be simple, and it couldn't be defensive, not something that would harm him, nothing like the spells young women were taught to protect themselves. He would watch for that, and easily disable anything she prepared. So she had decided on a very revolting defense, a spell that would merely drive him away. But it had to have a well-defined and carefully chosen trigger point, otherwise it might activate at the wrong moment; it wouldn't do to spew her lunch all over her handmaidens simply because one of them uttered the wrong phrase. She had settled on her breasts, for his eyes always strayed there. She'd set the spell to trigger when he overtly touched them, and only when she was sexually aroused, for she would never find him desirable unless under the influence of one of his compulsion spells.

She heard him marching across the floor toward her, so she opened her eyes. He'd wiped his face, but the former contents of her stomach still decorated the front of his tunic. He leaned down over her. "It was a spell, wasn't it?"

She thought of Olivia's predatory grin when she'd gained a point in some argument, and she tried to imitate her as she smiled up at him.

His face turned a bright, scarlet red. "You're insane," he screamed. He drew his foot back and kicked her in the stomach.

It hurt, and she curled up clutching her abdomen. She closed her eyes but kept the smile on her face.

The next time he'd be watching for a similar spell, so she'd have to think of something new, something different, something he wouldn't anticipate.

••••

Chrisainne wandered out through the open castle gates, walking slowly and trying to appear casual about it. She strolled through the market nestled against the outside of the castle wall, a long row of booths and stalls where one could buy just about anything of a practical nature. She wanted anyone who took note of her to believe she was just a young woman out for a breath of fresh air on a warm summer afternoon.

She glanced about to make sure she was not observed, then lifted her hand to her mouth and faked a yawn, Valso's magical coin hidden in the palm of her hand. She kissed it, then lowered her hand and continued walking, preparing herself for the king's displeasure. When Valso spoke she was careful not to react, but to continue strolling casually, glancing about at this and that.

What so abruptly interrupted our last conversation?

Your Majesty, please accept my most humble apology for that. I believe it was one of Lady Theandrin's wards, or a spell of some nature.

Is she on to you?

No, sire. And now that I've been alerted to her meddling, I've taken some pains to investigate carefully. I've found six wards embedded in the walls of Castle Penda, powerful constructs. I'd guess she's been reinforcing them for decades, and I suspect there are others that I haven't found.

Stay away from those wards; don't even attempt to find the rest.

Yes, Your Majesty.

Theandrin is a powerful witch, and no one's fool.

I'm aware of that, Your Majesty. I think that when you breach the castle wall with your power in this way, it triggers the wards to some degree, and she's grown suspicious. That's why I contacted you today from outside the castle walls.

Good thinking, girl. I'll not contact you again since I won't know whether or not you're inside those wards. But try to get outside the castle and reach me when you can.

Yes, Your Majesty.

And what of Lewendis?

He's ready. There will soon be blood on the border.

Valso withdrew from her mind.

As Chrisainne strolled casually through the castle gates and back into the yard, a young serving girl called out to her. "Lady Chrisainne! Lady Chrisainne!"

Lifting her skirts high, the girl ran across the yard, stopped and bobbed a quick curtsy. "I've been looking everywhere for you. Lady Theandrin wishes to see you immediately."

Chrisainne said, "I'll go right away."

She found Theandrin in her apartments standing by a window, tapping her finger on the sill impatiently. When she entered the room, the older woman turned and said, "Where have you been?"

Chrisainne couldn't guess what had sparked Theandrin's ire. "Why . . . just out for a stroll."

Theandrin spoke to her as if she were a servant. "I need more information about Lewendis. In fact, I need more information about everything."

Theandrin proceeded to give her a thorough tongue lashing, and Chrisainne now realized she could no longer stall her with bits and pieces of meaningless information.

••••

"Lord Mortal!"

Morgin opened his eyes, saw young Aethon running through the forest toward him, Erithnae walking at a slower pace behind the boy. He took in his surroundings, saw that he'd been sleeping while sitting on the forest floor on a bed of leaves, his back to a fallen log.

Aethon sat down beside him. "Why didn't you tell me you were the Unnamed King?"

"The Unnamed King?" Morgin asked as Erithnae approached.

She smiled at him, curtsied and said, "Your Majesty."

Morgin closed his eyes, sensed the forest about him, a part of him. He opened his eyes, looked into Erithnae's face and saw both Rhianne and Rhiannead there. "Yes," he said, "the Unnamed King."

Aethon was relentless. "Why did you keep it a secret?"

"I didn't," Morgin said. "I don't think I was the Unnamed King until this moment."

He stood and approached Erithnae. "You are my Rhianne, aren't you?"

She smiled again, and now all he saw was Rhianne. "Of course."

"And you're also the flighty, young girl Rhiannead, aren't you?"

"Of course."

He took her in his arms and kissed her, a soft, gentle, loving kiss.

••••

Morgin awoke a bit groggy, but feeling rather good for a man who should be dying, or, for that matter, already dead. In fact, on second thought, he felt rather refreshed, the way one would feel after a long night of deep, restful sleep: perhaps a little slow to wake, but healthy and whole and ready for the day to come.

He sat up in bed and took in his surroundings. He lay in a four-poster bed with a canopy suspended overhead. The mattress was so thick it almost swallowed him, with white linen sheets and a thick feather-stuffed comforter. Across the room a woman stood looking out a window through which the sun's rays slanted sharply. He realized it was not morning, but late afternoon.

Someone had dressed him in an elaborately embroidered, soft, cotton nightgown. He threw the covers back and swung his legs off the bed, then stepped down onto the stone floor, which appeared to be polished marble. The woman turned to face him, his Rhianne. She crossed the room and he took her in his arms. "I've been waiting for you," she said.

He said, "Are you Erithnae, Rhianne, or Rhiannead?"

She smiled, kissed his cheek, then brushed her lips lightly across his. With a sly grin on her face she said, "I am all three, but right now I'm mostly Rhianne."

He kissed her, much like he'd kissed her in the forest only a dream ago, soft and gentle. But he couldn't resist the taste of her, and as their tongues danced together, the kiss grew hot and passionate.

When they parted he said, "I've missed you."

She said, "And I've missed you."

"Why is it we can only find each other in a dream?"

"We'll find ourselves eventually," she said, and he saw the confidence in her eyes. "But right now, I'll settle for this dream."

She tugged at his nightgown, so he pulled at the laces at the back of her dress. She laughed, and he laughed with her. She was gowned in the elegance of a lady of the court, and her attire did frustrate them a bit. He removed one layer, then another, and another, and there always seemed one more to be removed. It took quite some time to peel all those fashionable layers of clothing off her. But they persevered. Together, they persevered.

••••

With morning sunlight flooding through the window, Morgin lay in bed with Rhianne sleeping in his arms. Or was it Erithnae, or Rhiannead?

The Unnamed King knows all names but his own. He thought how true that had turned out to be.

Rhianne stirred, sat up and stretched, naked above the blankets and wholly unconcerned about it. She turned and wrapped her arms around him and said, "You know you must return to the Mortal Plane, return to your Rhianne."

"You're not my Rhianne?"

She shrugged, brushed her lips across his cheek. "I am, and I am not."

"What happened to Rhiannead? Where is she?"

She reached out and curled a lock of his hair around a finger. "She was just a dreamer." The look on his face must have prompted her to continue. "She didn't really live here. She was just a mortal who was simply dreaming. You're the only mortal who really *lives* in the Kingdom of Dreams."

He noticed she hadn't included herself in that. "Even Rafaellen—he's just a dreamer?"

When she nodded it saddened him. He'd come to like Rafaellen; they'd faced death together, and that formed a bond of friendship even between the most different of men. And now that bond seemed elusive and artificial.

"All of them?" he asked. "Dreamers?"

"Yes, my love."

"And you? You said I'm the only mortal here. Are you a dreamer too?"

She laughed. "Oh, no, my dear. I am very real, but I'm not mortal. I'm the god-queen."

She leaned forward and kissed him. "There. Now wasn't that real enough?"

"Yes."

Her words had been meant to comfort him, but instead they left him feeling alone, so very alone.

16

The Return of the Fallen

STANDING AT THE window in her room, NickoLot watched the young men sparring in the castle yard below. DaNoel sat to one side, watching the contestants and waiting his turn, while NickoLot waited for the opportunity to plant her charms.

When his turn did come, she didn't immediately rush down to his room. She forced herself to be patient, watched old Beckett turn over the hourglass, and waited a bit for DaNoel to get into the match. Satisfied she would have the time she needed, she was about to turn and go, when DaNoel slipped, and his opponent's sword struck his arm. The sword's steel had been dulled to prevent injury, but it still opened up a nasty gash.

What a stroke of luck!

As the young men gathered around DaNoel, NickoLot turned and rushed out of her room. She hurried down the stairs, through the castle proper and out into the yard. Beckett was attempting to bandage the wound, but NickoLot elbowed her way through the young men and said, "Here, let me see that."

Beckett stepped aside, and she gripped DaNoel's arm, ignoring the blood. "That's a nasty cut," she said.

DaNoel gave her a skeptical look. "Since when have you been so concerned with my well-being?"

She tried to give him an Olivia look. "We may have our differences, but you're still my brother. Mother is much better at healing than me. You'd better have her look at this right away so it doesn't fester."

DaNoel pulled his arm out of her hands. "I'll do exactly that." He turned his back on her and walked away.

NickoLot looked down at the small puddle of blood cupped in the palm of her left hand. She'd deliberately let DaNoel's blood drip there, and had been careful to keep her right hand clean. She wouldn't plant the charms today. Now that she had his blood, she could recast them, make them much more powerful and set them another day. She closed her left hand, held it close to her side. As she headed back to her room she didn't care if anyone saw her hurrying on her way. She didn't have much time before the blood congealed, and certain, powerful spells required fresh blood.

She made only one detour. She stopped in the cook's herb garden and plucked a couple of basil leaves from small plants and several bay leaves from the tree in the center.

Up in her room she sat down at her writing table and carefully arranged the herb leaves in front of her. With meticulous care she dripped a few drops of DaNoel's blood onto each of them. She'd use them later for spells that required dried blood.

Using just her right hand, she retrieved the small chest she kept beneath her writing table, triggered the arcane lock that sealed it and opened it. From it she withdrew the handkerchief in which she'd wrapped DaNoel's hairs, and placed it next to the herb leaves. Through the years she'd collected a number of seemingly random items on the off chance she might use them in a spell or charm. She'd stored them in the chest and she searched through it now, looking for two shiny pieces of metal. She found them: two cheap, silver trinkets.

Silver, the conductor of energies, it absorbed many things but didn't store them, helped them flow in one direction or another. She tilted her left hand over one of the pieces, let three drops of blood drop onto it, was happy to see the blood still flowed cleanly. She'd prefer to put the customary seven drops on each charm, but there wasn't enough left. She repeated the process with the other piece, might have gotten a fourth or fifth drop onto it, but experience told her symmetry was critical for this spell. She wiped her hand on a cloth.

She hadn't anticipated working with blood, had to improvise as she worked. Now, how to proceed, what to do with this small boon, that was the question she must answer, and quickly.

••••

Morgin paced back and forth in the king's privy chamber. He couldn't forget the jackals, and he knew he couldn't ignore them.

"My king!" Morgin had been lost in thought. He stopped his pacing and looked toward the door. Erithnae had slipped into the room quietly. "Why so thoughtful?"

"The jackals," he said.

"Yes," she said. "They won't give up, will they? You said you've fought them before."

"Yes, a long time ago, and when I think about it, an old acquaintance keeps coming to mind. It's someone I've met in two different lives, and together we fought them."

"And this person?"

"Not a person, really. Metadan is his name."

She closed her eyes and lowered her head, almost as if the mention of that name gave her pain. "The foremost among the archangels, and for some centuries now, The Fallen One. You should summon him."

"Would he answer such a summons?"

"He would have no choice."

Morgin still didn't understand the powers of the Unnamed King. "Then let's get—"

The door to the room swung open and Kinardin entered. Morgin still hadn't grown accustomed to the fact that he didn't have to summon Kinardin; just think it and Castle Sabian would let the Lord Chamberlain know he was needed. Kinardin bowed with a flourish. "My king, what do you desire?"

Morgin had learned that if he didn't say it, Kinardin would hold the bow forever. "Rise. Please rise."

Erithnae said, "His Majesty needs help and he wishes you to summon Metadan."

Kinardin raised an eyebrow and cocked his head. "He can be a valuable ally, or a dangerous foe. But having fallen so far there is little chance he'll aid us."

Morgin shrugged. "There may be a way of convincing him."

"Very well," Kinardin said. "I'll take care of it right away."

He started to turn but Morgin said, "There's another thing." He'd been thinking about this now for a couple of days. In fact, he'd been obsessed with it. "Could you get me some obsidian? Enough to make a sword and a dagger?"

Kinardin frowned. "But will such a blade be of any use? Won't it be quite fragile?"

"It might," Morgin said. "I think I just have to make it the right way. I faced such a blade once, and I'm certain I'll have to face it again."

"As you wish, Your Majesty."

It occurred to Morgin that he needed Metadan's help, not his obedience. "One more thing," he said. "Don't summon Metadan, request his presence. And make it a polite request."

••••

As well as being a gentle lover, Lewendis proved to be quite discreet, and Chrisainne had come to appreciate him even more. When she stepped out into the castle yard, not realizing he and his border patrol were preparing to ride out, he glanced her way for a moment, but didn't succumb to any temptation to give her a surreptitious wink or an overly warm smile. Too bad she had to end their relationship, for there was no question it would eventually become a liability, but how? She couldn't just break it off; he might make a scene and expose her.

Her husband certainly knew about her liaison with BlakeDown, though they both pretended he did not. But he knew nothing of Lewendis, and she wasn't certain how he'd react if he found out. If he thought she'd taken Lewendis as a lover by her own choice, he might take it badly. Nor could she tell him Theandrin had forced her into the relationship. No, it would clearly be best to keep her affair with Lewendis just between him, her, and Theandrin, while she looked for a way to dispose of them both.

Lewendis and his men mounted up and rode out through the castle gates, stirring up a cloud of dust. Chrisainne hesitated for a few moments to allow it to clear, then walked through the gates, trying to adopt the air of a young woman out for a casual stroll. As she walked through the market nestled against the outer castle wall, she lifted her hand to her mouth, and under the guise of clearing her throat, kissed Valso's medallion.

Nothing happened for the longest time, and she'd even begun enjoying her stroll, was considering some of the wares offered in the market, when Valso entered her thoughts.

What is it? I'm quite busy, so make it quick.

Lewendis is ready to take action, she said. *Something should happen quite soon.*

Good! Very good! You've done well, but I must go.

As Chrisainne walked back to the castle, she returned to her thoughts of Lewendis. Once Theandrin, ErrinCastle and her husband were dead, and it was time to marry BlakeDown, Lewendis would prove to be a liability. But then she realized she might use him to accomplish some of her ends, and be rid of him at the same time. Theandrin with poison, ErrinCastle with an accident, then she could fuel Lewendis's desire for her and turn it into jealousy. With her husband standing in the way of her *true love* for Lewendis, they could not marry. If she could get the yokel to murder her husband in a fit of jealous anger—

She'd have to move carefully, make the fool appear to be an obsessed madman, and her the grieving widow. Once they hung Lewendis for her husband's murder, nothing could stop her.

••••

Standing at the window in her sitting room, Theandrin looked down at the castle yard below. She watched Lewendis and his men mount up and ride out to the border, watched the cloud of dust they raised slowly dissipate.

Her wards had been triggered quite regularly before she'd modified them to give her some sense of direction. Though once she'd altered them, nothing had occurred but that one, single incident that led her to Lewendis's room. She'd been exceedingly careful to show no mistrust of him, but had he somehow gained a hint of her suspicions? Even if he didn't know of her wards, a cautious man would understand the dangers of betraying his liege lord within the confines of his own castle, would conduct any covert activities outside its walls. But when not on border patrol Lewendis rarely left the sprawling confines of the castle grounds. No, nothing since that one incident; something just didn't add up.

Perhaps she should place some wards outside the castle walls. But that could prove to be a monumental task. Without the encircling nature of the castle to provide a well-defined enclosure, she'd have to blanket the countryside with them. Possibly, if she was careful and subtle, she could secretly place a small charm in his clothing, though she wasn't sure what to set as its trigger. She'd have to think on that carefully.

Just before she turned away from the window she noticed Chrisainne walking out through the castle gates. She appeared to be going for a stroll, or to do some shopping in the market. Theandrin was sorely disappointed in the information the girl had provided, but wasn't sure how hard to press her.

What was she going to do with that foolish girl? Probably what she'd done with all the rest: be patient and let BlakeDown tire of her. Once he did, he'd get rid of her and have another to replace her.

●●●●

Rhianne awoke, sighed with contentment and lay in bed. She'd been having the most wonderful dreams, very unladylike dreams. They'd also been most undreamlike, which she now understood was the nature of these dreams that weren't truly dreams. Each had ended with her and Morgin lying beneath the sheets in each other's arms, content and happy, though their joy had been shadowed by their fear of what the jackals might do to retaliate.

For several nights now she had had the joy of those dreams, each night a little different, but always the two of them laughing and cavorting like innocent children as they played at some very adult games. It was strange that she and Morgin found happiness only in her dreams, when in life they had found so little joy together. The hard part was that each morning she had to awake to *this* reality.

"Milady," Geanna said. "I see you're awake, and His Majesty wants you to attend an important meeting later this morning. So we must get you bathed and dressed."

Rhianne sat up in bed. "What meeting is that?"

"His Majesty hasn't informed me of the details."

Rhianne knew that to be at least partly a lie. She'd carefully tested the girl, said certain little mistruths when only Geanna was present, and most often nothing came of it. But once she spoke of how, as a child, she had loved the scent of the blossoms on the lime trees in her father's orchards, and a few days later Valso had mentioned her father's lime trees. But her father had no lime trees in his orchards. She had lied to Geanna, and by that simple, little, roundabout circuit of false information, had confirmed that Geanna regularly reported her words and actions to Valso. Apparently, she reported even the most trivial of things, such as lime trees in her father's orchards.

Rhianne had tested the other girls as well, and now knew exactly which of the them were, and which were not, Valso's spies. It was an exceedingly valuable piece of knowledge to have.

Geanna and her handmaidens dressed her carefully, wrapping her in layer after layer of clothing. It reminded her of the many layers Morgin had peeled off her that first night, and a smile touched her lips.

"You seem happy, my lady."

"Oh, just a fond memory."

The girls put her hair up, colored her lips and applied careful touches of makeup, then gowned her in one of those revealing dresses, reminding her once again of her failure to acquire more modest clothing. Once, she'd tried using a broach to pin a silk handkerchief to her dress to cover her cleavage. Valso had taken one look at it and ordered it removed. After that there'd been no more broaches in her suite.

"It's time. Is she ready?" There was no mistaking the harsh voice of the Kull lieutenant.

Rhianne turned, and with her chin held high, she stepped out of her boudoir into the sitting room. The Kull looked at her breasts hungrily, reminding her of the way Valso's eyes always settled last on her breasts. She didn't give the halfman the satisfaction of blushing.

Six Kulls awaited her out in the hallway, and it gave her some satisfaction that Valso felt the need to guard her so carefully. They escorted her down to the main floor of the castle, then through its labyrinthine corridors to the Great Hall. The massive main doors at its entrance had been thrown open, and there the Kulls peeled off and remained outside as she stepped across the threshold. She paused there for a moment.

Valso had chosen to have quite a number of his courtiers present this day. They lined the walls to either side, leaving a wide aisle down the center of the hall. At the far end he sat on his throne at the top of the dais, Carsaris standing beside him at his right hand, Salula at the bottom of the dais to his right. Clearly, he'd wanted to impress her, or perhaps cower her, so without waiting to be properly announced, she marched purposefully down the center of the hall. The herald hurriedly rapped his staff on the floor three times, and in a rush of words announced, "Her Ladyship, Rhianne esk et Elhiyne."

She stopped about 20 paces short of the dais, looked up at Valso, nodded her head and said, "Your Majesty." She curtsied, doing so with a flourish, though she did not bow her head and lower her eyes while doing so. And she did not wait for his permission to rise, but did so immediately and stood proudly. Valso looked at her for the longest moment as the Great Hall filled with the hiss of a hundred whispers. Beside him Carsaris took one fearful step back, as if he feared the king's anger might focus on him.

Valso opened his mouth to speak, and the whispers died. "Ah, the lovely Lady Rhianne. This should be an interesting morning. Please, take your place." He held out a hand, indicating she should stand at the base of the dais on his left.

Saying nothing, she crossed the short distance and turned about to face the court of the Decouix king. As if on cue, the herald at the far end of the hall rapped his staff against the floor three times and announced, "Magwa, queen of the jackal hordes, and mistress of the jackal court."

This time Rhianne knew what to expect. As before a strange and unruly retinue accompanied Magwa, all walking with the awkward gait of dogs who stood on their hind legs, but not like that of a trained pet, for their upright stature was clearly unnatural. As they drew nearer, Rhianne saw that three of the jackals following the bitch queen limped badly and wore bloodied bandages. And the right arm of one of them ended in a bound stump, his paw missing at the wrist. Rhianne's heart pounded up into her throat as she recognized the captain of the jackal troop who had abducted Rhiannead. For a moment she feared he'd recognize her, know she saw the events in the Kingdom of Dreams through Rhiannead's eyes. Would he reveal that to Valso?

"Magwa," Valso said. This time he did not stand and descend the steps of the dais. "I get the impression I'm not going to be pleased with the news you bring."

Magwa stepped forward and barked defiantly, "Three twelves of my best warriors. Three twelves of them I sent, and only a half-twelve return, and badly wounded at that."

Valso stared at her, a blank expression on his face. "It appears your dogs were not up to the task."

Magwa's retinue yipped and howled as she stepped forward and wagged a paw at Valso. "You said it would be easy, that you and your master's magic would protect them from the forest and the shadowwraiths, and without them there'd be no real opposition. Just go to the Kingdom of Dreams and retrieve the damn sword, that's what you said."

Valso leaned forward on his throne. "I have no doubt of my magic, so don't try to tell me it did not work. With my master supporting me, the forest could not have sensed your warriors."

"Oh it worked, exactly as you said it would. It was not the shadowwraiths or the Living Forest that defeated them. They were defeated because you failed to anticipate all of the opposition they faced. Had you done so we would have gone there in far greater force."

"And what did I fail to anticipate?"

Magwa stepped forward and said, "The one who fights with shadows was there."

Rhianne's heart went cold.

Magwa's retinue began yipping and howling loudly. Salula started, actually broke his calm and took an involuntary step toward her, and Valso stood with such speed it startled them all.

Valso threw his head back and laughed. He looked at Rhianne and said, "Of course his soul departed the Mortal Plane, he went to the Kingdom of Dreams. I must give him due credit for being rather imaginative in his choice of hideout."

To Magwa he said, "You still failed. Our master will not be pleased."

Spittle flew from Magwa's muzzle as she growled, "I killed him centuries ago when he wore the skin of a Benesh'ere, and I can do so again."

"I'm glad to hear that," Valso said. He marched down the steps of the dais, taking them two at a time. "You must go back, and as you said, in force. We'll assault the entire Kingdom of Dreams. We'll raze the castle and unseat the Unnamed King, if need be." He looked Salula's way. "And the good Captain Salula here will accompany you, with twelve twelves of his most cruel fighters."

Salula's lips turned up into a broad grin. Rhianne hated seeing such malice on the kindly swordsman's face.

Valso spun around to face Rhianne. "Your husband gives me great sport. I've always liked that about him. But I no longer have time to amuse myself with his trivial games, so we'll finish it this time."

Magwa stepped between Rhianne and Valso, approached her and stopped with her muzzle only a finger's breadth from Rhianne's nose. "The price you will pay grows with each day."

Only a few days ago Rhianne might have flinched at the threat in her words, but she no longer feared this jackal queen, not in the way she once had. Rhianne smiled just to taunt her. "The price my husband will exact from you grows daily as well."

The jackal warriors howled with rage. Magwa growled, leaned back and swung out. Her claws felt like hot brands as they raked across Rhianne's cheek. Rhianne staggered back a step, a runnel of blood from a gash on her face flowing down her neck and covering the front of her gown. But just to taunt the bitch-queen further, Rhianne ignored the pain and held her smile.

Magwa raised her paw to strike again, but Valso stepped forward and gripped her arm. She spun toward him and snarled, "Release me."

"Of course," Valso said, "but you'll not touch her again. She is still mine, and until she is yours, you will not harm her." As an afterthought he added, "That is, unless I tell you to."

Valso stepped around Magwa, almost as if he would place himself between the two of them to protect Rhianne. "That's a nasty cut," he said. "I'll have Carsaris look at it immediately. He's quite powerful, should be able to heal it with no scar."

At Valso's orders a servant produced a bandage to stem the flow of blood, and as Carsaris and the servant escorted Rhianne from the Great Hall her heart filled with joy. While they knew Morgin had survived Salula's obsidian blade, none of them yet knew he was the King of Dreams, nor that she could communicate with him through her dreams. And that gave them a small edge, no matter how slight. Perhaps she and Morgin might yet find some happiness.

17

To Fight the Obsidian

LEWENDIS ARRAYED HIS archers at the customary two hundred paces from the ancient rock wall that demarked the Elhiyne border. He watched the Elhiyne's doing the same, noted that they had doubled the size of their patrol, so once again they had parity.

He turned to his sergeant and said, "Give me your crossbow, armed and cocked."

The sergeant's eyes narrowed, but he said nothing. They'd had words last night about this, and Lewendis had reminded the fellow it was not his place to judge a nobleman's actions. The man put a bolt into his crossbow, cocked the mechanism and handed it to him. Lewendis hooked it to a buckle on the side of his saddle.

He watched the Elhiyne lieutenant ride out to the tumble of stones that had once been a wall, and though it was hard to be certain at that distance, he thought it might be DaNoel. If so, he'd been looking forward to this for some time.

He spurred his horse forward, and half way there noted happily that he'd been right; it was DaNoel. When he reined his horse in at the tumble of stones he turned it sideways, which made the crossbow hooked to his saddle less obvious.

"Lord DaNoel," he said.

"Lewendis," DaNoel said.

Lewendis swore inwardly, and decided then that DaNoel would acknowledge him properly before they parted. "It's *Lord* Lewendis to you."

DaNoel smirked. "Lord Lewendis, is it? So you're now making a claim to nobility?"

"I don't need to claim nobility. I was born to it."

"Were you now? I'll wager you were born in some hovel to a whore."

Lewendis felt bile rise in his throat. "My mother was no whore."

"Just because some nobleman chose to acknowledge a bastard begat on some trollop—"

Lewendis lifted the crossbow and leveled it at DaNoel, whose eyes widened. "You are rude and arrogant, and without honor."

"That may be," DaNoel said, showing none of the fear Lewendis had hoped to see. "But the question here and now is"—he nodded toward Lewendis's crossbow—"are you a murderer?"

No, Lewendis knew he couldn't just shoot the bastard. He did have a legitimate claim to nobility, but DaNoel had been born much higher than him. If he killed a member of the ruling family of one of the clans for just a few insults, he'd pay a dear price, possibly even his life.

"No," Lewendis said. "I'm not a murderer. But you are rude and arrogant, so maybe you'll learn a bit of humility if you have to walk back to your men."

Lewendis lowered the crossbow just a bit and pulled the trigger. The bolt thudded into the chest of DaNoel's horse. The animal reared, screamed and DaNoel jumped clear just as it collapsed beneath him.

"You maniac," he screamed.

Lewendis was furious with himself. He'd only intended to frighten JohnEngine, to get the satisfaction of seeing his eyes widen with fear, then perhaps bury the crossbow bolt in the ground. But he'd allowed the Elhiyne to goad him into a foolish act. For a peasant, killing a nobleman's horse would be a hanging offense. But while Lewendis need not fear the hangman's knot, there could be serious repercussions.

He pulled his horse around, turning his back on the Elhiyne. He touched his spurs lightly to his horse's flanks, and trotted away to the sound of DaNoel screaming curses at him.

••••

Morgin lifted the obsidian blade and dagger off the table in the king's privy chamber and examined them carefully. The first blade he'd made had shattered on impact, and yet Salula's blade had remained whole. On his second try he'd carefully inscribed runes on this blade and the accompanying dagger, using an emblem that had haunted him for most of his life: the symbol of the sunset king with crossed swords beneath it. Not the emblem Olivia had seen at his Naming, but the completed name, the name only he had seen. It was a sigil that filled his soul with terror. And yet, his instincts told him he must use that glyph on this blade. He'd completed the blade by instilling the runes with power. It had taken him several days, and now the time had come to test his craftsmanship.

For just an instant he thought he heard pipes. It came as a faint sound, as if from a far distance, a sad, sorrowful tune filled with grief and regret. It was a tune he'd heard before and knew well. But the instant ended and silence returned.

"A strange blade you hold there."

Morgin recognized that voice. Still holding both the blade and dagger, he turned to face Metadan. Dressed in his signature black leathers, but bearing no weapon, long dark hair framing an aristocratic face that could only be described as beautiful, the dark angel did not bend the knee, for he claimed no allegiance to the Unnamed King. But he did bow deeply with the elegance of the most fashionable courtier. "Your Majesty."

He straightened. The proudest and most arrogant of all the archangels, darkness still clouded his features. "You requested my presence, Lord Mortal, and I find it curious that you did not summon me. I would have been forced to obey, but I could have easily refused a polite request."

Morgin leaned back and sat on the edge of the table. "I don't need your obedience."

"Then what do you need?"

He extended the obsidian blade, held it with the point aimed at Metadan's chest as if they were about to duel. "I need you to teach me how to fight with this blade."

Metadan's eyes seemed to pierce Morgin's soul as he considered him carefully. Then he slowly crossed the room. He stopped with the blade's point just a finger's breadth from his chest and extended his hand, palm up.

Morgin lowered the point, then gripped the sword by the blade and reversed it, laying the hilt in Metadan's hand.

The archangel lifted the blade and regarded it carefully. "I see you've put quite a bit of work into this blade. But my master will not like it if I help you."

"Then perhaps we shouldn't tell him."

"It's that simple, is it?"

"Foremost of the archangels," Morgin said, "and now foremost of the Fallen."

His words clearly stung Metadan. "It might have been better had you summoned me. Then I could plead that I had no choice in the matter."

"But regardless of how you came here, by summons or request, you could still refuse my appeal for help."

"And you felt I might be more amenable if not forced. Give me one reason to help you."

Morgin knew one name that would carry great weight with the archangel, the one being Metadan loved more than his own pride, and the one being that loved him back so much, she now hated him. "Ellowyn would like it if you did."

Metadan didn't move a muscle, but his eyes shifted focus away from the blade, past it and into Morgin's eyes. "You've asked her?"

"No. But we both know she would."

"Aye, we do both know that." His eyes shifted back to the blade, and he seemed to take a special interest in the runes Morgin had placed upon it. "Interesting, that you've adorned this blade with your name."

"Is that what that symbol is, my name?"

"I find it ironic that you must ask such a question."

"*He knows all names but his own*," Morgin said. "I know the symbol, and I think I know the name it represents, if it is a name, but I don't think it's my name."

"Then what is your name?"

"If I knew that, I wouldn't be the Unnamed King. So if you think you know my name, why don't you tell me?"

"Far be it from me to enlighten you. But I must tell you that you cannot win while you deny your name. Victory can come only when you bear the burden of it."

"I'm the Unnamed King. I don't deny my name, I just don't know it."

Metadan's eyes remained locked on the blade. "Believe what you will," he said. He hefted it carefully and tested its weight. He turned to one side, slashed the blade to right and left, then lunged at an invisible opponent. He straightened and looked at the blade again. "But you have it wrong."

That surprised Morgin. "I've done everything I can to make that blade right."

"Oh, it's not the blade that you got wrong. It's your need that you misunderstand. You don't need me to teach you how to fight *with* this blade. You need me to teach you how to fight *against* it."

••••

After Metadan departed, the scent of brimstone hung in the air. Morgin lifted the obsidian blade and looked at the runes he'd placed there: the symbol of the sunset king with crossed swords beneath it. He'd spent the better part of his life wondering at the meaning of that symbol, wondering at the name it represented. Metadan thought he knew, but he really understood only the meaning, and not the name, though the archangel thought the two were one and the same. And Morgin had come to fear that was not the case. What if he didn't have a true name, just a meaning, a label no better than *Morgin*?

He bloody well knew the label the symbol represented, and he tried to say it now. "I . . . am . . ."

"I . . . am . . ."

"I . . . am . . ."

No, the Kingdom of Dreams would not allow him to claim that *label* as his name.

••••

DaNoel drummed his fingers on his thigh as he waited, he and his men well hidden by trees, brush and boulders. Their position gave them the high ground, about twice the height of a grown man above the Penda border: a small winding creek. On the Penda side, dense forest extended to within about 50 paces of the creek. Late the previous day

DaNoel and two of his men had snuck across and scouted the forest, confirming there were no easy trails among the trees within sight of the border. Lewendis and his patrol would be forced to ride within easy bow-shot.

Off to one side movement caught his attention, one of his scouts running in a low crouch behind the Elhiyne armsmen. The man dropped to one knee beside DaNoel. "They're coming, my lord. It shouldn't be long now."

DaNoel was beginning to doubt the scout's word when a Penda rider came into view about three hundred paces up the creek. He told the scout, "Tell the men to hold their arrows until I give the signal. And remind them that they're not to aim anywhere near Lewendis, and only at the horses."

Valso had made it clear that if DaNoel didn't take more aggressive action on the border, he might expose his treason to Olivia. He couldn't kill Lewendis, for while the fellow was born of a minor family, he still could claim the rights of noble birth. On the other hand, Lewendis had killed DaNoel's horse, so no one could blame him if he took payment in kind. Killing a few horses might anger the Pendas, which would get Valso off his back, but it wouldn't start a war, so he could avoid facing Olivia's ire.

The scout moved down the line of archers, stopping at each for a quick word.

One-by-one the Penda patrol rode into view, their horses ambling along at a comfortable pace. The trail by the creek forced them to ride single file, stretching them out nicely.

DaNoel got off his knees and rose into a crouch, staying hidden behind a boulder. He waited until the Pendas were directly opposite them, then stood, raised his arm, slashed it down and shouted, "Now."

The Pendas looked toward his shout as his men stood, arrows already nocked. They aimed and shot. The arrows arced out over the creek and sliced into the Penda patrol. One horse collapsed beneath its rider. Another reared with an arrow in its neck, screaming, its rider desperately trying to control it. The patrol broke up into a mass of bucking horses.

DaNoel had given his men orders to shoot only one arrow each, and not loose another without his signal. The Penda armsmen were disciplined, and with no more arrows arcing their way they quickly calmed their horses. DaNoel counted three horses down.

Lewendis shouted, "What insanity is this, Elhiyne?"

DaNoel shouted down to him. "I valued the animal you killed, so I'm taking payment."

He and his men mounted up and rode away, though it did concern him that two stray arrows had found Penda armsmen, and both men lay on the ground unmoving.

••••

Morgin back-stepped as the obsidian blade hissed past his face. Metadan spun and followed with the dagger, but Morgin sidestepped that and swung his sword at Metadan's shoulder. Metadan deflected Morgin's steel with obsidian, and a shower of sparks blossomed where the two blades met, settling down over both of them like a rain of hot embers in the night. They disengaged and stepped back a few paces, breathing heavily.

Metadan said, "In just a few days you've improved nicely."

"It's an unusual feeling when the two blades meet," Morgin said, "And I needed to get used to the sparks." Steel on steel rarely threw sparks, but against obsidian, each stroke was like steel striking flint.

Near mid-morning each day Morgin heard the faint sound of pipes in the distance, which he'd learned preceded Metadan's appearance. The Fallen One always arrived ready to exercise Morgin's skills against the obsidian blade, and they then practiced for the rest of the morning.

"You need to watch more closely for the off-hand blade," Metadan said.

"I know. That's how Salula got me the last time."

Metadan eyed Morgin for a second, but didn't ask him to elaborate. "But don't watch it so closely it distracts you from the sword."

Erithnae stepped into the room and said, "My lords, the queen of the jackals plans to return in force and lay siege to Sabian. And she'll bring with her twelve twelves of *halfmen*, and their leader."

Metadan asked, "And how do you know this?"

She looked at Morgin and smiled. "There is a woman who haunts my soul, a mortal, and she and he love each other very much. She was there when Magwa hatched her plans."

Morgin asked, "Did Magwa say how large a force she'll bring?"

"No, but you should know that your Rhianne is a prisoner of this Valso whom you both hate. And he now knows that you are not dead, but are here living among the dreamers."

He thought of Kinardin, but before he uttered a word the Chamberlain swept into the room. He began an elegant bow, but Morgin interrupted it. "No, forget that. We're going to be under attack soon. What defenses can we mount?"

Kinardin spoke as if instructing a child. "Sabian commands the Living Forest, and the two are always prepared to mount a powerful defense. And the shadowwraiths will aid us with unflinching support. And we have mortal armsmen aplenty."

"That won't do," Morgin said. "The jackal troop that kidnapped Rhiannead was invisible to the forest and the wraiths. It may be that only the armsmen can oppose this enemy."

"But Your Majesty," Kinardin said. "If the enemy comes in real force, that will not be enough."

"Until you acknowledge your name," Metadan said, "the Living Forest and Sabian will be that much weaker."

"You've found a name?" Erithnae asked.

Morgin couldn't hide his frustration as he spoke. "I know a symbol, not a name."

"You must show it to me."

Metadan crossed the room and stopped in front of her. He lifted the obsidian blade and held it close to her face. "See for yourself. He's adorned the damn obsidian with it."

Her eyes narrowed as she looked at the runes on the blade. "The sunset king! With crossed swords."

She looked at Morgin and said, "AethonSword."

Metadan nodded. "Yes. But it is not you or I who must acknowledge it." He turned away from her, walked to Morgin and extended the hilts of the blade and dagger toward him. Morgin sheathed his sword and took the two blades, and in that instant the archangel winked out of existence, leaving behind a column of gray smoke formed in the shape of a man that slowly dissipated into the air of the room.

Kinardin asked Morgin, "Do you know your name, my king?"

"No," Morgin snapped.

Erithnae said, "This Rhianne of yours believes that you do, but your fear of it is so great you cannot acknowledge it."

"I don't know my damn name," Morgin said. "I know that symbol, and I know what it represents, and that's not my name."

Erithnae crossed the room to Morgin. She reached out and touched his cheek, ran her finger along the line of his jaw. "I believe you cannot return to your Rhianne until you find your name and acknowledge it."

18

To Assault a Dream

LATE IN THE morning Rhianne sat on the couch in her sitting room and tried to sneak a few moments of sleep, a few moments in the Kingdom of Dreams. But as she drifted off she sensed a powerful force of nether magic. She opened her eyes and tried to flush the cobwebs of confusion from her mind. She felt it even now, a potent draw of power from the netherworld.

She stood, crossed the room to the balcony and stepped out onto it. The castle yard below, the city in the distance, nothing seemed out of the ordinary.

This power had the taste of a malign and vast intelligence, with hints of Valso's magic fluttering through it. No sorcerer could contain such power, and to do so did not demonstrate ability or strength, but rather a warp in the fabric of reality that should never be. She was reminded again of Morgin's semi-delirious ranting about a *vast chasm of power*, and for the first time she truly understood what he'd meant.

She turned away from the view of the city, determined to follow the scent of that power to its source. As usual, the Kullish guards waiting outside her suite stepped into place behind her, following her every move.

The power permeated the castle, but following a straight line toward it only led her to one dead-end after another, and she had to retrace her steps several times. At one point she turned down a corridor and came face-to-face with Haleen. They both paused and Haleen gave her a vacant smile. "My child is coming back," she said. "He'll be back soon, and then you can find happiness."

Mad, Rhianne thought. *Truly mad.*

Hoping the Mad Whore would not divert her from her search, she curtsied and said, "Lady Haleen."

Haleen looked down at her for a moment as she held the curtsy, then without another word stepped around her and continued down the corridor.

Relieved, Rhianne put the women out of her mind and continued her search. The scent of the power led her to a long corridor on the third floor of the castle, at the end of which two Kulls stood guard at a set of double doors. As she approached the half-men one of them stepped in her way and said, "His Majesty is not available."

That confirmed that Valso was in the room beyond. She'd never been in this part of the castle before, but the scent of that power had led her unerringly to these doors, so they must open into a workshop of some kind. In that moment the vast outpouring of power dissipated, and in a few heartbeats all that remained was a sense of corruption and malevolence.

"Tell His Majesty I wish to see him."

The Kull didn't respond, just stared at her.

"You know full well that if you don't at least give him the opportunity to send me on my way, he'll be angry."

The Kull continued to stare for a moment, then turned and knocked on the door. Several heartbeats passed before the door creaked open and a wan and haggard Carsaris peered out. His eyes seemed recessed deeper in his skull as if he'd been stricken by some illness, and his skin appeared even more sallow than usual. He glanced over his shoulder in a guilt-ridden, surreptitious way, and it struck Rhianne that he had the look of a man who lived constantly with fear.

Rhianne didn't give the Kull or Carsaris a chance to speak. "I wish to see His Majesty."

Carsaris hesitated, then nodded and said, "I'll ask him if he's available." He closed the door.

Only an instant passed before the door flew open to reveal Valso standing there. Where Carsaris had appeared sickly, Valso seemed invigorated. "Rhianne!" he said, elbowing his way between the two Kulls. "This is a lovely surprise. It's a real pleasure to look upon you after such hard work."

He took her arm and began walking down the corridor away from the door and the two Kulls. "You were drawn by the power, weren't you, like a moth to the flame?"

"What were you doing?" she asked.

He looked at her and smiled. "Just sending Magwa's army on its way."

Magwa's army! That could only mean he'd just sent them to the Kingdom of Dreams to assault Sabian. But to require so much power must mean that her army was vast indeed.

Valso said, "I've worked up an appetite. Let's have some lunch."

Rhianne wanted to rush back to her suite, to sit down on her couch, close her eyes and try to reach Morgin in her dreams. She needed to warn him that the army he faced must be enormous. But *she* had approached Valso, and now she was stuck with him. She'd have to suffer through lunch, then try afterwards.

••••

Kinardin organized the castle's defenses, so Morgin had little to do other than sparring with Metadan and the obsidian blades. The Lord Chamberlain refused to believe that any power could obscure the forest's perception of those within its bounds. But recalling how some magic had hidden the halfmen and jackal hordes from the forest and shadowwraiths, Morgin convinced him to send mortal armsmen out as scouts. Two days later several of them returned with reports of a large army approaching from the north, and Kinardin was beside himself when he heard that the forest was unaware of their presence and could do nothing to hinder them.

"I had hoped you were wrong, Your Majesty," he said.

Rafaellen said, "We saw the same with the jackal troop that abducted Her Highness. This is a mortal fight we face."

Morgin decided to take the fight to their enemy, so they organized 12 companies, each consisting of six twelves of mounted armsmen with a mix of swords, war axes, lances and bows. They planned on a simple strategy: strike swiftly at several points on the periphery of Magwa's army, then retreat and strike again later. They were badly weakened by the fact that the shadowwraiths could not fight their enemy directly, though they could carry messages swiftly from company to company. But when Rafaellen commented in an offhand way, "It's a shame we don't have more men who can hide in shadows like you," it gave Morgin an idea.

He recalled how the wraiths had helped shield him when he fought the jackal raiding party. "Maybe we do," he said.

He had Kinardin summon all of his lieutenants. He'd only come to the castle some days ago, so most of them were nameless men with faces much like any clansman. He recalled his conversation with Erithnae, recalled that they were dreamers all.

When they were assembled, Morgin summoned Soann'Daeth'Daeye with a whisper.

My king, the wraith said, dropping to one knee before him. He noticed several of the men looked away as if they feared the wraith.

"Rise," Morgin said, and the wraith did so.

Of the men who'd turned their heads, Morgin selected one who was older and asked him, "Why did you look away?"

The fellow hesitated, then said, "I . . . ah . . . don't rightly know. I—"

"We fear them," a younger man said, stepping forward. He was an average looking fellow of middle height. "We know of them, but before you came just a few days ago, I'd never seen one."

Several men grumbled their general agreement with the fellow. He continued, "They avoid us, hide from us, and it makes us wary of them."

The unknown was always a fearsome thing, but Morgin needed them working together. "What's your name?" he asked the young man.

"Tasmian, Your Majesty. Forgive me if I have offended you." He lowered his eyes.

"Nothing to forgive. Come forward. I want to try something, and you're probably not going to like it. At least not at first."

As Tasmian approached, Morgin turned to the wraith. "Soann'Daeth'Daeye, please envelope me in shadow as you did in the forest when we fought the jackals."

The shadowwraith moved like smoke in a light breeze, and in a few heartbeats had covered Morgin completely. There were several gasps, and some of the armsmen stood with their hands on the hilts of their swords as if they needed to come to the aid of their king.

"I am unharmed," Morgin said, "So there is no need to fear, and no need for swords. But I can see you quite clearly. Can you see me?"

Tasmian said, "Almost not at all, Your Majesty."

"So imagine what it would be like to move like this among the natural shadows of the forest."

Perhaps because he was younger, Tasmian saw the implications immediately. "I could dance death among my enemies with impunity."

Tasmian volunteered to let Soann'Daeth'Daeye envelop him, then he helped talk other men into giving it a try. When no one dropped dead or emerged from the shadows covered with boils from some strange malady, they soon had at least a dozen men from each company teamed up with a shadowwraith.

Morgin did not want to be a king sitting on a throne while men died for him, but when he told them he'd decided to lead one of the companies, Kinardin and several of his lieutenants threw a fit. Erithnae shut them up when she stepped forward and said, "He is the Unnamed King. We cannot fight a battle in the Kingdom of Dreams without him in the forefront."

"Aye," Rafaellen added. "And he knows these jackal warriors, knows their tricks, knows how to kill 'em."

With Erithnae and Rafaellen's support, his lieutenants reluctantly agreed.

As Morgin was checking Mortiss's harness and the provisions in her saddle bags, he saw Erithnae crossing the castle yard toward him, carefully avoiding the horse manure that dotted the grounds. She wrapped her arms around him and he pulled her tight, wishing she were Rhianne.

"Which one was it in there?" he asked. "When these men didn't want their king to personally lead them and ride into danger? Which one believed in me enough to see me ride to my own war, Erithnae, Rhiannead, or Rhianne?"

She kissed him on the cheek. "I don't know, but I think we're all one and the same, and have been for a long time. Though the one who truly knows you the best, that would be your Rhianne. And when this is done, you must return to her, for only then can you each be whole."

"And what of you when I return to her?"

She smiled, and was truly Erithnae at that moment. "I am new to the Kingdom of Dreams, and yet I have lived here and died here a thousand times, and will do so again. I will always be here when you return, and I think your Rhianne will be here inside me."

"And how do I return to her?"

"You must acknowledge your true name."

"I need to find it first."

She smiled, and looked at him like a young maiden intent on some mischief. Then she pulled him tightly against her and kissed him, one of those kisses that made him forget everything.

When they separated, she said, "I think you already have, AethonSword."

He shook his head. "You and Metadan think the label for that symbol is my name, but I know you're wrong."

"Then if you cannot acknowledge your name, you must acknowledge what you are. For that is something you have always denied."

••••

Morgin slipped carefully from one shadow to the next, following the jackal sergeant as he checked with each sentry. Concealed by a shadowwraith, one or more of his men had moved into position behind each of the nearby sentries, and they were all waiting for Rafaellen to give the signal. With his greater experience and affinity for shadows, Morgin had taken on the more difficult task of staying with the moving jackal sergeant as he made his rounds. Magwa's generals were clearly aware of his abilities with shadows, but he hoped they hadn't anticipated what he might do with the aid of the shadowwraiths.

Morgin and his shadowmen—as they had taken to calling themselves—had carefully scouted the encampment of the jackal army. Magwa's hordes had set up a temporary camp in the forest, a staging area from which to launch an assault on Sabian. When they marched south, which would be soon, Morgin had no doubt they'd devastate the forest.

It had taken an enormous amount of power to physically move twelve thousand jackal warriors and a thousand horses and their equipment off the Mortal Plane and into the Kingdom of Dreams. Morgin recalled the seemingly unlimited power he'd sensed in Valso, and he assumed the Decouix king had tapped it to accomplish the task. That frightened him, for he could not summon such power, and yet soon he must find a way to defeat Valso and his master.

Morgin spotted the next sentry about 15 paces ahead. But as the sergeant approached him, the cry of a jaymakaw echoed through the forest. No jaymakaw had ever flown through the branches of the Living Forest.

In response to the jaymakaw a shadow arose behind the sentry, an arm reached out from the shadow and slit the dog's throat. As the sentry gurgled out its last moments of life, the sergeant Morgin followed tensed and took a deep breath to raise the alarm. But Morgin stepped out of his shadow and buried his sword in the jackal's back. Quite a number of the jackal sentries suffered a similar fate.

Even at their quietest, on foot leading their horses by their reins, six twelves of armsmen produced a soft roar: the creak of saddle leather, the clop of hooves, a grunt here, a groan there. Rafaellen, leading his own mount and Mortiss, emerged with Morgin's company from the forest, moving hastily, for they all knew they had little time.

Morgin had just climbed into the saddle when somewhere nearby a jackal howled out a warning. Something had alerted them, so Morgin spurred Mortiss into a charge and shouted, "With me, charge."

The jackals did not have time to mount a proper defense, and Morgin and his men hit them unprepared. As they charged into the camp, Morgin slashed downward right and left with his sword. He cut down one jackal, wounded another, then reined in Mortiss. It would be suicide for his small company to charge deep into the middle of an enemy twelve thousand strong, so he kept his men near the perimeter of the jackal army. In the distance he heard chaos and pandemonium erupting at several places along the perimeter, and knew his other companies had likewise engaged the enemy.

A mounted Kull loomed out of the chaos and charged at him with a steel blade. The Kull lunged, driving the point of his sword toward Morgin's heart. Morgin ordered the steel to deflect upward and to one side, and to continue the lunge past him. The blade jerked in the Kull's grip and sliced just past Morgin's ear, pulling the halfman toward him. Morgin lunged and buried his sword in the Kull's chest. The Kull fell from his horse, and riderless, the horse trotted away.

Salula sat astride his horse not five paces distant, holding the obsidian blade casually by his side. It pulled at Morgin's heart to face his old friend this way, to see the swordsman's playful smile turned into the demon's snarling grimace. Where France's eyes had always glinted with mischief, Salula had corrupted them into sharp anger and hatred. And the joy the swordsman had found in every facet of life had been extinguished, snuffed out until not a hint of it remained.

"ShadowLord," the halfman shouted. He raised his obsidian sword and swung. Morgin met the blow squarely with his blade, and as steel and obsidian clashed in blow after blow, they lit up the forest about them in a continuous shower of sparks. With each stroke Morgin reminded himself he faced the demon captain of all Kulls, and not his old friend. But striking out at that face sapped his strength and resolve. If he won this contest he would only kill his dear friend France, and not the demon that haunted his soul. So Morgin changed tactics; he spurred Mortiss hard as he brought his sword down. Their blades met just as Mortiss rammed Salula's horse; the halfman's mount stumbled and went down.

"Retreat," Morgin shouted, and with his men following they charged out of the encampment and into shadows of the forest.

It had been a successful raid. They'd killed a few dozen jackals and destroyed some supplies. But when Morgin considered the odds arrayed against them, it had really been nothing more than a minor nuisance to Magwa's army.

••••

JohnEngine found DaNoel in the castle yard practicing sword skills with one of the armsmen. He was so furious he didn't ask them to stop, but barged between them, elbowing the armsman aside. He turned to DaNoel and shouted, "You said nothing happened."

At the sound of a nobleman shouting at the top of his lungs, the armsman decided he had business elsewhere.

DaNoel lowered his sword and said. "Nothing of import did happen."

JohnEngine wanted to hit him, to curl up his fist and bloody the idiot's nose. "Nothing of import! I hear rumors among the armsmen of a skirmish on the border, and when I investigate I learn you ambushed the Penda patrol."

DaNoel rolled his eyes. "Lewendis killed my horse, so we killed a few of theirs."

"The men report Penda armsmen were downed by your arrows."

DaNoel shrugged. "An accident."

"And you didn't report this accident before allowing Brandon to replace you on the border? Lewendis is a hothead, and Brandon has no idea what he's walking into."

DaNoel slid his sword into its sheath. "Lewendis is a peasant. He's not stupid enough actually harm a member of House Elhiyne."

"I'm not sure who is more stupid," JohnEngine shouted. "You or him."

He turned his back on DaNoel and headed toward the main building. He'd have to report this to Olivia, then send out a rider to warn Brandon. He prayed it wouldn't be too late.

19

Dream Under Siege

BLAKEDOWN HUDDLED WITHIN his cloak as he and his companions let their horses meander up the trail. Even in late summer a cold wind whistled through the peaks surrounding Tharsk. The sun had risen that morning in a diamond clear sky and should have warmed them nicely. But the icy wind found any gap in his clothing, or gusted up the back of his cloak, and every other twist in the trail led them into the chill of a shadow cast by a large boulder, or the slope of the hill above them.

Once again, after trading several messages with Valso, he and a small group had ridden up into the pass at Methula, supposedly to hunt the bighorn sheep near Tharsk. And once again he'd chosen his companions carefully. They spent three days truly hunting, then today he and a select group made the trek to Tharsk.

He paused and looked up at the fortress, silently cursed the monolith of black granite. He wanted to get this over with. During the colder seasons it was a place of black rock, white snow and cold winds. He hadn't realized that during warmer weather, without snow covering almost everything, it was simply a place of black rock and cold winds, with no real vegetation to break the monotony of the landscape.

This time no one called out from above, and they didn't have to identify themselves with fake names. As they approached the dark tunnel the portcullises simply rose with a clanking rattle of chains dragging across stone.

None of his companions spoke as they entered the tunnel. They found the massive stone portal at its center already open. They rode through it into the circular courtyard open to the sky, surrounded on all sides by high walls cut from the same black rock. Valso stood there huddled in a heavy cloak.

"Lord BlakeDown," he said. "I hope when this is done we'll meet under more pleasant circumstances."

"Aye," BlakeDown said, as he swung a leg over his horse's rump and climbed out of the saddle. He could almost hear his joints creaking in the chill.

BlakeDown approached Valso and dropped to one knee, lowering his eyes. "Your Majesty."

"No, no," Valso said. "Rise. Stand up and face me."

Surprised, BlakeDown stood. Valso gripped his hand, shook it and leaned in close, whispering, "When this is done you'll not bend the knee to me like some common nobleman. You'll bow to me as equals."

A rush of pride swept through BlakeDown, and he held his chin high, ignoring the wind that sliced past his throat.

"Come," Valso said, spinning about. "I have a warm hearth and a warm meal waiting for us, and mulled wine."

The king proved to be a man of his word. Once again the two of them dined alone, and as the good food and warm wine settled into his stomach, BlakeDown relaxed. He and this Decouix king were getting to know one another quite well.

When they'd finished the meal, BlakeDown stood to leave. As he donned his cloak, Valso also stood and said, "One more thing, Lord BlakeDown."

BlakeDown paused and said, "What would that be, Your Majesty?"

Valso's eyes darkened, and he looked at BlakeDown as if evaluating the temper of a steel blade. "If you find the opportunity to rid us of the Elhiyne thorn, I would be most grateful. The sooner you remove that old witch from the playing board, the sooner you will gain your throne."

BlakeDown couldn't hide a smile as he crossed the room, bent the knee to Valso, and kissed the ring of the King of the Greater Clans.

••••

With Lewendis on border patrol, Theandrin felt no need to hurry as she stepped into his room. She closed the door and turned to look the place over.

A small window in the far wall looked out onto the fields south of the castle. To her right the blankets on a single bed had been carefully arranged, were smooth and without wrinkles, a feather pillow against the headboard. Next to the bed, a pitcher and goblet rested on a night stand. To her left a small writing table contained two quill pens and a clay pot of ink, all carefully arranged with considerable attention to detail. She hadn't really noticed that about Lewendis before, but as she considered his room, she recalled he was always quite scrupulous about his appearance. He was not a fancy dresser, but she'd never seen him wear a blouse with a missing button, or a wrinkled collar. She'd have to be careful to leave everything as it was, to return anything she moved to its original position.

She crossed the room to a chest at the foot of his bed. It had a simple, mechanical lock which she defeated easily with a charm she'd prepared in advance. In the chest she found mostly clothing and a few other possessions. She carefully lifted out three blouses and two sets of small clothes, all meticulously folded. She arranged them on the bed in the order in which she'd removed them.

From a pocket hidden in the folds of her dress, she retrieved a folded linen handkerchief. She placed it on the bed and opened it, revealing five small charms she'd prepared in advance, using bits of her own hair and blood. She placed one charm on the shoulder of a blouse, then licked her finger to get a bit of saliva. When she touched the saliva to the charm, it flared brilliantly for a moment, then faded away and disappeared. When Lewendis wore that blouse, he'd have no idea he was carrying one of her charms.

When planning the preparation of these charms her thoughts had kept returning to the Vodah connection revealed by the first modification of her wards. She'd looked carefully into Lewendis's background; no Vodah there. It could be that he was communicating with a Vodah reporting to Valso. She'd settled on a Vodah trigger. If Lewendis wore any of this clothing and spoke with a Vodah, she'd know.

She repeated the process on two more blouses and the two sets of small clothes. Then she placed them in the chest, careful to return them to their original positions. She closed the chest, relocked it, and left the room.

••••

Brandon looked down at the ravine that marked the border between Penda and Elhiyne. On both sides the rocky, boulder-strewn ground sloped down to the bottom of a dry wash. The gully flooded regularly during the spring rains, frequently turned into a raging torrent. But now, in the warmer months of summer, it had run dry. The slope was a bit steep, but still easily navigable on horseback.

The Penda lieutenant arrayed his armsmen along the top of the opposite slope, and Brandon did the same on the Elhiyne side. He thought the fellow might be Lewendis, but he couldn't be certain at that distance. The terrain forced them to set up their positions within easy bowshot of one another, and that worried him. But while there'd been a little tension on the border of late, there'd been no real incidents for several years, so he put his worries aside, and started down the slope.

He didn't hurry his horse, let it pick its own way because of the rocky ground, guiding it only in the smallest ways. On slopped, rough terrain like this, a stumble could result in a bad fall. He focused on the ground, on the difficult footing, was carefully nudging his horse around a large boulder when an arrow thudded into the horse's neck. The animal screamed and reared just as another sliced into Brandon's upper arm with a fiery hot flash of pain. Arrows thudded into the dirt around them, another into the horse's chest, and he knew the animal would go down.

He had one chance to escape being crushed by its weight. He thought it was collapsing onto its left side so he threw his weight to the right, made a reasonably good leap from the saddle, but landed badly and twisted his ankle. He heard snapping limbs as the horse tumbled down the slope, and he thought he was about to follow it, but he slammed into a boulder and heard something in his chest crack. Blistering pain sent him to the edge of consciousness.

As arrows rained down around him and men shouted on both sides of the ravine, he tried to curl up into the smallest shape possible in the lee of the boulder. He heard steel arrowheads ping off the boulder and thump into the ground nearby. He prayed the boulder's size concealed him from the arrows, and since no more punched holes in him, it appeared to be working.

The pain in his chest was enough to tell him he'd done some damage there, and the blood he coughed up told him he should be concerned. The arrow in his arm had punched through the muscle, a length of shaft protruding from either side. His ankle throbbed badly.

The shouting had stopped, and so had the rain of arrows. Brandon wasn't stupid enough to peek over the boulder; he wouldn't see anything with an arrow in his eye.

"Lord Brandon."

He recognized his sergeant's voice. He stayed huddled against the boulder, took a deep breath to shout back, but a sharp, stabbing pain in his chest told him that wasn't going to happen. He lifted his left hand, didn't have to lift it high enough to expose it to the archers on the other side. One halfhearted wave, two, then he let it collapse against his side.

"We'll get help to you. Just stay where you are."

He drifted off for a while, had no idea how much time passed, but when he opened his eyes the sun had moved to a decidedly different part of the sky. His mouth had gone dry, his tongue sticking to the back of his teeth. He wanted water, became obsessed with the idea of a drink, would have traded his soul for . . .

"Cousin!"

Brandon struggled back to consciousness. Night had come.

"The Penda's have withdrawn . . . I hope. Sorry we had to wait for nightfall."

JohnEngine! Whispering.

"The men are bringing a stretcher down. We're going to get you out of here, get you to my mother for some healing. I rode hard to get here, and she's not far behind."

"Wathjer." It didn't come out well. Maybe he should try again.

"You've got a lung wound. Mother taught me a man with such a wound should drink nothing until we get him to a healer. But I'll wet your lips."

JohnEngine's fingers brushed across his lips with blessed drops of water clinging to them. Brandon sucked at them. JohnEngine repeated that twice, then said, "That's enough."

Brandon heard the armsmen scuffling in the scree of the hillside. "My lord," one of them said. "You're mother's here. She's waiting at the top of the hill."

"We're going to get you home, cousin. Alive and well."

••••

For two days Morgin and his 12 companies of armsmen raided the jackal horde. They hit them individually and in unison, striking at random during any hour of the day or night. And they were quite successful in that they suffered few losses, while whittling away at Magwa's army. But they were so badly outnumbered he knew these small victories would make no difference in the long run.

Apparently, Sabian had never been under siege. No enemy had ever reached the castle to lay siege to it, for the forest and the wraiths stopped them long before they got there. But now, with the forest and wraiths blind to this enemy, Magwa's army advanced steadily. Little by little the jackal horde drove them south toward the castle, and late in the evening of the second day the 12 companies retreated behind its walls. Morgin asked the forest to create a no-man's-land for three hundred paces from the castle walls, and the growth there simply ungrew. When the sun rose the following morning they were surrounded by a sea of jackal warriors.

Magwa's generals wasted no time, and as Morgin and the rest of the defenders manned the battlements at the top of the walls, the horde immediately laid siege to Sabian. The jackals had no siege engines, but they had the advantage of numbers. They charged the castle in a wave of jackal warriors that seemed unending. The castle's archers took a heavy toll among them, but that only slowed them and they reached the base of the wall well before midmorning. They started climbing, using the vegetation that formed the wall, and the convenient hand-holds it offered.

Morgin had never defended a castle under siege, and he learned quickly to keep his head down or risk taking an arrow in an eye. With his abilities as a SteelMaster he need not fear a steel tipped arrow, but many of them bore a sharpened flint warhead that could take his life as surely as they had taken Morddon's so long ago. He made one attempt to deflect all of the steel-tipped arrows coming their way, but there were hundreds of them raining down upon the castle, and he learned he could control no more than a dozen or so at any one time, so he abandoned the effort. The castle's archers took a heavy toll and jackal bodies piled up at the base of the wall. A little after midmorning the jackals retreated to regroup.

The horde gave them only the shortest time to lick their wounds, and at midday they charged for the second time. Morgin's archers slowed them briefly, but then they ran out of arrows and it turned into a hand-to-hand fight at the top of the wall. It wasn't too difficult at first, for they had the advantage of the high ground. They still couldn't ignore the jackal archers, so like the other men on the wall Morgin learned to keep his head down and watch for a jackal's paw clutching at the lip of the parapet. A quick chop with his sword, and with a wounded paw the jackal fell away. Then there came a moment when there were two paws clutching at the parapet, then three, then four, and by the time Morgin had chopped them away, a jackal had actually climbed onto one of the crenellations. Morgin dispatched him quickly, but another came behind him, and another.

The jackals might outnumber them tenfold, but at the top of the wall there were only so many who could come over the lip at one time, and the battle stalled there. Morgin and his companions held the line and refused to give ground, forcing jackals clinging to the wall to wait their turn to gain the top. Increasingly, those who did came up already exhausted, and it became easier to fight them back. Sabian's defenders fought for what seemed an eternity, but near mid-afternoon they finally repelled the onslaught and the jackals withdrew.

Morgin was reminded of Gilguard's last stand on the cliff above the river Ulbb so many centuries ago. He'd watched it through the eyes of the ancient Benesh'ere Morddon, his alter-ego in the past. He recalled that even though Gilguard and his Benesh'ere had outfought the jackals, the horde's numbers allowed each wave of jackal warriors to penetrate a little deeper and push the Benesh'ere line back. In the end the whitefaces had been overrun. Yes, the jackals had a sound strategy.

Morgin knew their respite would be brief so he climbed down from the battlements to get a quick bite. As some of the defenders scrounged arrows the jackals had shot at them, Morgin sat on the ground with his back to a wall. Erithnae, Rafaellen and Kinardin found him there chewing on some jerky.

As they approached, Morgin said, "I'm not much of a king, eh?"

"It's not you, sire," Kinardin said. "It's Sabian, and the forest, and the shadowwraiths. Never before have they been so defenseless. Whatever magic is blinding them must be truly powerful indeed."

"Aye," Morgin said, recalling Valso and the power he flaunted. "It is."

Erithnae sat down in the dirt beside him and took his hand. He liked the way she instinctively knew when to discard propriety. "But it is not as powerful as your name, my lord."

Her words infuriated him. "I've already tried to acknowledge it. I know what that sigil means, but this Kingdom of Dreams will not allow me to claim the name AethonSword. Give me a name I can claim and I'll gladly do so."

She frowned. "It won't allow you to claim that name, eh?" She leaned close and kissed him on the cheek. "Then if that is not your name, you must find within yourself your essence, your purpose, and acknowledge that."

She looked up at Rafaellen and Kinardin standing over them. "I wish to be alone with my king. Please leave us."

The two men bowed, backed up three paces, then turned and walked away.

Morgin's frustration crawled up into his gut. "I don't want to be a king. I never wanted this. And if I do find something to acknowledge, whether it's a name or a purpose, what more will be asked of me . . . and of Rhianne?"

"I know not, my king. But your Rhianne is a part of me, so I know that she will gladly bear the burden with you. And in any case, you and she cannot be free and whole until you find yourselves."

20

Come the Sword

WITH THE FAMILY assembled in Olivia's audience chamber, AnnaRail watched the old woman's expression as Roland reported the incident on the border. Olivia didn't take her eyes off DaNoel as she turned angry, then furious, then livid, and then calm. Open anger was always better than the calm.

DaNoel's eyes darted about like a cornered animal. Olivia spoke to him in a cold, hard voice. "This means war, you idiot."

DaNoel cringed. JohnEngine and NickoLot remained silent, smart enough to know not to draw the old woman's attention.

It had taken all of AnnaRail's skills to keep Brandon alive with a punctured lung. He would survive and recover, though he'd be in bed for days.

AnnaRail looked at DaNoel and couldn't hide her own bitter disappointment in her son. But as head of the clan, Olivia's fury could mean the loss of many lives. Anna-Rail said to the old woman, "Let's try to remain calm."

Olivia's gaze remained locked on DaNoel. "Calm," she said. "This fool has just started a war."

Roland had carefully interrogated DaNoel's armsmen while JohnEngine and AnnaRail retrieved Brandon. "Technically," Roland said. "Lewendis started it."

Olivia's calm evaporated. "Lewendis killed a horse. We could've settled that with payment. The war started when this moron killed armsmen."

DaNoel said, "We don't know they're dead, and it was an accide—"

Olivia rose and crossed the room in a heartbeat. DaNoel stood a head taller than her, but somehow she loomed over him. "Yes, we could have claimed an accident, had you reported the incident to us. But now they've attacked, wounded and almost killed the heir to Elhiyne."

AnnaRail wasn't terribly happy with her oldest son at the moment, but she had to control Olivia's anger. "The greater wrong has been done to us; as you say, the heir to Elhiyne versus a few common armsmen. I recommend we send a diplomatic mission to

Penda, sue for peace. If the Penda armsmen are dead or disabled, we can offer reparation."

Olivia's calm returned. She turned away from DaNoel and paced back and forth, considering AnnaRail's proposal. "We'll appear weak."

"Better that than open war."

Olivia stopped pacing and turned toward her. AnnaRail knew that look well. Olivia said, "Perhaps war wouldn't be such a bad thing, after all."

Roland said, "No."

Olivia smiled at him. "We can send messengers to the other Lesser Clans, make sure they hear our version first. The heir to Elhiyne versus a few armsmen; we were clearly wronged."

AnnaRail said, "War with Penda would be bloody and costly."

"Probably," Olivia said. "But if it weakened the ties between Tosk and Penda, it might be worth it."

They argued heatedly throughout the afternoon. Perhaps the only thing that stopped Olivia from going to war was that *everyone* in the family opposed her, though DaNoel didn't say a word one way or the other. He wisely kept his mouth shut, but AnnaRail was certain he too would prefer a peaceful resolution to this crisis. At least she hoped so.

They decided to send a messenger to Penda to pave the way for a diplomatic mission. It would have to be led by one of the most powerful wizards or witches in the clan, so that meant it must be either AnnaRail or Olivia, and AnnaRail was determined that it would *not* be the old woman.

••••

In midafternoon the Penda armsmen's barracks was nearly empty, and as ErrinCastle strode into it, the few men present stood in deference. He approached the sergeant who'd recently returned with Lewendis from the border, and had to think carefully to recall his name: Erlander. The fellow had risen through the ranks by dint of good and loyal service, and deserved to be treated with respect.

"Erlander," ErrinCastle said, trying to keep his voice calm and neutral. "A word with you alone, please."

The man bowed his head and said, "Certainly, my lord."

ErrinCastle led him out of the barracks to a corner of the castle yard where they could not be overheard. He turned to the man and faced him squarely. "I heard a rumor there was some sort of incident on the border." When the man's eyes lowered with guilt, ErrinCastle's gut clenched.

Erlander opened his mouth to say something, hesitated for a moment, then said, "I begged him not to do it, Your Lordship. But he wouldn't listen."

With those words, ErrinCastle's anxiety ratcheted up a notch. "Do what?"

Erlander wouldn't look him in the eyes. "Kill the Elhiyne's horse."

ErrinCastle prayed that the story would end there. "Just a horse? That's all?"

The armsman's gaze remained locked on his feet.

"By the gods, man," ErrinCastle demanded. "What happened? Tell me, everything."

As Erlander spoke and the story unfolded, ErrinCastle's anxiety turned into dread. When the man finished he asked, "Lord Brandon et Elhiyne? The Elhiyne heir?"

The man said, "I told him he shouldn't do it, but he—"

ErrinCastle cut him off. "Come with me, now." He spun about and marched across the castle yard with the sergeant in his wake.

When they entered the main building he intercepted a servant, who cringed when he saw the look on ErrinCastle's face. "Where's my mother?"

"I believe she's in the kitchen, Your Lordship."

"Get Lewendis," ErrinCastle said. "Find him no matter where he is. I don't care if he's sitting on the privy; tell him to report to my father's study immediately."

••••

Theandrin and the cook were discussing the evening meal when ErrinCastle marched into the kitchen with an armsman on his heels. Even before he spoke, Theandrin knew something terrible had happened.

"Please come with me now, mother," he said. "This is important."

She nodded. He turned and strode out of the kitchen, the armsman following, both walking so fast she had to rush to keep up.

Lewendis awaited them at the closed door to BlakeDown's study. He started to say something, but ErrinCastle cut him off. "Shut up and come with me."

Without knocking, ErrinCastle lifted the latch on the door and threw it open. Inside, a kitchen maid was in the midst of arranging a tray of food, with BlakeDown standing close behind her, his back to the door. At their entrance, BlakeDown started and stepped away from her, a guilty look on his face.

ErrinCastle looked at the maid, hooked a thumb over his shoulder and said, "Get out."

The maid scurried out, and ErrinCastle slammed the door behind her.

BlakeDown demanded, "What's going on? And you should knock first."

ErrinCastle turned on Lewendis and growled like an animal. For a moment Theandrin thought he might strike the man. Without taking his eyes from Lewendis, he said, "Erlander, repeat what you just told me. Every word."

As the armsman began his story fear clutched at Theandrin's gut. The poor man spoke only small bits and pieces of a horrifying story, but ErrinCastle interrogated him relentlessly, and as the tale unfolded, Theandrin's heart went cold.

Theandrin hadn't realized she'd crossed the room, but as the man finished his story she found herself standing so close to Lewendis she smelled ale on his breath. She struggled to keep her voice down, but failed miserably. "You attacked and nearly murdered the heir to Elhiyne?"

Lewendis cringed and lowered his eyes. Behind him she noticed BlakeDown cringe as well, as if he felt some guilt over the incident.

ErrinCastle demanded, "What were you thinking, man?"

Lewendis pleaded, "But he started it."

Theandrin demanded, "Brandon attacked you first?"

Lewendis shook his head. "No. it was DaNoel."

"DaNoel attacked you, so you killed his horse?"

"No, he didn't attack until after I killed his horse. First he just threatened me with archers."

ErrinCastle exploded. "You bloody idiot."

BlakeDown intervened. "Calm down, son. And you too, wife. This situation may not be as bad as it looks. It won't hurt to stand up to the Elhiynes, show them we're their equals, probably their betters."

BlakeDown's words stunned Theandrin. Was he stupid enough to want war with Elhiyne? What might he hope to gain by something so foolish?

And Lewendis! Surely he knew that splitting the Lesser Council this way was not just ill-advised, but an absolute disaster. He *must* be in the employ of Valso or one of his henchmen. He couldn't be that stupid; he must have acted with motive and purpose. And yet, he'd returned from the border two days ago, was undoubtedly wearing one or more of her charms. And he'd done nothing to trigger them. Was she wrong about him?

ErrinCastle interrogated Lewendis and the armsman, picked apart their stories and slowly reassembled the truth in minute detail. Theandrin listened to every word, watching BlakeDown closely through it all. Her husband brushed off each incident casually when he should have been furious with Lewendis. "It's a border," he said, "between two powerful families. Of course there's strife and tension there. There've been incidents before, and there'll be incidents again."

Theandrin had lived with BlakeDown for 30 years, and knew the man wasn't that stupid. He was stupid about wenching, but not about war. She concluded there must be some overt motive behind his desire for such a costly enterprise.

He continued speaking, "I don't like it that we appear to be the aggressor here. Aye, they killed a couple of our armsmen, but we attacked the heir to Elhiyne. The other Lesser Clans might consider that a disproportionate response, so we can't go to war with them just yet. Let's see if we can get them to respond more aggressively. We must appear to be defending our lands against a hostile neighbor."

ErrinCastle exploded. He and BlakeDown argued heatedly, sometimes shouting uncontrollably.

No, Theandrin thought. *BlakeDown isn't that stupid, and Lewendis is.*

So what was going on in her husband's mind? What was he up to? Why did he so badly want war with Elhiyne?

Then there was the question of Lewendis. The power in the charms she'd planted in his clothing dissipated with time and they'd soon be useless. But they no longer mattered because she'd come to realize he was truly an idiot, not smart enough to be a spy for the Decouix. Valso might be a snake, but he was too smart to suffer a fool like Lewendis. So if not the yokel, then who was the spy in their midst?

That night Theandrin slept poorly.

••••

Morgin sat with his back to the wall holding Erithnae—or was it Rhianne—in his arms, saying nothing. A roar in the distance drew their attention to the wall, and someone on the battlements shouted, "Here they come again."

Morgin kissed Erithnae one last time, then scrambled to his feet and sprinted up the steps to the top of the wall. The jackal horde had already crossed half the distance from their camp, barking and howling in anticipation of the victory to come. A flock of arrows arced out from the castle and dropped a few of them, but that was the last of their supply, so the wave of attackers quickly reached the base of the wall and started climbing.

As Morgin waited for the first of them to reach the parapets he thought of Erithnae's words: *. . . you and she cannot be free and whole until . . .* If the sigil he'd acquired at his Naming wasn't his name, then what did it mean? He knew the words it symbolized, but they weren't an *essence,* a *purpose.*

The first jackal reached the parapet and Morgin stabbed him in the eye. But more came right behind him, and though he killed them one after another, each forced him back a fraction of a step.

He ducked a sword thrust aimed at his face, swung out and chopped into a jackal's arm, severing it just below the shoulder. He kicked the dog aside and engaged another, trying not to think of Erithnae's words: *. . . you and she cannot be free and whole until . . .*

His blade bucked and jerked in his grip, hungering to be released, slavering for more blood. The sword had been quiescent for so long he'd almost forgotten the effort it took contain the evil within it. He'd long ago sworn that he would never again yield to it, never allow it even the slightest freedom to act on its own, and it was like a painfully knotted muscle in his power. He crushed it now, mercilessly and without hesitation.

Behind and to one side a jackal stabbed at him with a short spear. He slashed out and chopped the shaft in two, deflected a sword thrust and grabbed the jackal by the throat. The dog twisted in his grip and bit his arm.

. . . you and she cannot be free and whole until . . .

He heard Erithnae cry out, not a sound for his ears but a plea from her soul to his. He scanned the castle yard, saw her with Rafaellen and two armsmen surrounded by jackal warriors and backed against a wall. Rafaellen and the armsmen fought to defend her, and she fought beside them, slashing out at the jackals with a small short-sword. If she died here, and Rhianne were within her soul, he would lose both of them.

A halfman standing on the parapet above Morgin sliced down toward his head with a two-handed stroke. In that moment his anger and frustration boiled up in his soul. He released the hatred in his sword and allowed its bloodlust to take control of him. The blade deflected the Kull's stroke, then chopped into his side, cutting him in two. It sliced, cut and slashed, and he held onto it with all his strength, just as he'd done years ago in the sanctum when it had butchered a dozen Kulls: stab here, chop there, slice everywhere. And then he faced no enemy; the blade had cleared a section of the wall and bought him a moment's respite. But as he looked about and saw the jackal hordes swarming over the entire length of the wall, he knew it was hopeless.

He tried to spot Erithnae again, but the castle yard was filled with jackal warriors in such numbers he could see nothing of her.

. . . you and she cannot be free and whole until . . . What was his purpose? What was his essence?

"ShadowLord," Salula cried out, roaring with laughter.

It took him a moment to find the halfman in the chaos. Salula stood on a crenellation about 50 paces down the wall, smiling hatefully at him with his old friend's face.

. . . you and she cannot be free and whole until . . .

Salula crowed, "ShadowLord, we have won."

. . . you and she cannot be free and whole until . . .

He felt Erithnae die, felt it with his heart and his soul and every fiber of his being.

. . . you and she cannot be free and whole until . . .

He couldn't beat Valso and Salula by denying his true nature. "AethonSword," he whispered. Little by little he'd pieced together the meaning of that symbol, and though he knew it was not his name, something terrible crawled up his spine.

"AethonSword," he said, still speaking softly, but all of the action on the wall ceased, and a strange silence descended. The jackals and Kulls and armsmen had all sensed the beast as it arose within him.

He threw his head back and screamed at the heavens, "AethonSword." It came out as a challenge of defiance to the gods of all the planes of existence, and the silence ended with a deep roar as the forest came alive.

"I . . . am . . . the . . . AethonSword."

A nearby branch, part of the outer wall of the castle, reached out and wrapped around the neck of a jackal, snapping his spine like a twig, then tossing him over the wall like refuse from last night's chamber pot. The shadowwraiths coalesced out of the forest and wrapped themselves about the heads of halfman and jackal alike. It clearly blinded them, for they slashed about with sword and pike aimlessly, allowing armsmen to step in and kill with impunity.

Morgin stepped up to the wall and saw that down in the horde's main encampment confusion and bedlam had descended. The victory, so close at hand for the jackals, had turned into a rout. They fled through the forest as it and the wraiths hunted them down mercilessly. Those still on the wall tried desperately to climb back down, some even jumping from the wall to their deaths.

Morgin turned around and scanned the castle yard, looking for Erithnae. It was littered with corpses—jackals and halfmen and armsmen—but he had no trouble spotting her. She lay on her back where she'd been pinned to the ground by the long blades of three pikes, two in her chest, one in her abdomen. She had died because he didn't have a name to acknowledge and didn't know his purpose. He'd waited too long to find himself.

He felt so tired, a weariness of the soul that no sleep could banish. So he sat down on the parapet with his back to the battlements, and closed his eyes. He thought he might sleep for centuries.

21

The Return

ANNARAIL'S EYES SUDDENLY fluttered and rolled into the back of her head. She swooned, and Roland barely caught her in time to keep her from falling to the stone floor. They'd been standing in his study talking when they both felt a sickening shift in reality. And with his limited sensitivity to the arcane, if he felt it, whatever it was must have hit his wife like a storm of demons from the ninth hell.

He lowered her gently to the floor and sat down with her head in his lap. He tested the pulse at her neck, and sighed with relief when he found it rapid but strong, and not faltering.

The door to his study burst open and Olivia stormed in, godfire burning in her eyes. "What in netherhell just happened?"

"I don't know," Roland said. "Though even I felt it."

JohnEngine rushed in a moment later, clearly had the same question on the tip of his tongue, but when he saw AnnaRail, he said, "What happened to mother?" He crossed the room, knelt down beside her and picked up one of her hands.

Roland said, "It hit her especially hard, but her pulse is strong and I think she'll be all right."

Brandon limped in, one arm in a sling, using the other to lean on a cane. "What's going on?"

DaNoel was an instant behind him. "Yes, what happened? And what's wrong with mother?"

They all started shouting at once.

Roland shouted, "Will everyone shut up?" But his voice was just one more to add to the confusion.

Then AnnaRail sighed and took a deep breath, and that silenced them all.

Roland asked, "Are you okay?"

"Yes," she said, speaking in an exhausted whisper, like someone who'd suffered a long illness. "I'll be fine. I just need to rest."

Olivia loomed over them, and Roland was thankful she had the presence of mind to put her impatience aside and speak calmly. "What happened, daughter?"

Behind the old woman, NickoLot said, "Morgin's back."

Olivia glanced her way, and her eyes narrowed as she considered the girl's words.

"Yes," AnnaRail said. She took several deep breaths, and Roland felt her heart rate slowing as she calmed. "Morgin just returned to the Mortal Plane."

Olivia leaned forward. "Really!"

"And he brought that blade with him."

"Oh," Olivia said. "That is unfortunate."

"No," AnnaRail said, sitting up. "No, I think we no longer need to fear that blade." She looked carefully at them all. "But it's possible we must now fear Morgin."

Olivia demanded, "And where was he hiding all this time that we couldn't sense him."

AnnaRail said, "I think . . . I think in a dream."

••••

Rhianne opened her eyes and gasped. She'd been napping, sitting up on the couch in her sitting room, and the last thing she remembered was the jackal warriors in Sabian's castle yard, she and Rafaellen and two armsmen surrounded by them, fighting for their lives. Then Erithnae had somehow thrust her out of her soul with the thought, *You cannot die here with me.*

"Your Ladyship," Geanna said, rushing into the room. "His Majesty is coming."

Rhianne had trouble shifting her thoughts to the moment. Were they alive? Had Erithnae been killed? Had Morgin died? She had to go back to her dreams. She had to know.

"He'll be here any moment, Your Ladyship."

Valso! It took an effort to calm her racing heart. She stood and forced her thoughts away from the battle in the Kingdom of Dreams.

Geanna circled her slowly, examining her like a giftwrapped package. She stopped in front of her and looked unhappily at her chest. Rhianne glanced down and only then remembered the silk handkerchief she'd stuffed into her cleavage. She'd fluffed it out in an attempt to make it look decorative, but she'd only been partly successful. It did look out of place.

Geanna raised an eyebrow and said, "May I remove that, milady?"

Rhianne couldn't hide her anger and just stared at her.

Geanna put her hands on her hips and said, "You know . . . if you don't allow me to remove it now, he'll just have me do so when he gets here."

Rhianne pulled the handkerchief out of her cleavage and threw it to the floor. It fluttered down slowly, much less dramatically than she'd intended. Geanna visibly clamped her mouth shut, holding back some sort of retort.

"Rhianne," Valso said, walking into the room unannounced. "As always lovely."

Geanna bobbed a quick curtsy, then backed out of the room.

Rhianne curtsied more carefully than the servant, but as she rose the floor tilted, and reality changed so abruptly she gasped. Her knees buckled, and suddenly Valso's arms held her tightly. He lowered her carefully to the couch and called, "Geanna. Come here, now. The Lady Rhianne is ill."

She heard the patter of rapid footsteps, then Geanna leaned over her, breathing heavily. "Oh my lady, you look quite pale."

Valso said, "Get her some strong brandy."

Rhianne's hands trembled. Her knees trembled. She couldn't stop shaking. But deep inside, hidden from them all, she rejoiced. Morgin had come back. Her Morgin was alive again, and in this world, not in some strange dreamscape. He'd brought back the sword too, which should have terrified her, but it had now taken on a benign aspect, as if he had somehow tamed it.

Valso leaned over her, holding one of her hands. Geanna appeared behind him holding a crystal goblet filled with an amber liquid—brandy. Yes, he'd called for brandy.

Valso helped her sit up, but when he tried to hand her the glass her hands shook so violently she couldn't hold it. He held it to her lips, she took a small sip, and as the warmth of the brandy washed down her throat, her mind focused on one thought: Valso hadn't reacted. Had he sensed Morgin's return? Had he sensed the sword's return? The shift in reality had been so dramatic he couldn't have missed it.

The king stood, placed the goblet on a nearby table and turned to leave. He hesitated and turned back to her. "So your husband has returned, and without that sword. That means Magwa succeeded. She'll bring it to me, and there'll be nothing to hinder us."

After he left, her hands steadied enough to hold the glass of brandy. She took it and lifted it to her lips for another sip. Valso hadn't sensed the sword's return. What did that mean? And what of the sword; how had it changed? And how might she use Valso's ignorance against him?

••••

The late summer sun warmed Cort's face as she rode up the Gods Road several strides behind Tulellcoe, their horses moving at a comfortable walk. They'd gotten an early start that morning, and if there were no delays they hoped to make Durin before nightfall.

Without warning Tulellcoe brought his horse to a halt, didn't turn about to say anything, just sat in his saddle staring straight ahead. Cort allowed her horse to amble toward him, wondering as she approached if he'd spotted some danger in the road, or perhaps in the forest nearby. As she pulled up beside him he didn't acknowledge her, just sat there, looking forward with his eyes unfocused.

After several heartbeats he turned his head, looked at her and said, "Morgin's back." Without another word, he turned back to the road and nudged his horse forward.

Morgin's back! That was all he had to say! She could strangle the man.

"Now wait just one moment." She spurred her horse into a brief trot and caught up with him. "What do you mean *Morgin's back?*"

"Just that. He's back, on the Mortal Plane."

"And how do you know that?"

"I just do."

No, strangling was too good for the man. She'd have to think of something much more creative. She reined in her horse and brought it to a halt. "Stop right here and talk to me. Morgin's dead. How can he be back?"

Tulellcoe reined his horse in. "I don't know. He just is."

She'd still strangle him, but only after a creatively mean and nasty precursor. "If he wasn't on the Mortal Plane, then where was he?"

"Honestly, Cort, I don't know. I just felt his soul return, that's all. I don't know what shape he's in, or where he is. If I knew anything more, I'd tell you."

Well, maybe she wouldn't strangle him after all.

He said, "Maybe when we return to Elhiyne AnnaRail will know more. But for now let's just focus on helping Rhianne."

Tulellcoe must be roiling on the inside, but so like him to show nothing on the outside. And what did it mean that Morgin had died and then returned? That wasn't simply magic or power. No mortal had the ability to bring a soul back to the Mortal Plane once it had departed. Only a god could intervene on that level.

Okay, no strangling. She looked at the sun. "We should make Durin well before nightfall."

••••

Theandrin barely managed to keep her lunch down, gulped heavily and managed not to spew it over the carpet in her sitting room. In mid-day without attempting any kind of seeking or spell-casting, she'd had a spontaneous vision of a cloud obscuring the sun and casting a red Elhiyne shadow over Penda. She might have fallen had she not already been seated.

BlakeDown walked into the room, took one look at her and said, "You look ill, my dear. You should take better care of yourself."

She took a deep breath and felt better. She didn't want her husband inquiring further; for some reason she didn't want to discuss the vision she'd just had, so she asked, "How was the hunting?"

"Excellent." He seemed in an expansive mood. "I'll have a nice trophy or two out of it."

He glanced at the two girls sitting with her, obviously looking for Chrisainne. If she'd been present he'd probably have made up some excuse to send her on an errand, then follow her out to the stables to fuck her. He really needed to learn a bit more subtlety.

"Well," he said. "I have work to do." He turned and left, no doubt to find Chrisainne.

Theandrin considered the vision she'd just seen, and the shift in reality that had come with it. It had something to do with the young Elhiyne lord, the one with the reputation for shadows, AethonLaw. His name had been on everyone's lips for the past two years, though she'd heard he preferred another name, a peasant's name that she couldn't recall at the moment.

The vision hadn't felt ominous in any way. The red shadow had cloaked Penda completely, but not like some menacing shroud to be feared. Rather, she got the impression it had enveloped Penda to obscure it, to hide it from some menace in a protective way.

Odd that no one else in Penda had felt it, especially BlakeDown. A powerful wizard, a powerful sending, and yet he'd felt nothing. She'd have to think on that a bit.

••••

Morgin started awake and opened his eyes, saw nothing in the pitch black darkness where he lay. He was stretched out on his stomach, his arm extended, hand still gripping his sword. He rolled onto his back, stirred up a cloud of dust that filled his nose and mouth and eyes. Coughing and spitting, he sat up and called forth a bit of nether fire to burn in the air in front of him.

Nearby the skeleton king sat on his throne, and he realized he'd awakened in the crypt where he'd fallen after Salula had stabbed him. Had it all been just a dream: Rhiannead, the Living Forest, Sabian, Erithnae?

No, he decided. Yes, it had probably been a dream, but he'd learned long ago that his dreams weren't *just* dreams. They were all too real, and he couldn't excuse his failure to defend Erithnae by simply shrugging it off as a dream.

He stood and made his way carefully to the cave's entrance, and as he stepped out onto the shelf of rock in the side of Attunhigh, he saw why the interior of the crypt had been so dark. Dawn was just breaking over the horizon and deep shadow still enveloped the slash in the rock that opened into the cave.

Nearby a horse spluttered and neighed. *It's about time.*

Mortiss stepped onto the shelf of rock.

Morgin said, "I'm glad you're here, old friend. It's time to leave this mountain and its secrets behind."

22

The Fault in a Name

VALSO HAD SUMMONED Rhianne, but this time her Kullish guards took her up to the third floor of the castle. They turned down a corridor that she recognized immediately. Not long ago she had sensed a vast draw of nether power, and sniffing it out had led her to this hallway, and to the door at the far end.

She'd not been allowed to enter before, but now her guards led her straight to that door and opened it for her, admitting her to a large and spacious workshop. Scrolls were heaped on shelves along one wall, and the shelves on another contained bottles, vials and ampoules of all sorts. Valso sat in a comfortable chair with his heels up on a heavy work table, his ankles crossed, his hands behind his head, his fingers locked. Behind him the little winged demon snake sat coiled on a perch. The skeletal Carsaris stood looking out a window, his back to the room. When Rhianne entered the sorcerer did not turn around, but Bayellgae perked up, its wings fluttering, its head weaving from side to side.

Valso stood. "Rhianne. My lovely Rhianne."

He crossed the room, but as she started to curtsy he took her by the shoulders and pulled her upright. "No need for that here." He took her hand, bent and kissed it. "It's a lovely day, and soon it's going to get even better."

He turned around, speaking as he crossed the room. "I anticipate excellent news today. And a trophy. A valuable trophy, one I intend to destroy so it can no longer hinder us."

Still standing at the window, Carsaris said, "She's here. She just entered the castle yard. I've instructed the halfmen to bring her here immediately."

Valso paced back and forth, like an expectant father waiting for the birth of his heir, probably anticipating Magwa's triumphant return. Rhianne didn't know if she should be fearful or not. She stepped to one side, backed into a corner and decided to keep a low profile.

The door burst open and Magwa stormed into the room followed by two of her generals. "Your magic failed us," she barked, spittle flying with every word.

Valso stopped pacing and his eyes narrowed. Bayellgae's wings buzzed as it lifted off its perch and hovered just behind the king.

"Your protections were nothing," Magwa growled. "Twelve thousand jackal warriors—annihilated by that forest. Barely twelve twelves escaped."

Rhianne felt something nether enter the room—no, not the room, it entered Valso, a malevolent power so vast no mortal should have been able to contain it. She recognized it as the same nether power she had sensed before in this room, and it had taken up residence in Valso's soul. She struggled to breathe, the demon snake hissed, and Magwa cowered.

When Valso spoke, it was not his voice they heard. It sounded more like the grumble of an earthquake as he said, "You failed. Tell me what happened."

Magwa made a visible effort to put aside her anger. "When he claimed his name, the forest came alive. My warriors were no longer hidden or protected, and it butchered them."

Rhianne had sensed Morgin's return to the Mortal Plane, so he had somehow escaped. But Erithnae had thrust her out of her soul before the finish, and she didn't know how the battle had ended. She wanted to listen raptly to Magwa's story, but she cringed at sharing the room with the thing in Valso's soul, wanted only to escape and flee.

The thing that stood in the room looking like Valso spoke again in that inhuman voice. "He claimed his name? What name would that be?"

Magwa hesitated, as if afraid to speak the name, and when she finally did her voice came out in a frightened whisper. "AethonSword. He claimed the name Aethon-Sword."

The snake darted over Valso's head and hovered above the jackal queen. It hissed at her as she swatted at it. "Get away from me."

Rhianne would have enjoyed seeing the bitch queen cower, would have reveled in her discomfort were it not for that other presence that shared the room with them. If she had the ability to control shadows the way Morgin did, she'd hide in one now.

The thing that had entered Valso's soul left in a heartbeat. Valso threw his head back and laughed. "AethonSword," he cried, once again speaking with his own voice. "I should have known."

Emboldened, Magwa said, "Yes, you should have."

Valso continued to laugh. "All along that old witch Olivia had it wrong. Aethon-Law, AethonSword—yes, it all makes sense now. The foolish old woman failed to recognize the potential she had in her grasp, failed to use it as she should have. Well it's too late now."

Magwa spun and pointed a paw at Rhianne. "I demand payment now—her."

Rhianne's chest tightened and her pulse pounded in her throat.

Valso leaned back casually against the table and looked her way. His eyes tracked down to her toes, then slowly up to her face, and finally, as always, settled on her breasts. "We had a deal, Magwa: the lovely Rhianne in payment for a sword. Where's the sword?"

"I didn't get it. But only because you failed to protect my warriors as you promised. So I demand her as payment for the loss of twelve thousand."

Rhianne couldn't breathe as she watched Valso consider Magwa's demand.

"No," he said. "No sword, no pretty girl."

Magwa stepped toward him, stuck her muzzle in his face. "Then I'll put my claim before our master."

Bayellgae hovered over them both as Valso smiled, and a hint of that other presence brushed through his soul. "You already have. And you have His answer."

Magwa stepped back, lowered her eyes and cringed. Her generals whined like mistreated dogs.

Valso turned his back on Magwa in a show of arrogance. He crossed the room to the table, lifted a sheathed dagger off it. He stood with his back to them as he pulled the dagger from the sheath. Rhianne caught a glimpse of it and recognized an obsidian blade like that Salula carried. Valso looked at the blade as he said, "AethonSword."

He turned back to them and his eyes focused on Rhianne. "Come here, child."

The snake streaked across the room and hovered so close to her ear she felt the air moving from the fluttering of its wings. She resolved then that somehow she would find a way to defeat its venom.

Rhianne had no intention of obeying Valso, but that powerful, evil magic took hold of her, and her legs moved as if she were a puppet dancing on the end of Valso's strings. She struggled, tried to resist, but step by painful step she crossed the room, the snake drifting with her, the buzz of its wings in her ear. Valso didn't release her until she stood about half a pace from him, an intimately close distance. The snake settled on her shoulder as Valso lifted the dagger and touched the point lightly to her throat. He didn't cut or scratch her, but she learned the point of the blade was needle sharp.

He leaned down and placed a feather-light kiss on her cheek. "So Magwa failed, and the whoreson is back, but without the sword."

"He's back?" Magwa howled. "On the Mortal Plane?"

Valso pressed the flat of the blade to Rhianne's throat, and without cutting her traced the tip of the dagger from ear to ear.

"Massster, let me be the one to take her life."

Valso ignored the snake. "Don't worry, my dear. I still want you alive . . . for the time being."

"I'll find him," Magwa said. "Then kill him."

Valso looked her way. "No. You've failed twice now. I think you're just not up to the task."

Magwa said, "We still need that blade. Our master cannot manifest fully on the Mortal Plane until we control it."

Valso looked into Rhianne's eyes and she couldn't look away. "That name won't keep the whoreson alive for long. Smart of him to leave that sword in the Kingdom of Dreams where I can't get at it. But that's only temporary, because I have something he desperately wants. I have you."

He traced the flat of the dagger along her cheek, then down her throat to her chest. "You'll betray him, you know. Oh, not willingly, but nevertheless you will betray him. You'll point my dogs in his direction, and we'll hunt him down."

With a flick of his wrist he sliced through the cloth at the top of her dress, exposing more skin. "Then I'll send Salula and Bayellgae after him, not to kill him, more like hunting dogs sent to flush game."

Rhianne couldn't speak, couldn't move, could do nothing but stand there and tremble. She had thought that nothing could be more horrifying than Bayellgae, but that thing that inhabited Valso's soul made her want to run from the room screaming like a terrified child. Even after it had gone, now that she knew what to look for, she sensed a remnant of it always present within him, a black scar on his soul hungering to devour anyone who came near it. In his eyes she thought she saw a hint of madness, though she also saw that he reveled in her terror.

"He'll come for you, won't he?" he said. "And when he does I'll give him a choice: you, or that blade. And when I own that blade, I'll put this dagger in his heart. And then I'll have you all to myself."

••••

Rhianne couldn't stop trembling as the Kulls escorted her back to her rooms. As she stepped through the door to her sitting room, Geanna said, "Oh my lady, you're so pale. Are you ill again?"

Rhianne let Geanna help her to the couch.

"I'll get some brandy, my lady."

"No, just water."

Geanna left, and returned immediately with a goblet of cold water. Rhianne took a sip, then said, "Thank you. I wish to be alone."

Geanna curtsied and left.

When Valso had held that obsidian blade to her throat, she'd almost wanted him to plunge it into her, to end her life so she wouldn't have to face that thing he'd welcomed into his soul. For the first time she realized the magnitude of the battle Morgin would have to fight. *No*, she thought, *the battle Morgin and I must fight together*. To die now, even at the hands of another, would be cowardly.

Valso considered her bait in a trap for Morgin, knew he would come for her. Somehow she must get word to Morgin. Perhaps she could do that through the Kingdom of Dreams, but he'd now left that realm.

As her heart calmed, something Magwa said bothered her. She recalled the bitch-queen's words and carefully tried to remember everything she'd said. *He claimed the name AethonSword.* Magwa had said it, and Valso had accepted that. Both Erithnae and Metadan had believed Morgin's true name was AethonSword. Morgin had told Erithnae he'd tried to acknowledge that name, but the Kingdom of Dreams wouldn't let him. And now Valso and Magwa had made the same mistake. *So if not AethonSword,* she wondered, *what is Morgin's true name?*

••••

NickoLot sat at her writing table and examined her small store of materials. The bay and basil leaves had dried and withered, were now stiff and crinkly, the blood on them a dark, brown stain. Blood was an enormously powerful addition to any charm or spell-casting, and obtaining DaNoel's had been a stroke of pure luck. But *human* blood could be quite dangerous, and since she'd never worked with it before she'd forced herself to move with caution. Ordinarily she'd consult with Olivia or Anna-Rail, but the moment she asked either of them about such a black spell, they'd question her relentlessly, and that she could not allow. She'd done her research carefully, pouring through the scrolls in the library by candlelight in the wee hours of the morning.

She now knew that had she been able to use the customary seven drops of blood on each of the two silver charms, they'd be much more powerful. But still, once she triggered them, placed one in DaNoel's room and one in hers, they would conduct to her a sense of his activities there, perhaps even some of his words, if he concentrated on them hard enough.

She retrieved the small chest from beneath her writing table, opened it and searched through its contents for three pieces of dull, gray metal. Down in the bottom of the chest she found the crude lumps of lead, and placed them on the table, flat blossoms of melted metal she'd retrieved from the smithy.

Lead, the silent metal, it created a space empty of all sound and energies, could be used as a barrier to keep things in, as well as out. She wanted the lead charms to contain information, to store it and hold it for her.

Basil was frequently used to drive off hostile spirits. She and her spells could be considered hostile in this case, so the blood that had dried on the basil leaves would countermand that. She carefully manipulated a basil leaf over a lump of lead, bent it here and there, causing flecks of dried blood to flake off and drop onto the metal. She repeated that with the other two lumps, making sure that each held exactly seven flakes of dried blood.

Bay was often used as a protection against black magic. This spell was definitely on the black side of the arts, and again the dried blood would reverse that. She placed each lump of metal, with its flakes of blood from the basil leaves, onto a dry and crinkly bay leaf, then on top of the metal she added one of DaNoel's hairs. She fed power into one of the metal and bay leaf concoctions, thinking of her brother as she did so. The bay leaf began to smoke, then burst into flames. It burned until the leaf, blood and hair were consumed, leaving behind the lump of metal, but now strangely transformed so it appeared bright and shiny like polished silver. She repeated the process with the other two lumps of lead, then sat back to examine her work.

She'd find an opportunity to plant the charms properly.

••••

From the window in her private work room, Theandrin watched the moon slowly cross the night sky. She still had a bit of waiting to do, for it was imperative she use the power of midnight for this spell. And the trap she intended to set could be easily thwarted by a witch or wizard with even modest capabilities. Better to lessen any chance of being observed by waiting until all but a few sentries had retired to their beds.

She'd now looked more closely at Lewendis, paid more attention to his nature. He was just too forthright to be a spy for Valso, didn't have a clandestine bone in his body. She reminded herself not to forget that he was also just plain stupid, didn't have the brains to avoid making some mistake that would reveal hidden loyalty to another clan.

When she judged the time right, she turned from the window, crossed the room to her workbench and retrieved a carefully folded linen handkerchief and the two charms she'd prepared. She recalled the last time she'd walked out into the castle yard late at night, and the guard on the parapets who'd called down to her to ask if she needed anything. It wouldn't do to have him wake half the castle with a loud shout, so she activated one of the charms with a bit of saliva. Anyone who looked her way would find their attention deflected elsewhere, not as difficult as a detailed veil of illusion, but in the shadows of night, just as effective.

She activated the second charm, and a small flame blossomed in her hands, illuminating the room with light that only she could see. She'd also not be advertising her whereabouts with a candle or lantern.

She stepped out into the hall, walked down the stairs to the main floor and out into the castle yard. She'd given herself plenty of time, and didn't want to tempt fate, so she stayed in the shadows and worked her way around the edge of the yard to the main gates. It was a time of peace, so they were open. She slipped through them and paused just outside the castle's walls. She waited a bit for true midnight, but when it came, she knew with her witch's senses the time was right.

She opened the folded linen handkerchief and looked upon the six blue threads she'd wrapped within it: six threads for Penda, the sixth tribe, and blue, for the blue of Vodah. The stone of the walls had been laid hundreds of years ago, and while still strong and quite formidable, it wasn't difficult to find small gaps here and there in the mortar. She carefully wedged three threads in three separate places on the left side of the gates, then the three remaining on the right.

She stepped back to examine her handiwork. She'd spent days preparing those six charm-wards. They'd alert her the moment anyone of Vodah loyalty passed between them and through the castle gates.

23

The Fallen Revealed

LOW-LYING CLOUDS drifted in as dusk settled over the western shore of the Lake of Sorrows. Morgin guessed he was in for a bit of rain that night, so he set up camp early. He had two oiled, canvas tarps, the same material the Benesh'ere used for their tents. He draped one over the branches of a tree to give Mortiss some shelter, though he wondered if the nether horse felt discomfort as mortals did.

Don't be stupid, she neighed.

He wasn't sure what she meant by that, and really didn't want her to enlighten him, so he ignored the comment. He managed to erect a small lean-to, collect some dry wood and start a fire before the clouds released a slow drizzle. When he crawled into his blanket he was warm, out of the rain, and reasonably comfortable, but his thoughts went to the many tasks before him and sleep eluded him for a time.

When he awoke in the morning the rain had stopped and a clear, blue sky greeted him as he crawled out of his blanket. He picked up his water skin, walked down to the lake and splashed a little water on his face. While he refilled the skin, the familiar, sad sounds of a pipist's tune drifted through the forest, and when he returned to his camp he was not surprised to find Metadan standing in front of the fire waiting for him. The archangel had a broadsword buckled at his side. He placed a hand on the hilt of the sword and said, "Time for a lesson." He drew the sword and the blade dripped blood onto the ground, the blood of first legion, the angels he'd betrayed.

Metadan raised the sword and looked at it. "No, this is not the blade you must face." He flicked his wrist, and now he held the obsidian blade.

Morgin walked over to his gear and retrieved his sword. He and the archangel sparred for a good portion of the morning. When they finished Morgin walked down to the lake to wash away the sweat, and returned to find Metadan seated on a log in front of the fire, the pipes pressed to his lips, again playing that sad tune. The archangel had added fresh wood to the fire and stoked it nicely. Morgin was pleased to see that it burned with almost no smoke; it wouldn't do to advertise his presence.

He sat down on a rock on the opposite side of the fire and said, "Nice tune. But always so sad."

"You taught it to me," the archangel said. "Several centuries ago. Teach me a happy tune, and I'll play it."

Morgin recalled that as Morddon, the ancient Benesh'ere warrior, he'd known the pipes, and now he had a vague memory of teaching Metadan how to play them. "I don't know any happy tunes."

"Well then you should compose one."

"First, I have to find happiness."

Metadan nodded. "And how will you do that?"

Morgin knew what he had to do. "I have to kill Salula without killing my friend. I have rescue Rhianne, and beg her forgiveness for the way I treated her. I have to stop Valso."

Metadan looked at the pipes in his hand and they vanished in a heartbeat. "And let's not forget you have a prophesy to fulfill, and then you must right the last two wrongs."

Morgin recalled the sixth wrong, and that he must *free the soul of the Fallen One*. Metadan, the betrayer. After Metadan and Ellowyn had fought in the clearing near Csairne Glen, he'd told Morgin, *I am the Fallen Angel. I serve the Dark God who sits upon the throne of power in the ninth hell of the netherworld* . . . Morgin had no idea how he could free the archangel's soul.

••••

Rhianne's Kullish guards escorted her to the room on the third floor, which she now understood was Valso's workshop. When a Kull opened the door she saw Valso, Salula and Carsaris standing with their backs to her, their attention focused on something on the heavy work table. The little snake sat coiled on its perch.

As she stepped into the room, the skeletal Carsaris said, "I don't know if it'll work."

Salula glanced over his shoulder at her, and she cringed inwardly at seeing the demon look through France's eyes.

Valso said, "We have alternatives if it doesn't."

As the Kulls closed the door behind her, the three of them turned to face her. Valso strode toward her, saying, "My Rhianne, always so lovely." He took her hand and kissed it.

Without turning to the wizard he said, "Carsaris, bring it here."

Valso turned away from her as the wizard crossed the room. Carsaris handed him something, he turned back to Rhianne and raised his hand. Between thumb and forefinger he held a medallion like that Salula had used to control her. It would take her will, turn her into nothing more than an obedient dog.

"Please, no," she said, stepping back, bumping into the door behind her.

Valso smiled and stepped forward. "But it must be, my dear."

He reached forward, bringing the medallion toward her face. She closed her eyes, and when the cold metal touched her forehead she wondered why she felt such fear. She had nothing to fear here. She opened her eyes, looked into Valso's kindly face.

He said, "Now isn't that much better?"

She lowered her eyes and said, "Yes, Your Majesty."

Valso turned, saying, "Come, my dear."

She followed him to the center of the room, where he turned to face her. He reached out and took her by the shoulders. "Now let's see how well it works . . ."

. . . Spinning . . . spinning . . . spinning . . .

She sensed nothing but the need to find her Morgin. Her entire being narrowed to that one desire. She desperately wanted to find him, thought her heart might burst if she failed.

. . . Spinning . . . spinning . . . spinning . . .

Her Morgin was nowhere to be found, gone as if he'd never been. She slumped to the floor, sobbing openly, tears streaming down her face and dripping to the floor.

"No, it didn't work."

"I'm sorry, Your Majesty."

"Not your fault, Carsaris. Come, child."

She opened her eyes as a pair of strong hands lifted her gently to her feet, looked into Valso's face and said, "You are so kind, Your Majesty."

Valso reached out, touched her forehead, and when he withdrew his hand it held a shiny, metal object.

Rhianne staggered and backed several steps.

Valso turned away from her and crossed the room to the little snake's perch. "Hmmm, snake. You've tasted his blood, and he your venom. Can you sense him?"

The snake's head wove from side to side. "The connection isss there, Your Majesssty, but not ssstrong enough."

Valso considered the snake for a long moment. "I may be able to do something to enhance the connection, even if only a little. I certainly have enough bits and pieces of him from his stay in my dungeons to concoct something."

"What of his ssshadows, massster?"

Valso shook his head. "If you can't see through his shadows now, I doubt I'll be able to do anything about that. But strengthening a connection that already exists, yes, I should be able to do something there."

Rhianne's chest tightened with fear. If Valso turned the snake into a hound, what else might he do? When Morgin finally faced Valso, even though Morgin could no longer be killed by the little serpent's venom, might it tip the balance in some way?

Rhianne couldn't take that chance, and realized now that she would have to do something about the snake, but what?

Valso turned and looked at Rhianne, but he spoke to the serpent. "I'll do something to help you sniff him out. And when you go, take Salula with you. It's time to be rid of the Elhiyne once and for all."

••••

To approach the Benesh'ere camp Morgin rode around the south side of the Lake of Sorrows. Rounding the north side would have been shorter, but he'd have to pass close to the mining camp and Norlakton. Too much danger of being seen.

As night approached he stopped in the forest just south of the Benesh'ere camp, unsaddled Mortiss, ate a cold meal of jerky and hardtack, and slept wrapped in his blanket with no fire. He arose well before dawn, bundled his saddle and gear in the canvas tarps, then cut an armful of leafy branches and concealed the bundle beneath them. He continued on foot, wrapped in shadow.

He slipped past the Benesh'ere sentries as the first rays of sunlight brightened the horizon. He'd chosen his timing carefully, had arrived just before the camp roused, early enough that the shadows were still long and deep, but late enough that Harriok and Branaugh would be awake and breakfasting.

He stopped in a shadow near the entrance to their tent. "Harriok, Branaugh," he said, speaking softly so his voice didn't carry. "It's me, Morgin. May I enter?"

A couple of heartbeats later Branaugh threw the tent flap aside. She looked at him for a moment, then said, "They said you were dead. Apparently, they were wrong."

Morgin grimaced. "I'm not sure that they were."

She shook her head sadly. "Why am I not surprised that you'd say something like that?"

She stepped aside, holding the flap open. He crouched and walked past her into the dark interior of the tent, smelled roasted meat and warm bread. Harriok sat by a small brazier, something on top of it steaming, their half-finished breakfast in front of him. "Would you like some tea, my brother of the sand?"

Morgin unbuckled his sword, put it to one side and sat down opposite him. Branaugh sat down next to Harriok as he poured tea for the three of them. She retrieved an empty plate and asked, "Hungry?"

"I've had nothing but trail rations for several days," he said. "It smells wonderful."

She prepared a small plate, handed it to him, and as they ate they spoke of little things. LillianToc had finally gotten over Felina's murder at the hands of the Kulls, and he swam quite regularly in the lake, was teaching some of the other children to swim. Yim's father had allowed her to discard the debt collar, and she'd soon marry her warrior. The smiths were now making better steel than ever, thanks to the lore from the past that Morgin had recalled. It gladdened Morgin's heart to listen to the simple gossip of the tribe.

They told Morgin about JohnEngine and NickoLot's visit. Harriok said, "You need to let them know you're alive."

"I think they already know," Morgin said.

"So what do you need from us?" Branaugh asked.

Harriok gave her a disapproving look. "Need you be so blunt? Why do you think he wants something?"

She rolled her eyes, looked at her husband, then at Morgin. "If he'd come to visit, or to live with us again, he would have come openly. Instead, he's come like a thief in the night, so when he leaves no one will know he's been here."

Morgin said, "She's right. I do need your help."

Harriok shrugged and swallowed a piece of meat. "You have but to ask."

Morgin considered his words carefully. "I need to go out on the sands, and I don't have the skills to survive there on my own."

"Out on the sands?" Branaugh asked. "Why?"

"I have to go to Kathbeyanne, the city of glass."

Harriok froze in mid chew. "That's a fool's errand. What makes you think we won't end up like all the rest?"

"When you and I were out on the sands and saw the city on the horizon, I sensed its true position, and it was not where I saw it. I think I can get us there."

"It'll be hot this time of year. Why do you want to go?"

"I have to fulfill a prophesy."

Harriok looked to Branaugh. She rested a hand on his arm and said, "I think you must do this thing, husband."

Harriok nodded his agreement. "I'll put together the provisions, and meet you in your camp at dawn two mornings hence."

Morgin gave them careful directions to his small campsite, then wrapped himself in shadow and slipped out of the Benesh'ere camp before it came fully awake.

••••

Morgin danced sideways as the point of the obsidian blade thrust through the space where his chest had been a heartbeat earlier. He struck down with his sword, meeting the obsidian in a shower of sparks, driving its point into the dirt. Metadan recovered with inhuman speed, they disengaged and backed away from one another, Morgin breathing heavily, Metadan showing no outward signs of exertion. Apparently the archangel was not subject to the same physical limitations as those of a mere mortal.

"You're doing well," Metadan said. "You might even be able to face me someday."

"Will I need to?"

As they circled warily the archangel shrugged. "Who knows what fate awaits us!"

Morgin attacked, swung his sword down in a high arc that Metadan deflected easily. Morgin followed through with a thrust, catching Metadan by surprise and the angel back-stepped clumsily. Again they disengaged, and the angel nodded his approval.

They circled in a crouch, each evaluating the other, looking for an opening. Morgin was about to try another attack when Metadan frowned, stepped back, stood up straight and raised a hand to signal a halt to the match. He looked up to the sky and scanned it, turning slowly full circle. He stopped facing north, raised a hand to shield his eyes from the sun, and looked that way for several heartbeats. He tensed, turned to Morgin and said, "I must be gone."

Saying nothing further, he vanished, leaving behind a column of smoke in the shape of a man that dissipated slowly. Morgin took his cue from Metadan, stepped into the shadow of a tree, drew his shadowmagic about him like a cloak and waited. Mortiss must have sensed something, for she was nowhere to be seen.

He waited there unmoving for quite some time, sensed something nether approaching, then heard the buzz that reminded him of the wings of a hummingbird. A heartbeat later Bayellgae zipped into the clearing, darted about as if searching for something, then settled on the branch of a nearby tree.

Morgin waited as the snake sat quietly, its head constantly weaving from side to side. He forced his breathing to slow, dare not move, wondering what the little snake was up to. He heard a horse splutter and neigh somewhere nearby in the forest, found he was holding his breath without realizing it. He let the air out of his lungs slowly, careful to make no sound, heard the creak of saddle leather, and the clop of a horse's hooves at a slow walk. Moving at an easy pace Salula rode into the clearing. It tugged at Morgin's heart to see the face of the swordsman turned into a hard mask of expressionless stone.

"He wasss near," the snake hissed. "But now he isss gone."

Bayellgae zipped into the air and flew away. France—Salula, Morgin reminded himself—followed at an easy pace.

Morgin waited for quite some time, afraid to step out of his shadows. When Mortiss reappeared and walked calmly into the clearing, he took that as a sign that the demon snake and demon man did not wait in hiding nearby.

••••

Late in the afternoon Theandrin stood next to BlakeDown on the battlements. In the distance ErrinCastle led a small contingent of armsmen, escorting JohnEngine et Elhiyne, a carriage and six Elhiyne horsemen. When the Elhiyne messenger had come asking safe passage for a group led by AnnaRail esk et Elhiyne, ErrinCastle had insisted that he lead the escort, saying, "We're promising safe passage, and I'll not let some hot-head break our word."

The decision to send AnnaRail had been wise. Probably the second most powerful witch in the Lesser Clans, she was highly respected, and known for keeping a calm head. Theandrin had met her many times over the years, and knew the two of them could work together to defuse the border situation.

Theandrin and BlakeDown walked down to the castle yard and were waiting when the group rode through the castle gates. The men dismounted, JohnEngine walked to the carriage and opened its door, then helped AnnaRail step down. They exchanged greetings, though BlakeDown came across a bit gruff. She'd have to talk to him about that.

Theandrin had orchestrated this carefully, including the timing of their arrival. AnnaRail and JohnEngine were shown to their rooms, were given plenty of time to freshen up from their journey, then joined Theandrin, ErrinCastle and BlakeDown for a private dinner.

"How is Lord Brandon?" Theandrin asked. She and AnnaRail had traded quite a bit of information by messenger prior to this meeting, so she already knew the answer to that question.

"He's doing well," AnnaRail said. "Though it was close."

"How bad were his injuries?"

"An arrow wound to his arm," AnnaRail said, and Theandrin saw she was trying to keep any belligerence or accusation out of her voice. "A twisted ankle and two broken ribs. One of them punctured his lung. That was the most dangerous wound of all. But he'll heal."

BlakeDown leaned across the table and snarled, "Our two dead armsmen won't heal."

JohnEngine's eyes flashed and he started to say something, but AnnaRail put a hand on his arm and said, "It was an unfortunate escalation of hostilities, and we feel that both sides must bear some blame."

BlakeDown pressed her further. "So you accept blame for it?"

If Theandrin had been seated next to him, she would have kicked him. She said, "I think AnnaRail's point is that they do accept some blame, but not all."

AnnaRail smiled and didn't comment.

Theandrin continued, "Both sides acted imprudently. We have two hotheads to blame for that."

BlakeDown wouldn't keep his mouth shut. "But our hothead was a minor lieuten-ant, who may be disciplined. Yours, I believe, was your oldest son, a member of House Elhiyne."

AnnaRail continued to smile, though Theandrin could see she was finding it harder to do so. "My son's punishment is that he must face Olivia—daily."

Even BlakeDown cringed.

By the end of the evening they'd made no progress. The next day they met twice and fared no better. BlakeDown even introduced AnnaRail to Lewendis. JohnEngine bristled at the presence of the yokel, but kept his composure, though he made a visible effort to do so.

What was her husband thinking?

On the third day Theandrin orchestrated a carefully structured evening meal with just her, BlakeDown, ErrinCastle, AnnaRail and JohnEngine present. She had the servants set up a dining table in a small, comfortable room, made sure there was no brandy at hand, and instructed the cook to see to it that the wine was heavily watered. Alcohol would not be allowed to influence anyone's thinking, especially her husband's.

The meal started out pleasantly enough. She, AnnaRail and their two sons spoke of the coming winter. Both clans were well prepared, with plentiful grain stores and stocks of smoked and salted meat. But while they spoke her husband brooded silently, didn't join in the conversation, though at least he didn't glare at AnnaRail or JohnEngine. Why was he so intent on not finding common ground?

BlakeDown suddenly leaned forward and said, "Enough of this idle talk. We have an issue to discuss, and I'm tired of ignoring it."

In the silence that followed, both JohnEngine and ErrinCastle made visible efforts to control their anger. AnnaRail took a sip of wine and said, "You're right, Lord BlakeDown. We should deal with that issue before anything else. We should try to come to terms."

BlakeDown demanded, "Are you offering terms?"

"We certainly would consider offering some reparation to the families of the dead armsmen."

BlakeDown pressed her aggressively. "We're on the verge of war, and you offer reparation for a few unlanded armsmen?"

Theandrin decided to step in. "We don't need to be on the verge of war. We've had similar issues before, though I grant you it's been quite some time. And in any case, we have a common enemy in the Greater Clans, and they'd love to see us at war."

"Why do you say they are our enemy?" BlakeDown asked. "Certainly they are the enemy of Elhiyne, but I see no reason they need be the enemy of Penda."

JohnEngine stood and leaned forward, his hands on the table. ErrinCastle's mouth opened in surprise. Even Theandrin had trouble hiding her astonishment.

JohnEngine said, "You're insane if you think you can ally with the Decouix king."

Theandrin and AnnaRail both tried to speak, but BlakeDown shot to his feet, leaned across the table, his nose barely a finger's breadth from JohnEngine's. "And you're insane if you think you can draw Penda into your little war with Valso."

BlakeDown spun about, crossed the small room, kicked the door open and stormed out.

The next morning the Elhiyne's departed with nothing accomplished. And that evening Theandrin and BlakeDown had a monumental argument.

24

The One Shadow

CORT SPLASHED WATER on her face, wiped it with a towel and looked in the polished brass mirror on the wall. Behind her Tulellcoe was busy unpacking their gear, laying it out on the bed in their small room. She'd dearly love a real bath, but the inn they'd chosen in Durin was of medium quality. They dare not take a room in one of the better inns. Someone might recognize Tulellcoe.

They'd arrived the night before, too exhausted from the long ride to do anything but grab a quick meal in the common room, climb under the sheets and fall asleep.

"I could use some breakfast," she said. "And do you know of any place around here where I might buy a hot bath?"

Tulellcoe looked up from their gear, smiled, was about to say something when the knock on the door startled them both. Cort crossed the room, leaned close to Tulellcoe's ear and whispered, "You stand to the side where you're not visible from the hall and I'll answer it."

He nodded, lifted a dagger out of their gear and put his back to the wall behind the door. She stepped up to the door, opened it a crack and peered out into the hallway. A woman stood there in a long cloak with a hood thrown over her head, her face hidden by shadows beneath the hood. Behind her stood two Decouix armsmen. Her clothing spoke of money and the clan.

Cautiously, Cort asked, "What may I do for you, my lady?"

The woman hesitated, then spoke softly. "May I come in?"

Cort glanced at the two armsmen, and the woman added, "They're simply body guards. They'll remain out in the hall."

She turned her head and spoke over her shoulder. "Please wait farther down the hall. This is a private conversation."

The two armsmen strode to the end of the hall. The woman leaned toward Cort and whispered, "I wish to speak to Tulellcoe."

If this woman already knew, they had nothing to lose, so Cort stepped back and opened the door wider to admit her. She stepped into the room, Cort closed the door, the woman threw the hood back and turned to Tulellcoe. She had raven-black hair, an angled face drawn by strain and tension, though even then she was quite beautiful.

In a wispy, ethereal voice she said to Tulellcoe, "Darling, it has been a long time."

Tulellcoe's face softened with compassion. "Yes, Haleen, it has."

Cort knew that name, knew that Valso's sister stood before them.

Tulellcoe asked, "How did you know I was here?"

She took a step toward him. "Oh my darling, do you think it's possible for you to come to this city, and I not know it? Don't worry, I've told no one . . ." As an afterthought she added, ". . . especially not my brother." When she'd said that her voice had hardened with some unpleasant emotion.

She turned and looked at Cort, examined her carefully. "I see you have a new love." She smiled and turned back to Tulellcoe. "I'm glad. You deserve someone nice. But that means you haven't come to see me, so why have you come?"

"We're just passing through," Tulellcoe said.

She stepped toward him, reached out and ran a finger along the line of his jaw. "It's his wife, isn't it? My cruel brother is holding her captive, and you've come to rescue her. You were ever the gallant one, something I always liked about you."

Tulellcoe started to say something, but she held up her hand and said, "You needn't deny it."

She held her hand out, saying, "I made this for you."

Tulellcoe extended his hand, palm up. She dropped something into it and said, "It's a small charm. When you need help, touch it to your forehead and I'll know, and I'll meet you here the next morning, or I'll send a messenger with word on how we can meet."

She turned toward the door; Cort opened it and held it for her. She paused and turned back to Tulellcoe. "I'll help you get into the castle. You see, I hate my brother even more than I loved you. He took our child from me."

Tulellcoe gasped and staggered back a step as Haleen turned and walked out through the door.

••••

The Kingdom of Dreams had changed, had become a strange place of simple dreams without the clarity Rhianne had seen through Rhiannead's and Erithnae's eyes. She drifted without purpose, her dreams controlling themselves as dreams were want to do. She found Sabian deserted except for the occasional glimpse of another dreamer, translucent and only half there.

"My lady, you must awaken . . ."

She found no signs of the great battle that had nearly destroyed Sabian. There were no bodies lying about, neither jackal nor defender. The dirt of the castle yard seemed undisturbed, unmarked by foot or paw or hoof.

"My lady. Please. The king demands your presence. You must awaken."

Rhianne opened her eyes as Geanna shook her gently, forced herself to focus on the present. She needed to contact Morgin, and knew the only way she might do so was through the Kingdom of Dreams. But how could she get a message to him to meet her there when she could no longer control her dreams? She suspected now that her earlier sense of reality and control had come about only because he had been there.

Her handmaidens moved quickly, dressed her, combed her hair and set it elaborately atop her head, applied her makeup and had her ready for Valso in short order. Six Kulls escorted her to Valso's workshop on the third floor of the castle, where Carsaris and Valso waited, with the demon snake curled on its perch in the far corner. Valso sat on the edge of the heavy, wooden table he used as a workbench. Carsaris stood attentively nearby, and again she saw unease and fear in the sorcerer's demeanor.

When she entered the room, Valso said, "My lovely Rhianne, today you're going to see something quite instructive."

He turned to Carsaris and said, "Summon that recalcitrant archangel."

It appeared that Rhianne would not be the center of attention this day, so she slipped quietly to one side and put her back to a wall, trying to remain as inconspicuous as possible.

Carsaris didn't do anything obvious, but in a heartbeat a faint tendril of smoke appeared in the center of the room, accompanied by the smell of brimstone. The small coil of smoke swirled about, then thickened and grew until it took on the shape of a man. Bit by bit the smoke took on finer form and detail, and Rhianne recognized Metadan, whom she'd dreamed of through Erithnae's eyes.

The archangel bowed deeply to Valso, lowering his head and extending his arm with an elegant flourish. "You summoned me, Your Majesty?"

As the archangel stood straight Valso smiled at him pleasantly. "Metadan, I'm always humbled by your grace and beauty."

Metadan gave a slight nod of his head. "You flatter me, sire."

"Show me that sword of yours."

The archangel hesitated, and Rhianne noticed he carried no sword. "As Your Majesty wishes," he said. He held out his hand, and in a blink a magnificent broadsword appeared, its hilt in Metadan's outstretched hand. The blade dripped blood from the steel, drops of it splashing on the floor between Valso and the archangel.

Without looking over his shoulder at the snake, Valso said, "Bayellgae, is that the blade you told me about?"

The snake uncoiled and sprang off its perch, darted across the room to hover between Valso and Metadan. "No, massster. The blade I sssaw wasss the blackessst of night, a dark blade for a dark purpossse."

Valso's smile hardened and turned into a menacing grin. Then that thing Rhianne had sensed before entered the room. Valso seemed to swell, and his magic threatened to overwhelm her. When he spoke his voice came out in a rumble like thunder on the horizon. "You should not have chosen to defy me."

Metadan cringed, but said nothing.

That thing continued speaking. "It appears you can find him easily, on just a whim. And the snake tells me you are teaching him to fight the obsidian."

Metadan dropped to his knees. "But I—"

The thing roared, "Silence."

Metadan lowered his eyes.

Valso paced slowly around Metadan, speaking in that thing's voice, "What punishment shall you have?" As he spoke a wisp of smoke rose from one of Metadan's ears. "I thought you had learned the price for disobedience, but apparently I must teach it to you again."

Metadan raised his chin, his face contorted in a grimace, and he cried out, "Ahhh!"

Tendrils of smoke rose out of his mouth and nose, from his eyes and ears. He screamed, the sword vanished and he fell to the floor. He curled into a fetal ball, sickly yellow smoke coiling upward from his body. Rhianne thought he might burst into flames, but he simply continued to smoke and wither, screaming and begging, wasting away little by little. She closed her eyes and looked away, bile rising up into her throat as Metadan's pleas slowly diminished.

After silence filled the room, Rhianne waited several heartbeats, then opened her eyes. Valso stood over Metadan's withered corpse. In that thing's voice he said, "So, you can find him easily."

To Rhianne's utter horror the corpse opened its desiccated eyes and said, "No, master. When he wants me, only then do I feel the pull of his need."

Valso shook his head sadly. "Such a fool."

He looked up from the archangel's shriveled carcass, and again she saw madness in his eyes. He looked at her and said, "It appears I have many alternatives. I have the snake and Salula, and now I have the archangel. When next your husband needs his aid, he'll teach the whoreson a lesson of death."

••••

Morgin sat in his small camp south of the Lake of Sorrows and pondered the magic of shadows. In the Kingdom of Dreams when the jackal captain had taken Rhiannead captive, and Morgin had faced him in the clearing in the Living Forest, the shadow-wraith had helped him traverse a distance of 20 paces in an instant. Soann'Daeth'Daeye had stepped from one shadow to another, even though the shadows were separated. Morgin had assumed it was a thing only a shadowwraith could do, but the sensation he'd felt at the time had been both unusual and memorable, and that had haunted him. He decided to see if he could repeat that feat without the aid of the shadowwraith.

Morgin had chosen a small clearing for his camp, nothing as large as the clearing in which he'd faced the jackal captain, but he didn't need much room for this. He stood facing the ring of stones he'd assembled for a fire pit, closed his eyes and tried to recall every detail of the sensation he'd felt that day in the Kingdom of Dreams, a stomach twisting rush as if falling from a great height. He cast a shadow on the other side of the fire pit, cast one about himself and tried to repeat that feeling, but nothing happened. He tried several times, his frustration growing with each failed attempt. He finally gave up and decided to eat a light lunch.

It was while rummaging through his saddle bags that he recalled So-ann'Daeth'Daeye's words that day in the Kingdom of Dreams: *All shadows are but one. To walk in one is to walk in them all.*

He abandoned the thought of lunch and decided to try one last time. Again he cast a shadow on the other side of the fire pit and one about himself, but this time he didn't try to repeat that sensation. He simply decided that the two shadows were one and the same, and that all he needed to do to cross the distance was take a single step from one to the other. He did so, his gut tightened and he staggered as he felt the sensation of falling, but he caught himself, straightened and looked about from within his shadow.

It appeared that nothing had changed. He stood within one shadow facing another on the other side of the fire pit, his gear carefully stacked on the far side of the clearing. But then he recalled that when he'd started this experiment he'd been standing in the shadow near his gear with his back to it, not the one in which he stood now.

He spent the afternoon experimenting, trying to determine if there was a limit to the distance he could cross in a heartbeat. He had no trouble traversing 50 paces or more, but that was about the limit of the distance he could see through the forest growth. At one point he tried to picture a shadow in Elhiyne in an attempt to cross the intervening leagues without wasting days doing so, but that effort proved fruitless. He concluded that to step from one shadow to the next, he must see the other shadow. And that limited him to a distance of about a hundred paces.

That night, as he curled up in his blanket, he drifted off to sleep with a deep sense of satisfaction.

Morgin awoke just before dawn, ate a quick meal and packed up his gear. He'd just finished saddling Mortiss when Harriok arrived with Jack the Lesser riding beside him.

"Can't let you find Kathbeyanne without me," Jack said. "The two of you would probably end up walking in circles and eating sand."

"I thought it would be good to bring Jack," Harriok said. "He knows the sands better than me."

They'd brought one of the small pack animals they called a chakarra, primarily to carry extra water skins. The two whitefaces helped Morgin pack up his gear, he saddled Mortiss, and they headed into the forest east of the Lake. With the three of them on horseback, they made much better time than the tribe had in the spring, and reached the Plains of Quam by late afternoon.

Jack shielded his eyes from the sun and looked out at the flat, featureless landscape that stretched before them. "Might as well use the last few hours of sunlight. We can make a couple more leagues before nightfall." He nudged his horse into a walk.

Jack led, followed by Harriok with Morgin in the rear. But only about three hundred paces out onto the plains Jack pulled his horse to a halt, and sat in the saddle looking at something on the ground. When Morgin caught up to the whitefaces, he looked down and saw a few bones bleached white by the sun, among them a human skull. Most of the bones had been scattered by scavengers, but among them were a few rags of coarse, black cloth.

"Kull cloak?" Harriok asked.

Jack nodded his agreement.

Morgin stood up in his stirrups, tried to recall that night so long ago, hoped for some sort of distinguishing landmark. But out on the flat expanse of the plains, one location looked just like any other. He nudged Mortiss into a walk, and she meandered slowly eastward. After about 20 paces he spotted an old rusted sword lying in the dry grass and he pulled her to a halt. Harriok and Jack stopped beside him.

Morgin looked back at the bones and said, "Salula. Or rather, his host. Turns out I didn't kill the demon, just the human body he haunted."

Jack said, "Guess you'll have to kill him again."

Morgin thought of France and winced inwardly.

They rode east until the sun set, then stopped, lit a small fire with what little wood they could scrounge on the plains, and bedded down for the night.

25

Seeking the Prophesy

BLAKEDOWN REFUSED HER?

Walking casually through the market outside the walls of Penda, Chrisainne stopped and pretended some interest in a display of lace doilies.

No, Your Majesty. He didn't refuse AnnaRail outright, but argued against every point she tried to make. I could tell that she and Theandrin were quite frustrated by it all.

The workmanship in the doilies was actually quite good.

Excellent! Valso said. *Now I need BlakeDown to escalate the situation further.*

The woman behind the table displaying the doilies was a plain cow of a peasant. She perked up at Chrisainne's interest.

I'm concerned there, Your Majesty. Theandrin and ErrinCastle are pressuring him to act expediently. And he and Theandrin had a horrendous row after the Elhiyne's left. I'm sure it was about exactly that.

Chrisainne didn't really need another doily, so she smiled at the women, turned and continued on.

Damn! I need BlakeDown to act.

She slowed her pace. She dare not enter the castle grounds while in communication with Valso.

I think I can influence him, Your Majesty.

Good girl. Do whatever it takes.

Valso withdrew from her mind.

••••

Theandrin stood at the window of her sitting room looking down on the castle yard, her jaw clenched with frustration. Someone had triggered her charm-wards at the gates, someone of Vodah sympathies. She'd immediately rushed to the window and saw a few armsmen who had just passed through the gates walking into the yard. There was no one else close enough to have triggered the wards, and while she took note of the armsmen's faces, both were of low rank. They'd be absolutely useless as spies, could provide nothing more than rumors and base, castle gossip.

She stood there for quite some time trying to understand what had gone wrong. With her years of experience, she knew her spells and incantations, knew that her wards wouldn't have falsely triggered, and yet apparently they had. Once activated, they were now useless. She'd have to recast them.

She was about to turn away from the window when Chrisainne walked through the gates into the castle yard. Theandrin had noticed her before, walking out or back in, and as she thought back, she realized the girl had recently begun visiting the market outside the castle quite regularly. Chrisainne had reached the middle of the castle yard, and she was carrying no bundles. Perhaps she'd not found what she was looking for, or had just done a little casual shopping with no real intention of buying.

Vodah! Theandrin had not paid any attention to the girl's lineage. Could there be some Vodah in her background? When a woman took a husband and moved into his clan, as her loyalties shifted to that clan, her magic and powers naturally took on the new clan's aura. It worked the other way too, if for some political reason a man moved into his wife's clan. True loyalty carried with it a powerful tint. But if Chrisainne's allegiance hadn't changed . . . Could she have triggered the wards on her way out?

Theandrin decided she'd have to look into the girl's background, find out her original clan, and learn a bit more about her past. And she needed to keep pressure on the girl for more and better information.

••••

Standing at the window in her room, NickoLot looked down on the castle yard below, waiting with growing impatience for DaNoel to take his turn at sword practice.

Since planting one each of her silver and lead charms beneath DaNoel's bed, NickoLot had had to listen to the constant background din of his activities when in his room. The companion to the silver charm rested against the skin between her breasts, suspended by a chain about her neck and hidden beneath her dress. The silver charms weren't that strong, so the message the one in his room transmitted to its companion was most often just a weak impression of his activities.

The signal grew stronger when strong emotions or feelings were involved. One night, just after crawling beneath the blankets of her own bed, the sending grew strong and powerful and she thought she might be on to something. But then she realized DaNoel was just masturbating, and the thoughts he transmitted were quite disgusting. That night she lifted the charm away from her skin and placed it on the stand beside her bed, which dampened the signal nicely.

Today had been different. It had been midmorning, and she'd gotten so used to the background din of his activities it was like ignoring the drone of a fly buzzing near one ear. And then one single word had stuck out clear and sharp: *Valso*. Why the Decouix king, and why so emotionally charged?

When DaNoel began his turn at sword practice NickoLot turned immediately from the window and made her way down to his room, careful not to draw attention by hurrying. She used the prepared charm to open the spell lock on his door without deactivating it, stepped into the room and closed the door. It took but a moment to drop to her hands and knees, retrieve the lead charm from beneath his bed, and replace it with another.

She opened the door to his room just a crack and checked the hallway, stepped out, closed the door and reactivated his lock spell. She walked back up to her room, again careful not to hurry, sat down at her writing table and placed the shiny lump of metal on top of it. Lead, the silent metal, the container. She unbuttoned the stiff, high collar of her black gown, exposed the skin just above her breast and pressed the charm against it, then fed power into it.

. . . insane . . . war . . . Penda . . .

Disjointed words, or perhaps thoughts, flittered through her mind, clearly DaNoel's thoughts.

. . . can't do it . . .

Was he talking to himself, thinking to himself? It wasn't enough to act on, nothing even vaguely incriminating. But for some reason the thought of Valso had triggered something very strong in her brother.

She had one lead charm remaining. She decided to modify it. If she applied the white of Clan Decouix, could she sensitize it to anything DaNoel thought regarding Valso? She'd have to do a little research first, figure out the proper way to make the modification, then plant the charm in his room.

••••

Morgin awoke before dawn, and sensed immediately that the three of them were not alone. The small fire had long since burned out, he was tangled in his blanket and knew he'd be slow getting to his feet. The cold steel of a sword blade touched his cheek, and Blesset said, "Get up, Elhiyne."

Morgin moved slowly, rolled over and sat up. Jack and Harriok were already on their feet. When Morgin stood, Blesset touched the tip of her sword to his chest. Jack said, "Now Blesset."

She looked into Morgin's eyes for a moment, then lowered the sword and sheathed it. "I'm riding with you."

Morgin asked, "You want to go to Kathbeyanne?"

"No. I want to watch you waste yourselves on a fool's errand."

She turned and looked at Jack as if defying him to deny her. Jack shrugged and nodded toward Morgin. "It's up to him."

Morgin said, "Looks like she's riding with us."

They pushed the horses a bit and reached the sands after nightfall. To avoid the heat of the daytime sun they continued on, the glow of a half-moon guiding their steps as they rode down one dune and up another. It was a monotonous trek, and Morgin drifted off into a light doze.

As the sun rose the next morning Jack stood up in his stirrups to scan the horizon. All Morgin saw was an ocean of sand ending in more dunes in every direction. They were close to Aelldie so they continued on and reached the oasis well before noon, replenished their water skins, camped there briefly and moved on at nightfall.

In the middle of their second night out, Morgin felt that arcane pull again, at first a faint sensation, but it grew stronger with each step. At sunrise, while the whitefaces set camp he climbed to the top of a dune, shaded his eyes with his hand and saw the city of tall, glassy spires on the horizon. The three whitefaces joined him at the top of the dune.

Harriok shaded his eyes and said, "Kathbeyanne."

Jack said, "The city of glass."

Blesset said nothing.

Morgin stood facing the city squarely. He closed his eyes, but now he sensed its arcane magic off to the left. He opened his eyes, and still it appeared to be directly ahead. He closed his eyes again, extended his arm and pointed in the true direction of the city. "It lies that way. We'll sleep through the day. Then tonight, when none of us can see the mirage, I'll lead us to the true city of glass."

••••

Theandrin and BlakeDown hosted a small reception for Torthan et Tosk, heir to the House of Tosk. Chrisainne donned one of her most revealing gowns, and at the reception played BlakeDown like a finely tuned harp. She made sure she was always within his line of sight, never winked or did anything overt, but tempted him with little things. Several times, when he happened to look her way, she ran her tongue across her lips, slowly, provocatively. Once, when he was near, and with no one else looking, she leaned forward just a bit. She'd chosen this particular gown because it was cut low and slightly loose around the bodice. It tended to billow out when she leaned like that, giving him an enticing view of a lot of skin. With Theandrin and half his liege lords and their ladies present, he stayed on his best behavior, didn't dare try anything, but near the end he brushed past her and whispered, "I'll meet you later in your bedroom." He sounded almost desperate.

Chrisainne didn't want to meet him in her bedroom, not at first. He'd just slam her down on the bed, rut on her for a few moments, spill his seed and be gone. So as the festivities broke up she enticed Silaya et Tosk to join her in the west garden. Silaya was young, impressionable, and quite flattered at the attention.

The night was cool and comfortable as Chrisainne strolled down a path with the young girl. She pretended to be entertained by Silaya's naive banter, but kept an eye open for BlakeDown, knew he couldn't help himself.

On the far side of the garden she saw him step out of the castle proper and start walking her way hurriedly. But when he spotted Silaya he slowed his pace, and tried to appear casual as he approached them.

"Lady Chrisainne," he greeted them. "Lady Silaya."

They both curtsied, and Chrisainne took care to give him a good, long view down the front of her dress. When she rose and lifted her eyes to look in his face, he blinked and gulped.

He asked Silaya, "Did you enjoy yourself, young lady?"

"Oh, yes, Your Grace," she said, breathlessly excited and thrilled as only a young girl from the family of a minor lord would be.

"But aren't you a bit young to be out this late? I don't want your mother angry with me."

"You're right, Your Grace," she said, "but I was so excited to walk with Lady Chrisainne. With your leave, I'll go to my room now."

BlakeDown nodded his approval, she curtsied, and rushed away from them.

"Thank you for rescuing me," Chrisainne said. "I couldn't get rid of the poor girl. Otherwise I would have met you in my bedroom as you wished."

"That's all right," he said, though he almost trembled with the tension of his unsatisfied lust. "Let's walk this way."

They were in a public place, so he dare not touch her. She kept her pace slow, needed time to make this work. "How did it go with the Tosks, my lord?"

"They've reluctantly agreed to support me if I choose to act against Elhiyne, though I gave them a somewhat edited version of the events on the border. We must appear to be the wronged party."

"Will you act soon?"

"I don't know. Theandrin is against acting at all. And she's making my life miserable."

"Hmmm!" she said.

"What's bothering you?"

"Well . . . I shouldn't say, my lord."

"Out with it."

"Well . . . I mean no disrespect to your lady wife, but . . . and I say this as a woman myself, a woman who is as intelligent as any . . . but what do we women know of such things? We haven't trained in war, have no experience at it. How can we make proper decisions? Why . . . it would seem to me we're not even qualified to advise men like you, what with all of your experience and knowledge."

He stopped in his tracks and turned to face her, his chest swelling with pride. He was an easy one to flatter. "You're right." He spit each word like one might spit seeds from a melon. "I've been a fool."

"No, my lord, you're never a fool."

He turned back to the path and started walking. "I was a fool to consult Theandrin, and that won't happen again. It's time I did what needed doing."

At that point they reached the entrance to the castle, and once inside turned different ways. It would not do for him to openly accompany her to her bedroom.

When she closed her bedroom door, she didn't have long to wait. He knocked quietly, she opened it, he stepped into the room and clutched at her breasts before she even had the door closed. He pushed her on her back on the bed, lifted her skirts, groped at her crotch, tore her small clothes and thrust into her. He pounded in and out of her, his anger fueling his lust, was done in a matter of moments. He pulled up his pants and left.

She realized that, with him, she actually preferred it that way. It was quick and dirty and done with, and she didn't have to waste a lot of time flattering him and pretending she enjoyed herself. And he was gone.

Chrisainne was pleased with the night's work. She'd grown weary of Theandrin's constant badgering for more information. It would be nice to be present when Theandrin learned BlakeDown had decided to ignore her counsel, to see the look on the old witch's face.

••••

Theandrin carefully examined the doorway that led from the outer hall into her sitting room. She'd made six more of the blue-thread charms, and last night at midnight she'd placed them around the threshold: six threads for Penda, combined with the blue of Vodah. She'd started early that morning, had summoned the least likely candidates one at a time, first the two guardsmen she'd seen walking through the castle yard, then Lewendis. As each crossed the threshold into her sitting room, her charms confirmed her suspicions: none of them carried Vodah loyalties.

She turned to the young servant girl sitting in the corner sorting the spools of thread for stitching. "Would you kindly summon the Lady Chrisainne."

The girl hopped to her feet and bobbed a quick curtsy, saying, "Yes, milady."

She walked quickly out of the room, and Theandrin turned to the window overlooking the castle yard to wait. She'd looked into Chrisainne's background, learned that she'd been born Chrisainne et Vodah.

Time passed, and she concluded the girl hadn't found Chrisainne in her room and had to go searching for her. She was probably somewhere fucking BlakeDown, or the stable boy, or the stable master, or Lewendis, or whoever else she chose to spread her legs for.

When Chrisainne entered the room, Theandrin knew it instantly, for her charms triggered and rang a bell of triumph in her soul.

Behind her, Chrisainne said, "You wished to see me, my lady."

Theandrin turned and gave her a neutral look, careful not to give the slightest indication she now knew the girl was a spy for Valso. "Yes," she said. She wanted to see the little slut squirm. "What have you learned from Lewendis and my husband about the border?"

The charms had triggered rather strongly, and Theandrin was confident that when she had a chance to examine them more closely, she'd find that the girl's loyalties had remained unchanged.

Theandrin quizzed her unmercifully, learned a little, but nothing of significance, then dismissed her. The only question that remained was what to do with the girl. Certainly, at some point she would expose her, BlakeDown would undoubtedly have her removed, and they'd be rid of her. On the other hand, a spy who didn't know she'd been discovered could be of some use. Theandrin decided to let her continue without hindrance, but keep a close eye on her.

It occurred to her that overconfidence here would be unwise. She reminded herself to never forget that the little slut could be far more dangerous than simply a pair of spread legs. The girl was a reasonably strong witch, had no compunction about anything, and to forget that could be fatal. It would be wise to make certain preparations: something extra to protect herself and her family, and something special to control the girl if it came to that. Chrisainne was not a weakling when it came to spell-crafting, so it would have to be something powerful. Theandrin smiled as she considered what she might do.

26

Prophesy Thwarted

MORGIN WANDERED THROUGH the Kingdom of Dreams. The Living Forest opened a path before him that led to Sabian, but the castle was deserted now, no sign of its past inhabitants. He saw a ghostly image if a woman, partially transparent, wandering in a daze through the castle yard in a floor-length bed gown, realized she was a dreamer. There were many of them, appearing and disappearing as their dreams came and went.

Could he find Rhianne, talk to her, try to plan her escape from Valso? He wandered down to the room and the bed they had shared, longed to hold her in his arms again, and swore that he would let nothing prevent him from doing so. But how would she know to meet him here? They might both come here at random times and never cross paths.

Right now he lay asleep in a Benesh'ere tent out on the sands of the Munjarro, sleeping through the day. He needed to get this prophesy thing over with, so he could return to sleeping at nights. He'd have a much better chance of finding her then.

He went back to the castle yard, to the spot near the wall where Erithnae had died. With his boot heel he scratched a message in the dirt: *Meet me here at dawn*. He didn't sign it, trusted that she would know it was from him. He looked up at the walls that surrounded him and said, "Sabian, please preserve this for Rhianne's eyes, and if she comes to this kingdom, make sure she sees it." He wasn't sure if the castle could really control a dreamer that way, but he had to try.

He awoke in the late afternoon, spent the remaining heat of the day in his tent wondering if he'd ever see his Rhianne again.

After the sun set, Morgin and his companions packed up their camp and set out for Kathbeyanne. In the dark Morgin didn't really need to wear a blindfold, but doing so prevented him from trying to make use of the dim moonlight and his shadow sight, forced him to rely purely on his arcane sense of the ancient city. Wearing the blindfold, he pointed the way and they rode their horses at an easy pace across the sands.

Deep in his gut Morgin feared there would be no city when they got there, that even his magical senses were being misled by ancient enchantments. He'd said nothing to his companions of these fears, but the previous morning the city had appeared to be no more than a single night's journey. So he'd sworn to himself that if they didn't reach it this night, he'd abandon the search, and leave the city to its ancient ghosts.

Even blindfolded he could tell when Mortiss struggled to climb up the side of a dune, felt it when she reached the peak then started down the other side, only to climb another. He noticed a dim, yellowish light leaking through the blindfold, and realized dawn was approaching, and feared that he had failed again. Then Mortiss and the other horses topped a dune, and Jack said, "By the gods!"

Harriok answered, awe in his voice, "Aye, friend. By the gods!"

Morgin ripped the blindfold off and saw that before them stretched the ancient city. What appeared from a distance to be magnificent spires jutting toward the heavens, they now saw were nothing more than broken shards of glassy stone, jagged spikes testifying to the ruin of Kathbeyanne. Through the centuries the sands had encroached and buried many of the buildings, while most of those still visible were nothing more than tumbled blocks of broken masonry. With Morddon's memories, he realized that even though they still stood on dunes of sand, they were well into what had once been part of the city proper.

"You've done it," Blesset said, a note of awe in her voice. "You brought us to the city of glass."

Harriok said, "It's enormous."

Harriok had never seen a real city before. To Morgin's eyes, Kathbeyanne was now a mere shadow of what it had once been. With Morddon's memories to guide him, he thought he could find the old center of the city. "Come," he said, and nudged Mortiss forward.

As they moved off the sands and in among the crumbled, ancient buildings, Morgin thought he sensed life within the city, as if it hadn't been completely abandoned, but the feeling passed quickly. They came to an intersection of two large avenues. Blesset started and pointed up at the side of a partially intact building. "In that window up there."

On the second floor Morgin saw a dark, black square, heavily shadowed by the bright sunlight.

"I saw someone standing there looking down at us."

Jack spoke with a harsh note of skepticism. "I don't see anyone."

They continued on. Morgin now recognized this part of the city. The first time Morddon had come to Kathbeyanne, he'd walked these streets on his way to the palace of the Shahotma. He'd stopped in a weapons maker's shop to buy a sheath for the naked sword he was carrying, and he'd been appalled at the poor quality of the steel the man offered.

Harriok started, thought he saw someone standing in a doorway. Jack thought he saw someone looking at them from the depths of a dark alley. Interestingly enough, Morgin saw none of these apparitions, though his companions grew quite skittish, were jumping at every shadow they encountered. And then the street they rode down opened onto the magnificent parade ground at the center of the city. The vast open space was littered with blocks of broken masonry and wind-blown piles of sand. At the far end the once magnificent palace of the Shahotma had been reduced to a single, square facade. The balconies and balustrades no longer soared high above the city, and gone were the spires that reached toward the heavens. It saddened him.

Out of curiosity, Morgin led them to the barracks of the first legion of angels. They dismounted; Morgin didn't have to worry about Mortiss, and the well-trained Benesh'ere mounts would not wander. There was no longer a door on the opening at the front of the barracks. Standing just outside the threshold he saw that the roof had collapsed, filling the interior with rubble.

He stepped across the threshold and the rubble disappeared. The roof above him was whole and undamaged, the interior walls sported paintings and banners celebrating the victories of the legion, and a cool breeze promised a pleasant afternoon. He turned around and looked for his companions, but they too had disappeared, though through the doorway he saw that the parade ground was clear of all the rubble, and had returned to its original glory. He heard the sound of sad pipes, turned back and found Metadan standing in the center of the room.

The archangel said, "Magnificent, isn't it?"

"No," Morgin said. "This is just a memory. You're just a memory. The glory of Kathbeyanne is gone forever."

The memory of Metadan lowered his head and wept openly.

Morgin turned back to the door and walked out of the barracks. As he crossed the threshold the parade ground returned to its state of decay. He heard something behind him, turned and found his three companions emerging from the barracks. "Just more decay," Jack said.

Obviously, they had not shared Morgin's experience.

He looked toward the palace at the far side of the parade ground, felt drawn to it. "Come," he said to the whitefaces. "I think someone's waiting for me."

All that remained of the palace of the Shahotma was the front wall of the great throne room, with a gaping hole where enormous bronze doors had once stood. Inside, the remains of three walls and the roof formed an enormous pile of rubble.

Morgin said, "Wait out here. I think this is what I came for."

Like the barracks, when he stepped across the threshold the throne room returned to it past glory. Tapestries draped much of the walls, depicting the glories of the great Shahotma Kings. Where the walls were bare, they were colored with frescoes and gilt.

Morgin stood on one end of a long strip of red carpet that led arrow-straight down the center of the room, ending at the base of a high dais upon which rested three thrones. Someone sat on each of the thrones, but the distance was too great for Morgin to make out any details.

On either side of the red carpet courtiers filled the hall dressed in finery beyond imagining. And yet they were nothing more than ghostly specters of past glory, translucent and frozen in time.

In another time and place Morgin would have sought some means of escaping this dream, but he recalled Metadan's prophesy: . . . *in the city of glass, beneath the fires of the eternal sun, you will ask three questions, and you will gain three answers, and in them you will know yourself far more than any mortal should.*

Morgin stepped forward boldly and marched down the red carpet. As he approached the dais he saw that, like the courtiers, the beings that occupied the three thrones were ghostly specters. He realized they didn't truly exist, were just memories buried in the rubble of the great city.

In the throne on the right sat a woman of incredible beauty, but her splendor was cold and lifeless. The man on the throne in the middle shared her beauty, and its lifeless vacancy. But a monster sat on the throne on the left, a being with the head of a goat, and blood-red eyes. Morgin knew then that he looked upon three gods.

It occurred to him it was no coincidence he must also ask three questions. So he looked to the woman and asked, "Who are you?"

She smiled at him, though it was a look that made Olivia's coldest stare seem warm.

"I am Augis," she said, and Morgin realized the river south of the Lake of Sorrows had been named after a forgotten god. "And within me is the first goddess of Kathbeyanne, mistress and guardian of all that once was."

Morgin looked to the man on the middle throne. "And who are you?"

"I am Attun," he said, his voice booming through the hall, the namesake of the mountain Attunhigh. "And within me is the first god of Kathbeyanne, lord and guardian of all that is now."

Morgin looked to the monster on the third throne. He knew what the third question was supposed to be. And he knew what the answer would be. The woman: guardian of all that once was. The man: all that is now. The monster: all that *will be.* Morgin couldn't allow that. He knew that the gods had manipulated his life, a life that apparently had spanned centuries.

The monster, the Dark God, leaned forward with a look of greedy anticipation. He wanted Morgin to ask that question, needed Morgin to ask it. In that moment Morgin wondered what would happen if he didn't ask it, if he didn't blindly follow the dictates of the gods. Could he break that cycle of manipulation? What could they do to punish him, torture him at the forges for centuries, wound him, kill him? They'd already done that.

The Dark God snarled with rage. "Ask the question, mortal."

Morgin was confident that if he completed the cycle of the prophesy, the monster in front of him wouldn't simply manifest then and there to rule the Mortal Plane. The three beings he faced now were just memories; they had no real power over any plane of existence. *So why am I here*, he wondered. *What is the purpose of this prophesy?*

The monster said, "That's not the right question. You cannot know yourself until you ask the right question."

Morgin hadn't spoken his thoughts aloud, but somehow the monster knew them. He looked up at the dark god, leaning forward on its throne in anticipation of his words, and knew then the truth of this farce. The only thing or being these *memories* could influence was him, a simple, mortal man. They'd manipulated him throughout his life, led him down the paths they chose, and this charade was nothing more than an attempt to complete his training. If they taught him the taste of defeat again and again, he would come to accept it readily.

"Ask the question, mortal."

Morgin feared any words he might utter, so he simply turned and began walking back down the red carpet.

The Dark God's voice shook the walls of the great throne room. "Ask the question, mortal. Ask the question."

Morgin had only made it a few paces down the red carpet when the ghostly specter of the monster coalesced in front of him, the fires of netherhell burning in its eyes. "Ask the question, mortal. Fulfill the prophesy if you wish to know yourself."

Morgin said, "You're just a memory, and not a very good one at that." He drew his sword.

The monster looked at the blade and his eyes flashed with fear. He stepped back and grew less substantial with each heartbeat, until nothing of him remained.

As Morgin continued down the red carpet the monster's voice boomed louder and louder, "Ask the question, mortal." But with every step Morgin took it sounded as if it came from a far greater distance. It wasn't more than a hundred paces to the far end of the hall, and yet with each step it sounded as if he'd crossed leagues to leave the memories of the three gods behind. Just before he reached the entrance he sheathed his sword, and when he stepped out of the hall silence descended.

His Benesh'ere companions were waiting for him there. He glanced back over his shoulder into the great throne room, and once again it was filled with nothing but rubble and decay. Oddly enough, in breaking the cycle of prophesy, he now knew himself more than ever before.

He said, "There are no good memories left here. Let's go home."

••••

With three twelves of mounted armsmen and four twelves of archers to support him, BlakeDown sat on an old tree stump and watched his workmen move cartload after cartload of stones. He'd allowed the armsmen to dismount and relax, but had ordered them to keep their horses saddled and ready, and he'd sent scouts out ranging quite far. With nothing to do his armsmen and archers grew bored and sat about gossiping and gambling.

Here in the far western marches the border between Penda and Alcoa's lands had been demarcated by an old line of tumbled-down stones that had once been a wall. About five hundred paces south of the border a good-sized creek fed a large pond that made for an excellent watering hole for cattle, even in the dryer months of summer. BlakeDown had coveted it most of his life, as had his father before him, for with control of creek and pond he could expand his herds. Chrisainne had thought of the solution: simply move the border south so the creek and pond were on his lands. She was actually quite smart—for a woman.

One of his lieutenants stood and pointed. "There, my lord. One of the scouts."

BlakeDown stood, saw the scout riding hard toward them. "Tell the men to mount up and get ready." He had anticipated this.

One of the armsmen brought him his mount, he climbed into the saddle and had just settled there when the scout reined his horse to a halt in front of him.

"Your Grace," the man said, breathing heavily. "Three twelves of Elhiyne armsmen about two leagues west of here, approaching slowly. Probably Alcoa's men, led by a lieutenant, not Alcoa himself."

"Did you recognize the lieutenant?"

"No, my lord. We didn't get close enough."

After two days of moving stones the workmen had almost finished the job. They'd started at the western end near a small woodland, so BlakeDown now had a new border behind which to confront the Elhiyne patrol. And the woodland was large enough to hide his four twelves of archers.

BlakeDown turned to the leader of the archers. "Do as we planned."

"Yes, my lord."

The day before, as the workmen were just beginning to move the stones, BlakeDown and his lieutenants had planned for every possible approach the Elhiyne border patrol might make. The western approach, near the woodland, was the best of all for his purposes. The archers quickly concealed themselves in the brush of the woodland.

To the lieutenant of his armsmen, BlakeDown said, "Send two twelves of your men north. We won't need them for this, and I want them out of sight."

As the two twelves rode away, he and his remaining twelve rode to the new border near the woodland and waited there.

He first spotted the Elhiynes about a thousand paces distant, riding easily, probably anticipating a routine day patrolling the border. When they saw BlakeDown and his men, the Elhiyne lieutenant raised his hand and brought his men to a halt. BlakeDown couldn't hear him, but he saw him barking orders. Then they rode forward and stopped about 20 paces short of the new border.

"What is this?" the man demanded without introducing himself.

BlakeDown kept his voice calm and even. "What is what?" He looked from side to side. "I believe this is nothing more than a routine meeting on our mutual border."

The Elhiyne had trouble containing his anger. He swept a hand out, indicating the line of stones. "This is not our border."

"Why, I do believe it is," BlakeDown said, grinning. "Our border has been this line of stones for centuries."

The Elhiyne's eyes fluttered with anger and disbelief. "But you've moved the stones." He pointed to the workmen moving the last cartloads of stones. "You've changed the border."

BlakeDown pointedly looked up and down the line of stones. "I do believe I have. And so we have a new border. There's no reason we can't continue as before."

The man looked at the line of stones, the workmen, the pond and the creek. Last of all he looked at BlakeDown's single twelve of men. BlakeDown could almost see the wheels turning as the man realized that, with his three twelves, he had the Penda's outnumbered. He calmed and said, "I must insist that you withdraw your armsmen, and have your workmen return the stones to their original place."

BlakeDown hardened his voice, "You may insist all you want, but the stones are moved, and they will remain moved."

The Elhiyne drew his sword, and his armsmen followed suit. "If you do not withdraw willingly, then I will have no choice but to force you to do so."

BlakeDown drew his own sword, did so slowly and carefully, and his men followed suit. "Then force away," he said.

He and the Elhiyne locked eyes, a silent challenge during which BlakeDown made sure the man saw he would not flinch.

The man shouted, "Charge," and spurred his horse.

BlakeDown raised his own sword, slashed it downward and cried, "Now."

The archer's in the forest rose from their hiding places and four twelves of arrows hissed through the air, feathering man and horse alike. The battle was over in a dozen heartbeats, and BlakeDown and his armsmen had not even needed their swords.

There remained a few wounded Elhiyne still alive, but BlakeDown's men dispatched them quickly.

27

Treason Revealed

WHEN THEY REACHED The God's Road east of the Lake of Sorrows, Morgin and his Benesh'ere friends paused to water their horses and share a meal of trail rations. They sat in a circle within the forest, and as they ate, Jack said, "There's been a strangeness about you since we left Kathbeyanne. Something happened there, didn't it?"

Morgin hadn't told them of Metadan's prophesy, nor of his experience in the city of glass. He did so now, and when he finished Blesset demanded, "So you refused to ask the third question? Have you broken the chain of prophesy?"

They all knew her concern was the seventh wrong. Clearly she feared he would fail to right it and free the Benesh'ere.

Jack said, "Watch your tongue, girl."

She stood. "If he fails at one prophesy, will he fail at others?"

"He didn't *fail*," Harriok said. "He chose not to follow their whims. He's taken control of these prophesies, and that strengthens my confidence in him."

They argued throughout the brief meal, and neither Harriok nor Jack could convince Blesset that Morgin wouldn't cheat them of their freedom. And Morgin couldn't be certain she was wrong.

They parted there, the three Benesh'ere returning to their camp, Morgin heading south to Kallun's Gorge. Before he could right the seventh wrong, he had to figure out how to right the sixth, and he had no idea how he might do that.

They'd already used up most of the day so he camped that night in the forest south of the lake, awoke the next morning feeling confident and renewed. There was no question in his mind that he'd done the right thing by not asking the third question.

He looked about, didn't see Mortiss, figured she'd probably found a bush full of berries to dine upon. He thought it might be good to exercise his sword arm, hoped that Metadan would show up that day. He was thinking about a light meal of trail rations when he heard the familiar sound of the pipes. He looked up to see Metadan striding toward him carrying his naked sword in one hand, not the obsidian blade but the sword that dripped the blood of the first legion. The archangel's eyes were pinched and strained, and he trembled as if struggling under a great weight.

"Is something troubling you?" Morgin asked as the angel approached.

Morgin heard Mortiss's hooves pounding on the forest floor an instant before she cried a nether scream of fear and anger. She burst into the small clearing at full charge and he dove to one side to avoid being ridden down. She continued past him, charging at Metadan, and as she slammed into the archangel she and he disappeared in a flash.

Morgin jumped to his feet and drew his sword, trying to look in all directions at once and wondering what had just happened. Metadan appeared in front of him, his sword already swinging around in a flat arc aimed at taking off Morgin's head. He ducked and threw his own sword up, clumsily deflecting the blow, which bought him the instant needed to regain his balance and drop into a defensive crouch.

Metadan's eyes glowed with hellfire as Morgin demanded, "What are you doing?"

Metadan screamed and charged, swung his sword with both hands in a high arc. Morgin back-stepped, parried the blow, and struck back. Their swords rang as they traded blows back and forth. Then they disengaged and circled in a fighting crouch.

Morgin demanded again, "What are you doing?"

Metadan ignored him and charged in. The archangel fought without his usual finesse, simply slammed strike after strike at Morgin with feverish insanity. Morgin tried to control the steel in Metadan's blade, but it was as dead as the first legion, and he found no life in it to answer his commands.

Metadan came in with a series of blows that were easily predictable. Morgin deflected them, then thrust at the angel's chest. It would have been a death stroke had Metadan not vanished in a puff of gray smoke.

Morgin heard a twig snap behind him, dropped, spun and kicked out, caught Metadan in the knee where he'd reappeared at his back. The archangel grunted with pain and staggered backward. Morgin swung his sword out, and again Metadan vanished.

Morgin knew what to expect, knew that Metadan would appear behind him in an instant, decided that two could play that game. He cast two shadows, one about himself, another behind where he knew Metadan would reappear, and with no more than a thought stepped from one to the next. The archangel reappeared as expected and slashed his sword through the first shadow. Now behind him, Morgin thrust with his sword's point, but the archangel disappeared an instant before the steel passed through him, slicing through the smoke he'd left behind.

Morgin stepped into another shadow just as Metadan reappeared behind him. Their contest turned into a strange dance of smoke and shadows, the angel disappearing an instant before Morgin's sword struck the column of smoke he'd left behind, then reappearing behind Morgin to strike at him. Each time Morgin disappeared into a shadow a hair's breadth ahead of the angel's steel, then stepped out of another behind Metadan. They repeated the sequence a dozen times, and as Morgin tired he recalled how Metadan could fight on with no sign of fatigue. It was a game he could not win, so Morgin ended it by casting a shadow well outside the small clearing, stepping into it, and not stepping out. He held his silence and his breath.

Metadan hesitated in the clearing, disappeared and reappeared several times in different places. He finally stopped, stood in the middle of the clearing and cried, "I must take your life Lord Mortal. It is not by my choice, but until death frees me I must bend to the will of my master. I will come for you again, and you will not again escape me." He disappeared and did not return.

Morgin waited in his shadow until well past noon. Even when Mortiss walked into the clearing calmly and without hurry, he retained his shadows as he saddled her, gathered up his gear, and rode towards the Gorge. He didn't think he would again be practicing his sword skills with Metadan anytime soon, though he wondered what had brought on the angel's sudden change of heart.

••••

Rhianne's handmaidens had just dressed her for bed in a floor-length nightgown when Geanna entered her boudoir and announced, "His Majesty wishes to see you."

Rhianne looked down at her nightgown and said, "But I'm not dressed."

"Don't worry," Geanna said. "We have an excellent robe for you that will be modest and appropriate."

Rhianne was skeptical until Geanna produced a floor-length robe quite like something Olivia might wear when receiving someone in her small audience chamber. It was heavy with brocade, hooded, with a double flap on the front tied off by laces. It concealed her completely toes to chin, covered her much more than the gowns she was forced to wear on a daily basis.

Valso awaited her in her sitting room, seated comfortably on a couch. When she walked into the room he stood, took her hand and kissed it, bowing with a flourish. He could be quite elegant, as long as one didn't know to look for the evil beneath the surface. And she could not deny that he was handsome; her handmaidens twittered constantly about his striking features.

"Rhianne, my dear," he said, stepping back and admiring her. "Even prepared for bed, without the paints and makeup you ladies place such store in, even then you are lovely."

He reached out and ran a finger lightly across her lips. His touch sent a thrill through her, and she steeled herself to be ready. But then she realized she was being foolish, overreacting to her own natural response to the touch of a handsome man.

There was nothing to fear this night, especially since she was bundled up nicely with almost no skin showing. And yet she hungered to feel that thrill again.

She forced herself to turn away from him, took two steps and tried to still her racing heart as she said, "What may I do for Your Majesty?"

He put his hand on her shoulder, though she hadn't heard him cross the distance between them. She noticed then that Geanna and the girls were conspicuously absent. She turned around and felt a desire to be closer to him so she stepped forward. He had a kingly profile; she reached up and touched his jaw and that thrill ran through her again.

Noooooooooooo!

He leaned forward and kissed her lightly on the lips, and her vomit spell didn't activate. With his lips only a hair's breadth from her face, he said, "I see you're disappointed that your little spell didn't work this time."

He shook his head sadly. "I found the vomiting spell easily, and deactivated it. You should have thought of something new and original, something I wouldn't anticipate."

She tried to keep the look on her face neutral, but he must have seen something there. He leaned back, cocked his head and said, "There's something else, isn't there? I saw it in your eyes just now."

He stepped back, putting a little distance between them. "What is it? Tell me?"

She felt an overwhelming desire to keep nothing from him. "Boils," she said. "When you touch my breasts I'll break out in boils, disgusting pustules oozing yellowish ichor. The vomiting spell was just a feint."

"Oh you little vixen," he said. "I would have found that quite disgusting, and it certainly would have dampened my ardor."

She felt the tendrils of his magic fluttering at the edges of her soul. "There it is. I've found it. And quite nicely done too, difficult to spot."

His magic washed through her and the spell she'd spent so much time preparing dissipated. In a heartbeat it was gone.

Noooooooooooo!

He took her in his arms, kissed her, and she responded passionately. "Now we're going to truly enjoy ourselves. Or, at least, I will."

Noooooooooooo!

He led her into the bed chamber, unlaced the robe Geanna had provided to cover her up. She stepped out of it willingly and he tossed it aside. She tugged at his pants, desperately driven by desire beyond anything she'd ever felt. He turned her about, undid the laces of her nightgown and dropped it to the floor. She felt not the least bit modest standing there naked in front of him.

Noooooooooooo!

He tugged at his own pants, finished the job she'd started, pulled off his tunic and threw it aside. He wrapped her in his arms and kissed her. She felt his penis against her belly growing erect, and for some reason she found a tiny bit of humor in that. A chuckle escaped her lips.

He pressed her on her back on the bed, climbed on top of her, groped at her crotch and tried to stick his finger in her. That was even funnier, and she couldn't contain a short laugh. He hesitated and looked at her oddly, then resumed his groping.

They were both breathing heavily now, panting and groaning, and that was the funniest thing of all. A full-throated laugh burst out of her, then another, and another.

"I'm so sorry, Your Majesty," she said, gasping for air, gulping and giggling like a young girl. She tried desperately to find nothing funny in the look on his face, but she hiccoughed, and that sent her into another round of wild laughter.

He pushed up off her, and she noticed his penis was growing limp, and that brought on even more laughter. She could hardly breathe she was laughing so hard, her stomach muscles straining with the effort.

He slid off her, stepped off the bed, a look of horror on his face. He swung out and slapped her, and that too was funny, though it didn't mask the pain of the fiery burn on her cheek.

He slapped her again, and the pain brought her memories back in a rush. The vomiting spell had been a feint, and the boil-spell a double-feint. The laughter spell had been easy. The hard part had been the memory spell to make her forget. She had to forget both the memory and laughter spells so completely he couldn't make her tell her own secrets.

He hit her in the jaw with his closed fist. His face had blossomed a bright red and tears streamed down his cheeks as he screamed and hit her. It was all so funny, even when she ended up on the floor, and lay there laughing as he kicked her and beat her into unconsciousness.

••••

NickoLot stood on the battlements and watched the armsmen marching toward the Penda border. Two days ago a messenger from Alcoa had arrived with news that BlakeDown had moved the border to take possession of a strategic water supply, then massacred one of Alcoa's patrols. Both clans were now fortifying the border, though no one had yet declared open war.

She stood there for quite some time, waiting as the marching armsmen disappeared over the horizon. She waited further, then heard a shout down in the yard, the rumble of horse's hooves, and below her a large company of mounted Elhiynes rode out through the castle gates, DaNoel among them.

In the wee hours of the morning her charms had alerted her to the mention of Valso's name in DaNoel's room. But the castle had been a beehive of activity, and she'd waited through most of the day for the men to leave. With DaNoel now out of the castle, there was no need to hurry, or even to lurk about as she walked down to his room. She retrieved the lead charm that she'd sensitized with Decouix white, and returned to her own room.

She repeated the process of unbuttoning the stiff, high collar of her gown, placing the charm against her skin and feeding it with her power.

. . . act now to stop him . . .

. . . keep my name out of it . . .

. . . fear not my friend . . .

NickoLot's heart almost stopped beating, and she felt a tear roll down her cheek; a two sided conversation of thoughts, one DaNoel, and the other Valso. Her brother, a traitor, not just conniving or sneaking about, but out-and-out treason. This would break AnnaRail's heart as nothing else could.

She sat there for quite a long time, even as her room darkened with the setting sun. She debated back and forth, a schizophrenic argument between her and herself; should she tell her mother, could she tell her mother? Finally, with a heavy heart, she buttoned her high collar, stood, and carrying the charm as proof, walked out of her room.

At the door to AnnaRail's apartments she hesitated, was about to knock when Olivia's voice stopped her, "Hold, child."

Olivia marched down the hall toward her, didn't stop as she reached her, but took her by the upper arm in a painful grip and dragged her down the hallway with her.

"What are you doing?" NickoLot demanded.

"We're going to talk, girl, before you break your mother's heart."

The old woman's words stunned her. Did she suspect? Did she know? NickoLot was still struggling with that as Olivia shoved her into her audience chamber, followed her in and slammed the door. Only when they were alone did the old witch calm down.

Olivia's eyes narrowed as she demanded, "How much do you know?"

Nicki threw the question back at her. "How much do you know?"

Olivia leaned toward her with godfire in her eyes. "This is my castle, child. I know everything that goes on within its walls. I know about your little charms and your experiments, though I hadn't anticipated you discovering the truth so quickly."

"Then you know that . . ."

Olivia waited for her to finish, and when she didn't the old woman said, "That DaNoel's a traitor? Of course I know. I suspected as much before Valso escaped our tower, and I knew for certain the day DaNoel killed that guard."

"You've known all along?"

Olivia turned her back on her, strode to a window and looked out into the darkening night.

Nicki demanded, "Why didn't you say something, stop him?"

Olivia sighed. "And break you mother's heart? No, I'll not do that. In any case I've been using DaNoel to feed little bits of false information to Valso. We can use him to our advantage, and at the same time we need not destroy your mother, whom I value more than you can imagine."

Compassion! Never had NickoLot thought to hear compassion from the old woman.

"Let DaNoel's secret remain ours," Olivia said. "If we're careful we can keep him from damaging the clan, and from killing your mother with grief."

28

War to Come

THEANDRIN'S DEMANDS AND impatience had grown into outright threats, and Chrisainne knew she could no longer wait. She had done her homework, had carefully researched poisons and toxins, concoctions and contagions. And having lived now at Penda Court for some months, she knew the methods Theandrin employed to protect the Penda ruling family from any attempted poisoning. She'd experimented a bit, had found that incoming food and drink supplies were carefully checked on arrival, and each member of the family maintained certain charms to warn them of any dangers when eating. Most importantly, Theandrin was a bit careless about the wine and water decanters in her own apartments. She checked them in the morning, and once or twice during the day, but she didn't check each individual glass served to her. Anyone who poured her a goblet of wine or a cup of water in her own apartments was a trusted retainer.

Chrisainne had settled on an herb frequently used to relieve a woman's cramps during her menstrual cycle. A good witch could strengthen its effects if her cramps were unusually severe. A *very* good witch could reverse the effects as well as strengthen them, and alter them significantly. It had taken considerable effort to concoct her potion, a deep burgundy distillation that would disappear nicely in a glass of red wine. A drop or two in Theandrin's drink, administered repeatedly over the cycle of a single moon, would show no ill effects. But a cancer would grow slowly in her womb, and in about six moons she'd die a rather painful death. No one would suspect foul play, for a death of that nature was not uncommon in a woman Theandrin's age. It would be a sad loss for the entire clan, and Chrisainne would be there to comfort the family during their time of grief. It might even be fun to seduce ErrinCastle before she killed him. After all, he was quite handsome.

She'd learned quite a few new tricks in her studies, and after Theandrin, she could put some of them to use getting rid of the Penda heir, BlakeDown, Lewendis, her husband—anyone else who got in her way.

Today Theandrin had asked Chrisainne to join her for a pleasant afternoon of stitchery, and she'd invited a few other young ladies. It was time to be rid of the older woman.

She knocked on the door to Theandrin's apartments, was admitted by a servant.

"Chrisainne, my dear," Theandrin said, standing and greeting her warmly. They kissed lightly on the cheek, and Chrisainne sat down at her stitching hoop.

The other two girls were quite young, and obviously thrilled to be invited to join the preeminent lady of the clan. They giggled and chatted, and at one point Theandrin leaned close to Chrisainne and whispered, "Thank you for joining us. I'm glad of some mature conversation."

Chrisainne smiled and said, "It's my pleasure, Your Ladyship."

The afternoon dwindled away rather pleasantly and Chrisainne had begun to think no opportunity would present itself, when Theandrin breathed a heavy sigh, and said, "Dinner's approaching, and I feel like a glass of wine. Chrisainne, will you join me?"

"Certainly," Chrisainne said, standing. She spoke as she crossed the room. "What would you like, red or white?"

Chrisainne reached the small table containing two decanters and some goblets, noticed happily that one decanter held water and the other red wine. Before Theandrin could answer, Chrisainne turned back to her and said, "I'm sorry, but it appears there's only red today. Would you like me to go to the kitchens and get you some white?"

"No, no, red will be fine."

Chrisainne poured wine into two goblets, and with her back turned to the rest of them, she slipped the small vial out of her sleeve. In a quick motion she'd practiced a hundred times, she removed the stopper, let two drops of the liquid fall into one goblet, replaced the stopper and returned the vial to her sleeve. She was rather proud of how quickly and smoothly she'd done it.

She turned, crossed the room carrying the two goblets, handed one to Theandrin, and sat down next to her. Theandrin lifted the goblet toward her lips but hesitated, glanced momentarily at a ring on her finger. She lowered the goblet, looked at the two young girls and said, "It occurs to me that it is getting rather late. You two should run along and return to your mothers, while we older women enjoy our wine."

The girls hopped to their feet, kissed Theandrin on the cheek, bobbed a quick curtsy and left.

To the servant girl sitting in the corner, Theandrin said, "Run down to the kitchen and tell the cook I'll be down shortly to discuss dinner."

With a quick curtsy the servant girl followed the two youngsters. Now that they were alone, Chrisainne thought Theandrin would renew her demands for information, but the older woman seemed to be in a pleasant mood this day.

"Ah," Theandrin said. "Alone, finally. I'd like to show you something."

She rose, stood over Chrisainne and held out her hand. Chrisainne noted three rings on her fingers. "Look at this one," Theandrin said, pointing to the ring on her index finger, which contained a pale, white, colorless stone.

"It's a lovely ring," Chrisainne lied.

"No, it's not. It's normally lavender, and then it's lovely. But I recently treated it with some special spells. It loses all color when I hold poison in my hands."

Chrisainne started, trying to think quickly, but before she could say anything Theandrin swung out and slapped her so hard she tumbled from her seat onto the floor, her goblet of wine splashing across the carpet. With her head spinning she managed to get to her hands and knees, but the older woman grabbed her hair from behind and pulled viciously, lifted her up to her knees. Theandrin then slapped something against the skin exposed above the top of her gown.

Chrisainne looked down and saw a trinket of some dull metal stuck to her chest. It pulsed once with a faint, yellowish glow, but she felt nothing.

"Lay down there and don't move," Theandrin said. "And say nothing."

Chrisainne's muscles turned into water and she collapsed onto her side, then flopped over onto her back. She couldn't move, and when she tried to speak the muscles of her throat contracted painfully. She realized an enormously powerful compulsion spell was forcing her to obey every word Theandrin uttered.

Theandrin loomed over her, leaned down and looked in her eyes. "You might have gotten away with it had I not discovered you're working for the Decouix. But once I knew, I took extra precautions. I'm afraid you're not going to survive this, girl."

Chrisainne lay so strongly imprisoned in the older woman's spell her heart didn't even beat rapidly in response to the fear that crawled up her gut. She tried to resist the spell, opened her mouth to plead for her life, but her throat muscles constricted so badly she couldn't breathe.

Theandrin said, "Shut your mouth and say nothing."

Her teeth clamped shut so quickly she bit her tongue.

••••

As Morgin rode west to Elhiyne, he made good use of Mortiss's ability to cover great distances through the nether ways. With Bayellgae, Salula and Metadan all hunting him, he felt safer in the netherworld, though he knew the dangers of spending too much time there. His connection to reality, to the Mortal Plane, would slowly erode, and he'd find it difficult to return.

He reached the foothills below Kallun's Gorge late in the afternoon. The trail that led up to the Gorge had been well marked, and while it was a bit treacherous in spots, he could trust Mortiss's abilities and his own shadow vision, so he continued on. He'd taken this trail once before, riding down it to face Illalla's army alone. Those events of only a few years ago felt as if they were part of a distant past, while his memories of Morddon's life centuries ago seemed only yesterday.

Near midnight the trail leveled off just short of the Gorge. Exhausted now, he recalled that there was a waystation on the east side, and he hoped to rest there. He dismounted, and holding Mortiss's reins he walked forward, spotted the faint, orange-red glow of a flickering fire illuminating the boulders ahead. He must have made some sound or noise, for Samull, the son of the waystation's keeper, stepped out onto the trail, groggily rubbing his eyes and peering through the darkness.

"Good even', sir."

Samull and his father Durado had been kind when Morgin had thought he had no friends. "It's me, Samull, Morgin."

"Ah, Lord Morgin. We heard you was dead." He spun about and shouted, "Da, it's Lord Morgin. And he ain't dead."

Durado stepped out of the fire's glow, also rubbing the sleep from his eyes. "Lord Morgin. Tis late. You must be tired."

Samull took Mortiss to feed her, while Durado led Morgin between two boulders toward the glow of the fire. They emerged into a large level space, sheltered on all sides by rock walls and boulders. Masons had cut a shelf into the rock for seating around the fire pit. The fire hadn't been banked, and it emitted enough light to cast the faint glow on the boulders Morgin had spotted earlier.

As Durado tossed a couple of logs on the fire, sending a shower of sparks upward, he said, "We keep the fire burning so late travelers like you can see their way. Wouldn't want no one stumbling past it and stepping into the gorge."

Durado fed him a simple meal of porridge with a little sugar to sweeten it. Seated on the rock shelf, with a full stomach and his blanket wrapped about his shoulders, the warm fire in front of him, Morgin drifted off to sleep . . .

He searched through the Kingdom of Dreams for Rhianne, asked Sabian to reveal her to him if she was dreaming. He wandered on, dreaming and not dreaming . . .

Just before dawn something woke him, something nether, something near and dangerous. The fire in the sheltered space at the top of the gorge still gave off some warmth and a dim glow, but it had dwindled. Morgin stood, stepped into the shadow of a boulder and reinforced the shadow with his magic. A moment later Bayellgae buzzed into the small space, flitted about then settled on the branch of a large bush. Salula walked out from between two boulders and approached the fire. He extended his hands to warm them. Metadan winked into existence beside him.

Salula growled, "Was he here?"

The snake hissed, "Yesss, but I can no longer sssenssse him."

Metadan said, "Nor can I."

"There isss life nearby," Bayellgae hissed, "and I hunger."

Salula shook his head. "Stay away from the old man and the boy. We don't want to advertise our presence. He's probably headed for Elhiyne, and we need to catch him before he gets there."

Salula turned and marched back the way he'd come. Metadan winked out of existence, leaving behind a column of smoke. Bayellgae took to the air and followed Salula.

Morgin waited in his shadow until well after sunup before stepping forth. They were ahead of him now. He'd have to move cautiously.

••••

Morgin saw no sign of Bayellgae, Salula or Metadan on his way to Elhiyne, probably because Mortiss followed her paths through the nether ways. Each time it grew harder to return to the Mortal Plane, almost as if he had some special affinity for the netherworld. When reality finally came upon him he sat astride her east of the village near Elhiyne.

He noticed immediately that something was wrong. There were no hands in the fields and in the distance he saw no activity in the village. He didn't want to be recognized or questioned, so he pulled the hood of his cloak up over his head, cast a shadow about his face to augment that cast by the sun, and rode through the village at a trot.

Once before he'd ridden blindly into Elhiyne without listening to his instincts, only to learn that Valso and the Tulalane were occupying it with a company of Kulls. This time he stopped at the edge of the no-man's-land, dismounted, pulled a shadow about him and slipped into the woods there.

The castle gates were open, but armed sentries stood watch at the battlements. Dusk was approaching, and the late afternoon sun cast a long shadow behind one of the open main gates. It was over two hundred paces distant, just out of range of a bow, though not a Benesh'ere longbow. He wasn't sure he could do it, but he must try. *To walk in one is to walk in them all.* He closed his eyes, decided that the two shadows, that in which he stood, and the one in the distance behind the castle gate, were one and the same. He staggered as he felt that falling sensation.

"Bloody Penda's deserve what we give 'em."

"Let's just hope we be doing the givin', and not them."

Morgin opened his eyes. He stood in the shadow of the gate below the wall, two sentries on the battlements above talking about something to do with Penda. They weren't looking his way, would never have considered that someone could just appear at the base of the wall without crossing the no-man's-land. Keeping a shadow wrapped about him, he stepped around the edge of the gate and into the castle yard, hugging the wall and the shadows there. The castle yard, always a beehive of activity, was completely deserted.

Tightly wrapped in his shadows he made his way to the castle proper. It too was nearly deserted, though he spotted NickoLot walking down a hallway, carrying a candle to light her way. He slipped into a shadow behind her and followed.

She made her way to Roland and AnnaRail's apartments. She stopped at the door, knocked, and a moment later Roland opened it. Behind Roland Morgin spotted a shadow in the far corner of the sitting room. *To walk in one is to walk in them all.*

He stood now in the shadow in the room, watching NickoLot step through the door, and Roland close it.

"Will we be ready at dawn?" Nicki asked.

AnnaRail walked into the room and said, "We have to be."

Roland said, "Mother won't like us showing up."

AnnaRail waved a hand in angry dismissal. "I care not what your mother wants."

Roland frowned and raised a hand to silence her. They tensed as he carefully looked around the room. His gaze settled on Morgin's shadow, he visibly relaxed and said, "There's no need to lurk in shadows, son."

Morgin sighed, dropped his shadowmagic and stepped forth. AnnaRail's eyes widened, then she stepped forward and wrapped him in her arms. Nicki wrapped her arms around both of them, and Roland his around the three of them.

When they parted Morgin asked, "Where is everyone? What's happening?"

From the three of them he heard a story of steadily escalating tensions on the border with Penda, then skirmishes, a massacre of some of Alcoa's men, and now open war.

Roland said, "Olivia and BlakeDown are gathering armies on the border, preparing for battle. We've been forbidden to attend because we've openly opposed her."

Morgin asked, "What about Wylow and PaulStaff?"

"They don't want war any more than we do," Roland said. "But with Tosk sworn to Penda and Inetka sworn to Elhiyne, when Olivia and BlakeDown go to war, the others must back them."

Nicki said, "This will destroy all of the Lesser Clans."

AnnaRail added, "We're leaving at dawn to try to stop this madness."

Nicki said, "But I fear we'll not succeed, not even in our wildest dreams."

Her words stung Morgin, and he said, "Perhaps it is only in a dream where we may succeed."

29

A Soul Freed

MORGIN AND ROLAND scrounged up a quick meal from a frightened cooking staff, and the four of them ate in the kitchen. Then they retired, hoping to get some sleep, planning to leave at first light. Morgin lay down in JohnEngine's bed, though he knew his sleep would not be restful.

Sabian awaited him in the Kingdom of Dreams. "Sabian, help me find PaulStaff," he begged.

Morgin found himself standing over the Tosk clan leader, who lay on a cot in a tent near the border, his small contribution to the army camped around him. It felt strange to walk in another man's dreams, stranger still to twist them and knot them, to distort them into fear and terror.

Next he visited PaulStaff's lieutenants, then BlakeDown and his lieutenants. He followed that with Olivia and Wylow and their lieutenants, felt bad about delivering such terror to JohnEngine and Brandon, who deserved better.

It was a long night's work. He finished by going to Sabian at dawn. The message he'd scratched in the castle yard remained unchanged, but he stood there alone, no Rhianne to be found.

Roland woke him at dawn, saying, "Come, you need to see this."

Roland led him up to the top of the parapets, and with the sun just rising over the mountains in the east he saw a lone rider seated on a horse at the edge of the no-man's-land. Rider and mount stood absolutely still, well out of bow-shot. The rider threw his head back and laughed, a harsh, guttural roar that echoed off the surrounding hills.

NickoLot and AnnaRail stepped up beside Morgin. AnnaRail said, "There is something nether about this."

"Yes," Morgin said. "Salula. And the little snake won't be far away."

Roland put a hand on Morgin's shoulder. "We still have enough armsmen to take down one Kull."

Morgin shook his head. "Not this Kull. This is my responsibility, and I've avoided it too long."

Nicki asked, "What of the snake, and its venom?"

Morgin couldn't see the little monster at that distance, but heard it hovering near Salula. "I've tasted its venom and lived, so it cannot kill me. But no one knows what it can do to someone who's survived its venom, so I think that uncertainty will make it hesitate. It might strike at me in desperation, or to save its master, but not to save Salula. I think it will only observe and report back to Valso. So let's give it something to report."

AnnaRail asked, "Why do I sense that France is involved in this?"

Morgin hadn't considered it, but now realized that none of them would have any reason to know. "France is now Salula's host. I can only guess, but I suspect Valso forced it upon him."

"Oh dear," AnnaRail said. "Can you kill the demon without killing the host?"

Morgin had lain awake at night pondering just that. "The last time I killed the host without killing the demon, and I think it was because I killed him on the Mortal Plane. Perhaps if I drag him into the netherworld, I can kill the demon there."

"How will you do that?"

Morgin had considered that carefully. "I have a particular shadow in mind."

••••

As the carriage pulled to a stop, sitting in its dark interior Theandrin heard the shouts of armsmen and the thud of horses hooves. Across from her Chrisainne sat obediently silent.

One of BlakeDown's lieutenants opened the carriage door and held out a hand to assist Theandrin. She took it and climbed down onto the muddy grass that had been chewed up by horses' hooves and the boots of marching men. The tents of her husband's army dotted the fields about her, groups of armsmen riding horses back and forth on some errand or another, and foot soldiers drilling in squads.

Behind her BlakeDown's lieutenant said, "And you, milady."

Theandrin turned around, saw that the man held his hand out to assist Chrisainne, who sat unmoving. In the grip of the compulsion spell, the girl couldn't move until Theandrin allowed her to.

"You may take his hand," she said, "and allow him to assist you."

As the lieutenant helped the girl, Theandrin scanned the camp, saw BlakeDown's banner fluttering in the air above the largest pavilion. Once Chrisainne stood beside her she said, "Walk beside me and say nothing."

They stepped around puddles of mud and piles of horse dung as they made their way to the pavilion. Some of BlakeDown's junior officers emerged from it as she approached. They all looked unusually tired and drawn, though she knew no real fighting had yet occurred, only small skirmishes. One of them stepped aside and held the tent flap for her. "Your Ladyship," he said.

Within, BlakeDown and PaulStaff leaned on a table reviewing maps with some senior officers. Theandrin spotted a small stool, pointed at it and said, "Chrisainne, sit there, say nothing, and don't move." The girl obeyed without question.

BlakeDown and the other men turned to look her way. She thought they all looked rather haggard and drawn, with gray, washed out complexions. She said, "When you're finished, my dear, I have something important to discuss with you."

BlakeDown glanced at Chrisainne with an uneasy look.

Theandrin crossed to the far side of the pavilion and helped herself to a tin cup of water. She turned about and waited, sipping on the water, and after some brief discussion, PaulStaff and the other men excused themselves politely and left. BlakeDown turned her way, his hand resting on the hilt of the broadsword strapped to his side.

"You look tired," she said. "Almost ill."

"No sleep," he said. "Just nightmares, and always about that Elhiyne."

"That Elhiyne?"

"Yah, the one calls himself ShadowLord. I'm going to have to kill him. So what's so important you made the trip all the way out here?" He glanced at Chrisainne. "And with her?"

Theandrin crossed the room to stand in front of the girl. "She has an interesting tale to tell, husband. And I have her under compulsion so she'll tell the truth."

"Your spell crafting is powerful. Isn't that a bit harsh?"

Theandrin said, "She tried to murder me with some very nasty poison."

BlakeDown frowned, clearly couldn't justify such actions in a young girl who was supposed to be enamored with him. To Chrisainne he said, "You tried to kill my wife?" The compulsion spell forced Chrisainne to answer only Theandrin's questions, so she remained silent.

Theandrin said, "Chrisainne, ignore him and answer my questions when I ask them. And do so truthfully, with no dissembling or misdirection."

Theandrin had already interrogated the girl rather thoroughly, knew the details of her work for Valso. "You have been spying on us for someone else. Is that correct?"

The girl spoke in a toneless voice. "Yeth." The poor girl had bitten her tongue quite badly and it had swollen a bit.

Theandrin glanced BlakeDown's way and saw his brow furrow.

"Who have you been working for?"

"King Valso."

"What were his instructions to you?"

"I was to seduce your husband."

"Did you enjoy seducing my husband?"

"No."

"Why?"

Chrisainne struggled for a moment, a valiant effort to resist the compulsion spell, but it ruled her completely. "He ruts like a pig."

BlakeDown grunted, interestingly enough, sounding a bit like a pig. Theandrin controlled the look on her face carefully, had to suppress the smile that wanted to form there.

"What else did Valso tell you to do?"

"Encourage him to distrust ErrinCastle's choice of lieutenants for patrolling the Elhiyne border."

"What?" BlakeDown demanded, stepping forward.

Theandrin put out a hand and stopped him. "Tell me the reason you were to do this."

"King Valso wants war between Penda and Elhiyne."

"Why does he want such a war?"

"It will weaken all the Lesser Clans and make them easy to conquer later."

BlakeDown shouted, "But he promised me—"

He lunged at Chrisainne and Theandrin stepped in his way. Her husband had a horrible temper, and he'd likely beat the girl into unconsciousness, but she wanted BlakeDown to hear more, so that must wait.

"Hold off," she said. "We can punish her later." She looked at him pointedly, and didn't try to hide her contempt as she asked him, "And what did Valso promise you?"

A sulking look crossed his face. "It was a private agreement between him and me."

When BlakeDown got stubborn like this, she'd get nothing out of him.

He nodded at Chrisainne. "She looks like she wants to speak."

Theandrin turned and saw the girl's eyes flash. She clearly had something to say, and was angry enough, and stupid enough, to blurt out something indiscreet. Perhaps they could learn more. She chose her words carefully, chose a phrasing that would make the spell force the girl to speak from her heart. "Speak you mind, girl."

Chrisainne shouted at BlakeDown, "I would have made a much better wife to you than this cow."

That statement surprised even Theandrin. Clearly, she hadn't learned everything the girl had to reveal, and apparently hadn't asked all the *right* questions. And from the doubtful look on BlakeDown's face he hadn't yet made the right connection. Theandrin needed to help him do so. "Hmm! You clearly intended to poison me, but you couldn't have taken BlakeDown as your husband while you had one of your own. No doubt you intended to poison him too." It was not a question, so the spell did not compel the girl to answer her.

Theandrin wondered how far the girl's plans for poison went. "And what else would you have been to my husband?"

"I would have given him strong heirs."

The wide-eyed look on BlakeDown's face told her he was starting to put the pieces together. She still needed to help him along a bit. "But my husband already has an heir."

Chrisainne realized her mistake and her eyes widened.

Theandrin asked her, "So what plans did you have for our son?"

The girl struggled in the merciless grip of the spell, shook as she tried to resist it, finally blurted out, "I was . . . going to . . . kill him too."

BlakeDown roared, "What?"

Theandrin threw out an arm to hold him back. "So you would murder me, murder your husband, murder our son, wed my widowed husband, bear him new heirs . . . and then what?"

Chrisainne shook uncontrollably, tears streaming down her cheeks. "Poison . . . him . . . too."

Theandrin had gotten what she needed from Chrisainne, so the time had come to let BlakeDown punish the girl. She expected him to strike her with his fist or his open, gauntleted palm a few times, didn't think he'd beat her into unconsciousness yet. As BlakeDown's eyes bulged and his face turned red, Theandrin stepped back a pace, just in case a drop or two of blood spattered her way. She didn't want to ruin her gown.

BlakeDown roared with fury. In an instant he drew the massive broadsword at his side and swung it high over his head in a two-handed grip, the muscles of his shoulders and arms bunching with the effort. Chrisainne's eyes widened, and held in the grip of the compulsion spell she could neither move nor flinch. She sat there stiff-backed with her mouth open as he brought the steel edge of the blade down on the top of her head, cleaving it in two, splitting her face cleanly down the center, the blade stopping only after it had cut half way down through her chest. Blood sprayed outward and covered everything. It dripped from Theandrin's face and hair and arms. She looked at BlakeDown, his face screwed up in a blood-spattered grimace of rage.

Chrisainne hadn't fallen from the stool. The sword buried in her chest, and BlakeDown's two-handed grip on the hilt, held her sitting there. He lifted a boot, pressed the heel against one of her breasts and kicked out. The girl tumbled backward off the stool, ended up with the shoulders of her split torso on the floor, her hips still up on the stool, her legs splayed at odd angles.

"Well," Theandrin said. "She died as she lived—legs spread." She retrieved a delicate handkerchief to wipe the blood from her face, but it really wasn't up to the task.

She turned to BlakeDown, who stood there staring dumbly at the girl's corpse, blood dripping from his eyebrows, nose and chin. "And so, husband, you now know the real purpose of this war you and Olivia are so intent upon."

••••

Morgin rode Mortiss at a slow walk out toward Salula. The halfman waited unmoving, and as Morgin drew closer he spotted Bayellgae hovering above him. Morgin stopped about ten paces from them. Behind them he saw Metadan appear momentarily, then vanish.

"So," Salula said, "You think you're finally man enough to face me."

It hurt to hear that hard, dead voice coming out of France's mouth. Morgin didn't respond, just locked eyes with the halfman. Salula nodded, then dismounted, drew the obsidian blade and waited by his horse. Morgin dismounted, drew his sword and waited by Mortiss.

Salula swatted his horse's rump with the flat of his sword and the animal trotted away. Mortiss simply vanished.

Morgin wondered what role Metadan would play in this as he bent into a crouch. He and Salula squared off, circled slowly, Morgin conscious that the elusive archangel could appear at any moment.

Salula came in with a series of quick strikes that Morgin parried, sparks erupting where the steel and obsidian met. They disengaged and circled again.

Morgin thought he might be able to defeat Salula, but he'd have to kill France to do so. He hadn't come up with a better solution, and death would at least free the swordsman's soul from the grip of the demon. He pulled a shadow around himself, cast one behind Salula, stepped into it with that falling sensation, stepped out of it only to meet Metadan face-to-face.

He charged in under the archangel's guard, butted him under the chin with his head, knocking him into Salula. Metadan and the halfman stumbled away, turned on each other and traded two quick sword blows. Morgin noticed that the dead steel of the blade that dripped blood did not strike sparks from the obsidian.

Metadan staggered, looked about as if coming to his senses, turned on Morgin and attacked. Morgin back stepped, parrying the archangel's strikes, sidestepping to keep Metadan between him and the halfman so they couldn't take him on two-on-one. He stepped into one shadow, stepped out of another behind Salula, but Metadan winked into existence beside the halfman and struck at Morgin.

Caught by surprise Morgin deflected Metadan's blade clumsily as Salula thrust at him. It would have been a killing strike, but Metadan struck the halfman's sword aside with his own, and it merely sliced across Morgin's ribs. Then the archangel turned on Morgin and attacked him.

Metadan appeared crazed, as if he could not make up his mind who he wanted to kill. One strike he aimed at Morgin, and the next at the halfman. Morgin used his shadows, stepping into one, then out of another, but he was tiring. Metadan blinked in and out of existence, and the two danced around the halfman, Morgin never knowing who Metadan would attack next.

Metadan's sword hilt thudded painfully into Morgin's shoulder, staggering him. The archangel winked out of existence just as Salula stepped in and thrust at Morgin's heart. But a heartbeat before the blade pierced Morgin's chest, Metadan appeared directly in front of it, knocking Morgin backwards. Morgin saw the tip of the halfman's sword punch out through the archangel's back.

The three of them froze, the halfman's sword piercing Metadan's chest, the archangel with a look of joy and wonder on his face. He smiled, said to Salula, "Thank you."

He reached out, stretched his arms to their full extent and clamped both hands around the wrist of Salula's sword hand. He staggered forward, a small step, pulling the blade deeper into his chest. Salula, with a look of horror on his face, tried to resist, but Metadan's two-handed grip would not yield, and step by step Metadan walked the length of the blade, until it was buried to the hilt in his chest.

The archangel turned his head and looked at Morgin. "Take him. Now."

The archangel was giving him his chance. He stepped into one shadow, and out of another behind the halfman. Holding his sword in one hand, he gripped Salula by the back of the neck with the other, recalled a shadow he'd stepped into in a far distant past, a shadow cast by the flat-bed cart upon which SheelThane had been chained as Magwa's prisoner. *To walk in one is to walk in them all.* He wrapped him and Salula into a shadow, and stepped with that falling sensation from one to the other.

He and the demon sprawled out of the shadow beneath the cart in a deserted jackal camp. They were deep in the netherworld, in the ninth hell, and now the demon wore its true nature: the head of a snake, torso of a man, the cloven hooves of a goat, and for arms the clawed talons of a vulture.

Stunned, the demon looked down at itself and cried, "What have you done?"

Morgin pulled his belt knife, a blade he'd personally forged in the Benesh'ere camp, a blade he taught to speak with the single voice of a SteelMaster. He commanded the steel in the blade, it shot through the air and thudded into the demon's chest. Buried to the hilt, the flesh in contact with the blade smoked, hissed and sputtered. The demon cried out, tried to grip the hilt, but when its taloned hands clutched the steel they burst into flames.

The demon staggered, cracks appeared all over its body emitting flame and smoke. It cried out a wail of agony and pain, collapsed onto its hands and knees. A bright flash of blood-red fire blinded Morgin momentarily, and when he could see again nothing remained but a smear of sickly, greenish ichor and ash.

Morgin staggered and leaned against the cart to catch his breath, hoping his strategy had worked, praying that by taking the demon deep into the netherworld he'd separated it from France.

Mortiss trotted into the abandoned jackal camp and neighed, *Well done. Time to take you back.*

••••

Mounted on Mortiss, Morgin found Ellowyn sitting on the ground at the edge of the no-man's-land. Metadan's empty black leathers lay in her lap, one white feather resting upon them. As Morgin rode up to her she looked up, her cheeks smeared with tears. "Thank you," she said. "His soul is now free."

Morgin dismounted. Like the other deeds he hadn't really righted any wrongs. He'd simply stumbled into them and they'd righted themselves. "I didn't really free him," he said. "He freed himself."

She looked down at the feather in her lap and stroked it gently. "That's why he's finally free."

AnnaRail sat on the ground near France, who lay curled in a fetal ball, his eyes closed, his cheeks wet with tears. She stroked his blond hair and looked up as Morgin approached. "I did what I could to heal him. He's resting comfortably now, and I think he'll be okay."

"Yah," France said, his voice weak and faint. He didn't open his eyes. "I'll be okay, lad. Just need a little time."

Morgin sat down on the ground next to him, took one of the swordsman's hands and held it against his own breast. He had his old friend back, and tears coursed down his own cheeks as he said, "Good. I'll need you tomorrow at the Penda border."

France opened his eyes. "The border?" he asked. "Why the border?"

"Olivia and BlakeDown want to have a little war, and I have to stop them."

France reached up and wiped the tears from Morgin's cheek. "I'll be there, lad."

AnnaRail glanced Ellowyn's way. "Who is the strange woman?"

Morgin looked at the archangel. "An angel I met in a strange dream."

She raised an eyebrow at the cryptic response.

"I have to go to Durin," he said, "to see to Rhianne. After that I'll come to the border, and we'll end this war before it starts."

"Tulellcoe's in Durin," she said, "hoping to do something about Rhianne. But to Durin and back, that'll take a twelve of days."

Morgin recalled the feeling of stepping out of a shadow here on the Mortal Plane, and into the shadow beneath SheelThane's flatbed cart in the netherworld. He'd crossed levels of existence and centuries of time in the blink of an eye. There had to be a way to cross leagues of distance on the Mortal Plane in a heartbeat. If not, he'd fail Rhianne.

He shook his head. "No, I'll take care of Rhianne, and meet you at the border tomorrow morning. After we stop this war, we have another to fight."

30

Hardened Resolve

SITTING ON A couch wrapped in a blanket, Rhianne could barely lift her head. Valso hadn't abused her sexually as the Kulls had that night so long ago, but the physical beating had been far more vicious, and he refused to allow her a healer. Hopefully, that meant he'd given up on seducing her. When she'd looked in a mirror that morning her face had been swollen, puffy and bruised, nothing like the pretty trophies Valso liked to keep around. She'd healed the worst of the injuries herself—a broken nose, broken arm, some broken ribs, and something bleeding internally that would have killed her had she not addressed it—but the combination of the beating and healing had left her as weak as a kitten.

Rhianne had visited the Kingdom of Dreams several times now since Morgin's return, but each time found it deserted. And the dreams had continued to lack the sense of reality she'd felt when she'd been there with Morgin. Twice now, for just an instant, she'd thought she'd seen some sort of message scratched in the dirt of the castle yard, but both times the dream had shifted just as she turned to investigate. She now knew she had no control of her dreams unless the Unnamed King walked his realm to give it life.

"The king is in a foul mood," Geanna said, as she rushed into Rhianne's sitting room. "And he's coming here now."

The girl knelt down in front of her, took her hands and tried to rub warmth into them. "You must appear strong. He relishes weakness, especially in women."

Geanna's attitude toward Rhianne had changed, and so had that of the other girls. Rhianne suspected they could no longer rationalize their romantic notions of a handsome king with a man who beat a woman so cruelly. Broken bones and internal bleeding were just not on their list titillating fantasy.

Rhianne heard Valso long before he walked into the room, heard him coming her way, at first his voice a faint sound muffled by the walls of the castle. He ranted and screamed at the top of his lungs, and as he came closer the volume of his rage increased.

She smiled at Geanna and said, "Help me, please."

The girl helped her sit up straight. "The blanket," Geanna said. "It makes you appear weak."

Rhianne removed the blanket from about her shoulders and handed it to her, then adjusted her gown carefully. She finished only an instant before Valso marched into the room, waving his arms about, Carsaris and Magwa following fearfully in his wake.

"Metadan," he screamed. "And Salula."

He charged across the room toward her and she thought he would hit her. It took every bit of willpower she had not to flinch, to keep the look on her face impassive and cold. She had determined that she would die, rather than show him any fear or weakness.

He leaned down until his nose almost touched hers. With his eyes bulging, his face red, he shouted, "Metadan—and Salula—and Chrisainne too."

She didn't know any Chrisainne, but apparently something had happened to Metadan and Salula. Rhianne noticed Geanna, little-by-little taking tiny back-steps across the room, her head bowed, eyes focused on the floor, instinctively putting distance between her and the enraged king. Magwa and Carsaris had stopped just within the room, well out of Valso's reach. None of her handmaidens were visible. Rhianne was effectively alone with Valso. At another time she might have goaded him with a nasty grin, but dare not try something like that now. "What about them?"

"They're dead," he said, continuing to rant, drops of saliva spattering her face. "You and your husband killed them."

She considered arguing the point. How could she have killed anyone while confined to this castle as a prisoner? She was curious about one point. "Is the demon Salula dead, or just his host?"

Valso straightened, swung out and hit her with a roundhouse slap. It rocked her to one side, and she almost lost consciousness. But she'd gotten her answer, or at least part of it.

She had trouble focusing as Valso continued to rant, screaming and shouting while he marched back and forth across the room. She kept her face impassive, but inside she was too frightened to do anything but sit there and hope he didn't focus on her again.

He stopped and froze, surprising them all, then cocked his head to one side as if listening to something. He stood that way for a moment, then with a calm that belied his earlier fury, he said, "Yes, excellent."

He turned to Rhianne, smiled, and calmly crossed the room to stand over her. He leaned toward her, leaned close and said, "My master is now going to take a personal interest in the whoreson. Apparently, your husband connects to the netherlife quite frequently . . ." Rhianne felt that thing enter Valso's soul. ". . . and when next he ventures there, on any level beyond the Mortal Plane, I will be waiting for him."

Valso straightened, turned, and calmly left the room with Magwa and Carsaris on his heels.

Metadan and the demon Salula dead—it must have been Morgin. She hoped he'd found a way to kill the demon without killing France, though if he'd had to kill the swordsman as well, it must have been a mercy.

She sensed that something had changed, a subtle shift in the relationship between the planes of existence, and she had no doubt it was Morgin's doing. Soon he would come for Valso—there was no question of that—and Rhianne now knew it was up to her to make sure he had an open and clean field of battle. Carsaris was too riddled with fear, and Magwa too cowardly to interfere directly. No, it was the little snake that Rhianne feared most, not just for her, but for what it might do when Morgin finally faced Valso's master. She must find a way to neutralize it, to prevent it from interfering. But first, she had to find a way to warn Morgin to stay away from the Nether Plane.

••••

Standing on the parapets Morgin recalled the shadow beneath SheelThane's cart in the netherworld. Dragging Salula to that shadow in the abandoned jackal camp had been an instinctive act, and now he must repeat a similar feat, but how? He looked out across the no-man's-land to the edge of the trees where that morning he'd fought Metadan and Salula, tried to remember how he'd stepped from a shadow there to one in the netherworld. *To walk in one is to walk in them all.* He'd pictured the cart and its shadow in his mind's eye, and in the unchanging daylight of the netherworld, where the sun never set and shadows never changed, it had been easy to recall the shadow in every detail. Was that the limitation, that he had to know the shadow well enough to picture it precisely?

He turned around, looked down into the Elhiyne yard and noted several shadows. He paid particular attention to one near the outer wall that wouldn't dissipate as the sun crossed the sky. If this worked, he'd return there.

He closed his eyes, and tried to recall the yard in Castle Decouix where he'd fought so many Kulls in gladiatorial combat as Valso's prisoner. During those contests he'd longed to use his shadowmagic, had looked at every shadow within those walls with envy, and remembered them even now. Was that the key, he had to know the shadow he was going to step into, picture it in his mind? By now it would be mid-morning in Durin, and he recalled a shadow beneath a stone stairway that descended from the parapets. He must have seen it a hundred times, and at this time of day it was always deep, dark and inviting. By late afternoon sunlight would fill the space and that particular shadow would disappear, but others would form elsewhere to replace it. He pictured it now, while he pulled a shadow about him—and he took that step.

He almost gasped at the falling sensation, but he swallowed any outcry. A cacophony of sounds assaulted his ears as he steadied himself and opened his eyes. Hidden deep in his shadow, a squad of Decouix armsmen marched past him, servants ran here and there, and swords rang out in the practice arena. It was a far cry from the nearly deserted castle he'd just left behind. He huddled in his shadow and pulled the hood of his cloak over his head. He waited, ready to jump back to Elhiyne if necessary, if he could, but after a hundred heartbeats no one raised the alarm, so he breathed easier.

He could guess where Valso kept Rhianne, probably on the second floor not far from where he'd imprisoned Morgin. But he'd not paid close attention to the shadows there at the time, and couldn't recall any now. He'd have to move slowly, work his way into the castle shadow-by-shadow.

Across the yard the sun filled a narrow path between two buildings with deep shadow. Since he'd lived here for many months he knew the layout of Decouix, and that lane led to servants' quarter and the kitchens. It was not wide enough for two men to walk side-by-side, so he'd be taking a chance that no one happened to be coming the other way, but it was still his best bet. He closed his eyes, stepped from his shadow to the shadow in the narrow lane.

He kept his shadowmagic wrapped tightly around him as he moved quickly down the lane toward the kitchens. He'd almost reached the end of the way when a young boy came around the far corner trotting on some urgent errand. Morgin stopped and pressed his back to a wall, tried to occupy as little space as possible as he huddled in the shadow there. When the boy jogged past him his elbow brushed across Morgin's gut and the boy noticed it. As he stopped and turned, Morgin stepped across the lane and pressed his back against the opposite wall, concentrating on his shadow magic.

The boy retraced his steps and carefully examined the shadow where Morgin had been standing a moment ago. He ran his hands up and down the wall, shrugged when he found nothing, turned and continued on his way.

Morgin stopped in a shadow near the entrance to the kitchens and peered around the edge of the doorway. He needed to go through the kitchen and out the other side to get into the castle proper, but there were cooks, undercooks, scullery maids, and other members of the staff busily preparing the mid-day meal. He was considering retracing his steps to try another way into the castle when he spotted a shadow on the far side of the kitchen near the other exit. He closed his eyes and stepped into that shadow, then slipped out of the kitchen, taking it with him.

He used that technique repeatedly, crossing occupied rooms in an instant by stepping into a shadow on the far side. Unfortunately, inside the castle proper, without the aid of the sun to darken the shadows, they weren't as distinct and well defined. It took the rest of the morning to work his way up to the second floor.

He stopped at the end of a long hallway that had no exterior windows and was dark even in mid-day. The few shadows he could use were cast by wall sconces, and poorly defined. He was considering his route when a woman stepped into the corridor at the end. She came his way slowly, stopping every step or two to peer into a shadow, and rub her hand up and down the wall there, almost as if searching for someone in hiding, likely searching for him. That intrigued him, so he held his position and waited. If the need arose, he could step to another shadow in an instant. As the woman got closer he recognized Haleen, Valso's sister.

She stopped only a few paces from him, looked his way, but a little to one side as if she sensed him in some way but couldn't really see him. "Child," she whispered. "You must leave. Valso is having her watched too closely. Your . . . uncle is staying at an inn called The Weary Bard. It's on the south side of the city. Come back to this same spot just after sunset and I'll help you find her, though . . . she may surprise you." She turned around, straightened her shoulders, walked back down the hallway and disappeared around a corner.

Haleen had been an ally once before, had helped him escape from this same castle a little less than a year ago. He stepped into a shadow five paces away, noted that the shadow in which he'd been hiding was cast by the light of a wall sconce, would probably still be there after sunset. He noted several more like that as alternatives.

He'd have to trust Haleen, though as he left the castle he wondered about her last words.

••••

Morgin didn't walk the streets of Durin, he stepped from shadow-to-shadow, traversing the entire length of long avenues and streets in a heartbeat. If he could see the shadow, he could step into it, no matter how far away it might be. But he didn't know the city, and was forced to repeatedly ask directions of other pedestrians, many of whom had never heard of The Weary Bard. He finally found the place late in the afternoon, stepped out of his shadows and walked openly through the front entrance.

The innkeeper was a small, bookish fellow with eyes pinched into a squint. Seated at one of the tables in his own common room, with scrolls and parchments in front of him, he appeared to be tallying goods. Morgin tried to sound casual as he said, "I'm supposed to meet a couple of old friends here, man and woman; she's a twoname, wears breeches like a man."

The innkeeper said, "Carries a small sword too, right."

"Yah," Morgin said. "That's her."

"They got a room upstairs, though they're out now. Been out all day, go out every day, usually come back before dusk. You can wait, if you want. But if you sit at a table you gotta buy something."

"Nah," Morgin said. "I'll come back later."

Morgin turned and walked to the front entrance, opened the door, took one step out, slipped into a shadow and stepped back into the inn just before the door slammed shut. The innkeeper didn't look up from his lists of goods. Morgin worked his way through the shadows at the edge of the common room, then up the stairs and into the upstairs hallway. He reinforced his cloak of shadows and waited.

Leaning against a wall at the top of the stairs, Morgin grew drowsy and had almost dosed off when he heard the front door of the inn open and close. He heard the innkeeper say, "Fellow came by asking about you," and concluded Tulellcoe and Cort had returned. He walked to the back of the hallway where the shadows were deep.

As the two of them came up the stairs Tulellcoe said, "Other than Haleen, only my family knows we're here."

Cort topped the stairs just ahead of him. "You think it was one of them?"

They stopped at a door in the hall and Tulellcoe produced a heavy, iron key. Morgin stepped out of his shadows and said, "It was me."

They both started and stepped apart. Cort dropped into a defensive crouch and produced a dagger; Tulellcoe rested a hand on his sword. Morgin held his empty hands out and stepped out of the shadows, walking slowly. "It's just me, Morgin."

Cort grinned and put her dagger away. "I should have known you'd come for her."

She bounded across the few paces separating them, plowed into him and wrapped him in a joyous hug. "It's so good to see you," she said as she planted a big kiss on each of his cheeks.

When Cort released Morgin, Tulellcoe gripped him by the shoulders, held him at arm's length and looked him over carefully. Tulellcoe was not the kind of man to wrap someone in a hug, but Morgin saw the emotions racing across his face. "You're a changed man. I'll bet you have a strange tale to tell. Welcome back, nephew."

He turned to the door, opened it and Morgin and Cort followed him into the room. Cort sat on the edge of the bed while Tulellcoe leaned casually against a wall and Morgin retreated to a corner. Cort wanted to hear everything that had happened since they'd parted almost a year ago. "There's no time," Morgin said, conscious of the approaching dusk. "I have to get back to the castle. Haleen is going to help me rescue Rhianne."

Cort leaned forward. "*Get back* to the castle. Your were *in* the inner keep?"

"Yes, at mid-day."

Tulellcoe asked, "And you spoke to Haleen?"

"Somehow she knew I was there. She's always had some delusion that I'm her long lost child." Morgin described his brief encounter with Valso's sister. He knew that Tulellcoe and Haleen had long ago been lovers, and it clearly pained Tulellcoe to listen to him now.

"How did you get into the castle?" Cort asked. "We've been nosing around it for days, managed to get inside the outer bailey, but no further. Haleen offered to help us, but we're not ready to play that card yet."

"I learned a trick . . ." Morgin hesitated, recalled how angry Tulellcoe got at obscure references to strange happenings, decided to forge ahead anyway. ". . . in the Kingdom of Dreams. Apparently . . . I'm the Unnamed King."

He saw the look that passed between them, the kind of look one might share when concerned about the sanity of a friend. They didn't roll their eyes or anything overt, but clearly thought him unhinged. It was time for a demonstration.

He cast a shadow in the far corner of the room about six paces away. He pointed at it. "Do you see that shadow?"

They both looked that way and Cort asked, "One of yours?"

Morgin wrapped himself in a cloak of shadow, stepped into the one in the far corner, stepped out of it and said, "Yes, one of mine."

Cort gasped and shot to her feet. Tulellcoe started and stepped away from the wall he leaned against.

Morgin continued. "This morning I stood on the parapets of Elhiyne. I'm learning that I can cross leagues in a heartbeat, if I know a shadow is there, and I know its shape and location. If I don't, then I have to see it."

Cort whistled through her teeth as Tulellcoe asked, "And you crossed from Elhiyne to Decouix in a single morning?"

Morgin shook his head. "In a single heartbeat. And not directly into Decouix. The only shadow I could recall was in the outer bailey, but I worked my way into the castle proper shadow-by-shadow. I memorized a few shadows there so I can get back when I need to."

He needed to make sure he could really do what he planned, and Cort was about Rhianne's size. "I need your help," he said to her. "An experiment. I need to try something I haven't done before."

She cocked her head and gave him a doubtful look.

"I don't think it'll hurt you," he said. "If it doesn't work it'll just fail."

Tulellcoe said, "You *don't think*? That's not—"

Cort interrupted him. "Okay, I'll help, what do you need?"

Morgin walked to one corner of the room, saying, "Join me over here."

When she stood beside him, he said, "If this works you'll feel a falling sensation. Ready?"

She nodded.

He placed a hand on her shoulder, cast a shadow in the far corner, wrapped one about the two of them—and stepped.

"Ah!" Cort said.

He extinguished the shadows and he and she now stood in the far corner of the room.

"Wow!" Cort said. "That was amazing."

The room had a single shuttered window, and through its slats he saw darkness descending on the city. "I have to go. Haleen promised to help me find Rhianne. I'm going to bring her back in the same way. But I need a familiar shadow that I know will be here."

Cort stood, walked across the room and lit a lamp. They placed it on the floor, and Tulellcoe draped his cloak over the room's only chair, then positioned the chair so the lamp and cloak cast a large, dark shadow in the corner. "Will that do?" he asked.

"Perfectly," Morgin said. He walked into the shadow.

31

A Little Surprise

WITH DUSK APPROACHING, exhaustion weighed heavily on NickoLot as she, France and her parents rode toward the Elhiyne encampment, though saddle sores weighed more heavily. Compared to the other three, her riding skills were limited. If the poor swordsman hadn't been near collapse when they'd left Elhiyne that morning, she would have held them back, or been left behind. As it was, France barely managed to stay in the saddle.

No one challenged them as they rode through the camp's perimeter, then through it to the pavilion flying the Elhiyne banner. Roland dismounted and handed his reins to a groom, then helped AnnaRail out of the saddle. When he turned to Nicki she had a moment of panic, not sure she'd be able to dismount. "My back side is not feeling so good," she said, trying not to grimace visibly.

He did grimace. "I'm sorry, Nicki."

He helped her down, and when she stood on the ground she thought it might be a while before she could walk like a lady again.

Roland looked past her and she followed his gaze, and almost forgot her own pains. France climbed out of the saddle like an old man, leaned on his horse and rested his forehead against it.

AnnaRail approached him and put an arm about his shoulders. "I can give you strength, swordsman."

He took a deep breath, and it surprised them all when he nodded, for they all knew he did not abide magic. AnnaRail closed her eyes, concentrated, and a moment later France stood a bit straighter. He swallowed, craned his neck from side-to-side, as if stretching the kinks out of it, then said, "Let's get this over with."

The look on Roland's face turned angry. He nodded, turned, and the three of them followed him into the pavilion.

They found Olivia in council with Alcoa, Wylow, Brandon and JohnEngine, all bent over maps on a table. To one side DaNoel stood with a tankard of something to drink in one hand. Without preamble Roland shouted, "I'll not stand by and allow you to destroy the clan with this war."

Nicki had never heard anyone shout at grandmother that way, and couldn't help but cringe in anticipation of the explosion that would certainly come. She looked about the pavilion, instinctively seeking a place to hide, like a mouse scenting the presence of a large cat nearby.

Every head in the tent turned Roland's way. Olivia looked up from the maps and said, "Oh posh! It's just a war, son. We'll have a few skirmishes, they'll kill a few of us, we'll kill a few of them, and then it'll be over. No harm done."

As everyone competed to shout the loudest, Nicki stepped back and looked on. Something bothered her about Olivia, her brothers, cousins and the other lords of Elhiyne. They all looked ill, with washed-out complexions and dark bags under blood-shot eyes.

She noticed Brandon edging his way quietly toward her, still limping badly from the incident on the border. He hadn't joined in the shouting. "Nicki," he said, wrapping his arms around her and hugging her tightly. He sounded exhausted.

When he released her she examined his aura, saw nothing there that would indicate illness or injury. "What's wrong?" she asked. "You look ill."

He shook his head, as if having trouble thinking, and said, "Didn't sleep well last night. Nightmares."

"But a nightmare or two shouldn't affect you this badly."

"Not a nightmare or two, but continuously all night. Started immediately every time I closed my eyes. Must have awakened ten or fifteen times with night terrors. And always about Morgin."

"He came back, you know, to Elhiyne, yesterday."

She could see Brandon had a hundred questions he wanted to ask, but Abileen, a sergeant of men, entered the tent and approached them. Brandon turned his way and acknowledged him. Abileen said, "A messenger from Penda, my lord. They want to talk."

••••

Morgin huddled in a shadow near the top of the stairs waiting for Haleen. He'd chosen a different shadow from the one she'd found him in earlier. He didn't think she intended to betray him, but it never hurt to be cautious. If armsmen suddenly rushed that shadow thinking to catch him, they'd find it empty and he'd have a few precious moments to escape.

He saw movement at the far end of the hall, but it turned out to be a servant girl walking hastily on some errand. She rushed past him and down the stairs, completely oblivious to him standing there.

It was well past sunset so he had the advantage of darkness, but he'd been waiting for quite some time and was growing impatient. Haleen was late, and he wondered now if she would show. If she didn't, he'd have to find Rhianne on his own.

More movement at the far end of the hall drew his attention, Haleen walking briskly his way, no armsmen visible. She'd have to walk past him to get to the shadow she'd found him in earlier that day. He still wanted to see what she intended, so he decided to wait and watch, to reveal himself only when sure of her motives. But as she came near she hesitated, came to a stop, then slowly and deliberately turned to look his way. Somehow she sensed his presence.

"You are a cautious one," she whispered.

"It keeps me alive."

She cocked her head. "You do have good reason to move with care. My brother is vicious, and deadly."

"You're late."

"It was necessary to wait for everyone to retire."

She looked up and down the hall, then said, "Stay in your shadows and follow me." Without waiting for an answer she turned and continued on her way.

Morgin danced among the shadows in her wake as she led him deeper into the castle. He recognized some of the corridors, but during his imprisonment here he'd rarely walked them at night. They appeared vastly different cloaked in the shadows of darkness and the occasional flaming sconce, and he wasn't certain he could find his way back out.

She stopped at a set of high double doors, lifted the latch on one and opened it slowly. She looked back his way and nodded for him to follow. He slipped through the door behind her and closed it, taking care to avoid making any noise.

Morgin took in his surroundings. He stood in a small vestibule that opened into the sitting room of a suite. An open window on the far side admitted a shaft of pale moonlight. For Morgin that was more than enough illumination.

He followed Haleen past the sitting room and into a short hallway. She stopped at an open door, leaned toward him and whispered, "Servants sleeping in this room." She pointed to a closed door beyond the servant's quarters and said, "Your lady is behind that door. I'll spell the servants so you won't be disturbed." She slipped into the servant's room.

Morgin lifted the latch on the closed door and eased it open, glad that its hinges didn't squeak. He stepped through and closed it, turned about and took in his surroundings with his shadow sight. The banked fire in a large hearth emitted a wan, orange illumination. He noted two high-backed comfortable chairs near the hearth, a makeup table with a mirror and a small chair, and dominating the room a large canopied bed. His Rhianne would be there.

He crossed the room, but the bed was empty.

"I'm over here."

••••

Rhianne awoke in the night and sensed Morgin somewhere in the castle. She'd sensed him earlier that day, and prayed that he would not endanger himself by coming for her. Then in a blink he had left, but she knew he'd return. Now that he was back, this time he would find her, and she needed to prepare herself mentally to confront him.

She climbed out of bed, still stiff and sore from Valso's beating, though she'd improved greatly in just the last day. She threw on a heavy robe, crossed the room and sat down in one of the high-backed chairs in front of the hearth, then triggered the spell she'd concocted to hide the bruises on her face. Morgin was not the type to take one look at her bruises, rush to Valso's suites and openly challenge the king to something misguidedly heroic. But still, if he saw how she'd been treated, he'd resist even more strongly when she told him she could not leave with him, not yet.

She didn't have long to wait. She heard him lift the latch on the door, open it, step into the room, close it, then cross the room to her bed.

"I'm over here," she said.

In a heartbeat he stood in front of her. She rose and stepped into his embrace, and as he wrapped his arms around her he said, "To find this one moment in time I would march across the Plains of Quam a hundred days, struggle through the oven of the Munjarro's sands for a thousand."

He held her in silence for a moment, then whispered, "I've missed you."

"I've missed you too," she said.

"I love you."

"I love you too."

"Let's go. I can take you away from here in my shadows."

She hesitated, and as she did so he frowned. "I can't," she said. "My duty lies here."

She leaned away from him and looked into his face, and now she did see the pain there. "What do you mean?" he asked.

"After you leave here you're going to return, aren't you? With an army. You'll take Durin, so you can fight Valso and his master. But the little serpent is too dangerous to leave unchecked."

"No," he said, sounding like a little boy again, tears streaming down his cheeks. "Stay away from Bayellgae. His venom would consume you. What can you do against him?"

"I have an idea, but I must remain here to make it work."

"No, we've waited so long for this."

"And we'll wait a bit longer." She felt tears flooding her own eyes.

He squeezed her tightly, kissed her gently on the neck, and she heard him inhale her scent with a long, deep intake of breath. "I can't allow you to do this."

She felt his tears dripping on her bare shoulder. She ignored him and said, "Be wary of the Nether Plane."

"What do you mean?"

"Now that Salula and Metadan are gone, Valso's master is looking for you there. If you venture to any level beyond the Mortal Plane, he can probably harm you."

"I can't avoid it completely, but I'll be careful."

She said, "And there's something else you must know, my darling."

She'd thought about this long and hard, knew that she was likely the only person who truly understood the blade, because she now truly understood her Morgin. She recalled that moment when she'd first seen him on the shelf of rock in the side of Attunhigh. She'd thought that when Salula spun her, Valso's spell compelled her to track the blade, when in fact it compelled her to track Morgin. "There is no power in the blade. It is but a thing of steel."

He leaned back from her, looked into her eyes with a deep frown on his brow. She continued. "The power we all sensed . . . and feared . . . it was yours. It was the power in your soul, and you needed to learn to control it."

"No," he said, shaking his head. "It was evil and malevolent."

She ran a finger down the line of his jaw. "No, it was tormented and in pain, and when you didn't control it, it struck out. And now you're the one in control. I'm so proud of you. When this is done we'll make a life together."

"Yes," he said. "We'll go back to Elhiyne."

She shook her head. "No. I can't live under that old woman's thumb. Perhaps you can find a little cottage somewhere, with a brook or a stream nearby, and far from Elhiyne." She knew she was fantasizing, understood it would likely never come to pass.

"There's one more thing," she said.

He leaned away from her to look in her face, held her gently by her shoulders. The dim light from the fire in the hearth glinted off the moisture on his cheeks. "What?"

"I need a little of your blood. Just a few drops."

"Why?"

She hadn't known what she would do, still wasn't exactly sure, but the seed of a plan had begun to form. She said, "A little surprise for a little snake."

••••

Sitting on the bed and sharpening her dagger, Cort watched Tulellcoe pace back and forth in their little room, growing increasingly impatient with every heartbeat. They'd waited well into the night for Morgin to return, and yet nothing. Tulellcoe was not good at waiting.

"Where is he?" he demanded. "He should have been back by now."

"Calm down," she said. "I'm sure he's all right."

"Something must have happened. Something must have gone wrong. Where is he?"

As if answering his question, Morgin stepped out of the shadow in the corner—alone. Tulellcoe crossed the room and gripped him by the shoulders. "Where's Rhianne?"

Morgin seemed stunned as he said, "She wouldn't come, said she has to stay to fight the demon snake. She said a lot of things."

Cort was struck again by how much the two men looked alike.

"No," Tulellcoe said. "You shouldn't have listened to her."

Morgin looked at Tulellcoe and the stunned look on his face disappeared, as if he'd just come to a decision. "No, uncle, she is strong, much stronger than you realize. Much stronger than I realized."

Morgin stepped back from Tulellcoe. "She and I have a battle to win. I'll have an army here in a few days; six armies, in fact. I need you to prepare at this end. I'll be back tomorrow and I'll need a horse. The three of us will ride south, so provision the horses with trail rations." He nodded toward the lamp on the floor. "We'll need that lamp, so make sure we've got a good supply of oil for it."

He turned, walked to the shadow in the corner but stopped and looked back at them. "I'm not sure when I'll be back tomorrow, but try to maintain this shadow all day."

Cort nodded, saw Tulellcoe do the same.

Morgin stepped into the shadow.

••••

Morgin didn't know any shadows on the border where the Penda and Elhiyne armies had gathered to destroy one another, so when he stepped into the shadow in Cort and Tulellcoe's room, he sought out a shadow at Castle Elhiyne. It was late, well after sunset, so the shadows in the castle yard had long ago disappeared. But when not under siege, a guard shack just outside the main gates was always manned, with a torch burning outside it that cast a small shadow in the lee of the shack. He stepped into that now.

As he stepped out of the shadow in front of the main gates Mortiss spluttered. *You're late.*

"Sorry," he said. "We have to get to the border before dawn. Can you manage that?"

She didn't answer, basically implying that, *of course she could.*

He climbed into the saddle and she put a nether wind in his face. He recalled Rhianne's warning about the Nether Plane and Valso's master. He sensed something probing at the edge of his soul, but Mortiss chose ways just below the Mortal Plane, not deep in the netherworld, so perhaps that protected him.

Mortiss neighed, *You are right to fear the Dark God in his realm.*

The netherworld was a part of him now, and he wondered how that had come to pass.

You've always been nether.

For the first time he found traveling the nether ways difficult. Something constantly pawed at the boundaries of his awareness, as if he was protected in a cage with some beast trying to break in. By the time Mortiss delivered him to a low hill overlooking the border, exhaustion weighed heavily on him. He arrived just before dawn and the sun had yet to rise. In the dark the campfires of the two armies dotted the landscape below him.

Before leaving Rhianne, Morgin had told her he would briefly check Sabian's castle yard at dawn each morning. If she needed to communicate with him, he would meet her there. He didn't think she'd be there since he'd already spoken with her earlier that night, but he'd promised, so he detoured briefly into the Kingdom of Dreams. He waited alone in Sabian's yard until Mortiss stomped a fore hoof into the ground. *Dawn has come to the Mortal Plane.*

32

The Lie in a Name

BRANDON WOULD HAVE liked to keep BlakeDown and Olivia apart, but the old woman insisted on meeting the Penda leader personally. They'd agreed to meet at dawn, with an escort of six twelves each; the escorts would hold back two hundred paces while the leaders met in the middle. Each leader was allowed to bring his or her heir, plus one member of the ruling family, plus a senior lieutenant or captain. BlakeDown was not a man normally given to rational discourse, so Brandon was curious why he'd chosen to talk first.

Theandrin, ErrinCastle, PaulStaff and his son, and an older officer Brandon didn't recognize, accompanied BlakeDown. Olivia brought with her Brandon, Wylow and his son SandoFall, and AnnaRail and France, though AnnaRail had forcefully asserted her authority to be sure she and the swordsman were part of the group. They met in the middle between the two escorts, and all remained mounted.

"Well, BlakeDown," Olivia said, "why the change of heart?"

"No change of heart," he said. "I thought it only right to give you an opportunity to petition for peace."

Theandrin gave BlakeDown an angry, piercing look that would have made Brandon flinch had it been aimed his way.

"We have no desire to petition for peace. You're the one who sent the messenger and wanted to talk, so talk."

BlakeDown opened his mouth, but before he could speak Theandrin said, "We have learned that Valso wants this war, wants to see us weaken each other."

Olivia's horse pranced sideways a step, but the old woman calmed it quickly, and Brandon recalled that as a young girl she'd been an accomplished horsewoman. "I could have told you that," she said.

Theandrin nodded. "Yes, we all know Valso's proclivities, don't we? But need we cater to him?"

"Valso is always a concern," Olivia said, punctuating her words with a level of arrogance Brandon would never attempt to imitate. "But we are here because of another issue: the unprovoked attack upon the heir to Elhiyne."

BlakeDown nudged his horse forward a step and said, "The attack was provoked."

"Provoked by an incident with a minor lord of Penda." Olivia said, her voice dripping with scorn.

"Nevertheless," BlakeDown said. "Still a lord of Penda."

Olivia threw her head back and laughed. "Very well then, we shall attack ErrinCastle and you attack one of the lesser lords of Elhiyne. I might even provide you with one to attack. Then after we've bloodied your heir and nearly killed him, we'll be even."

BlakeDown's eyes narrowed and his face turned red.

"Alternatively," Olivia continued. "We are due reparation. Make payment, and we'll all walk away from this."

BlakeDown reached to the sword strapped to his saddle. ErrinCastle reached across and tried to stay his hand, but he shook ErrinCastle off and drew the broadsword. "Never," he shouted, as swords were drawn by the armsmen on both sides.

Brandon turned about in his saddle and held up a hand to stay the Elhiyne armsmen, and ErrinCastle did the same to the Pendas. BlakeDown roared, spurred his warhorse sideways, bumping ErrinCastle's mount and almost knocking him from the saddle. He turned back to his armsmen and shouted, "Advance."

••••

Morgin climbed into Mortiss's saddle in Sabian's yard, and she returned him to the low hill overlooking the two armies. It was a little after dawn when he nudged her into a canter and headed down toward the border. As he rode he spotted two large troops of mounted armsmen each holding position about two hundred paces from the border. The troop on the far side carried BlakeDown's banner, while that on the near carried Olivia's. He estimated about six twelves in each troop, and between them a dozen individuals on horseback were meeting on the border. Had someone finally been touched by sanity and decided to talk instead of spilling blood?

He was about half way there when he sensed the pull of power and felt the anger accompanying it. With so many memories to guide him he recognized that anger: Olivia was about to kill someone.

Morgin knew he had to get there immediately and stop this before blood was spilled. His first thought was to spur Mortiss hard and race down there to intervene, but then he realized there was a better way. He reined Mortiss to a stop and said, "I think we need to arrive on a nether wind, and quickly."

••••

"Hold," Brandon shouted. "Hold."

With six twelves of Penda armsmen charging toward them, and six twelves of Elhiynes charging up from behind, all with swords drawn, they were about to find themselves in the midst of a bloodbath. France snarled, "I'll protect AnnaRail, you take Olivia."

Brandon reined his horse to the side and spurred it toward the old woman. But a black cloud of shadow descended upon him and a monster from netherhell appeared in front of him, a demon horse twice the size of any mortal horse mounted by a demon rider wearing a twisted, fanged, distortion of Morgin's face, and carrying a blood-red talon the length of a man's arm. It was the demon he'd dreamed about in his nightmares. It opened its mouth and cried out a scream that sent waves of fear coursing through his soul. His horse bucked and kicked beneath him, and it was all he could do to stay in the saddle as it carried him away in a panicked charge. The animal galloped west for a hundred strides before he got it under control, but it still took every bit of horsemanship he had to calm it and bring it to a halt. He reined it about and took in the carnage where they'd met the Penda's.

Everyone had suffered the same nightmare, and the armsmen on both sides had been scattered over an area about a thousand paces wide, most of them unhorsed. France, AnnaRail and Theandrin remained in the saddle back at the meeting point, had apparently been unaffected by the apparition. BlakeDown was on his butt on the ground beneath Theandrin's horse, a dazed look on his face. Brandon spotted Olivia and Wylow about a hundred paces away walking their mounts back and helping SandoFall, who was horseless and limping badly. In the other direction ErrinCastle helped PaulStaff up off the ground. There was no sign of PaulStaff's son, or BlakeDown's senior officer.

In ones and twos they all reassembled at the meeting point, without their armsmen to back them. As BlakeDown climbed to his feet Brandon noticed his hands were empty, no broadsword, and a quick glance about produced no sign of the blade.

They slowly reassembled at the border, some standing, some astride their horses, no one willing to break the silence. Then Olivia opened her mouth to say something, but before she spoke a shadow descended upon them all, blinding them. Brandon had a moment of fear, but the apparition didn't reappear, and the horses didn't panic. The shadow lifted, and there, seated upon his horse in their midst, was Morgin.

France said, "A bit dramatic, don't you think, lad?"

Morgin shrugged. "But effective."

Morgin had changed considerably since Brandon had last seen him, as if in the year or more he'd been gone he'd aged ten. Again Olivia started to say something, but Morgin raised a hand, silencing her. "Hear me, and listen."

Olivia eyed him skeptically, then closed her mouth and nodded.

He continued. "I am the Unnamed King, and my realm is the Kingdom of Dreams." He looked at BlakeDown, then back at Olivia. "Stand down now, for if you don't, the war you fight will always be in your dreams."

BlakeDown stepped toward Morgin, the muscles in his jaw bunched. He spoke through gritted teeth. "You gave us those dreams?"

Morgin nodded. "Yes, Lord BlakeDown, I did."

Clutching his arm to his chest and in obvious pain, PaulStaff said to BlakeDown, "My men and I are withdrawing. I didn't want this war in the first place."

"And I and my men," Wylow said. "We're withdrawing as well."

Morgin shook his head and said, "No, we're going to Durin. I'm going to end this now, and all of the clan leaders need to be there."

"Impossible," BlakeDown said. "That's a six-day forced march. We're not equipped for that. We don't have the supply lines."

"Ride east," Morgin said, "and I guarantee you'll be in Durin in far less than six days."

Spittle flew from BlakeDown's mouth as he snarled, "I'm taking my men west, back to my castle."

Morgin leaned forward in his saddle, leaned down toward BlakeDown and spoke calmly. "You're going to learn that as you ride west your nightmares only get worse. On the other hand, the farther east you ride, the sweeter will be your dreams. Take these armies east—no supply wagons, just donkeys and pack horses—and meet me at dawn, tomorrow, in the shadow of Attunhigh."

Olivia cackled with laughter, and Morgin disappeared into a shadow.

••••

Hidden within his shadows Morgin slipped into the Elhiyne army's encampment, then into Olivia's command pavilion. He extinguished his shadows, grabbed a chair and sat down at the map table to wait for them to return from the meeting point. He looked at the maps strewn across the table, and a small piece of charcoal caught his attention. He picked it up, then drew the sigil of the sunset king in one corner of the table top. Beneath that he added the two crossed lines that symbolized the balance of clan law. He did not add the additional lines that made them look like crossed swords.

He contemplated that symbol, the name that had been his for so long but was not truly his: AethonLaw. He had always known that was not his name, and had feared what his true name might reveal. And he now knew that his fears were well founded.

He heard the rustle of skirts and the soft patter of a woman's step crossing the floor behind him. Olivia leaned over his shoulder and looked down at the symbol he'd scratched. "Hmmm! Contemplating your name, eh?"

Morgin shrugged, not willing to waste time informing her it was not truly his name, and not willing to suffer the argument that would ensue.

"Exactly!" she said, a strange response to his shrug.

She stepped around him and into his field of view. Then she lifted her hand, palm up. "May I have the charcoal, grandson?"

He wasn't sure what she intended to do and suspicion clouded his thoughts. Nevertheless, he placed the charcoal on her open palm.

"Let's contemplate your real name," she said, and with two rapid strokes she added the lines that looked like cross-guards on swords. She finished by calling him, "AethonSword."

Morgin flinched so hard he almost toppled over in his chair. He stood to face her. "You saw ElkenSkul draw the last two lines? You knew all along?"

She gave him that irritating, condescending, all-knowing smile of hers. "Of course I saw. Of course I knew."

"Then why didn't you speak up? Why did you allow me to be misnamed?"

She shook her head and sighed sadly. "Child, such a name would only be given to one destined to be the Shahotma King. And had the other clans learned that you had been granted that name, you would not have lived past the next full moon. We would have had assassins trying to breach our defenses at every turn. You needed time to grow, to develop your powers and your mundane martial skills, so you could defend yourself."

"But why didn't you at least tell me? I spent years looking for the meaning of that symbol."

"It would only have frightened you back then. And you were a timid enough child as it was. No, the burden of such a name would have been too much, and you might never have come into your power."

She too had made the mistake of thinking he bore the true name of AethonSword. And while he knew she, along with Erithnae and Metadan, was wrong, he wasn't about to open that argument with her. He turned away from her, found AnnaRail standing in the open entrance to the pavilion, Roland behind her, tiny little NickoLot peering around from behind the two of them. "I'm sorry," AnnaRail said. "Had I known of her deceit, I wouldn't have let you live with such uncertainty?"

AnnaRail walked into the room, followed by Roland and NickoLot. Behind them came JohnEngine and Brandon. JohnEngine burst around his parents, came at Morgin like a charging bull, wrapped him in a bear hug and tried to lift him off the floor. Morgin was larger than him, and he barely succeeded, but they got a good laugh out of it.

Brandon slapped him on the back and shook his hand, saying, "Back from the dead. You always were full of surprises."

France had slipped into the tent and stood near the entrance. Morgin approached him and put a hand on his shoulder. The swordsman smiled, and Morgin saw that glint in his eye again. "You look a lot better."

"Yah," the swordsman said. "Your mother's healing has some benefits. But damn, I hate magic."

Brandon said, "Thank the gods you averted this idiotic war."

"Oh child," Olivia said. "There was never going to be any war. I wouldn't have allowed it."

"But—" Brandon said. "But you—you did everything you could to start a war."

Olivia let out a dramatic sigh. "Haven't you learned yet that everything is so much more complicated than the way it appears?" She pointed at Morgin. "He needed an army, and I gathered one for him. In fact, if you look closely, you'll see I got him two."

To Morgin she said, "You should thank me."

Morgin said, "Thank you, grandmother. But what do we have out there, the two armies together, maybe four or five thousand men?" He recalled the walls of the Decouix city. "I need far more than that to breach the walls of Durin."

"How will you get them?" Nicki asked.

He looked at the tiny woman, remembered how he'd liked making funny faces at the little child, now a powerful witch. "With the help of three of the most powerful witches in the clans, I hope to add seven thousand to that number. Will you help me, Nicki?"

"Of course."

He turned to AnnaRail. "And you?"

She simply nodded.

He turned to Olivia. "And you?"

The old woman smiled. "I'm intrigued, grandson. What are we going to do?"

Morgin was at a loss. He hadn't figured out how he would get the three women east of the Worshippers in a single night, and it was imperative that he do so. He didn't know a good shadow there, so that wouldn't work. On Mortiss he could ride the nether ways, but she couldn't carry all four of them.

A common armsmen stepped into the pavilion, approached Olivia and dropped to one knee. The man was literally trembling with fear. "Your Ladyship, I— I—"

"What is it?" she demanded. "Spit it out."

"Dogs, Your Ladyship. Giant dogs, three of 'em, bigger'n horses, with eyes and teeth that glow. And they talk. They asked for the Unnamed King."

They all turned to Morgin with a questioning look.

Outside the tent a horse neighed. *I invited them*, Mortiss said.

"Not dogs," he said. "That would be WolfDane, the hellhound king, and a couple of his subjects."

To Olivia he said, "Tonight you're going to learn to ride the nether ways with me."
She started, and he realized it was the only time in his life he'd ever surprised her.

••••

DaNoel wanted nothing to do with the monsters Morgin called hellhounds, and from the fearful looks on people's faces, he wasn't the only one. He stepped back, putting as much distance as he could between him and the beasts. Since there'd be no war, maybe he could find one of the camp-followers, have a little fun.

Where have you been?

He cringed at the sound of the Decouix's voice in his head. *Watching the whoreson. He averted your little war.*

What do you mean?

DaNoel heard the frustration in Valso's words. *There are rumors everywhere. According to one, you had some Penda whore working for you, convincing BlakeDown to start a war. But BlakeDown killed her yesterday.*

She was a tool, and sometimes a tool fails and is discarded.

I assume you plan to discard me too.

Oh no, not at all. You're much too valuable to me.

Especially since Morgin killed Salula, and now I'm all you've got left. Incidentally, France is back among us, and apparently quite healthy.

DaNoel sensed Valso's anger flare, felt him struggle to suppress it. Never before had Valso's emotions come through their link so clearly, and he wondered if the Decouix king had lost some of his control. *None of that matters.*

All of your plans are failing, and none of it matters. I think not.

Blinding pain shot through DaNoel's head and he staggered, barely managed to keep his feet. *Please, stop. I'll be discovered.* The pain snapped off. DaNoel sat down at one of the campfires to catch his breath.

I could kill you with merely a thought, or even better, let you live with intense pain for years. So don't push me. What is your brother planning?

It irritated him that Valso insisted on calling the whoreson his brother. But as the vestiges of the pain slowly receded, DaNoel new he'd have to give the Decouix something. *He's combined the Penda and Elhiyne armies, and he's going to bring them to Durin.*

How many men?

Four to five thousand.

That's nothing, Valso said. *It will take ten times that to breach the walls of this city. And it'll take six or seven days to get here.*

He says he can get this army to Durin in far less time than that, and everyone's wondering how he plans to do it.

He does, does he?

DaNoel could almost hear Valso's thoughts churning. The Decouix continued. *He's going to use the nether ways. To transport an army that size he'll have to, and he'll have to go deep, and my master will be waiting for him.*

••••

Rhianne's Kull escort opened the door to Valso's workshop and held it for her. She stepped into the room with no idea what to expect, and tried to be ready for anything. Valso was expounding on something, while Carsaris and Magwa listened raptly. Or perhaps they only pretended to listen, for if the king felt slighted in any way, someone always died. Rhianne took note of the little snake coiled on its perch in the corner, Valso's favorite executioner.

"Rhianne, my lovely Rhianne." Valso crossed the room, took her hand and kissed it with a flourish. She never trusted his exuberance, for he could turn dark and angry in a heartbeat.

"I was just telling Magwa and Carsaris that your husband is coming, and he's bringing an army."

He turned, took her arm and marched her across the room. "But it's a paltry army. Between Magwa's forces and mine, we have him outnumbered five to one. And we have Durin's walls."

Magwa said, "My generals tell me it will take fifty thousand men to breach the walls of this city."

Valso released Rhianne's arm, leaned toward her and kissed her gently on the cheek. "I don't have to seek out your husband, because the fool is coming to me. He's giving me exactly what I want."

Rhianne said, "But every—"

Magwa barked, "Silence."

"No, no, no," Valso said. "Let her speak."

She hesitated, knew she would pay a price for her words, but it was up to her to carry the battle to Valso. "It seems to me that every time you think you have him defeated, he surprises you."

Valso blinked, and his eyes narrowed in thought, then his smile slowly disappeared. He frowned, then he lashed out and hit her. She fell to the floor, managed to keep from striking her head on the stone.

As Magwa and Carsaris cringed and stepped back, he stood over her and screamed, "You are insane, woman."

At the sound of his fury the little serpent shot off its perch and dashed across the room. "I'll kill her for you, massster."

Now was the critical moment. If Rhianne was going to bring her plan to fruition, this would be her only chance. Valso stepped back and she rose slowly to her feet, cringing beneath the snake as it hovered above her. She tilted her head slightly to one side, exposing the side of her throat. "Then do so, little snake," she said, "for I care not if I live."

It was a lie, a gamble, a calculated risk that Valso would want her continued presence for his gloating. The snake darted toward her, its fangs extended dripping venom. In the same heartbeat that thing that haunted Valso entered his soul and he shouted, "No."

He swung out. The snake darted around his arm and halted just above Rhianne's throat, hovering, drops of venom dripping from its fangs onto her skin.

"Do not defy me, little snake," Valso's master said as fiery pain erupted on Rhianne's throat, accompanied by a hissing crackle where the venom had touched her.

"Back away," Valso said, and the little snake retreated.

Rhianne grimaced with pain. When Valso saw that, he produced a delicate handkerchief and tossed it to her, saying, "Get that healed."

Carsaris stepped forward. Valso held up a hand. "Not you. I need you too much here, now."

To Rhianne he said, "Go find another healer, or heal it yourself."

Rhianne took the handkerchief and rushed out of his workshop, but she went to her own suite, not to a healer. Geanna and the girls tried to hover over her, but she kicked them angrily out of her room. She retrieved a small mirror, and carefully wiped the remaining venom onto the cloth. Ignoring the burning pain on the side of her throat, she retrieved another handkerchief from the bottom of a chest. On it were the dark stains of Morgin's blood, seven drops now dried and brown. Since taking them from him, she'd carefully prepared them with all the magic she could summon without being detected by Valso.

She rubbed the two pieces of cloth together, mixing the dried blood and venom, blood from a man in whose veins the venom had flowed. Then she stuffed the two handkerchiefs into a goblet from her nightstand, and poured water over them. She carefully lifted the two pieces of cloth out of the goblet and wrung them dry over it, leaving it half-filled with water that had taken on a faint, brownish tint. She fed power into the water and said, "Let the fire of the venom flow with the chill of ice." Then she put the goblet to her mouth and drank the contents, praying that the essence in Morgin's blood that now protected him from Bayellgae's venom would keep her alive.

Her stomach cramped up, spasming in an effort to reject the concoction, but she held it down as she slumped to the floor. Geanna found her there and called in Carsaris.

33

Exile Absolved

RIDING ON THE back of a hellhound through, as Morgin called it, the nether ways, Nicki decided she would have a little talk with that brother of hers. Earlier that morning, outside Olivia's command pavilion, Morgin had politely introduced them to WolfDane, the hellhound king. Then WolfDane had introduced Nicki to Lord KarlDane, one of his subjects, all nice and polite and formal. Hellhounds! Nether ways! How many more surprises was Morgin going to spring on her without warning?

The armsman hadn't exaggerated—just the opposite—the hellhounds dwarfed a normal horse. As she'd stepped out of the tent Nicki hadn't known what to expect, but when she saw the enormous beasts with golden-yellow eyes and teeth that glowed, massive canines that could snap her spine with a shrug, fear washed through her. How was she going to ride an unsaddled monster?

With a nether wind in her face, she leaned forward on its back, kept her eyes closed, her fingers buried in its fur gripping fiercely, her legs straddling its spine. Oddly enough, her saddle sores from yesterday's ride didn't bother her in the least. The nether beast must emit some aura that helped her stay mounted without discomfort, or maybe its fur simply cushioned her. And while the night had a chill to it, the warmth that radiated off the massive animal comforted her, and she drifted off into a pleasant doze . . .

Standing in the midst of a vast forest, a dark canopy of leaves overhead, Morgin said, "You've nothing to fear. Come, let me show you the Kingdom of Dreams. It's near dawn and I have to check for Rhianne."

Nicki looked around at the forest, couldn't mask the awe in her voice as she said, "The Kingdom of Dreams!"

"Yes," Morgin said, though he sounded tired. "I'm the Unnamed King. Didn't you hear me tell everyone that?"

"Yes, but I—" Nicki couldn't find any words to express how she felt. She spun toward him and said, "When this is done, you're going to sit down with me and tell me everything."

He smiled and nodded. "Okay, but it's a long story."

She noticed he had dark bags under his eyes. In the shadows of the forest canopy she hadn't noticed them until she looked closely. And he walked like an old man. "What's wrong?"

He grimaced. "The nether ways have become . . . difficult."

He threw his shoulders back and once again stood straight and tall. "Come, let me show you Sabian."

He took her hand and led her to the strangest castle she'd ever seen, walls, turrets and parapets all made from the life of the Living Forest. It was a wonderful dream, marred only by the way Morgin seemed so weary.

"Nicki, wake up."

She opened her eyes, had trouble leaving her dreams. She sat up, still straddling the monstrous beast, Morgin standing beside her. She looked about, saw that they'd entered the Benesh'ere camp, whitefaces walking about everywhere. The sun had just risen and hung low on the eastern horizon.

"Let me help you down," Morgin said. He reached up, took her by the waist, lifted her off the monster's back and set her down beside it. Nicki thought he looked tired, exhausted, or was that just part of a dream?

Olivia laughed like a school girl. "That was exhilarating. Grandson, you'll have to let me do that again, some time."

They gathered in Angerah's tent with several senior members of the black tribe, where they were served a breakfast of warm tea, fruit and roasted meat—she wasn't sure what kind. Nicki ate in silence.

Speaking to the Benesh'ere, Morgin said, "I need you to gather the entire tribe, every man woman and child. Don't overlook a single soul, have them ready to travel, and meet me at Gilguard's Ford."

The Benesh'ere sat silent and unmoving. Angerah said, "Where are we going, SteelMaster?"

Morgin said, "It's time to ride to Durin."

Several of them nodded solemnly, as if those words held some great significance for them. Nicki paused, for the Benesh'ere couldn't ride to Durin, and then she realized the import of Morgin's words. Oh, she was definitely going to have a talk with that brother of hers.

••••

Mounted again on the back of a hellhound, Nicki followed Morgin through the netherworld up the steep slope, AnnaRail and Olivia behind her on their mounts. They gained altitude quickly, then the terrain leveled off into a flat expanse of rock, and they stepped back onto the Mortal Plane. She watched Morgin shrug off his weariness, and she worried about him, thankful they'd spent only a short time in the nether ways.

Around them stretched a wide plateau with little soil to support vegetation. The occasional stunted tree and small clump of brush grew here and there among the boulders and loose rocks of black basalt.

Morgin led them to the edge of the plateau. He dismounted, helped her off KarlDane's back again, and as he put her down she noticed a trickle of blood on his upper lip.

She said, "You have a nose bleed."

He touched a finger to his lip, examined the blood for a moment then wiped his lip with his sleeve. He started to turn away but she grabbed his arm and said, "What's wrong?"

He grimaced and said, "The nether ways . . ."

"Then stay out of them."

"I can't, not completely, not if we want any chance of victory."

They approached edge of the cliff carefully, eased their way toward it slowly, all of them but Olivia in a crouch. Nicki wanted to get down on her hands and knees, but the old witch would never approve. Below them, in the distance, the Plains of Quam stretched to the horizon.

Morgin pointed east. "You see the Ulbb there."

The river formed a jagged line zig-zagging its way east.

Still pointing, Morgin said, "Now see that ridge south of it, and south of the ridge the jagged line of overgrown brush that looks like another river."

"What is it?" Nicki asked.

"Centuries ago," Morgin said. "That's where the Ulbb flowed."

When Morgin explained what he wanted them to do, even Olivia was taken aback. "That will take quite a bit of preparation, grandson, and enormous power."

"I know," Morgin said, and there was nothing cavalier about the way he said it. "That's why I need you three."

••••

At the base of the cliff Morgin selected a large boulder with a good shadow on its north side; it would be there most of the day. He pulled Mortiss to a halt, dismounted and said, "Wait here. I'll be back about mid-afternoon."

She neighed, *Don't be late.*

He stepped into the shadow, stepped out of the shadow in the corner of Cort and Tulellcoe's room. The older man stood at the room's window, and there was no sign of Cort.

Tulellcoe turned away from the window and said, "Cort's with the horses now, holding them ready. We figured you'd be in a hurry. I've already paid for our room, and the lamp, so we're set to go."

They extinguished the lamp, retrieved Tulellcoe's cloak from the back of the chair, met Cort down in the street, and rode south. Morgin led them to the forest south of the city, and as they rode he outlined his plan to them. They were politely supportive, but clearly didn't believe he could do it.

When Haleen had helped him escape from the Decouix dungeons, she'd brought him to this forest in a carriage, and left him here. Tall pines grew sparsely, with little undergrowth between them, and a carpet of pine needles blanketing the dirt. It was a perfect place to conceal an army—six armies—and with the tall pines casting shadows everywhere, perfect for what he needed.

They hurriedly set up a small camp. He couldn't use the natural shadows of the trees, for they'd change with the movement of the sun and disappear when it set. In the shadows of a cluster of pines they lit the lamp and placed it on the ground. They hung Tulellcoe's cloak from a tree branch, and positioned it so it cast a tall, wide shadow.

Morgin said, "Keep this shadow here tonight and through tomorrow morning."

He stepped into the shadow, then stepped out of the shadow on the north side of the boulder.

Mortiss neighed, *We don't have much time.*

Morgin expected there to be delays in gathering up the Benesh'ere and not missing a single soul, but when he rode into their camp near the Lake of Sorrows he found it deserted. There were no tents, and the only thing that moved were swirls of steam and smoke rising from hundreds of quenched campfires. He turned Mortiss east and headed for the God's Road.

Seven thousand people walking or riding, with an untold number of heavily packed chakarras, left plenty of signs of their passage. The dirt of the road had been churned up by boots and hooves, and the wild grasses on either side had been trampled out of existence.

Just south of Gilguard's Ford the tribe had bivouacked along the sides of the road, sitting or lying wherever they found a comfortable spot, leaving a narrow passage up the middle of the ancient highway. As Morgin rode through them no one greeted him, called out or cheered. No one tried to question him; they simply rose up as he passed by and stood in mute anticipation. Angerah, Jerst, Harriok, Branaugh, Jack and all the other Benesh'ere he'd grown close to were waiting just south of the ford.

He reined Mortiss to a stop and said, "We ride east."

Blesset scowled openly and several of them frowned, but no one questioned him. Those with horses mounted up, while the rest followed on foot. They traveled through lightly wooded forest, which after about a league opened up into open grassland. He spotted the ridge he'd pointed out to the three witches from the top of the cliff, the ridge he'd seen when retrieving Jack the Greater's body after the poor fellow had tried to cross the ford. Morgin led the Benesh'ere up to its crest. He continued east for another league, with the banks of the Ulbb on his left, and on his right the ancient riverbed through which it had flowed centuries ago.

As Morgin rode, his gut tightened with fear. Olivia, AnnaRail and NickoLot might fail, in which case his whiteface friends would be sorely disappointed, and Morgin would not have the army he needed to breach the walls of Durin. But the greatest danger was that the three witches would succeed, and Morgin would learn that he'd misinterpreted the riddle of the seventh wrong. In that case he'd have to watch seven thousand men, women and children bleed out through their eyes, ears, noses and mouths. If that happened, he swore he'd stay until the last of them died; he owed them that much.

He had them stop and cluster on the crest of the ridge. He rode around the tribe slowly, making sure that everyone stood on raised ground between the riverbed of old, and that of the present. Then he rode to the top of the crest and stopped in their midst. In the distance the black, basalt cliff loomed above them.

AnnaRail had prepared a little charm for him, a small silver trinket connected by her arcane magics to one she carried. He retrieved it from a pocket, looked at it for a moment, then touched it to his tongue, activating it with a bit of saliva. She would know they were ready.

He started counting heartbeats, was going to count to a hundred, but only made it to ten when he saw a massive piece of the cliff slump away from it. A few heartbeats later he heard a rumble like distant thunder. The sound grew, and as it became a roar many of the whitefaces covered their ears with their hands. Then the ground shook, the horses panicked, and for many it had been a mistake to remain in the saddle. Some were unhorsed as the ground beneath them became unstable, but the shaking reached a peak, then subsided, and silence returned.

Morgin closed his eyes and waited. The Benesh'ere waited silently with him. He counted a hundred heartbeats, then another hundred, and another. Someone nearby coughed, Blesset harrumphed, someone else cleared his throat. A word was spoken here, a question there, and slowly the crest of the hill filled with the sound of fear, disappointment, and regret. But beneath the sounds of seven thousand people Morgin listened to the sound of the river. Facing west, his right ear picked up the sounds of its flow, the soft crackle of water breaking over a rock, or splitting around a large root. And little-by-little those sounds died, until his right ear heard nothing. Then his left ear picked up the sound of a wave of water flowing over dry land, a strange sort of popping sound.

He opened his eyes and looked south at the ancient dry riverbed, and the wave of water washing down through it. He looked down at his whiteface friends, waiting to see if he'd been wrong, to see the pain and blood and death, but none came. Morgin recalled the ancient riddle: *the Benesh'ere will not be free until they stand north of the Ulbb, but the Benesh'ere cannot cross the Ulbb until they are free.*

Jerst said it. "I did not cross the Ulbb, but I stand north of the Ulbb, a free man."

••••

Blesset had tears in her eyes as she drew her sword, raised it high and shouted, "We ride on Durin, now."

"No," Morgin said, and even Jerst and Angerah showed their impatience by looking askance at him.

Morgin said, "That's at least a four-day forced march, with children. Separate out the warriors and I'll have them there much quicker than that."

Angerah frowned and said, "Did you learn nothing during your time with us, Elhiyne?"

Jerst said, "On the March, did you not see even the smallest child carrying a weapon against the Kulls?"

Morgin lowered his head and said, "Forgive me. I forgot." He looked up, locked eyes with Blesset, smiled and said, "But I can still get you there tonight."

She actually smiled, something Morgin had never seen.

To Jerst he said, "Line up your people into a single-file line. All riders should lead their mounts on foot."

As Jerst issued orders and got the tribe organized, Morgin looked at Blesset and said, "Would you like to go first?"

She smiled again. He thought it would be nice if she did so more often.

Morgin cleared a space about four paces wide, then cast a shadow there large enough for a horse to walk through. He raised his voice and shouted, "Spread the word. We're going to a forest about five leagues south of Durin. When each of you gets there, spread out and make camp among the trees."

Holding her horse's reins, Blesset faced the shadow and said, "I'm ready."

Morgin stood beside her, put his hand on her shoulder and said, "Walk forward with me."

They stepped forward into the shadow, and their second step took them out of the shadow cast by the lamp and cloak. Tulellcoe started, and Morgin said, "Disperse them as I bring them through."

He turned around and stepped back through the shadow.

It was slow work, walking each whiteface through the shadow one-by-one. He took them alone, or with a horse or chakarra. After he'd walked about a hundred through, he found that he didn't need to go all the way through himself. He stood half-in and half-out of the shadow on the crest of the hill north of the new course of the Ulbb, and all he needed to do was place his hand on the shoulder of a whiteface or horse or chakarra, and keep the hand on them as they passed into the shadow. By midnight he stood alone on the crest of the hill, so he stepped through the shadow into the forest south of Durin.

Cort said, "Amazing!"

In the night he saw hundreds of small camp fires dotting the landscape of the forest.

"What next?" Tulellcoe asked.

Morgin said, "Get some sleep, then be ready with this shadow at dawn. Time to get another army . . . or two."

He turned and stepped back into the shadow.

••••

Riding Mortiss through the nether ways, Morgin returned to the top of the cliff to retrieve AnnaRail, Olivia and NickoLot. He found the three of them huddled about a small camp fire, the hellhounds resting on their haunches nearby.

Warming her hands at the fire, NickoLot said, "I'm hungry. Got any food?"

Morgin looked at the three women, then at the hellhounds. No rider in the clans would venture even a short distance from home without a minimum of trail rations in his kit. But in their haste, none of them had considered that the hellhounds didn't carry saddle or kit. He rummaged through Mortiss's saddle bags, retrieved what trail rations he had and split them four ways. They ate quickly, then mounted up and returned to the nether ways.

Morgin had come to realize that the deeper Mortiss took him into the netherworld, the faster she and the hellhounds could travel. They had to meet the Elhiyne and Penda armies in the shadow of Attunhigh at sunrise, and with only a few hours remaining before dawn, she had to go deep indeed to get them east of the Worshipers in time.

As he feared, the beast he'd encountered in the netherworld hammered at his protective cage even more forcefully, and each blow rattled his soul. He had a vision, saw again the being who'd sat upon the third throne in Kathbeyanne, a monster with the head of a goat, and blood-red eyes. But when he'd visited Kathbeyanne the creature had been no more than a memory clinging to the rubble of the great city. Now it felt all too real as it assaulted him, and hurt him . . .

"Morgin, wake up."

At the sound of AnnaRail's voice Morgin opened his eyes. He sat in the saddle, slumped forward on Mortiss's back, the three witches standing beside the nether horse, his face sticky with tears. False dawn lit the landscape, though the sun had yet to rise.

He sat up, wiped the tears from his face with his hand, looked at his hand and saw only blood.

AnnaRail put a hand on his knee. "You're bleeding from the eyes. I sensed that the Dark God was close as we traveled the nether ways, but I couldn't help you."

He looked about. To the east Attunhigh loomed over them, and to the west the two armies marched their way.

Olivia said, "Wylow, PaulStaff and BlakeDown will be here shortly. They mustn't see you looking like that."

Feeling like an old man Morgin climbed down out of the saddle. He retrieved his water skin, AnnaRail poured water into his cupped hands and he scrubbed the blood from his face.

"How do I look?" he asked.

NickoLot said, "You look fine."

Olivia shook her head. "She's being nice. You look like netherhell, though there's no blood visible, so that'll have to do."

A group of four scouts from the approaching armies rode up to them. "Thank the gods we've found you," their leader said. He dismounted and bowed deeply to the three witches. "Lord BlakeDown feared you would not return."

Olivia said, "Lord BlakeDown complained the entire way, I'll wager, and was hoping we'd give him an excuse to turn back to his castle."

The scout leader lowered his eyes. He glanced at Morgin, but looked away and said, "He tried to go west, but the dreams stopped him."

He sent two of his men back to the army to report that they'd found Morgin and the three witches, and that they were all well. The two scouts rode away at a gallop. A few heartbeats after they reached the army, a large contingent of mounted riders broke away from it and rode toward them. BlakeDown rode in the lead, and he reined his horse in a few paces from Morgin. "Blast your damn dreams! We can't assault Durin with this army. It's too small."

Morgin nodded his agreement and said, "You're right." That made them all pause. He continued, "The entire Benesh'ere tribe is waiting for us in a forest five leagues south of Durin. We're going to join them."

BlakeDown spluttered, "But the Benesh'ere can't— They can't just—"

"They can now," Morgin said. He turned his back on the Penda leader, walked ten paces east and looked at the approaching army. The sun was just beginning to break over the Worshippers, and it turned the wan light of the false dawn into a patchwork of shadows and brightly lit countryside. Morgin felt the enormous shadow of Attunhigh wash over him; it stretched for leagues.

He stepped from that shadow into the shadow in the forest south of Durin. Tulellcoe and Cort were seated at a small fire, and they both stood as he stepped out of the shadow. "Tell the Benesh'ere to break camp. We'll be coming through shortly, so have everyone form up in the open land north of this forest." He turned around and stepped back into the shadow of Attunhigh.

With Attunhigh's enormous shadow enveloping the entire army, Morgin simply walked among them, touching them and sending them through to Tulellcoe and Cort. Only a few hours after dawn he'd moved the last of them to the forest south of Durin, so he and Mortiss stepped through to join them.

34

Ancient Friends

RHIANNE'S KULLISH GUARDS escorted her down to the ground floor of the castle, then out into the castle yard to a carriage. The Kull lieutenant opened the carriage door and said, "Get in."

"Where are we going?" she asked.

"You'll find out when we get there. Now get in."

She stepped up into the carriage and sat down. The Kull closed the door, leaving her alone in the dark interior. The door had a simple window through which she saw the Kulls mount horses, then the driver snapped his whip and the carriage lurched forward. A few heartbeats later the carriage raced through the gates of the outer bailey and into the city.

She hadn't been allowed outside the walls of the castle since returning to Durin with Salula, which meant something was happening to make today different. As they passed pedestrians in the streets she looked into their faces, hoping to see some indication of an unusual event, but all seemed normal, just another day in the sprawling city.

The carriage pulled to a stop, the Kull lieutenant opened the door and said, "Get out."

She ducked her head, stepped through the door and onto the cobbles of a wide square at least a hundred paces across. Something about it struck a chord of memory, but she couldn't place it. Only when the Kull led her around the carriage did she realize they'd taken her to the main gates in the outer wall of the city. She turned back and looked again at the wide square, recalled that when she'd returned to the city it had been an open market, filled with stalls and vendors hawking their wares. And now it had been cleared, for some reason.

"Don't delay," the Kull lieutenant said.

She turned back to the wall and craned her neck to look up, saw smoke rising into the sky from fires outside the wall. The Kull pointed to a doorless archway in the wall to one side of the gates. It was filled with dark shadow.

"That way," he said.

Inside the archway she found a spiral staircase of stone steps worn by centuries of use. She climbed upward step-by-step, wondering what she would find at the top, circled four times before reaching the top of the wall. She stepped out of an archway onto a wide parapet behind Valso, Carsaris and Magwa, who stood looking at something outside the wall, pointing and gesturing. Carsaris said something about ". . . the Benesh'ere . . ."

The Kull lieutenant stepped out of the archway behind her and said, "Your Majesty."

Valso turned toward them and his eyes brightened. "Rhianne, my lovely Rhianne." He crossed the space between them and kissed her hand with a flourish.

When he looked up she saw the madness in his eyes quite clearly.

Valso threw his head back and laughed. He leaned close and hissed in her ear, "I can see the awe and wonder in your eyes. You see the god within my soul, don't you?"

He took her arm and marched her to the embrasures on the wall, and swept an arm outward. "Magnificent, isn't it?"

A flat plain extended outside the city for a thousand paces, though just outside the walls lay a swath of ash and smoldering wood about three hundred paces wide. She had to think back to recall that there had been a bustling market of ramshackle stalls there.

"We burned the outer market," Valso said. "Can't have them in the way when the city's under siege."

Siege, he'd said. For the first time she took note of the wave of people and horses emerging from the forest in the distance. They had spread out across the no-man's-land and were slowly approaching the city. She leaned out and looked down to the ground, only now realized that the walls of the city stood more than twice as high as the walls of any castle she'd seen.

Carsaris said, "It appears he's freed the Benesh'ere."

"Still," Magwa barked, "There can't be more than twelve thousand, and I'm counting the children among them."

Carsaris said, "Do not discount the Benesh'ere young."

"He's right," Valso said. "My halfmen can tell you the spawn of those crazy desert men have separated more than a few of them from their demon counterparts. But Magwa is right in her own way. It doesn't matter, even if it were twelve thousand fully-blooded warriors, that's nothing against these walls."

Rhianne had to admit that, while she was not trained in the science of war, even she could see that Morgin's army was too small to breach the walls of Durin.

Carsaris said, "It bothers me that he didn't use the nether ways to get them here. How did he get them here?"

Valso turned and vented his anger on the skeletal wizard. "It doesn't matter. He can't breach these walls."

He changed in an instant, went from angry to happy and exuberant. "I almost regret that your husband is such an idiot. What fun is there in stepping on the toes of a fool?"

Rhianne considered his words carefully. "But my husband has never been a fool."

Valso looked her way and his eyes narrowed, and for an instant she thought she saw fear there. She continued, "And every time someone thinks him the fool, it is they who learn the fool's lesson."

Valso's eyes flashed with open fear, and he let that thing into his soul. It spoke in that voice that was not Valso's, "I care nothing for this city, for it is the Mortal Plane I will rule."

He loomed over her, his eyes flaring with the red fires of his hatred. She tried to look away, but he reached out and gripped her throat, lifted her and held her with her toes barely brushing the stone of the parapet. Holding onto his wrist she struggled to breathe as he pulled her face close to his and forced her to look into his eyes. In them she saw armies of tormented souls, broken and twisted by his hatred. In them she saw her fate, and that of the entire Mortal Plane.

He tossed her like a rag doll onto the stone of the parapet. Her head slammed against the battlement and she lost consciousness.

••••

"There's no bloody way we're going to take those walls," BlakeDown said.

Morgin looked past BlakeDown at the walls of Durin as Olivia responded. "I'm sure my grandson has a plan. After all, he defeated Illalla nicely at Csairne Glen when we were heavily outnumbered."

Morgin left BlakeDown and Olivia to their argument. The two were so wrapped up in their mutual animosity, and their constant struggle to gain the upper hand, that neither paid him the least bit of attention. Still holding Mortiss's reins he walked forward to the edge of the ash-charred ground. The impenetrable walls of Durin loomed three hundred paces distant, and well out of bowshot.

He'd considered bypassing the walls, sending warriors through shadows directly into the palace. But he now had enough experience to know it would take hours to transport the entire army. At best, he'd get a few twelves into the palace before Valso realized what he was doing, and a few more into the inner bailey, but that would put them in the midst of an overwhelming force of jackal warriors and Decouix armsmen. Morgin couldn't fight Valso with the odds stacked so heavily against them. He needed an army at his back, with Valso and Magwa's armies neutralized, and to accomplish that he'd have to take the city step by step. But first he had to take the walls, and he knew he couldn't breach them with an army of twelve thousand, needed four or five times that, plus engines of war, ladders, and all the paraphernalia of a siege.

Standing at the edge of the ash-covered ground, he could make out a small group of people on the parapets at the top of Durin's wall just over the main gates, though the distance was too great to discern any detail. For several heartbeats he sensed the enormous well of power Valso had shown him, and that told him the Decouix king stood there looking down at him. He sensed Rhianne there as well, guessed Valso was delighted at the paltry size of the invading army, was probably bragging how he would crush it. It would be so like the Decouix to drag her there to listen to his gloating.

At the thought of Rhianne Morgin recalled her words. *There is no power in the blade. It is but a thing of steel . . . It was the power in your soul, and you needed to learn to control it.*

He gripped the sword's hilt and pulled it from its sheath. He held it up to look at it, let the sun glint off the old blade. He'd never looked at it through the eyes of a Steel-Master before, realized now that somewhere deep inside he had feared doing so, had feared the truth he might find. He examined the old steel from tip to hilt, then lifted his left hand, snapped a fingernail against the blade, and the ping of the metal rang in his ears. He took up the sound, strengthened it, listened to the steel sing, and it did so with a single voice, then he let the sound die. The blade had clearly been forged by a Steel-Master, forged by him. He said to it, "You are my self-forged blade."

Like a fool, all his life he had sought to control the power in the blade, and it took Rhianne's insight to show him the truth. He looked at Mortiss standing quietly beside him. "She was right."

She neighed, *Of course she was.*

While he'd been focused on the blade, NickoLot, AnnaRail and France had come forward to stand beside him. He noticed his Benesh'ere friends had gathered around to watch. They stood about him in silence, though he was thankful he saw no reverence in the looks they gave him, just determination, and expectation.

Somewhere behind him he heard Olivia and BlakeDown coming forward, heard them easily because they continued their argument unabated. Wylow and PaulStaff stepped up beside him, looking toward the walls of the city. Without looking at him Wylow said, "He's right, you know. With what we have, if we try to assault those walls, they'll crush us."

PaulStaff said, "Aye, lad. What are you going to do?"

Morgin had considered using his shadows to attempt to open the city's gates. If he knew a shadow near the gates, he could transport a small force of Benesh'ere there, and take the defenders by surprise from behind. With the gates open they wouldn't have to throw themselves against the walls, which would be futile. But he didn't know any shadows near the gates.

He considered stepping into a shadow he knew in the castle, then working his way from shadow to shadow to the city gates to identify a shadow there. But it had taken him hours to work his way across the city to find Tulellcoe and Cort in the inn, and they couldn't afford to wait hours. At the moment they had the element of surprise. It hadn't taken any preparation to send the city guard out to burn the ramshackle market outside the walls. But if he gave Valso enough time to organize sorties, the battle would be in the open fields outside the city. Badly outnumbered, they would lose that fight.

Morgin turned to Mortiss and said, "What do you think, an aerial assault?"

She neighed, *Excellent idea.*

••••

NickoLot had begun to wonder at Morgin's sanity. Several times now she had watched him speak to his horse as if it were human. He frequently asked the animal its advice, though all he ever got from it was a splutter or a neigh. But somehow that seemed to satisfy him, and now he looked up to the sky expectantly.

NickoLot looked up, looked where he was looking, and saw a flight of birds, tiny black specs against the bright blue of the morning sky, probably a murder of crows. They circled, descending slowly, gliding downward on a dry thermal without flapping their wings, just circling and descending and drifting closer. She began to discern shape and detail, and there was something wrong about these crows. Their bodies were distorted and strange, and certainly larger than crows, probably more the size of a vulture or an eagle. Then she noticed that each had a creature riding on its back. She squinted, and realized the birds' riders were human shaped and human sized. Only when two of the strange birds settled to the ground in front of them, a smaller one carrying a rider and a larger one riderless, did she truly comprehend their size. She gasped and stepped back a pace, for these birds were not birds. Behind her she heard others cry out and utter sounds of amazement.

The animals in front of them were part eagle and part lion, odd misshapen creatures larger than any horse, coal black from head to foot, with blood-red eyes. The larger, riderless one bowed its head to Morgin and said, "Your Majesty."

As more of the winged eagle-lion animals settled to the ground around them, the rider on the smaller one climbed down from its back and approached Morgin. She was the most beautiful woman Nicki had ever seen, but it was a sterile beauty without the warmth of mortality. She had a broadsword strapped to her side, and she carried a bow and a quiver of arrows. She dropped to one knee in front of Morgin and said, "Your Majesty, I brought all 11 legions."

He said, "Ellowyn, please rise," and she stood.

He asked her, "Will WolfDane be joining us?"

"Aye, my lord," she said. "He has much to settle with the queen of the jackal court."

Morgin turned to Olivia and BlakeDown, and indicating the beautiful woman he said, "I'd like to introduce the Archangel Ellowyn, commander of the second legion of angels."

Olivia smiled, while BlakeDown stood dumbfounded, his mouth open like a simpleton.

The larger of the strange eagle-lions laughed and said, "You have changed since we last met, no longer the sad and lonely Benesh'ere warrior."

"And this," Morgin said, indicating the enormous half-bird, "is TarnThane, the griffin lord."

Morgin turned to the smaller of the two griffins, bowed deeply and said, "Your Majesty."

To BlakeDown and Olivia he said. "This is SheelThane, Queen of the House of the Thane. We met 12 centuries ago, in a dream."

Nicki was sooo going to have a talk with this brother of hers.

••••

Rhianne regained consciousness laying on the walkway of the parapet. She lay there for a moment, trying to forget the horror she'd seen in Valso's eyes. The power Valso—or rather his master—commanded was so overwhelmingly immense, she and Morgin had little chance of defeating it. Morgin would die on the battlefield below throwing his army against these walls, and she would die in this city at Valso's pleasure.

As she struggled to her feet Valso rushed over to her and helped her up. "I'm so sorry, dear Rhianne, but when you taunt me, you must suffer the consequences."

Her legs still felt a little weak, so she reached out and put a hand on a crenel to steady herself. Magwa pointed up to the sky and said, "Look."

Rhianne craned her neck to look in the direction the bitch-queen pointed, saw what looked to be a murder of crows high in the sky, but instinct told her otherwise. AnneRhianne, an ancient Benesh'ere princess, had haunted Rhianne's dreams, and she knew these half-birds for what they were. Back then she had thought her dreams were just dreams, but she had since learned otherwise, and it seemed that every day she would learn that lesson again.

Standing next to her Valso said, "Hmmm, I hadn't anticipated the Thane, or the Legions. Clever of him. So we'll lose a few more jackals and armsmen than expected, but they'll never take these walls, will they, Carsaris?"

The skeletal wizard held up an arrow, his eyes clouded with fear. "We have the means . . . to deal with the Thane, sire."

The jackal warriors around them began yipping and howling like mistreated dogs. Far behind Morgin's army a massive pack of enormous dogs larger than horses emerged from the woodland, loping forward to join the invading army.

"No," Magwa shouted. "Not the Dane." She swung toward Valso. "You didn't tell us we would have to fight the Dane pack."

Valso dismissed her complaints with a wave of his hand. "They can't reach you at the top of these walls, can they? All they can do is stand below and howl while you rain arrows down upon them. Defend the wall at all costs, and we'll crush them here."

••••

Riding on TarnThane's back was anything but pleasant. As Morgin and the legions of angels approached the walls of Durin from high above, he found the view magnificent, but the griffins didn't tolerate saddles. The bony ridge of TarnThane's spine made sitting up straight an unpleasant feat, so he clung to his bow, hugged the griffin's neck, and prayed he wouldn't fall.

With every angel carrying a bow and arrows, they should have had the advantage of height. They could stay high enough to remain out of range of arrows from below, and rain arrows down on their enemy from above. But as the leading edge of the assault approached the wall, arrows shot up from below with impossible speed, and griffins tumbled out of the sky to their deaths.

Morgin spotted a small clutch of people on the parapets just above the main gates: Valso, Rhianne, Magwa, Carsaris and several Kulls. It angered him that Valso would expose Rhianne so, but then he noticed that Valso deflected all the arrows that came their way with some sort of magical shield.

TarnThane stayed high and banked to one side, circling the wall just above the gates. Morgin saw one of Valso's wizards standing on the wall next to a bowman. The bowman handed him an arrow, the wizard did something to it, handed it back to the bowman, and when the bowman released the arrow it shot upward like a bolt of lightning.

Morgin pulled an arrow from his quiver, nocked it, and asked the steel arrowhead to strike true. He drew the bowstring back, aimed and released the arrow. It streaked through the air, pierced the wizard's heart and he tumbled off the parapet, leaving the bowman with nothing but simple, mundane arrows.

As Morgin looked for another wizard-bowman pair, TarnThane flapped his massive wings and rose higher. "Remember your purpose here," he called back to Morgin.

"You're right," Morgin said, realizing he'd lost sight of his primary goal. He wasn't riding on a griffin's back to kill enemy wizards. "Get me closer."

As TarnThane lowered his head and dove, Morgin's stomach climbed up into his throat. He gulped, recalling that the ancient Benesh'ere warrior Morddon had considered all of the griffins *crazy half-birds*. TarnThane pulled out of the dive and sliced through the air just above the wall, low enough to cause several bowmen there to duck. Behind the gates Morgin saw a wide, cobbled square bordered by the gates on one side and buildings on the other three. The square was empty of all but soldiers marching through it. They looked up as he and TarnThane streaked overhead. He sensed a steel-tipped arrow cutting through the air toward them, told the steel to deflect and it did.

"I got what I need," he said to TarnThane.

The griffin banked steeply and turned back toward the army of the Lesser Clans.

35

Shadows of the City

AS THE BATTLE above the wall raged on, TarnThane settled to the ground in the midst of Morgin's army. Morgin climbed off the griffin's back, glad to be back on solid ground.

"Did you find it?" Jerst asked.

"Aye," Morgin said. "An alley between two buildings, about a hundred paces from the gates. And no one is paying it the least bit of attention. But I found something better too."

France handed him a short, sharpened tree branch. "Draw it out for us, lad."

The clan leaders and many of their lieutenants gathered around. Morgin squatted down and carefully drew in the dirt what he recalled of the square, the buildings, and the byways just behind the gates of the city. As he drew he said, "There are several entries into the city, but we're going to concentrate on the main gates. On both sides of the gates, about 20 paces from them, there's a shadowed archway in the wall at ground level. Above each is another shadowed archway on the parapets. I'm guessing that they're connected by stairs, but it doesn't matter because I can use the shadows in all of those archways, and the shadows in the alley."

Jerst had claimed the right to lead the assault on the gates and open them, and Morgin felt it right to oblige him. There could be nothing more frightening for the defenders than to suddenly have towering Benesh'ere warriors appear among them, wielding swords and war axes.

Sitting on TarnThane's back on the flight back, Morgin had thought this through carefully. He'd been looking for one shadow, hadn't considered that he might find several he could use. He finished by saying, "I'm going to send the first two twelves out through the archways on top of the wall. Tell them to cause as much havoc as possible."

He looked specifically at Jerst. "But Valso is holding my wife captive up there, so be careful. And if you can, rescue her."

The warmaster nodded, and Morgin continued. "The next 24 I'll send out of the alley. Tell them to head up the street toward the center of the city. Like the first 24 their job is to draw attention away from the gates. The last two twelves I'll send out through the archways at ground level near the gates. Their job is to open the gates. Then I'm going to repeat, sending each group reinforcements until the gates open."

He looked up at the faces leaning over him, all looking down at the crude sketch he'd scratched in the dirt. He looked pointedly at BlakeDown, Brandon, Wylow and PaulStaff. "Stay out of bowshot, but when the gates start to open, charge with mounted troops in the lead, foot soldiers following. We have to take those gates without losing our army beneath the walls."

As the leaders dispersed to brief their armsmen, France gripped Morgin's arm and said quietly, "The real battle here today, it isn't for the city, is it?"

Morgin paused and looked his friend in the face. It brought joy to his heart to see the glint in the swordsman's eyes again. "No, my friend," he said. "We're taking the city only so I can get to Valso. The real battle will be Rhianne and me against that thing he's allowed onto the Mortal Plane."

France nodded and grinned. "Well then, lad, you and me, all the way."

Morgin owed France the truth. "But we can't win that battle, because I haven't found my true name."

France looked over Morgin's shoulder at the clan leaders. "The old witch says your true name is AethonSword."

Morgin shrugged. "And in that, she's wrong. Trust me, friend. Find a place to hide when this is done, because I don't think it's going to end well."

••••

Morgin stood at the edge of the charred ground and faced the gates of Durin in the distance. On his immediate right the hellhound pack sat on their haunches, silent and intent, their eyes focused on the gates of Durin. A hundred paces farther to the right the army of the Lesser Clans had assembled, while the Benesh'ere had formed up a hundred paces to his left. In front of him stood a little over two hundred Benesh'ere, organized into squads of 24 warriors each, all on foot without their mounts.

Morgin had told Jerst, "Regardless of how this ends, the responsibility of the Benesh'ere is to make sure no Kulls survive this day."

The warmaster had simply smiled and nodded.

Jerst had lined up the first squad of whitefaces in front of Morgin in two rows of 12, Jerst and Blesset each leading a twelve, all facing Morgin. The rest of the squads were lined up in similar fashion behind them. Earlier, Morgin had cast a few shadows a dozen paces apart then practiced this maneuver with Jerst and several of his warriors.

They needed to move warriors through Morgin's shadows at a pace much faster than a walk. Behind the whitefaces the battle above the wall continued without letup.

Morgin nodded and Jerst drew his sword. The Benesh'ere behind him and the armies to the sides did the same, drawing swords, hefting war axes, readying pikes. The hellhound pack merely rose up off their haunches, but remained silent, still focused on the gates of the city.

Morgin closed his eyes and concentrated his power. He thought of the shadows in the two archways at the top of the parapets, then he pictured a shadow behind him taller than any whiteface and six paces wide. He opened his eyes, glanced over his shoulder and saw the darkness hovering there. He stepped back so he stood half in and half out of that shadow, extended his arms and held his palms out to either side just within the shadow.

Morgin nodded, and Jerst and Blesset broke into a run, an easy jog that the warriors behind them duplicated. Jerst passed into the shadow on his right, Blesset on his left, both of them lightly slapping his palms as they went past. Morgin sent each out through one of the archways at the top of Durin's parapets. As the warriors behind them jogged past him they slapped his palms just as they entered the shadow behind him, and he sent them to follow Jerst and Blesset.

••••

When the first arrow shot her way, Rhianne cringed, knowing she would now die, but at the last instant it jerked to one side. All about them griffins carrying angels swooped and dove, loosing arrows at jackals and armsmen. An arrow struck one of the black half-birds diving toward them, it folded its wings, and angel and griffin slammed into the battlements with such force they dislodged a crenel. Angel and griffin tumbled to the ground below and lay still.

Valso had conjured some sort of dome-like shield about her, him and a dozen Kulls. Outside it Magwa shouted orders at her commanders, while Carsaris directed a cadre of wizards magicking arrows. Griffins and angels fell from the sky, crashed to the earth and were quickly swarmed by Decouix armsmen. Rhianne had no training in war and battle tactics, but even she could see the griffin-mounted angels would not be sufficient to take the wall.

Valso grabbed her arm and pulled her toward him. He shouted to be heard above the noise about them. "You know this battle means nothing."

She didn't answer him, for she always learned something when she let him boast.

"The only thing that counts is that your husband is coming to me, and he's bringing that sword."

Still, she held her silence.

"My master forced the whoreson to forge that blade, tormented him for centuries, so it is my master's self-forged blade. It would not hold such malevolent power otherwise."

Valso's reasoning was twisted, but perhaps true. Now was not the time to tell him there was no power in the steel Morgin carried, that the malevolent power had been housed in Morgin's soul.

Rhianne suddenly heard steel blades clashing just outside Valso's protective ring of Kulls, a sound she should not have heard at the top of the wall. Standing on tip-toes, she saw the white face and black hair of a Benesh'ere warrior, swinging his sword at a Kull, more of them pouring out the archway she'd emerged from earlier.

"Blast!" Valso said. "Damn his shadows."

She sensed that thing enter his soul. She recoiled from him, but still holding onto her arm he pulled her close, and she felt him draw an enormous flow of power. Reality slipped away, the sky shifted from blue to a wan, orange, and the air about her grew hot and humid. A monster stood over her wearing the head of a goat with blood-red eyes. He shoved her aside hard enough that she fell to her hands and knees on ground that was now dry dirt. Valso and his master had dragged her and his Kulls deep into the netherworld.

The monster spoke in that voice she'd heard come from Valso's lips recently. "He can have the wall. We'll finish this in the heart of my power."

Reality slipped back into place and they returned to Valso's workroom high in the castle, his Kulls in a ring about them. Valso no longer wore the head of a goat. He pointed at Rhianne. "Get her back to her apartments, and guard her closely."

As two of the Kulls grabbed Rhianne, lifted her to her feet and hustled her to the door, she heard him issuing orders. "Have everyone light torches, and carry them through the halls. If you see a shadow, get rid of it with the light of the torch, and cast a shadow elsewhere. I want every shadow in the castle constantly shifting and changing."

••••

After Morgin sent the last of Jerst and Blesset's twelves to the top of the wall, he nodded at the next squad. As they jogged toward him he shifted his focus to the shadow in the alley, sent the second twelves through there. The next squads he sent out through the archways at the base of the wall. Then he repeated the sequence, two twelves to the top of the parapets, two through the alley, two more through the archways at the base of the wall.

His hands grew sore at being slapped by so many Benesh'ere palms, while he kept his eyes focused on the gates of Durin. They began to open, though they moved slowly and ponderously, and he still had four squads left. Everyone must have been as focused as him on those gates, for several voices in the armies to both sides called for the charge, and the combined might of the hellhounds, the Benesh'ere and the four Lesser Clans surged forward.

Several of the whitefaces in front of Morgin hesitated and looked over their shoulders, but Morgin shouted, "Keep going." They turned back to him, and squad by squad he sent them through to the shadows behind the gates. The last of the Benesh'ere slapped his palms and disappeared into his shadows.

Silence now surrounded Morgin as he stood there alone, three hundred paces from the wall, all the noise and violence now in the far distance.

He didn't like it that Nicki and AnnaRail would ride to battle, but they were powerful witches, and were needed to support the armsmen. They would kill foes, and heal friends.

Mortiss neighed, *Shall we join them?*

Morgin looked to his right where France stood, holding the reins of Mortiss and his own horse. "You and me, lad."

••••

Mounted on their horses, Morgin and France paused side-by-side just inside the shadow of the alley a hundred paces behind the gates. The ground between them and the gates was strewn with dead: Decouix armsmen, jackal warriors, Kulls, Benesh'ere, griffins, with the livery of an angel draped across each massive griffin carcass. Morgin spotted Jerst high up on the parapets as he cut down one of the wizards magicking arrows for the bowmen. Near him Blesset traded blows with a jackal warrior, her off hand clutching at her side where her tunic was soaked with blood.

Morgin reinforced the shadows in the alley, scanned the wall and quickly identified several of Valso's sorcerers. But most importantly he spotted Carsaris. He dismounted, strung his bow, nocked an arrow, aimed at the skeletal wizard and drew the string back. "Strike true," he said, concentrating on the steel arrowhead. He released the arrow, watched it arc high above the square and descend slowly toward the wall. It punched into Carsaris's back just as a bowman handed him an arrow to magic. The wizard staggered, clutching at the shaft protruding from his back, faltering backward step-by-step. Then he tumbled from the wall and smacked into the cobbles of the square. In quick succession Morgin killed four more wizards. Morgin hadn't killed all of Valso's sorcerers on the wall, but without Carsaris's leadership, and with fewer magicked arrows holding them back, the angels and griffins took their toll of the defenders.

Down at the gates a squad led by Harriok and Jack the Only were hard pressed by jackals and Decouix armsmen. A few of them pushed on the gates, opening them much too slowly, while the rest fought at their backs, defending them with sword and axe and pike. The gates were not completely open when Harriok screamed at the top of his lungs, "Now." At his command all the whitefaces in his squad jumped to both sides of the gateway as if laying down in defeat. Still standing in the middle of the partially open gates, the Decouix defenders hesitated, and in that instant the hellhounds hit them.

WolfDane came through first, lifted one of the defenders in his jaws, gave him a shake, snapped his spine and tossed him aside. In only a few heartbeats the hellhounds cleared the gates and loped into the open square behind it, followed by Harriok and his squad. The jackal warriors took one look at the Dane pack, turned and ran yowling with fear, leaving only Decouix armsmen and a few Kulls to fight on.

France said, "It worked nicely, lad."

Morgin had given orders that the hellhound pack would be first through the gates. Long ago they had helped Morddon, the ancient Benesh'ere warrior, and through his eyes Morgin had seen the panic that flooded through the jackal horde when they faced the Dane. The hellhounds cleared the square, then spread out into the streets around it. Behind them came the Benesh'ere who swarmed up onto the wall, and quickly cleared it of defenders.

Morgin climbed into the saddle, and he and France spurred their horses into the square. They met WolfDane first. The hellhound was so much larger than a horse that even mounted on Mortiss, Morgin's eyes were on a level with the Dane King's.

Morgin said, "Your Majesty, we thank you for your aid."

"Your Majesty," WolfDane said in the deep, growling voice of a hellhound. "We thank you for the opportunity to hunt the bitch-queen's hordes."

Morgin said, "Then hunt well."

WolfDane loped off to join his pack hunting down jackals in the streets.

••••

Where are you?

DaNoel flinched. *I'm at the rear of the mounted troops.*

He'd decided it would be safest to stay near the rear, less chance of a stray arrow shortening his life.

Make your way to the front immediately.

DaNoel didn't like that. *Why? You're going—*

Blinding pain hit him, felt as if something had punched a hole through his soul. *All right . . . all right . . . I'll do it.*

The pain disappeared in an instant.

The whoreson has proved unpredictable. I want your eyes and ears on him, and relaying everything to me continuously. We'll stay in contact until this is done.

36

The Self-Forged Blade

A WIDE AVENUE named The King's Way wound in a meandering path from the city's main gates to the Decouix castle. Valso, and before him Illalla, had used it to parade vanquished enemies through the city. Morgin had ridden it once, a captive of Tarkiss, one of Valso's lords, though he'd not been openly paraded before the people of Durin. He'd simply been a package trussed up neatly and delivered to the king.

Morgin was tempted to use one of the shadows he knew in the Decouix castle and go straight there, but that would be a foolish whim, leaving dangerous armies at his back. *Stay the course*, he reminded himself. They'd taken the wall, now take the city, and in the process neutralize the jackal hordes and Decouix armsmen.

He sent the majority of the griffins and angels directly to the castle to continue the aerial assault, kept six twelves behind to help as they advanced. With the Benesh'ere and the hellhounds ranging through the streets ahead of them to hunt Kulls and jackals, Morgin's army progressed slowly up the wide avenue. They moved cautiously, had to stop repeatedly to dispatch archers on a roof or a balcony, or in the dark shadows of open windows. The six twelves of griffin-mounted angels helped immensely in that.

With squads out ahead of them clearing the way, Morgin rode with France and his family, though DaNoel was nowhere to be seen. It was a group among whom he felt safe, a group he trusted, even Olivia, the scheming old witch. The other clan leaders also chose to ride with family and trusted lieutenants, perhaps because now they all sensed the enormity of the power at Valso's command, and it cowered them as much as it cowered Morgin. With the combined might of the most powerful wizards and witches of the Lesser Clans, Morgin knew they still could not defeat the power of a god.

At that thought Morgin reined in Mortiss and brought her to a halt. They all halted with him, looking at him with a mixture of surprise and uncertainty. Without looking at anyone in particular, he said, "Valso will soon command the power of a god, and he knows that all of us together cannot defeat him."

He looked around, didn't see false confidence in any of their faces, saw only defeat. Their doubts reminded him of his own, and he wondered why they should all die with him. "You should all go back. This is my fight. I'm the one he wants dead."

NickoLot dug her heels into her horse's flanks, and in the press of riders in the street she forced other riders aside until her mount stood beside Morgin's. With an angry grimace, she struck out and punched him in the shoulder with her fist. It hurt, and Morgin said, "Owe."

With tears in her eyes and shaking her hand, Nicki said, "Owe, owe, owe that hurt. You idiot, owe."

Rubbing his shoulder Morgin asked, "Then why did you do it?"

"Because you're an idiot." She continued shaking her hand. "Hellhounds, archangels, griffins, we're going to have a long talk and you're going to tell me all about this when this is done." She choked back tears. "You and Rhianne are going to fight this thing we all now sense, and we're here to support you." She swept a hand out, didn't realize she almost knocked Olivia out of her saddle. "The clans, these nether beings, I saw it in a vision. We can't fight the battle for you, but we must be here to support you, even if it's only to bury you when we're done."

She leaned toward Morgin, holding her injured hand pressed to her breast. "Now," she said, placing great emphasis on the word. "Your responsibility is to figure out a way to win."

AnnaRail said, "Let me see that hand, Nicki."

Olivia said, "A prescient vision! You didn't tell me about that one. What else have you been up to?"

••••

"The king has sent for you," Geanna said, tears in her eyes, her voice trembling so badly she barely got the words out. "Your guard will take you to him."

Rhianne reached out and took the girl's hands in hers.

"I'm sorry," Geanna said. "I'm sorry I spied on you. I should never have done so. I didn't realize what he was really like."

"That's all right," Rhianne said. She pulled the girl close and held her tightly.

The Kull lieutenant harrumphed and said, "The king does not like waiting."

Rhianne released Geanna, turned and walked out into the hall where her six Kull guards surrounded her. They led her down to the throne room, and peeled away from her just before she stepped through the high double doors. Courtiers lined the walls to either side, though they were strangely silent, with none of the background murmur that would normally issue from such a large crowd. And to a man and woman they all lowered their eyes, focused them intently on the stone floor beneath their feet.

At the far end of the room Valso sat on his throne atop the dais, the little snake coiled on his shoulder. Rhianne held her chin high as she stepped forward, and tried to keep any hint of fear from her features. As she slowly walked the length of the room Valso sat silently, motionlessly. She stopped at the base of the dais and refused to curtsy or bow, refused to show any courtesy whatsoever.

Valso stood, wagged a finger at her and said, "Come up here, girl."

She had no choice but to obey, for her legs were not hers to command, and one by one she climbed the steps. His power made her walk right up to him and stop only a fraction of a pace from him. He leaned down and she felt the wind from the snake's tiny, fluttering wings as Valso kissed her lightly on the cheek. Then he smiled and spoke in that voice that was not his. "When this is done, you will come to me gladly, without the need for spells or artifice. And you will bear my children, the children of a god. And I will rule the Mortal Plane."

He leaned away from her and said, "Stand beside me. Your husband comes."

••••

Castle Decouix loomed above everything at the center of the city. It stood alone, with a wide parade ground separating it from any other structure, and surrounding it on all sides. There were two motes, one immediately beneath the wall, and another at the outer edge of the parade ground, separating the empty stretch of land from the city proper. A drawbridge had been lowered over each of the two motes, and the portcullis in the main castle gates had been raised.

Morgin stopped just short of the first bridge and looked up. Griffins perched on every tower, peak and gable of the castle, hundreds of them, while hundreds more filled the air above it. Bodies lay strewn haphazardly about the parade ground: Kulls, armsmen, Benesh'ere, jackals and griffins. Quite a few of the defenders had been dismembered. He recalled how a half-bird's talons, each the length of a man's arm and razor sharp, could slice and rend those on the ground as a griffin swooped past. Morgin nudged Mortiss forward, and riding beside him France did likewise. As Mortiss's hooves pounded on the planks of the bridge Morgin steeled himself for what was to come.

Behind him he heard only the hooves of a few horses on the bridge, not the hundreds that should have been following. He stopped and looked back, saw that only Olivia, Roland, AnnaRail, JohnEngine, NickoLot and Brandon had spurred their horses out onto the bridge. Behind them, the rulers of the Lesser Clans sat astride their horses, DaNoel among them. They'd stopped just short of the bridge.

That so many members of his family had come forth heartened and saddened him at the same time. It felt good to be *not alone*, and yet he didn't want them to die with him and Rhianne.

Olivia turned about in the saddle and looked back. "Blast all of you to netherhell," she cried. "This is your fight as well."

They all lowered their eyes, except for a simple soldier named Abileen, a sergeant of men, a man without power. He held his chin high and spurred his horse forward, a simple act that shamed all those behind him. Morgin turned back to face the castle, ignoring them; they would come or they would not.

He had cleared the bridge, and was several of Mortiss's strides out onto the parade ground when he heard more horses following. Apparently, shame was a powerful incentive.

Morgin crossed the second drawbridge and entered the high archway that passed through the outer curtain wall of Castle Decouix. In the outer bailey Jack the Only, Harriok, Jerst and Blesset waited with a few hundred Benesh'ere. Kull and whiteface bodies littered the ground everywhere.

Jack said, "SteelMaster, there's good hunting here."

With the whitefaces ranging in front of them, Morgin and France rode unmolested into the inner bailey. Morgin sensed Valso's power hovering at the edge of his own, restlessly anticipating the confrontation to come. As he dismounted in front of the steps at the entrance to the castle proper, Abileen spurred his horse forward, and quickly dismounted near him. He held out a hand. "I'll see to your horses, my lords."

Several Benesh'ere sprinted up the steps as Morgin and France handed him the reins to their horses. From within the castle they heard the ring of steel, a grunt or two and a shout.

Morgin and France climbed the steps together. Inside they found the Benesh'ere standing over the bodies of four Kulls and two whitefaces.

Jerst said, "Good hunting, indeed."

France turned to Morgin and asked, "Where to now, lad?"

Morgin considered the question. "Valso will be in the throne room. I know the way."

••••

It bothered Rhianne to stand at the right hand of the Decouix throne. To anyone who didn't understand the control Valso exercised over those about him, it might appear as if she willingly supported him, though undoubtedly that was exactly what he wanted. She sensed Morgin's presence in the castle, sensed him coming, and didn't want him to see her this way.

While Rhianne stood there unmoving—unable to move—Valso sat on his throne, one elbow on an armrest, his chin resting in the palm of the hand it supported, one leg extended casually outward, resting on its heel. He remained unmoving and silent, statue still, and his silence permeated the entire hall.

Rhianne started when she heard the dim ring of steel out in the corridor beyond the hall. Valso didn't flinch at all, didn't so much as blink. She thought about it and realized he hadn't blinked in quite some time, had sat there in unnatural stillness. She sensed that thing within his soul, now always a part of him.

The sounds of the struggle outside the hall ended quickly, and a few heartbeats later two Benesh'ere stepped through the entrance at the far end of the hall. More followed, they fanned out and Valso's courtiers edged away from them. Then Morgin stepped into the hall.

He wore the same simple garb he had that night he'd come to her here in the castle, a Benesh'ere robe belted at the waist that ended at mid-thigh, loose-fitting breeches tucked into calf-high boots, the sheathed sword hanging at his side. The blade had entered the room—anyone with power could sense it—though she thought she might be the only one present who knew it was not the steel at his side that they sensed.

Morgin walked toward the dais with the royalty of the Lesser Clans following him almost timidly. He didn't march or stride like a king, he simply walked down the length of the hall. Even when he was too far away for her to see his eyes, she knew he looked at her the entire way. Olivia and the other clan leaders stopped midway down the hall, but Morgin continued and halted about ten paces from the base of the dais. He smiled at her, and in that look he told her he knew she did not stand willingly at Valso's side. And that freed her of Valso's hold.

She began drawing power, drawing as much as she could and held it within her soul.

••••

Morgin looked up at Valso, sitting on his throne with the little demon snake perched on his shoulder. If he had any hope of defeating the Dark God, it must be on the Mortal Plane. He needed Beayaegoath to manifest fully here and now.

Rhianne stood beside Valso as still and unmoving as a statue. But when he smiled at her, she broke out of the stillness and smiled back.

"How quaint," Valso said, standing.

Morgin thought it interesting that Valso's eyes didn't meet his, but remained focused on the blade at his side. He said, "I brought you something." For emphasis he lifted his left hand and rested it on the hilt of the sword. "Something I know you desperately want."

Morgin reached across with his right hand and drew the blade, slid it out of the sheath slowly, allowing the scrape of steel to fill the silence in the hall. Valso hissed, tried to step back, but the back of his legs bumped against the throne. The little snake took to the air and shot toward Morgin. It stopped less than a pace away and hovered at eye level.

The knowledge that he could survive Bayellgae's venom did nothing to still the fear in Morgin's heart. While it might not kill him, he didn't know what harm it could do, and was not foolish enough to assume he could ignore it. "I've tasted your venom, Bayellgae. You cannot harm me."

The snake retreated a pace and hissed, "No one hasss ever sssurvived my venom, ssso you don't know that, do you?" It darted back to the dais and hovered near Rhianne.

Morgin lifted the sword and looked at it, knew every nick and scratch on the plain, unadorned blade. He looked past it at Valso and said, "You fear this blade."

Valso stepped forward, his eyes flashing with anger. "I fear nothing."

Morgin said, "I wonder if it's flawed."

He reached up with his left hand and snapped the nail of his middle finger against it. It rang softly with a faint, dull ping. Morgin took hold of that note, amplified it, brought it and the memories that came with it forth: his captivity in the Dark God's hands, the forced labor over the steel, the quest for the perfect blade. He remembered the days at the forges, days that turned into years, then into centuries, the laughter and scorn of a god looking upon a mere mortal without pity. The memories came back to him as the intensity of the note grew to a glorious crescendo of pain. Waves of heat flooded outward from the blade; the crowd in the hall cringed away from it; Valso cringed away from it.

This blade contained no flaw. It sang with the single pure note of the SteelMaster's forging. But Morgin continued to build onto that note, strengthening it, aligning it with a resonance that shook the core of his soul, feeding it all the power of the last of the SteelMasters. It tore at his ears as the hatred and torment he'd carried all his life flowed out of him and into the steel, and just when he thought he could take no more, the blade melted down its entire length, the note ended abruptly, and the steel dribbled to the floor where it puddled into a misshapen lump of slag. Morgin stood holding nothing but a bladeless hilt, and for the first time his soul was clean and free of pain.

Throughout the room people gasped and cried out. Even Valso started and his eyes narrowed, as if he couldn't believe what had just happened. Only Rhianne failed to react, didn't move in the slightest. She simply smiled and nodded approval.

Behind Morgin, Olivia cried out, "What have you done?"

Morgin looked at the bladeless hilt, and felt as if shackles that had bound him throughout his life had been broken away. He tossed the hilt forward, where it clattered on the stone floor and came to rest at the base of the dais.

Valso threw his head back and crowed with laughter. He took the steps of the dais two at a time, with the little snake hovering just behind him. Rhianne followed more slowly, taking each step carefully. At the base of the dais Valso bent and picked up the hilt. He held it up and laughed. "I am free. No one can stop me now."

He looked at Morgin with blood-red eyes. "You fool, now there is nothing to hinder me."

Morgin drew power as he watched Valso change. He pulled it from every level of existence, pulled it from the stone of the building, from the ground and the earth beneath it.

Valso roared with laughter, and with each heartbeat he grew in height. His head transformed slowly, his mouth extending into a muzzle, his teeth lengthening into vicious canines. His pupils elongated horizontally until he looked at Morgin with blood-red goat-slitted eyes. The monster with the head of a goat now towered above them all.

To one side DaNoel shrieked, dropped to his knees, put his hands over his ears and cried, "In my head, in my head, nooooo." AnnaRail rushed to his aid as he slumped to the floor.

Morgin focused on Beayaegoath above all else. He turned back to the dais as the monster tossed the bladeless hilt carelessly to the floor. It clattered at Morgin's feet, and the Dark God spoke in his true voice. "You are a fool, mortal. You've destroyed my self-forged blade, the one thing that could defeat me."

Morgin tried to still his racing heart, tried to appear calm and unconcerned as he bent down and picked up the bladeless hilt. He looked at it and said, "No. This was my self-forged blade, and I needed to destroy it."

The monster strode forward, stopped a pace in front of Morgin. He stood half again as tall as a man, and he towered over him. He reached out, gripped the front of Morgin's tunic and lifted him until their noses almost touched.

With fear crawling up his gut, Morgin tried to appear calm as he held up the bladeless hilt and said, "Your self-forged blade is not some trivial thing of mere steel, but one of flesh and blood and bone, forged in the hell of your hatred."

The Dark God frowned.

Morgin looked into the Dark God's soulless eyes and said, "The blade you should fear is me."

He released his power.

37

The Truth in a Name

THE BLAST OF power Morgin released stunned Rhianne, sent a shockwave through the hall that knocked many senseless. Rhianne would not have believed that a mere mortal could contain such power and live. She had managed to stay standing, saw that Olivia, AnnaRail, NickoLot and those who commanded the most power had done the same, and from the looks on their faces they too were stunned by the inhuman strength Morgin had shown. Others struggled back to their feet while many did not rise. She held onto the power she'd summoned, knew there were two things she must do, and that now was not her moment.

Morgin had wrapped his hands about the Dark God's throat and they staggered back and forth as the monster tried to dislodge him. Bayellgae hovered above them, darting about as they fought, but leaving the battle to its master. Morgin and Beayaegoath threw arcane magics at each other, power that could easily incinerate the strongest wizards and witches in the clans. But it bounced off the two of them the way water sizzles and spits off a red-hot iron.

Beayaegoath roared with fury, "You cannot defeat me, mortal." Then it writhed and twisted, and turned into a monstrous snake that coiled around Morgin, crushing him. Morgin screamed and cried out, beating against the enormous serpent with wave after wave of raw power, while the little demon snake hovered above them and cried, "Yesss, massster."

Still, Rhianne's moment had yet to come.

Olivia, AnnaRail and NickoLot combined their power and threw it at the monster. The three of them together did not match the waves of arcane force that Morgin poured forth, but they beat at it, adding their magics and arcane energies to his. And still it held against them all.

BlakeDown, Theandrin and the other leaders of the clans joined their might to the battle. Even Vodah and Rastanna wizards joined in, and Rhianne understood that while they could live with Valso's proclivities, none of them wanted to be subject to the Nether God's dark whims.

Beayaegoath weakened slightly. Rhianne sensed it and knew that the little snake did too, and would now act. Bayellgae's venom was not a physical poison but a truly magical toxin. She rushed forward, and as the little demon darted toward Morgin, its jaws open, its fangs exposed, she released the blood-spell she'd prepared from Morgin's blood and its venom, and stepped in its way. Only now would she know if the spell worked.

The snake slammed into her and its fangs punctured her throat. She gripped its body just behind its head and held it there so it couldn't escape and attack Morgin. It writhed and coiled around her wrist, pumped its venom into her while it fed on her blood, sucking it down greedily. Her legs weakened and she trembled as the cold of the nether poison washed through her veins. She dropped to her knees, felt consciousness slipping away, focused all of her energy on holding the snake to her throat, and feeding power into the blood-spell. And then suddenly she felt an abiding warmth where cold had washed through her a moment before. The snake choked and coughed, stopped pumping venom and sucking blood. As the blood-spell took hold she felt cold pumping out of her and into the snake, while blessed warmth continued to flood her soul.

Where the snake had coiled about her wrist it felt as if she'd plunged her arm into an icy snow bank. She pulled the snake from her throat and looked at the coils. The tiny serpent had turned a whitish-blue, was clear like the coldest of ice, and had gone completely motionless, as if she wore a bracelet of ice in the form of a snake coiled about her wrist.

She dropped to the floor and slammed her wrist and the little snake against the stone. It shattered into a thousand pieces that rose up into the air and swirled into a maelstrom, then dissipated into a cloud of smoke. She heard a faint nether cry that dwindled slowly to silence.

The throne room was far from silent. Morgin and the Dark God were still locked in battle and the monster had weakened. Its power hadn't diminished, but as Morgin and the clans threw more arcane forces against it, it appeared as if the monster couldn't match it. It shifted out of the form of the serpent, and back into the form of the goat-headed giant. The edges of its shape grew faint and indistinct as it attempted to drag Morgin into the netherworld, where he could not defeat it.

Rhianne acted, for this was her other duty. She shifted into the lowest level of the Mortal Plane, and threw out the power she'd accumulated, a shield between it and its realm. The monstrous god slammed into her, and her physical body knew pain, while her soul held the shield in place.

"Nooooo!" the Dark God screamed.

The monster's anger ripped through her soul, and she felt blood streaming out of her eyes, ears, nose and mouth. But from somewhere deep within she found more power, and while the Dark God beat at her, she held, blocked it from drawing fully on its sources of nether power.

She staggered, felt her body weakening while her power remained strong and whole. An odd, distant piece of her noticed that her arm was broken, a white splinter of bone jutting out of the middle of her forearm. It hurt immensely, and yet it did not weaken her. She and her Morgin could fight this monster, and defeat it.

"No," it said. "You and your husband are such fools. You know nothing of the power of a god."

He forced her to look into his eyes as they flared with blood-red fire. Once again he showed her the armies of tormented souls, broken and twisted by his hatred. Her heart skipped a beat as the monster smothered her magic and power. It skipped another, and another . . . then stopped altogether.

••••

Morgin struggled to breathe. With the Dark God's hands clamped about his throat holding him well off the floor, his legs dangling beneath him, he only managed to force a tiny whisper of air into his lungs. What a fool he had been to think he and Rhianne could defeat a god.

"You dare to defy me?" the monster roared, holding Morgin's face only a hand's breadth from its goat-snouted head. It shook Morgin like a child's plaything, and he thought the bones of his spine might snap any moment. "Speak your true name, mortal."

Morgin couldn't breathe, let alone speak. He felt consciousness slipping away as he tried to pull air through a throat constricted by the Dark God's iron grip. All he managed was a sickly gurgle, and when the monster heard that it threw its head back and roared with laughter.

"Finding it difficult to breathe, are we? But I so want to hear this wondrous name from your own lips."

Beayaegoath relaxed his grip slightly, just enough for Morgin to pull a faint gasp of air into his lungs.

"Speak your glorious name, AethonSword. Speak it now, for it will be the last word you utter."

Morgin had to try. If he could somehow claim that name, even though he believed it was not his true name, perhaps it would lend him strength and he could salvage something. Morgin struggled to speak. He opened his mouth and croaked, "I . . ."

"Speak it," the Dark God shouted, shaking him like a child's doll.

"I . . . am . . ."

"Yes," the monster cried. "I will take joy in hearing the defeat in your name."

"I . . . am . . . named . . ."

"Now, fool, speak the name."

Morgin tried to say *AethonSword*, but it would not come. He hung in the monster's grip, his mouth open, uttering no sound.

"No, mortal," the Dark God said. "I won't let you claim a false name in my presence. You can use only your true name against me, and you don't have one."

As little motes of unconsciousness danced in front of Morgin's eyes, he understood now that he'd spent a fruitless lifetime searching for a name that didn't exist. AethonSword, AethonLaw, Morgin, one-by-one he'd been given those names, and he could taste the falsehood in each of them. He'd come from the streets of Anistigh, a nameless, filthy, diseased child. He'd never had a true name, and now he never would . . .

Never had a true name . . .

As the monster roared, gloating in its victory, a bright flash of memory showed him the streets of Anistigh so long ago.

Never had a true name . . .

Cutting the purse.

Never had a true name . . .

Running through the streets, one step ahead of the mob.

Never had a true name . . .

The blind alley.

Never had a true name . . .

And he realized he'd always looked in the wrong place.

••••

Nicki struggled to get to her feet, almost couldn't do it but somehow managed. She stood in the middle of the Decouix throne room, staggering like a drunkard. Nearby Olivia had only made it to her hands and knees, though AnnaRail stood over her, helping her up. Beayaegoath had summoned a massive outpouring of energies that swept all of their combined magics aside, a simple demonstration of how little their mortal powers mattered when pitted against that of a god.

One wall of the room had crumbled, crushing many beneath massive blocks of stone. Dust filled the air like a thick fog, and Morgin, Rhianne and the monster were nothing but hazy figures in the distance, though she easily heard the Dark God's rumbling voice.

"Speak your glorious name, AethonSword. Speak it now, for it will be the last word you utter."

Somehow she had to help. Nicki staggered forward, and as she closed the distance the fog-like dust parted. The Dark God stood at the base of the dais, holding Morgin up off the ground by his throat. Blood had streamed from Morgin's eyes, ears, nose and mouth.

Rhianne lay in a crumpled heap of gown and petticoats at the monster's feet. She struggled to rise, but one arm seemed to have a new joint in the middle of the forearm, and when she put weight on it she cried out and fell back down.

Nicki staggered forward as the Dark God shook Morgin again. Morgin tried to say something, but clearly in immense pain his words came out in a barely audible croak. "I . . . am . . . named . . ."

Morgin hung in the Dark God's grip, his mouth open but saying nothing. Nicki watched fear and defeat appear in his face as the monster shouted out its triumph. But then Morgin's brow furrowed in thought, and a sudden moment of clarity appeared in his eyes. He whispered, "I am named Rat."

"What?" the Dark God said, frowning. "What kind of a name is that?"

Morgin shimmered, the edges of his shape grew faint and indistinct, and he shrank, growing smaller as she looked on. His clothing shifted in a strange way, and she heard it tearing, ripping into misshaped pieces. Nicki couldn't believe her eyes, for as each heartbeat passed, Morgin shifted and changed, until the Dark God held a filthy, malnourished child dressed in a cloak of dirty rags.

The Dark God grimaced with a look of distaste, then dropped the child. The little boy landed on his feet and looked up at the monster standing over him, his face smeared with dirt and offal.

Beayaegoath looked at the dirt and excrement on his hands and said, "You're filthy." It lifted a hand high, and swung it down toward the child with a blow aimed at taking off his head. But as the monster's hand reached the spot where the child stood, the boy vanished.

The Dark God frowned, and in that instant the boy reappeared behind him, reached into his cloak of filthy rags, and withdrew the wicked little knife Nicki had given him in a dream. He stabbed out, burying the ugly blade in the god's thigh.

The god screamed as a ray of intense, white light poured out of the wound, followed by an eruption of smoke and flame. The child jumped forward, wrapping his arms and legs about the monster's waist. He plunged the blade into the god's back and the monster screamed again. The child used the blade embedded in its back as a climbing spike, and pulled himself up. The monster roared with pain and staggered about, trying to swat the little being from its back. But its efforts proved futile and the boy climbed and stabbed, climbed and stabbed, each wound emitting a ray of intense light, and smoke and flame. Finally the boy reached the top of the monster's back, grabbed the hair on the god's head, pulled himself up so he was kneeling on the god's shoulders, and plunged downward with the knife, burying it in the god's eye. In that instant, both filthy boy and nether god winked out of existence.

Nicki stood there stunned, unable to move, trying to comprehend what had just happened. Rhianne's whimper brought her back to the dust filled throne room. She staggered forward, bent down and helped Rhianne stand. Like Morgin, Rhianne had bled out through her eyes, ears, nose and mouth, and her face was a ghastly, red mask. But the tears that now flowed from her eyes were normal, clear, salty drops of water. She trembled with pain as she asked, "Where is Morgin?"

Roland walked out of the clouds of dust, with AnnaRail beside him supporting DaNoel. Nicki's brother stood bent like an old man, his hands cupped over his ears, his arms and legs shaking with a fearsome palsy. He kept repeating, "In my head, in my head."

Roland said, "Let's get her out of here so your mother can help her."

AnnaRail was by far the better healer, so Nicki nodded. They headed for the doors at the end of the room, she and Roland supporting Rhianne between them, AnnaRail supporting DaNoel. But something snagged at Nicki's dress. She looked down and found Rat walking beside her, tugging at her skirt. She stopped, and AnnaRail and Roland stopped with her, giving her a quizzical look. Nicki nodded down at Rat and they both followed her gaze.

"Leave the city," Rat said. "Do not dally. A god is dying this day, and the city will not survive."

Nicki met her parent's eyes, one then the other, saw her own fear mirrored in their faces.

AnnaRail shouted, "Olivia, BlakeDown, Theandrin, we must leave the city now, and quickly."

Olivia had been helping Theandrin and she stopped, looked at them, and opened her mouth to say something. AnnaRail cut her off, "Don't ask questions. If you value your lives evacuate the city."

A wave of intense heat warmed Nicki's back and shoulders. She looked down, and Rat no longer stood beside her. She looked back, and where the little boy and Beayaegoath had vanished earlier, a white-hot ball of flame had appeared, as if a small sun had blossomed in the throne room.

Roland picked Rhianne up as if she weighed nothing, turned and sprinted for the door. Nicki helped AnnaRail with DaNoel and they followed, the intense heat behind them growing with every step.

When they reached the drawbridges over the two motes they were slowed by hundreds of others swarming across them, with many in the water swimming desperately. Nicki looked back, saw that the central keep had collapsed in upon itself. It didn't really burn, it just appeared to melt, turning the stone of the building into molten lava.

They ran on horses and on foot, shouting for all the residents to evacuate the city. By the time they staggered out through a gate in the city's wall, Nicki could barely put one foot in front of the other. They didn't stop until they had put several hundred paces between them and the city walls. Then they succumbed to exhaustion and sat down unceremoniously on the ground.

They watched thousands boil out through the many gates of the city. Among them loped a lot of odd-looking little dogs. Each had a sharp snout, large pointed ears that stood erect, and a long, bushy tail like that of a fox. Nicki realized she was looking at jackals, not jackal warriors, for without the Dark God's power to sustain them, they had reverted to their natural shape.

Stragglers continued to trickle through the city's gates, but tens of thousands did not make it. They spent the afternoon watching Durin consumed by the death of a god.

38

Forever and a Day

SEATED ON A large rock that JohnEngine had found for her, Rhianne warmed her hands by the fire and listened to the sounds of the Elhiyne army camped around them at the Lake of Sorrows. Across the fire AnnaRail sat with DaNoel's head in her lap, stroking his brow. Roland sat beside her, his arms around her shoulders. NickoLot sat next to them, wringing her hands. All three of them had tears in their eyes.

DaNoel started and tried to sit up. "In my head, in my head, in my head . . ."

AnnaRail said, "There, there, son, it's all right." She soothed him and he slowly calmed, though he'd lost control of his bowels again and the smell drifted on the night air.

Without Morgin to send them back through his shadows, the armies of the Lesser Clans had gone south down the Gods Road to return to their homes. They were equipped to travel, and had used very little of their supplies going north to Durin, so they didn't go hungry. They'd even decided to leave behind a modest force of armsmen drawn from all four of the Lesser Clans. AnnaRail and Theandrin were adamant that someone had to organize and police the survivors of Durin, who were homeless and without food. Their bellies would complain, but Olivia claimed she could make Rastanna and Vodah contribute some supplies, so no one would starve, or fall prey to the inevitable banditry that would arise.

In the middle of the third day of travel Penda and Tosk had split off to cross the Worshipers at Methula, while the rest continued to the Lake of Sorrows. Tomorrow, those of Elhiyne would turn east to Kallun's Gorge, while Inetka headed south and the Benesh'ere stayed at the lake. There was much debate among the whitefaces about what they'd do in the future.

Rhianne chewed on a piece of jerky and longed for a hot meal of roast pheasant, anything but journeycake, water, and dried or heavily salted meat.

Limping badly, JohnEngine walked into the light of the fire and sat down next to her. He stuck his hands out to warm them and said, "The jerky does get rather tiresome, doesn't it? Now you know what it's like to eat it day after day."

She wasn't going to complain. "It'll do until we get home."

"How's your arm?"

AnnaRail had reset the bone in Rhianne's arm, sealed the wound, splinted it and wrapped it, and created a charm to kill the pain. "It no longer throbs; the pain is manageable."

Brandon stepped into the light, the stump of his left arm heavily bandaged. When the wall of the throne room had come down a heavy block of stone had crushed his hand, but it was his off-hand, so it could have been worse. He would make a good clan leader. "How is Morgin?" he asked.

For two days she'd had only a strong sense of Rat, but no Morgin, and that had frightened her, had frightened them all. Then in the early hours of yesterday her sense of Morgin had returned, and Rat had gone. "He's okay," she said. "I think he was hurt badly, but Rat healed him." She didn't say it, but she thought Rat might never return.

Only AnnaRail had come away from that throne room with nothing beyond minor cuts and bruises. She assured them all that JohnEngine's limp would heal, but there was nothing more she could do about Brandon's hand. Roland now had back pains that AnnaRail treated regularly, Nicki had a nasty gash on her shoulder, stitches holding it closed. Olivia had taken to walking with a cane, though she remained as imperious as ever. And then there was DaNoel.

Olivia marched into the light of the fire, leaning on her cane, but with her head held high. Rhianne suspected she leaned a bit more heavily on that cane when no one was present. "How is DaNoel?" she asked.

AnnaRail looked up and said, "We can no longer get any food into him, though if we could I'm not sure it would be right. I doubt he'll last more than two or three more days."

Olivia took a breath and looked down at DaNoel, who lay in AnnaRail's lap, drooling like a child. "We'll be back at Elhiyne in two days. We'll bury him there."

Rhianne saw an odd look pass between Olivia and NickoLot, almost as if they shared a sense of relief. They too probably believed it was better to let DaNoel go, rather than extend his suffering. That was kind of them.

France stepped into the light beside Olivia, and in the accent of a refined nobleman he said, "Your Ladyship. A private word?"

Olivia's brows rose. "Certainly, swordsman." She glanced at those seated around the fire. "But you can speak openly here. We're all family."

"About my wages, Your Ladyship. I hadn't contracted for such hazardous duty, so I think a substantial increase is in order. And of course, it should be retroactive."

Olivia's eyes turned calculating. "But you'll no longer need to give my grandson lessons in swordsmanship, so that's a substantial decrease in your duties."

"Oh no, Your Ladyship. He is still an exceedingly poor swordsman . . ."

As France and Olivia haggled over his pay, Rhianne thought, *Two more days to Elhiyne. Will Morgin be there waiting for her? Will she ever see him again?*

••••

Rhianne dreamed that Morgin's lips touched her cheek with a feather-light kiss. Once they'd returned to Elhiyne she'd had similar dreams, and it always hurt to awake and find he wasn't really there. She kept her eyes closed and lay there, thankful for the comfort of a real bed after so many nights sleeping in a blanket on the dirt near a campfire.

She must have drifted off, for again she dreamed that Morgin's lips touched her cheek.

"It's not a dream," he whispered in her ear.

She started, rolled over, tangled her legs in her sheets, and there he was leaning over her. He'd lit a candle so she could see, and he bent down and touched his lips lightly to hers. He didn't pull away from her, and with their lips barely touching she asked, "Why didn't they tell me you'd returned?"

"Because they don't know. I came in a shadow."

"Where have you been?"

He frowned as if recalling something painful. "I was Rat for a while. It's not easy killing a god, and I needed to heal for a bit."

The frown disappeared and he smiled. "And then I had to find a place for us, a very special place."

He lowered his head and kissed her on the neck, lowered it further and kissed her on the chest just above her breast, lowered it further and kissed her breast, sending a thrill through her. "Come with me now," he said, and with her heart pounding she was ready to go anywhere he wanted. "I'll take you to the place I've found. It's a beautiful little cottage by a babbling brook. It needs a bit of work, but nothing a powerful wizard and witch can't handle."

She asked, "I hope it's far from the old woman."

He shook his head. "No, it's not far. We can ride there in less than a day, or step there in less than a shadow."

She didn't do a good job of hiding her disappointment as she said, "You know, she wants to have you crowned king of all the clans."

He gave her a mischievous grin. "She has to find me first. And that she can't do unless I want her to. My family and yours will only be a shadow away when we want to see them, but those same shadows can hide us from her just as well."

He kissed her, not a soft kiss but a hot passionate one. "Come with me now," he said. "That cottage is waiting for us."

A thought hit her. "Does it have a nice, soft, comfortable feather bed like this?"

He frowned. "No, not yet. But if that's what you want I'll get one soon."

She wrapped her arms around his neck, pulled him down and kissed him again with even more passion. She gasped as his hand touched her breast. "Soon is not soon enough," she said. "We're finally *not* in a dream, so perhaps tonight we can make good use of *this* feather bed."

He ran a finger down her neck, then across her chest above the top of her nightgown. "You're right," he said, brushing his lips across hers. "The cottage can wait."

••••

And so ends *The Gods Within*, in which Morgin and Rhianne have found each other, forever and a day.

Dramatis Personae

The Name of the Sword

Clan/Tribe	Color	Ward	Leader
Decouix	White	Tertius	Valso
Rastanna	Gray	Undecimus	Valso
Vodah	Blue	Duodecimus	Valso
Elhiyne	Red	Octavus	Olivia
Inetka	Yellow	Nonus	Wylow
Penda	Green	Quartus	BlakeDown
Tosk	Violet	Primus	PaulStaff
Benesh'ere	**Black**	**Septimus**	**Angerah**

The Greater Clans

- Decouix (dominant among the Greater Clans)
- Rastanna
- Vodah

The Lesser Clans

- Elhiyne (dominant among the Lesser Clans)
- Inetka (sworn to Elhiyne)
- Penda
- Tosk (sworn to Penda)

Clanless

- The Benesh'ere, the exiled tribe

Personae Decouix

- Valso—only living son of Illalla and Merriketh, and King of the Greater Clans
- Illalla—former King of the Greater Clans (deceased)

- Merriketh Alaella—wife to Illalla and mother of his children
- Mikal—Valso's older brother, murdered by Valso
- GregorDan—Valso's older brother, murdered by Valso
- Tarran—Valso's younger brother, murdered by Valso
- Haleen—only living daughter of Illalla and Merriketh, called *The Mad Whore* by some
- Andra—minor Decouix nobleman
- Thandin—an emissary to Elhiyne
- Degla—minor Decouix nobleman
- GeorgeAll—minor Decouix nobleman
- Carsaris—an advisor to Valso and one of his most powerful sorcerors
- Geanna—a handmaiden to Rhianne

Personae Rastanna

- Oubba—Commander of Tharsk, the fortress at Methula
- Carri—Oubba's wife
- Tarkiss—Oubba's son
- Andrew—an old country nobleman
- Stetha—Andrew's son

Personae Vodah

- Xenya—a young noblewoman with a rebelious attitude regarding Valso
- Alta—Xenya's brother

Personae Kullish

- Salula—Captain and commander of all Kulls
- Verk—a Kull captain, subordinate to Salula
- Mook—a simple Kullish guardsman
- Brakke—Kull officer in command of the Kullish forces at Tharsk
- Salya—a Kull lieutenant in Durin
- Qartan—the Kull lieutenant that kidnaps Felina

Personae Elhiyne

- Olivia—Head of Clan Elhiyne
- Bertak—Olivia's father (deceased)
- Hillell—Olivia's mother (deceased)
- Karlane—Olivia's husband (deceased)
- Malka—Olivia's oldest son and heir to the leadership of Elhiyne (deceased)
- Marjinell—Malka's wife

- MichaelOff—oldest son of Malka and Marjinell (deceased)
- Brandon—youngest son of Malka and Marjinell
- Jinella—born Tosk, now Brandon's wife
- Roland—Olivia's youngest son
- AnnaRail—Roland's wife
- DaNoel—1st child of Roland and AnnaRail
- Annaline—2nd child of Roland and AnnaRail
- JohnEngine—3rd child of Roland and AnnaRail
- NickoLot—4th child of Roland and AnnaRail
- Morgin—adopted child of Roland and AnnaRail
- Rhianne—the 4th of Edtoall and Matill's four daughters, and now Morgin's wife
- Hellis—Olivia's younger sister, took her own life in suicide (deceased)
- Tulellcoe—Hellis' only son, conceived by Illalla in an act of rape
- Vergis Caladan—an alias used by Tulellcoe
- Alcoa—Marchlord of the western reaches that border on Penda
- Eglahan—Marchlord of Yestmark, sworn to Elhiyne
- Packwill—a scout, sworn to Eglahan of Yestmark
- Annen—bastard son of Eglahan
- Abileen—a sergeant of men
- Dannasul—a childhood friend of Morgin and JohnEngine
- Durado—an old man who maintains the waystation at Kallun's Gorge
- Samull—Durado's son
- Gorguh—Elhiyne stable master
- Erlin—Elhiyne stable boy
- Valken Surriot—a *twoname* who fought with Eglahan at the battle of Yestmark
- Seurrak Aldwith—an alias used by the Surriot
- Cortien Balenda—a *twoname* who fought with Eglahan at the battle of Yestmark
- Thenda Sa—an alias used by the Balenda
- Hwatok Tulalane—a *twoname* advisor to Olivia (deceased)
- France—a common swordsman
- Rindal—an alias frequently used by France

Personae Aud

- Aiergain—Queen of the free port city, aka the Queen of Thieves
- Pandorin—a lieutenant in Aiergain's guard
- Sacress—Aiergain's physician
- Terrikle—a manservant provided to Morgin

Personae Penda

- BlakeDown—Head of Clan Penda
- Theandrin—BlakeDown's wife and first lady of Penda
- Doagla—an alias used by BlakeDown when he meets Valso at Tharsk
- ErrinCastle—Blakedown's oldest son and heir to the leadership of Penda
- Anja—a very young girl of minor status
- Tarare—a nobleman known to be a mouthpiece for BlakeDown
- Chrisainne—born Vodah, married minor Penda lord, seduces BlakeDown for Valso
- Perrinsall—ErrinCastle's cousin, and trusted to keep a calm head
- Lewendis—distant relative of BlakeDown's and a bit of a hothead
- Erlander—a sergeant of men

Personae Inetka

- Wylow—Head of Clan Inetka
- Carmet—Wylow's wife
- SandoFall—Wylow's oldest son and heir to the leadership of Inetka
- Edtoall—a minor Inetka lord and father of Rhianne
- Matill—Edtoall's wife and mother of Rhianne

Personae Tosk

- PaulStaff—Head of Clan Tosk
- Torthan—heir to the House of Tosk
- Silaya—a very young noblewoman

Personae Benesh'ere

- Angerah—ruler of the Black Council
- Merella—Angerah's wife
- Jerst—WarMaster of the Benesh'ere tribe
- Blesset—Jerst's daughter
- Jack the Lesser—a bowman and scout
- Harriok—Jerst's oldest son
- Branaugh—Harriok's wife
- LillianToc—Jerst's youngest son
- Jack the Greater—Jack the Lesser's twin brother
- Delaga—a common swordsman
- Fantose—a common pikeman
- Chagarin—the Master Smith
- Baldrak—a smith

- Felina—Baldrak's daughter
- Surnarra—a smith
- Yim—an impressionable young girl
- Tamlea—a young girl
- Tallik—a young bully
- Satcha—the cook for Jerst's extended household

Personae Celestial

- Augis—a mythical goddess, guardian of all that once was
- Attun—a mythical god, guardian of all that is now
- Unnamed King—knows all names but his own
- Erithnae—god-queen and consort to the Unnamed King
- Aethon—the last Shahotma King

Personae Angelicus

- Metadan—an archangel, commander of the first legion, and The Fallen One
- Ellowyn—an archangel, commander of the second legion
- Laelith—a faerie
- Cynaban—Metadan's senior lieutenant

Personae Common

- Raffin—a merchant, also known as Fatpurse
- Mathal—a fruit vendor
- Ott—a peasant
- Gulk—Ott's wife
- Ikth—Ott and Gulk's son
- Darma—captain of the *Far Wind*
- Bakart—first mate of the *Far Wind*
- Braunye—a peasant girl sold to Rhianne in exchange for healing her father's cow
- Chiren Tesha—guardmaster of a merchant caravan out of Anistigh
- Katha—leader of the scouts reporting to Chiren Tesha
- Jokath—a common thief that preys on travellers on the Gods Road
- Mistress Syllith—Rhianne's alias in Norlakton

Personae Nether

- Beayaegoath—the Dark God and ruler of the ninth hell of the netherworld
- Bayellgae—the venomousss demon flying sssnake
- ElkenSkul—the demon *namegiver*

- Mortiss—Morgin's unusual horse, also known as the DeathWalker
- Soann'Daeth'Daeye—a shadowwraith that Morddon meets outside Kathbey-anne
- Shebasha—a great sand cat whose soul is haunted by a demon

Personae Ancient

- Morddon—a bitter and angry Benesh'ere warrior, and Morgin's alter ego
- AnneRhianne—a Benesh'ere princess and Rhianne's alter ego
- WindHollow—a young Benesh'ere boy and AnneRhianne's nephew
- Gilguard—warmaster of the Benesh'ere
- Sarker—a Benesh'ere scout
- Takit—a Benesh'ere scout
- Bendaw—a Benesh'ere scout
- Binth—the pipist, Morddon's father
- Eisla—the SteelMistress, last of the SteelMasters, and Morddon's mother
- Jander—a Benesh'ere warrior, one of Gilguard's senior lieutenants
- Magwa—the jackal queen, aka the bitch queen, and queen of the jackal court
- TarnThane—the griffin lord
- SheelThane—the griffin queen
- AuelThane—a griffin warrior
- TearThane—a griffin warrior
- WolfDane—the hellhound king
- KarlDane—a hellhound lord
- Perrik—a nobleman with a flawed blade

Personae Kingdom of Dreams

- Sabian—the castle and seat of power of the Unnamed King
- Kinardin—Lord Chamberlain of Sabian
- Rhiannead—a young witch, betrothed to the Unnamed King
- Rafaellen—the captain of Rhiannead's escort
- Tasmian—a young lieutenant of the Unnamed King

Acknowledgements

I'D LIKE TO thank Karen for fixing all my dotted t's and crossed i's, and for both supporting my dream and being my most valuable critic, Kelley Eskridge for helping me turn an ok manuscript into something I can be really proud of, and Steve Himes, and the whole team at Telemachus, for getting a quality product out the door.

Books by J. L. Doty

Series: The Dreadmark Covenants
Dread Child (available 3/1/2024)
Dread Spirit (6/1/2024)
Dread Soul (9/1/2024)
Dread Lord (12/1/2024)
Series: The Treasons Cycle
Of Treasons Born
A Choice of Treasons
Stand Alone Novel
The Thirteenth Man
Series: The Gods Within
Child of the Sword
The SteelMaster of Indwallin
The Heart of the Sands
The Name of the Sword
Series: The Dead Among Us
When Dead Ain't Dead Enough
Still Not Dead Enough
Never Dead Enough
Series: The Blacksword Regiment
A Hymn for the Dying
A Dirge for the Damned
A Prayer for the Fallen
A Requiem for the Forsaken
Series: Commonwealth Re-contact Novellas
Tranquility Lost

About the Author

JIM IS A full-time SF&F writer, scientist and laser geek (Ph.D. Electrical Engineering, specialty laser physics), and former running-dog-lackey for the bourgeois capitalist establishment. He's been writing for over 30 years, with 19 published books. His first success came through self-publishing when his books went word-of-mouth viral, and sold enough that he was able to quit his day-job, start working for himself and write full time—his new boss is a real jerk. That led to contracts with traditional publishers like Open Road Media and Harper Collins, and his books are now a mix of traditional and self-published.

The four novels in his new coming-of-age epic fantasy series, *The Dreadmark Covenants*, are scheduled for release beginning in early 2024.

Jim was born in Seattle, but he's lived most of his life in California, though he did live on the east coast and in Europe for a while. He now resides in Arizona with his wife Karen and Julia, a little being who claims to be a cat. But Jim is certain she's really an extra-terrestrial alien in disguise.

Visit the author's website at https://www.jldoty.com/
Contact the author at jld@jldoty.com

9 781953 757043